A. R. Horvath
presents

Birth Pangs:

FIDELIS

A.R. HORVATH PRESENTS

BIRTHPANGS
THE SERIES

"I consider that our present sufferings are not worth comparing with the glory that will be revealed in us. The creation waits in eager expectation for the sons of God to be revealed. For the creation was subjected to frustration, not by its own choice, but by the one that subjected it, in hope that the creation itself will be liberated from its bondage to decay and brought into the glorious freedom of the children of God. *We know that the whole creation has been groaning as in the pains of childbirth right up to the present time…*"

Book 1

FIDELIS

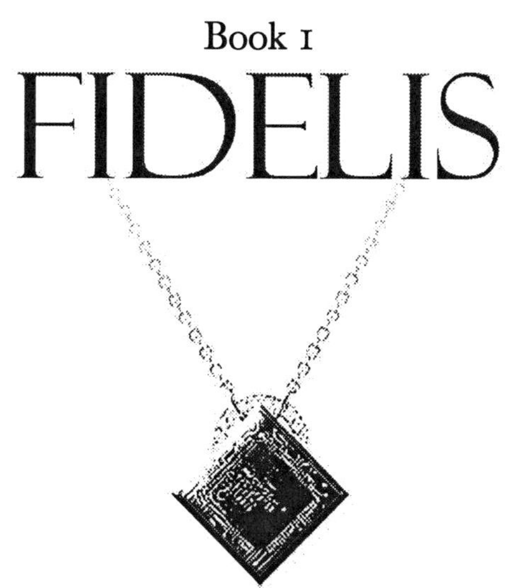

www.birthpangs.com

Prospective agents may contact the author at
interest@birthpangs.com

www.birthpangs.com

Published by Suzeteo Enterprises
www.suzeteo.com

First Edition.
Published in the United States of America

Cover by Elijah St. Cloud
www.elijahstcloud.com

ISBN-9# 0-9791276-1-0
ISBN -13# 978-0-9791276-1-8
Printed in the United States of America.

Thanks especially to my wife, whose patience knows no end. Thanks also to those who read various versions of this book, providing valuable feedback every step of the way.

Most of all, thanks to *the* Author and Perfecter…

Faith is the *substance* of things hoped for, a demonstration of matters unseen…

In your struggle against *corruption*, you have not yet resisted to the point of shedding your blood. And you have forgotten that word of encouragement that addresses you as sons…

Endure hardship as discipline; God is treating you as sons- his very own children. For what son, what child, is not disciplined by his father? Does a *loving* father fail to discipline?

== Chapter 1 ==

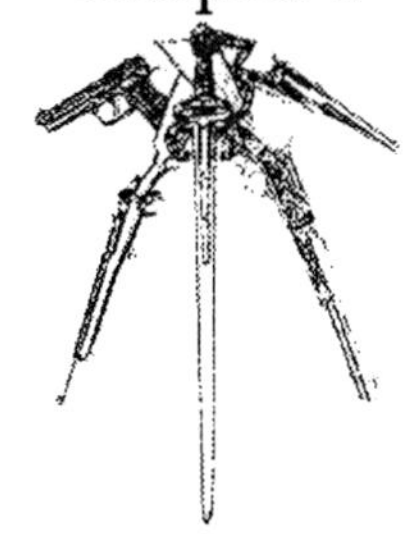

"Hold steady, son," his father whispered into his ear. Fides could hear the soldiers talking carelessly as they passed by on the road. Hidden in the weeds and grasses, the two of them watched as the deadly parade went past them. At last the men were out of sight.

Fides was fourteen years old. He and his father had been getting close to home when they had heard several soldiers up and around the bend. His father had pushed him off into the bushes on the side of the road and put his hands on his shoulder, both soothing him and holding him down.

After a few minutes more, even the sounds of their diverse foreign talk was heard no more, too. His father lifted him to his feet. "Let's get home," he said.

"Couldn't you kill them?" Fides had asked. His father looked at him, surprised.

"Do you think it is so easy to kill a man?" his father asked him, probing the intent behind the question.

"But don't you know how to fight?" Fides wondered, worried that he had asked an embarrassing question.

"That's not what I mean. It's one thing to have the skill, it's another to have the will," his father explained, deciding that Fides' question was not meant in a bloodthirsty manner, but as a question about his own character and the morality of the world. His father continued, "Some men kill because they like it. Those are rotten men, Fides. Whether or not there is ever a right time to kill at all, I don't know. But I only... that is... don't kill unless you really have no choice, son. If you can run, that's a choice. If you can hide, that's a choice. I know what men will say if you do that, but I want you to be able to close your eyes and not see what I see when I close my eyes, or see what I see when I look in the mirror. Do you understand?"

Fides nodded. He didn't know if he agreed, but he nodded. Of all the things his father had told him over the years, he thought he did understand this.

+ + + + +

"Hold steady, son," Fides whispered into his youngest son's ear. He put one hand on his son's shoulder while his other hand clutched the sharpened rod that served as his favorite means for self-defense. Thirty years had passed since Fides' own father had protected him from a lurking threat by throwing him into the brush. Fides was acutely aware of the parallel, and had vague recollections of what was on his mind the last time he was in such a situation. He and his son had been walking through the woods to their old shed when they were surprised to find that others were already there. Five men seemed to have taken up residence in it. Fides had shoved his son to the ground behind some bushes. Now they were both peering through the leaves at the rough looking interlopers.

As Fides was trying to decide whether or not he should confront the men, another memory surfaced.

+ + + + +

Away. He was running away. His mother had yelled, "Run!" and he did. His father had been off to war for some time at this point. Fides was only ten or eleven years old. It was with great shame that he found himself running through the woods now. There were two men not far behind him. He could hear them crashing through the branches. Fides was moving silently because he had the advantage of knowing the woods and also because he was able to duck the low branches. He knew if he could get to the shed, he might be able to barricade himself inside it.

An eleven year old fleeing two grown men is not shameful. That was not why Fides was ashamed. Mainly, it was because his father had put his hands on his shoulders before he left and charged him with the defense of the family. In retrospect, Fides considered that, "Help your mother," was probably not a mandate for defending the family, but that is how he chose to take it. While there were two men after him now, there were four others clawing at his mother. He had left her. In his fear, he had set aside his father's charge and instead was rushing headlong through the brush. He was too young to be able to imagine what his mother was enduring, but old enough to know it was terrible. And he had left her to face it alone.

The men were catching up.

Fides fell into the small clearing that sheltered the shed. If he had only fallen once, he might have gotten away. He slipped again, however, on some leaves. He slid head first, arms outstretched. As he climbed to his feet, two heavy hands fell on his shoulders and he found his face stuffed back into the vegetation. The two men were not happy.

"Think you're faster than us, boy?" one of the men sneered.

"Made us run! You're going to pay for that!" the other man gasped, out of breath. Fides found himself pulled to his feet, but only for a moment. The first man slapped him so hard he fell backwards onto his back and had the wind knocked out of him. He tasted blood and wondered if he was going to die. The man hauled Fides to standing again, but this time took him by the arm and threw him across the clearing. He rolled awkwardly over his arm and yelped in pain. The two men laughed. Fides knew how a mouse felt after the cat had gotten hold of it. In theory, he was far enough away he could try to make another dash for the shed but now there was a sharp pain in his arm hindering him. Fides couldn't think of anything else to do, so despite the pain, he started to crawl. The men were standing over him now, guffawing.

"Come on, finish him. We want to get back and see mom, right?" one said to the other. Fides didn't know what that meant, but he knew it couldn't be good. His shame at running away surged through him again. There was a spark of righteous rage, too. He wanted to protect his mother. On the other hand, he knew his rage could have no outlet. He allowed the shame to overcome the rage, deciding that he would prefer death rather than standing before his father to explain how he had let disaster fall upon his mother and family. He heard a knife being pulled out of a sheath. He bent his head and waited for the blow.

"Picking on a boy? Is that the new mark of a real man?" a silky voice washed over the clearing. The man paused and decided to delay his execution of Fides, but he didn't want him running off, either. He struck Fides on side of his head, sending him reeling to the ground. Fides lay stunned on the ground, struggling to gather his awareness. He struggled, too, to determine the gender of the voice of his savior, but concluded it was probably a woman's voice. He overheard the conversation as blood flowed into his eyes and cobwebs cluttered his mind.

"Who are you? Where are you? Come out and I'll show you the mark of a real man!" one of the fiends declared.

"Oh, I believe that. Why slay a boy when you can slay a woman!" the silk voice replied.

"Oh, you won't get off that easy, my dear," the other man snarled. The two were patrolling the inside of the clearing, peering into the woods around them in an attempt to find the origin of the voice. Fides was peering, too. "Show yourself, or show yourself a coward!" the man dared.

Suddenly, there was a loud crack. Fides thought he saw a man fly through the air near him. The other man's mouth opened in shock, but another cracking noise followed on the heels of the first one and the man found himself knocked to the ground.

The first man rolled over, holding his head. He scanned the clearing to try to find his assailant. Seeing no one, he deduced that he must have been struck by a rock. "Are you just going to throw things at us? We'll find you soon enough and I doubt your aim will be so good with my hands around your neck."

"Big talker," the voice said smoothly. The men had both found their feet again and were advancing in the direction (so they thought) of the voice. Fides thought he could hear a lilting whistle on the wind which he thought was just his ears still ringing from getting struck on the side of the head. The men still couldn't see their assailant, and Fides couldn't see much of anything. The men seemed nervous.

The first man gathered up his courage, "Yea, that's right. I'm a big talker. Give me a chance to show you I'm bigger than talk and you'll regret it."

"Or," countered the voice, "you could let the boy go and simply walk away." The men snickered in response and maintained their slow patrol of the clearing.

"We'll find you. It is just a matter of time," the first man answered her. "You go finish off the boy and I'll find the woman," he told his friend. His friend turned toward Fides. Fides could vaguely make out the form of the man approaching him. He grimaced in anticipation of the man's arrival, but his grimace evolved into awe.

Fides could see the man approaching him, but then it seemed as though the air between them began to quiver. Fides wiped the blood from his eyes to try to see clearly. He sat up, but found that his daze remained. He became dizzy and a pain shot through his head and he had to lie back down to await his fate. He turned towards the scene to try to see what could be seen while in his battered state. Fides realized he must be hallucinating. There appeared to be a woman in the clearing… with a sword?

The men chortled greedily, but the lady only coaxed them into attacking.

Fides heard the sound of the struggle but his vision could not be trusted. The woman was evading every blow. The men were angry. It seemed to Fides that the shadows of the shed seemed to be ill-defined. He struggled to make sense of what he was seeing. She really did seem to have a sword- now she had plunged it into the soil and was engaged in hand to hand combat. There was a loud snap. One of the men now had a broken arm. He howled in pain and rage. He fell to the ground, writhing. The other man had turned around to see his friend fall to the ground, but did not see the cause. He had his knife out.

"Shall we have a battle of blades, then?" Fides heard her ask the man softly. She had her sword in her hand, now. The man was determined to not be intimidated by a woman, though. He mustered up whatever contempt he had left in his body and lunged at her. From Fides' perspective, she did not appear to move at all. It was as though the man simply threw himself onto her blade. He made a final noise and gave a last gasp and fell to the ground, dead. The other man was still in agony but stood up, furious. He reached for her, but only briefly. He met a slashing blow and he too fell to the ground, finished. The woman looked down on the men with sadness. Fides sat up again and gazed at her. Finally, their eyes met, but only briefly. The blood ran down into his eyes and he became dizzy. He was sure he was delirious. She began talking to him, her words wafting through the fog that was Fides' consciousness.

"Go home, Fides," she said soothingly. Fides suddenly remembered that his mother was still in danger. At the same time, he realized he'd be no match for the men that remained, and was in no condition to fight his best, besides. The woman felt his fear. "All is well at home. Go home, Fides." She was gone. Or was she? Fides could hear a melody on the wind. Despite his corrupted vision, he was suddenly certain she was still present.

"Are you an angel?" Fides asked, testing his suspicion that she was still near.

Indeed, she was still present somewhere, perhaps lurking on the edge of the clearing. She laughed, "Not at all! Pray that you never see an angel! Terrible! Terrible to behold!" Fides heard her voice all around him.

"Then what are you?" Fides cried into the air. Despite the murkiness of the scene, he thought that she had been terrible to behold. Perhaps it was only the atmosphere around her that he perceived. She reeked of nobility.

But the woman only laughed, "I am human, just like you."

"You may be human, ma'am, but if you are, then I must not be," Fides said slowly, trying to look at her through his pain.

"I can see how you would think that," she agreed. "Realize that there is more to Man than the eye can see."

"I don't think there is anything more of me to see. I don't think there is more than a disgraceful little boy," Fides moaned, thinking again of his flight from danger.

"Sometimes we must defer judgment to those who are in a better position to know. You are certainly more than a disgraceful little boy. You can put your faith in that," she encouraged him.

"Are you magical?" Fides persisted. Fides thought that he must be out of his mind. The woman chuckled again. Despite the opportunity to make fun of him, her chuckle was completely good-natured.

"Your race always treats as magic what it does not at first understand. When it finally understands a matter, it heaps contempt on it as though it were something always self-evident to intelligent, sophisticated people. Yet, the wondrous does not cease to be wondrous just because one knows what made it wondrous or 'magical' in the first place," she explained to him patiently. She continued, "Your race then takes it to the other extreme, reducing the wondrous to the banal, thus failing at the end to understand in the slightest the very thing it understood- at least in part- at the beginning."

Fides contemplated these words. She talked to him as though he could understand what she was saying. Though he could not understand her, her thinking he could encouraged him. There was a change on the wind. Though he could not see much of anything, he could tell that she was preparing for a final departure. Fides struggled to find words that might prompt her to linger. He very much liked her even though he would be hard put to explain why.

"What... what is your name?" he stammered at last.

She laughed again. It wasn't a mocking laugh. It was innocently mirthful. "My name cannot be translated into your tongue. Maybe someday you will know the language by which it is understood, and you will know me. Peace, boy. Go home, Fides." Fides felt her hands on his face, stroking his hair. She wiped the blood from his eyes, and his sight and his awareness sharpened briefly. She was beautiful. She drew even closer to him. Her eyes were unnaturally bright and she looked deep into his eyes; he thought she was examining his soul.

"It is bright in there," she said. Fides felt her warm breath on his cheek and ear, but then his dizziness overcame him again. He collapsed. The breeze lost its song and Fides was sure he was alone. He slept, and the ringing in his ears was gone when he awoke.

Hours later, Fides managed to get home. He found his mother bruised and shaking but nonetheless safe. The bodies of the four men who had tried to have their way with her were scattered in the yard outside the front door. His mother said nothing about what had happened and she didn't ask him how he had escaped danger. Fides considered the possibility that perhaps his mother had been helped just like he had been helped. Over the years he would reason that this was almost certainly what had happened, but she never talked about it, so he never asked.

When his father came home from the war, parts of the story emerged. To Fides' utter disgrace, his father learned that when the family had been attacked, Fides had run. It did not take long for his father to sense Fides' shame. He reasoned with Fides.

"Your mother told you to run, right?" his father had asked. Fides nodded. "There were six of them, all grown men, right?" Fides nodded again. His father grabbed him by both shoulders and looked him in the eye, "If you can avoid a fight, son, you should. If your mother tells you to do something, you should do it. Some wars are not worth fighting. Some are, I suppose, but most aren't. If you can get away with not fighting, that's the choice I want you to make, you understand?" Fides received the restoration gratefully. His father didn't take him to be a coward. Despite this, Fides secretly felt that he should not have run.

Fides' father never talked about his own fighting. When the topic would come up, his father would gaze off into the distance. Fides didn't ask him about it, but then, he was probably not old enough to hear about it anyway. On occasion, his father would say things like, "War is a terrible thing. Is there such a thing as a terrible peace?" Sometimes he would say things like, "The pride of a nation goes before its fall." Fides had always pondered his father's statements but did not usually understand them.

Fides remembered again the one that he did understand. His father had said, "If you can run, that's a choice. If you can hide, that's a choice. I know what men will say if you do that, but I want you to be able to close your eyes and not see what I see when I close my eyes, or see what I see when I look in the mirror. Do you understand?"

+ + + + +

These memories flowed back to him with startling clarity as Fides was trying to decide whether or not he should confront the men. Interestingly, though he remembered well how disoriented he was at the time, today he seemed to recall other details from that event decades earlier- by the very same shed he was looking at now. His father's counsel to avoid violence if it was at all a choice percolated into the forefront, too. While not a violent man, more than once Fides had been forced to defend himself. He was strong and agile and perfectly able to hold his own. Five men, though? That is a trick. He'd have to protect his son, too. Not realistic. Did he have a choice? Yes, he did. "Let's get home," Fides finally said to his son.

As they were walking home, Fides heard his own voice in his mind asking his father, "But don't you know how to fight?" He wondered if his son was now considering the same question. If he was, he didn't say anything. Fides used their short walk back from the shed as an opportunity to reflect on the fact that the world had not gotten any better since he was young. There was no electricity anymore. Gasoline was scarce. Grocery stores were either closed, or nearly empty. Lawless men and refugees alike were loose on the land. They were living in a dangerous time.

One day, not too long after the discovery at his shed, Fides was out on the road tinkering with his car. He had run out of gas right at the edge of his property. Instead of just putting more in and taking it up the driveway, he put up the hood and was messing with the distributor cap to see if he could get better fuel efficiency. These days, there was always a steady stream of refugees making their way past their home, usually heading west. This day was no exception. A stranger came over to talk to him.

"Do you have any water?" the man asked plaintively.

"No, I'm sorry. We use a community well, and we used up our allotment for the day already. We have none left. Sorry," Fides replied, genuinely sorry. Fides did have some water stored away in case of emergency, but he was not going to give that away. It was a hundred yards away in any case.

"Well, thanks anyway." The man paused. He looked as though he had something else on his mind besides water. Fides noted the man's lingering presence and did not return to his labor. At last the man spoke again, "Have you heard about the African disease?"

Fides was taken off guard by this line of questioning. His look must have effectively communicated confusion, because the man began explaining himself. "Over in Indianapolis people are talking about some new disease that melts people from the inside. Nobody lives. But nobody knows how they got it, either. I heard it from a man who said he was trying to get west ahead of it. Said he was from Pittsburg, and that he heard about it from somebody from New Jersey."

"Is that why you are going west?" Fides asked casually, trying to hide his eagerness for the conversation to come to an end. He wasn't so sure he wanted to be talking to anybody from the east if there was in fact some new disease loose from that direction.

The man shook his head. "No, I was going west, anyway. No good reason to stay over there. Everything is strictly controlled nowadays, you understand."

Fides did understand. He said as much, and after a moment or so the man made his way down the road. Fides took the opportunity to push the car farther down the dirty path that served as his driveway. If there really was a new disease, there were sure to be even more refugees coming his way. Besides the fact that he didn't want to risk being exposed to the disease himself, he knew that one of them would likely want his car, and try to take it.

Fides considered this new development over the next few days. Even taking into account the chaos that already formed the backdrop of Fides' existence, this was a particularly ominous twist. The rumors accumulated: the Disease had been intentionally released; it was, by all accounts thus far, one hundred percent fatal; no one knew how it was contracted. Fides discussed the matter with his wife, Melody, and emphasized that at this point it remained only a rumor. This was little consolation. Even if one part in one hundred of what they heard was true, there were terrible things afoot. The most telling indicator that there was a new threat was that the atmosphere of life around them had changed. The climate within the community had changed. Fides and his wife knew that something had caused the change. It didn't matter that they didn't know exactly what the cause was. Whether the cause was known or not was irrelevant to the fact that they were breathing the effect.

In light of this change of atmosphere in their community, they agreed that it might be a good idea to stock up on supplies in case they needed to hunker down again. Over the years, it seemed they were always hunkering down over rumors. It was tedious. However, the thickening stream of refugees that passed by their house made it painfully clear that at least some of those rumors must have merit. They tuned into the radio, but the official station had no information on the matter, and they didn't live in an area where they could pick up outlawed stations. They were stuck with rumor as their best source of information.

Fides was a construction worker making a pretty good living. Skilled individuals were not so easy to find anymore. He worked with a handful of other men to build just about anything that a person might want. That was how he got his car. He did a job installing an indoors bathroom by himself and the only way the gentleman could pay him was trading away his car. His partners were jealous, but since it wasn't as though it was easy to obtain fuel, it was mainly a novelty. Thankfully, he had collected a number of items in the course of his business that were useless to him but useful for trading for fuel.

His crew did customized jobs for people all over the Terre Haute region. They were in high demand. Setting aside the fact that there was a lack of skilled labor, the skills that Fides and his fellow crewmates possessed would have been considered exceptional even in times of plenty. Fides' home was a good demonstration of Fides' own skill. It looked from the outside like a run-down old country house. That was intentional. He didn't want people thinking there was incentive to come exploring. Of course, this tactic was well known, but with the type of traffic common in his parts, something was better than nothing. Fides' defenses were a bit more than nothing. Inside the shell of the building he had reinforced the walls and windows so that it would take tremendous effort for someone to bust in uninvited. Indeed, it was much like an above ground bunker. He had adapted the roof so that it would collect rain water, which was then piped to a large container in the basement. If anyone tried to scale the exterior walls, he had sliding panels that he could move, giving him the ability to poke, slice, and jab. He had never needed to do this, but he was ready. When one considered the ingenuity he had employed to erect Fortress Fides, one can imagine the skills he brought to bear on the job. His crewmates were also exceptionally skilled, though they each had their own strengths.

Not long after first hearing about the Disease, Fides' partner dropped by to talk with him.

"We've got a job, Fides!" Ed declared happily.

"That's terrific," Fides said. "What is it?" Ed's face betrayed a glimmer of apprehension.

"Well, it's interesting, really. We've been specifically asked for. There is a general contractor out of Chicago who sent someone looking for us. He was instructed by the owners themselves to hire us specifically," Ed explained.

"Well, that's flattering. Out of Chicago? Chicago is quite a trip, Ed," Fides hesitated. It would take a week at least to get to Chicago the way roads were these days. The crew owned a good number of vehicles, so in theory the trip could be made. One of the reasons why they were in such high demand is because of their ability to travel. Finding fuel was not always easy, but in many instances they could be paid in part by fuel. There were deposits of fuel all over the place, even if they weren't sizable. Working vehicles were becoming less and less common, however, so much of the existing fuel was actually going bad over time. Still, just because they had vehicles and fuel it did not mean that a trip as far as Chicago would be quick. It would be long and dangerous.

"No, not Chicago, actually," Ed answered him. Fides could still see the apprehension playing on Ed's face. Fides waited for Ed to continue. "It's out by Peoria, actually."

"Peoria! That's no closer!" Fides exclaimed.

"But you don't understand! There is so much money involved in this, you wouldn't believe it. Look!" Ed produced a small, yellow slab of metal. It was obviously heavy. Fides took it in his hands.

"Is this gold?" Fides demanded, incredulously.

"It absolutely is," Ed smiled.

"This could really come in handy," Fides thought. Precious metals were in many cases useless these days because people needed necessities more than treasure, but there were still many situations where it was helpful, too. Fides had another thought, "Why do you have this? Did they pay us before we've even accepted the job?"

"That's just it, Fides. That's not the payment for the job. That's not even the down payment for the job. That's only your share of the down payment for the job!" Ed declared victoriously. Fides was stunned speechless. That gold bar was worth ten times what his normal take from a job was. Here it was being offered not as final compensation, but merely as a down payment. Ed continued, "Every man on the crew now has a gold bar just like that in their hands. I'm telling you, this is the big one. This one will make us set for life! Not only is there more gold to be had, but silver, too. Also, stuff we can really use. Cars, building materials, ovens, blankets, sheet glass, tools... all sorts of stuff!" Ed anticipated his next question, "Yea, it will take us a week or a little longer to get there, but once we're there, my understanding is that the whole job will only take us three to six weeks. We're only talking about being gone for two months and look at this payoff! The general contractor sent us a box of gold bars to prove to us that this is legit. In fact, he said that even if we decide not to take the job, we can still keep the gold. They must be rolling in it! Think of it, Fides! Set for life!"

Fides chatted with Ed a little more to find out some of the finer details. Fides knew that the rest of the crew would be ready in a heartbeat, but most of them did not have families to think of. Fides also knew that Melody would not want him to be gone for two months right now. Being gone for long stretches of time was part of the job, but it wasn't good timing if there really was a new disease on its way into the area.

Fides went home and put the gold bar on the kitchen table. Melody was outside tending the garden. When she came in, she washed her hands, and sat down at the table. "What's that?" she asked, pointing at the gold bar.

"Look at it," Fides smiled. "Pick it up."

Melody picked up the bar, but not before she dropped it, surprised at its weight. "Is this gold?" she exclaimed.

"Yep, it's gold, honey!" Fides said. Then he began to explain the situation to her. As he expected, her attitude soured the more he explained.

"More refugees were passing through the area, Fides," she said. "You know the disease is probably real. That's why we've been stocking up, getting ready to seal ourselves up again. You can't be gone right now!"

"But Melody, look. We'll be set for life! They paid each of us in gold bars just to consider this job!" Fides reasoned.

"I don't want you to even consider it!" Melody blurted out.

"Eight weeks and then I'll be back, and it will be for good. No more jobs, ever! Plus, they need me," Fides answered emphatically.

"They need you! What about me and your family?" Melody replied, angrily. Their children heard them arguing but after coming to see what the fuss was about, decided it was better to stay out of the way. The argument descended into loud shouting. He and his wife roamed from room to room like two warring armies seeking out strategic high points: here advancing, there retreating. It was not that he didn't understand her position. He did. In truth, he didn't really want to do the job, but his partners were depending on him. They each brought unique strengths to their projects and it would not be easy for them to compensate for not having him. He had a strong sense of loyalty, commitment, and even professional pride compelling him to go. It was also dangerous to travel in these times. He was needed to help provide security. Just as a mere matter of duty, he felt obliged to help them. These arguments did not go over very well. It was hard for Fides to put some of the intangible realities he felt into words. She couldn't understand the sense of duty he felt for his friends, quite apart from the apparent great pay-off involved.

When it was all said and done, it was up to Fides to make the decision. He remembered how his father had been away for so long and how at the time he had felt abandoned. It was as dangerous now as it was then. He recalled the recent shed incident. On the other hand, his father had been gone for two or three years. He would only be gone for two months at the most. Also, his father had been gone for a noble reason. While it was true that his own venture would 'only' be a building project, it was a building project that promised to bring security to his family for as far as the future could be seen. Fides remembered, too, that in a very real way, he and his mother were not completely alone just because his father was gone. Perhaps some help would still remain for his family if Fides was gone? Fides decided to go.

The days before making the trip were spent in strained silence. The day before they were to leave, Ed brought by one of the construction vans so Fides could load his tools into it. The van couldn't come up Fides' driveway, so Fides and Melody and his children were working together to carry his supplies out to it. While they were loading it, a large group of refugees passed by. A grieving family caught their attention. Fides had never seen such a forlorn family. It broke his heart. He delayed them and offered them water, which they gratefully accepted. The absence of a father and husband was conspicuous and unsettling. He exchanged a painful look with Melody and both looked away from each other sharply. Soon, the family moved on.

Later that afternoon, another group of refugees, much larger and moving much more quickly than the one they saw in the morning, rushed past them. Despite the group's great haste, a tall, lean man lagged behind the rest to warn Fides and his family about why they were fleeing.

"People are dying to the east," he said curtly. "It comes on suddenly, and if it comes on, you may as well crawl off into the woods and die," he told Fides. He paused, and looked from Melody to Fides and then to their children, and said cryptically, "Some things we don't want anyone to see, but some things certainly should not be seen by children." The man ran off to catch up to his group, leaving Fides and his family to absorb this troubling word. Fides tried to put it into perspective. They had been hearing all sorts of things. The haste and tone of voice, however, brought a sense of foreboding that was probably more dramatic given the fact that Fides was leaving them all the next day. Fides' family would have to deal with whatever else came down the road- without him. Fides fought back an uneasy feeling in the pit of his stomach.

The next morning the rest of the crew arrived at his house. Melody glared at each of his partners wickedly. Nobody said much as they loaded up the final items. Their caravan consisted of two vans, a truck hauling fuel, a truck hauling assorted building supplies, and another truck with their tools and other miscellaneous items. When everything was loaded at last, Ed tried to make some apology to Melody. But Melody turned her head away violently, looking instead, it seemed, at a single leaf in a tree near the edge of the property. Ed looked extraordinarily uncomfortable. Finally he grunted, turned on his heels, and got into the fuel truck to wait for Fides.

Fides approached his wife carefully. She turned to him quickly and fell into his arms, crying very, very softly. "Come home very quickly, Fides. Very quickly. I love you so much." With that, as though a levy had broken, his children felt like they could rush into his arms. His four children, finally sensing permission to show emotion supporting either parent, cried bitterly in his arms. Fides wondered if being gone for two months constituted an abandonment. He felt miserable.

Fides knew that his crew was probably getting impatient but he also knew that they wouldn't dare honk their horns. Fides soaked up his family's affection. Unable to bear it any longer, he choked back a tear of his own, grabbed his suitcase, and joined one of his partners in the passenger seat of one of the trucks. Even the vehicle noise seemed dampened in the emotion of the moment.

The journey west took about as long as Fides thought it would. There were the normal conversations speculating about what it must have been like to travel on intact roads and conversations trying to establish directions, but other than that the group traveled in suppressed silence. As a group, they had once been as far as Champaign. Frank had been further, apparently, but more to the south. It was flat land, but the roads were rough. There were large gaping holes in the pavement and occasional huge cracks. The trucks especially had to take special care. They would stare, as discretely as they could, at the numerous refugee cities that existed along the route. Every now and then there would be a large group of people traveling on foot and it would take some time for their carts out of the way of the crew's vehicles. Every four or five hours or so, they'd see another car or truck heading in one direction or another. Occasionally they'd see a caravan like their own. On either side of the road were the forgotten skeletons of abandoned vehicles. The group remained fairly pensive throughout the trip. Everyone perceived that events in the east were bubbling viciously and that they could in fact bubble over before they got back.

They reached Bloomington on the sixth day. They spent the seventh day passing through Bloomington's neighborhoods. They replenished some of their supplies and chatted with the locals. They reasoned that they might be able to make Peoria the next day. That night, they set up their camp a few miles outside the western limits of Bloomington. They established a night watch schedule and eagerly went to bed. The next morning there was a distinct sense that tension had been released. It was probably the fact that they knew they would be at their destination that day that allowed them to relax. There would be something to actually do rather then talk, or rather as they had been doing, sitting quietly. Their hands could work and their minds freed to think about things other than... whatever was happening to the east.

The caravan finally left the old interstate system somewhere in the area of Peoria about three that afternoon. Fides contemplated the steady decline in the quality of the roads as they got closer and closer to their destination. When they were very near and the road was nothing more than packed dirt, he marveled at the dark green of the forest he was in and wondered just what kind of facility it was that they were going to be working on that was tucked away in such an environment. The road opened up into a large clearing and in that large clearing were dozens of people and the strangest looking building foundation that he'd ever seen.

There were people milling about that appeared to be packing up their own materials and getting ready to depart. The apprehension he saw on their faces was similar to the apprehension he was feeling. It appeared that everyone knew that death was percolating to the east, and if history over the last one hundred years predicted anything, it would eventually spill out onto the western plains. There was subdued conversation throughout the camp. Fides' own group pulled their vehicles around one edge of the clearing where there were several buildings. Ed jumped out of the truck he was in and entered one of the buildings.

Fides took this time to examine the strange cement structure that he assumed he was going to be building on top of. Evidently a large structure was envisioned. About as wide as a football field and half the length, it appeared to be very close to an actual square. The foundation came up about two feet off the ground. It looked almost as though previous workers had just laid the concrete down right on top of the ground, but as he studied it, he could tell that the concrete did go down into the dirt. In the middle of the foundation was another raised square, coming up about another two feet. Finally, in the very middle of these two squares, one inside the other, was a cement structure about eight feet high. This structure looked like a shed of some kind, but from where he was sitting in the vehicle, he could not see a door to it. It looked like a cement cube.

All at once it occurred to him that he was looking at a bunker of some kind. It was not the bottom he was looking at, but rather the top. Just as this occurred to him, Ed came out of the building he had entered, followed by a great number of extremely odd looking people. They went out together to the presumed bunker and talked quietly for awhile. The tallest of the group was dressed in a long, flowing, orange robe. He was also the one talking to Ed. A significant part of the group appeared to be Muslims from the Middle East. This was a shocking development, indeed. Fides continued looking at the members of the group, and he noticed that his friends had now also taken an interest in this odd collection of individuals. He let out a sharp gasp when he noticed that three or more of the individuals were definitely Chinese. Such people as these were rarely seen in their area.

"Look at that, Frank. Chinese," Fides breathed quietly.

"I see them," Frank said nervously.

"I didn't know that there were any Chinese left in the United States," Fides whispered. Frank merely grunted. What were Middle Eastern Muslims and Chinese doing in the middle of Illinois in this day and age? After this shock had faded some, Fides continued his analysis of the group. About as shocking as his initial discoveries, he realized that another four or five members of the group appeared to be Roman Catholic priests. Wearing black pants, black shirts, and white collars, he decided that if they were not Roman Catholic priests they were definitely clergy from some other Christian denomination. Another handful appeared to be orthodox Jews. There were some others that he couldn't identify. Ed handled the strangeness of the situation with real tact. He didn't seem to show any kind of discomfort being around such an unusual group. They had to be foreigners. The state-approved religion didn't allow for such disparities in appearance. Fides should know. He had once applied to be a minister in it.

At last Ed made his way back to his crew. The group of religious foreigners slowly walked the perimeter of the bunker while Ed explained to the team what was going on.

"Alright, fellahs," Ed began. "You probably guessed that we've got a construction project that is a bit out of the ordinary. First, let me tell you about who we are working for. You already know that we are actually sub-contracted by this big shot firm out of Chicago and by special request. Apparently he is around here somewhere, but no one has seen him today. You guessed right if you guessed that he was hired by this group of religious people. So, that's who we are working for, in a sense."

"Ed?" Lonny, a short haired, burly man, gasped.

"That's right. None of these guys are part of any legal church. I don't know anything about them other than what I observed. I also don't know what's under that concrete, and they ain't going to tell us and I'm thinking that I don't really want to know. One thing is for sure, they've got money." At that, Ed pointed to another side of the field where there were a number of piles covered by tarps. Fides hadn't thought much of those piles when he had first seen them. He assumed they were just construction materials. Ed continued, "Under those tarps is gold, silver, fuel, oil, food, and more. We get whatever is leftover after the crews that are here right now take their share. As you can see, there is no way those crews can take it all. For that matter, there is no way that we'll be able to take it all, either, and we've got five vehicles. Those guys have enough here to get it done."

"Well, what are we supposed to do?" Fides asked.

"You are never going to believe this, fellahs. They want us to build a house on top of that... that... thing," Ed answered.

"That's insane!" Fides objected.

Frank laughed sharply, "Didn't they know we couldn't bring enough building materials to do that big of job?" Frank was under the belief that the house was going to be as big as the entire concrete foundation.

Ed raised his hands defensively. "Now wait guys. No, get this. We are building a regular sized house right in the middle of that concrete platform. If you look closely you can see that there are places where we can put the framing down into the concrete. We'll cover up that middle building-like thing jutting up in the middle. I don't know what it is. It doesn't have a door. Anyway, when we are done, it will look like a house plopped down onto a parking lot. Don't ask me, fellahs. I don't understand it. But the plans are pretty simple. They don't want any plumbing, they don't want any electrical. They just want us to put up a very basic, two-story house that more or less will cover that smaller raised concrete platform. In fact, it sounds like we are just putting up a shell of a house."

Frank was scratching his head. Fides had a blank look on his face. Mel had a tortured smile on his face, as though he had been about to laugh when a canary flew into his mouth. Finally Lonny spoke up. "Well, Ed, I don't want to sound unappreciative exactly, but why do they need us to put up a shell? Just about anyone can do that, one would think. And why pay us so well for such a simple job?"

Ed shrugged, "Apparently, on the other side of the woods over there is another large pile of supplies. Those piles have a lot of building materials, like shingles and siding. Good stuff, apparently. Not scavenged stuff. Stuff apparently from some of those factories still going up in Chicago. They've given us a pretty amateur looking plan for the inside, but they do have some specifications. I don't understand the purpose of some of them. Except for putting in the floor on the second level, we aren't even putting up any dry wall. I mean, in some places we aren't even making full walls. Just putting in the frames and leaving them as is. From the specs it's clear that it's the outside they are most concerned about, and I think we would be wise not to ask why. They want it to look like a real farm house. From the outside. If you get my gist."

A sense of realization swept over them. Yes, this was a bunker of some sort. The house that they were building was meant to conceal what was underneath. They were only covering up a part of it, and probably some folks would come later to cover up the rest. The crews that were here before probably worked on the insides, and now their crew would work on the outside. Fides decided that they probably had been rotating crews in for some time. Obviously they didn't want any one group to know too much about the bunker and they knew that they couldn't keep the workers from inferring that there was a bunker here. The reason for the generous payment was not merely to buy their skill, but also to buy their silence. Insane, Fides thought to himself again.

Eager to get started, they began unloading their stuff. They set up a small campsite near where they had parked and worked to get their affairs organized. While they worked they could see that the remaining crews had completely packed up. Fides' crew watched as finally the previous crew was allowed to pull back the tarps on the massive piles of compensation. There was hooting and hollering as they poured over the piles as though they were looting. The other crew had brought several flatbed trucks with them. They were stacking items as high as they safely could while still being able to tie the stuff down. After about three hours of gleeful shouting and packing, they rolled out and were gone.

Initially, Fides and his crewmates had resented the fact that the other crew had been allowed to get such access to all the good stuff. However, after the crew left and before the tarps were pulled back over all of the piles, they could see that there was plenty more of just about everything. In fact, after seeing all this, Fides was confident that they could not possibly take even a quarter of what was left in those piles. He started wishing they had brought another truck. Also, he started feeling a little less upset about leaving his wife and family. If this worked out, they were not going to have to scavenge again, ever. They might be able to buy their needs- actually buy them, rather than barter for them- for years into the future. From a risk versus reward point of view, he began to feel better about his decision. He also had an uneasy thought cross his mind: how can these piles be just sitting around, apparently undefended? Wouldn't earlier crews return to take more? By force? Fides decided he'd keep an eye out for danger.

One of the good things about this project, as Ed explained it, was its overall simplicity. They needed to pay special attention to detail in regards to the exterior, but as long as certain features were in place in the interior, they needed only assemble the framing. When finished with their own part, it would be possible from some angles to stand on one side of the 'house' and see straight through all the wood beams to the other side. By their estimation, it would only take two weeks, at the most, and then they could load up and return home. They joked together that they weren't bringing any building supplies back with them. Only their tools would return. They wanted lots of space available for 'loot.'

The next day they got to work. Frank was the one in charge of working off of the blueprint. Fides was glad it wasn't him, because simple or not, the blueprint was not well-made. Frank appeared to be very unhappy with the roughness of the plan, yet how exacting certain features were expected to be. Frank had snapped to Ed that if they (presumably the outlaw religious people) wanted such attention to detail then it was their job not to skimp on the plans themselves. Naturally, Ed was sympathetic.

It felt good to run the generators and start assembling the exterior walls. Using their air-powered nail guns, they were able to put together pretty good sections in short order. It took some time to get an efficient system set up. They had brought a bit of lumber of their own, which had to be pulled off the truck, but they also had to venture out to the makeshift warehouse that was on site to get the rest of the lumber that they needed. Once all the pieces were in place they assembled the walls very quickly. They spent that day merrily creating framed walls, joking, and chatting with each other. Only occasionally did they spot any member of the strange group that they had seen the day before. When they turned in for the night they were exhausted, but their minds were clear. There is nothing like hard, physical labor, to bring peace into a man's soul.

On the third day, Fides discovered why it was that they didn't have to worry about people coming back to take more loot by force. It would become clear that there was ample protection nearby. The morning began normally enough. When the crew woke up, they were quite ready to get moving on the job so they could get home. No quiet banter; it was all business. Fides had a headache and felt a little warm. They made some coffee over the open fire and fried some potatoes. Fides felt uneasy as the coffee percolator rattled the pot. Some black liquid seeped out of the edges, and Fides couldn't help but think that this was a good metaphor for whatever was happening to the east. He tried not to think about this much. It was better to keep his mind on the job at hand. His crewmates seemed to have the same attitude.

A couple hours after lunch, there was a loud crashing noise in the forest not very far from where the make-shift warehouse stood. This was followed by loud creaking noises, more crashing, and... Fides couldn't quite believe it... the sounds of horses. Everyone stopped what they were doing to stare towards the sound. He couldn't see into the forest to see what the cause was, so he didn't know if they were in danger or if there was only another mystery to be revealed. Frank held his air gun to his side, ready to deploy it as a weapon if necessary. They all waited.

Suddenly, the door to one of the larger buildings where the foreign crowd lived burst open. The foreigners emerged, looking very serious. They walked toward the noise without any apparent sense that there was any imminent danger, though with definite purpose in their steps. About thirty yards from the edge of the woods, they stopped and waited. The crashing noises had stopped and were replaced by other kinds of crashing noises. Fides decided that this must be people actually walking through the woods. It was still an awful lot of noise. There was clanking and crushing sounds. It must be quite a few people. The clamor dwindled away short of the edge of the woods, however, so Fides and his crew still couldn't make out the source of the commotion. At last, there was motion among the branches.

Fides and his crewmates nearly fell over when they saw emerging from the wood line, about forty yards away, twenty men dressed in military fatigues. Such attire was not completely out of the ordinary. But...

"Fides," Frank whispered fearfully. "They have guns."

Even Ed's face had gone white. Of course, they had all seen guns before. Every now and then state troops would come through Terre Haute and sometimes they would have weapons. Also, some of his friends still boasted that they owned their father's old hunting rifles, but he had only seen one with his own eyes. But every one of these men were armed with military issue weapons. These were not simple citizens wearing fatigues. It was obvious they were professional soldiers. A sense of eliteness radiated from them. Fides could sense it and was initially a little afraid of it, but ultimately he decided it was just plain cool. He had a sudden urge to ask if he could join.

The leader of this group strode over to the tall man in the orange robe and gestured towards Fides and his crew menacingly. The tall man seemed unfazed, and after a moment the military leader apparently relented. Lonny exhaled. "I thought we were goners, there," he said quietly. Lonny was perched on top of one of the frames that they had only just fixed to the bunker roof, joining two frame walls together at right angles.

Frank talked without moving his lips: "I don't think they were expecting us to be here."

The two groups held a conference while Fides and his friends watched them uncomfortably. The military men stared back at the crew. They did not seem to be angry, but they did seem to be saying, "Isn't your job to build things? So, why don't you?" At least, Ed must have perceived it that way, because suddenly he said, "Ok, guys, let's get back to work."

Just at that moment there were more crashing noises in the forest. They all turned again to see what would emerge this time. These noises were not like the first initial crash that had been the military men. Suddenly a troop of about ten horses trotted out of the woods, crushing small trees as they went. Apparently these were armored horses, and perched on them, looking magnificent, were ten bold-looking older men with long hair down to their shoulders. And swords in sheaths at their belt lines. Fides heard a yelp and a crash behind them. Lonny had fallen off the wall in surprise.

Nobody seemed to pay any attention to Lonny's fall, but Fides thought he saw a trace of a smirk on the face of one of the soldiers. Lonny picked himself up as Ed muttered over to him something about not becoming the center of attention.

"Come on guys. Really, we should get to work. Really. Now," Ed implored. But this sight was really too much. People with guns? That was strange but not unfathomable. Men on horses? With swords? With armor on the horses? With armor on the men? Had anything like it ever been seen? Maybe four, or five hundred years ago, perhaps. But in America? If it had been seen, it was too long ago to recount, and there could be no doubt that the swordsmen of the past did not often (or for long) share the field with men carrying guns.

An especially well built man- for lack of a better word, Fides decided he needed to call him a knight- trotted his horse over to where the tall man in the orange robe was talking with the military commander. An animated conversation between the three leaders ensued. After only a few moments, they were shouting at each other, and Fides wondered whether or not it was really a good idea that they remained on the scene. After another few moments, it seemed as though something had been settled. The military man made a gesture into the woods and three soldiers emerged a moment later, with a prisoner in front of them, all bound up.

"Oh no!" exclaimed Ed. "That's Bill Huxley! That's the one who contracted us," Ed exhaled, beginning to tremble. Fides agreed that this could not be good. If their boss had now become a prisoner, what was to become of them? Frank appeared to be counting the nails left in his nail gun. He heard Mel whisper scornfully, "What are you going to do Frank, nail 'em?"

The three soldiers presented Bill Huxley to the leaders and another argument ensued. This time, the only shouting done was done by Bill, a large plump looking man, who quite obviously didn't appreciate having his dignity attacked. Only the tall man responded to Bill. The military commander and the commanding knight remained silent. Bill kept shouting. "I wish I could hear what they were saying," Ed grumbled under his breath.

Bill's fevered shouting continued for a few more minutes. At last it sounded again as though something had been settled. Some command from the tall man in orange robes must have taken place, because suddenly the three soldiers untied the ropes around Bill's hands and torso. Bill stared back at them with contempt, a slight smile of victory playing at his lips. There followed, apparently, another command. A strong looking man stepped forward from out of the group of foreigners. He appeared to be one of the Roman Catholic priests. With a start, Bill started lumbering towards Fides and the construction crew. The priest followed a step behind him.

"Good Lord, Ed. What have you got us into?" blurted out Mel. Frank was checking his nail gun again; he was not going down without a fight. Lonny seemed to be looking for a weapon of his own. Ed shushed them up.

"It's just Bill and that priest coming. Relax. The soldiers are staying where they are." But Ed didn't seem all that confident of things, either. After not more than a moment, Bill and the priest came and stood at the foot of their part of the construction project. They walked back and forth, examining each of them. Ed was whispering pleas for calm. Finally, Bill stopped closest to Ed, Fides, and Lonny. Frank's finger quivered. Mel had his hand on a hammer. The other members of the crew, Steve, Phil, and Robert, were nearby, still holding up the two framed walls they were holding up when the forest first belched soldiers and knights. Bill surveyed the group for a moment and finally his eyes settled on Fides.

"This one alright?" Bill grunted. The priest, a good-looking man who no doubt had made many women jealous of his calling, also sized him up. Fides was growing uncomfortable under this scrutiny. He could not even begin to guess what all the attention was about. Surrounded by what appeared to be knights with real swords, soldiers with real guns, and believers of real religions, he felt completely disoriented. Besides that, he felt naked and vulnerable. The priest was taking his sweet time. There was a flash of eye contact with Fides, but if there was any message intended, Fides did not catch it. The priest turned on his heels and began marching back towards the strange assembly that he had originated from.

"You there," Bill called at him gruffly. "You need to come with us." He had small black eyes that looked like tiny, dense marbles. There was no twinkle in these eyes. Fides could imagine no appropriate reaction to this command, so he did what his instincts told him to do: he did nothing. Bill repeated himself, "Alright, let's go."

Ed appeared suddenly to be roused into action. "Now what is this all about? You can't come over here and start ordering members of my crew around. Who do you think you are? Explain yourself!" Frank and the rest of the crew were suddenly right behind Fides, and he felt strengthened by the show of support. Ed was now in Bill's face, jabbing his finger into Bill's chest. "I don't know what's going on here- and I've seen some strange things before- but this takes the cake, and now you are singling out my crewmember..." Fides listened as Ed started to lace his tirade with profanity and he glanced nervously over at the pool of gunmen. He wasn't sure, but he thought he saw some of their trigger fingers twitching.

"Hold on, Ed," Fides suddenly blurted out. He didn't want his friends' deaths on his conscience. He asked himself how bad could the matter be if a priest was involved? Fides stepped past Frank, who had slowly moved into position in front of him. "Thanks Frank, really. Really, thanks. No, look Ed. I'll go see what the deal is. It's not a big deal." Fides stood before Bill. He didn't realize that Bill was so much shorter than both him and Ed, and he was suddenly filled with an additional spurt of courage: "If there is trouble you have in mind for me, sir," he glared at Bill, "rest assured I'll make every effort to sort you out proper."

There was a brief moment of silence. Fides thought that maybe behind those beady eyes there was some machinery of thought in motion, but Bill showed no outward signs of introspection. Bill grunted one more time, "This feller will explain things to ya when he gets back." Bill turned and walked back to the assembly of militants. It suddenly occurred to Fides that he ought to follow, and so he did. He shot a re-assuring look back to his crewmates and hastened to catch up to Bill. He decided that he didn't want to meet that strange group on his own, much preferring to arrive before them with Bill.

As he got closer he was able to see all the parties more easily. The knights looked even more like knights than they did before. They appeared to be wearing breast plates with a bloody colored 'x' across the front. They really did have swords. He could see also that they had daggers in sheaths wrapped around their limbs in various places. One had a knife tucked in a sheath affixed to the outside of his boot. Another had a short knife strapped to his left arm. Easy enough to get to with the right hand, Fides considered.

He was surprised to see that the soldiers had patch insignia that was similar to those worn by the knights. They too had knives strapped to themselves all over the place, but they also had the traditional fixings: grenades, canteens, ammunition. Both groups seemed to be filled completely with exceptionally proud men. They were all either sitting or standing ram-rod straight. Each had a determined glint in his eye. When he finally turned to examine the group of religious people, he noticed the same determined gaze on their faces, as well. But he didn't have as much time to study them, because suddenly they were talking again.

"You'll get what you want when this feller returns," Bill was asserting to the tall, orange-robed man, who nodded grimly.

"I hope you get what you want where you are going," Tall Man intoned. There was no threat in the voice. It was steady and cool and unperturbed by the emotion that Bill was wearing on his sleeve. "And as agreed, Father Frederich will accompany you both. He will complete the transaction, or witness it, and return with this one. What is your name, sir?" the tall man gently asked him.

"Fides, sir. Fides."

"Father Frederich will return with Fides and you will have your reward, and everyone will be satisfied," Tall Man continued. Bill returned to his normal style of communication and grunted his approval. Fides stood there waiting for some sort of explanation about what was going on, but nothing appeared to be forthcoming from anyone.

The tall man addressed the soldiers and knights all at once, "Return to your outposts. Very soon we will have what we need. Mr. Huxley, please ask the crew you have hired to continue their work. It is very important that they finish it. And then you may go." With that, the soldiers and knights disappeared again into the woods. The assembly of 'believers' followed Tall Man back into the larger structure. Bill, Father Frederich, and Fides were left alone.

"I'll be right back," Bill muttered briskly, and stalked over to Ed. Fides smiled when he saw Lonny rubbing his back in pain. He couldn't hear him, but he knew he was moaning and complaining about his fall, and probably expressing outrage that none of the crew offered to catch him. The rest of them were in animated conversation with Ed. Frank in particular did not seem very happy at all. When Bill got there Fides could tell that he had imparted his message very undiplomatically because Frank's face became beet red and he blurted out something. Bill threw up his hands, said something, and stalked back towards Fides and the priest. During that whole time, Fides and Father Frederich had stood quietly together. Neither ventured a word with each other.

Having imparted his message to Ed, Bill stalked back past Fides and the priest without speaking to either of them. Father Frederich glanced at Fides and followed Bill off towards the old warehouse they had seen before. Again, Fides was left to figure out on his own that it was time to walk. He had had an opportunity to look at the priest while they were waiting and he found him to be a remarkable looking man. For lack of a better way of putting it, and with an eye towards preserving his own manliness in making the observation, Fides decided that Father Frederich had what could be described as "Hollywood Looks." He was a sharp looking man whose casual demeanor did not fool Fides one bit. This priest was not to be trifled with.

Fides half-walked, half-jogged, to catch up to the other two. He glanced back behind him just as he rounded the corner to go behind the warehouse and he could see that his friends were starting to return to work. They passed another clearing that was behind the warehouse and found a path into the forest, which they followed for only a minute or two before it opened up into an additional clearing. This was no ordinary clearing. Fides pinched himself: Was that an airplane? Is this an airfield? His heart jumped and he tried to say something, to object, to inquire, to protest, but nothing came out other than a gurgle. The gurgle caught Father Frederich's attention, and the priest turned and offered a reassuring look. They strode across the landing strip to a hangar. There was a pair of soldiers walking circles around it that didn't pay any attention to the three of them.

Inside, Fides saw a private airplane. Fides had seen an airplane once, but it had been a long time ago. A man, presumably the pilot, was sitting at a desk nearby, his feet propped up on it. He was leaning so far back in the chair without falling that Fides was sure the laws of physics were surely being violated. The pilot did not seem surprised to see them approach.

Father Frederich turned to address Fides. "This gentleman here..." the priest said, pointing at Bill, "...does not feel like he is safe in this area anymore. He wants to be taken to a place that he considers safe. You and I are going to accompany him on that journey. Your presence is part of an agreement to bring along a neutral party. Both sides here are concerned about having their commitments broken by the other. You will come with us on the trip. We will return not much more than a day from now. If all goes well, that is. When we arrive at our destination, Mr. Huxley will give you something that we want, which will therefore assure you safe passage home. Does that sound about right, Mr. Huxley?"

"Yea, you've got it." Bill did not seem very enthusiastic.

"You see, Fides, as rude as this man may seem, and I won't necessarily try to completely dissuade you of that impression, he did have your interests in mind as well as his own. He wanted to make sure that you would get back safely. Any attempt to remove that necklace without the right combination will cause the necklace to explode, destroying it and killing you. Since the necklace is a critical necessity to this site's operations, it is in our interests to make sure you return alive. For now, Bill is wearing it, presumably because he fears someone here plans on killing him." Bill looked at Fides, waiting for this information to soak in. Fides was just realizing the implications as Father Frederich motioned them along, "Come. Let us go and finish this."

The pilot leaped out of his chair with a shout, "All fueled up!" He yanked the door to the passenger area open, and waited for the three of them to climb up. Bill went first. Fides was on his way when Father Frederich grabbed his arm.

"Hold on a second, Fides. We may need these," the priest said mysteriously, opening a large cabinet near the pilot's desk. Inside was a rack filled with beautiful large swords, very similar to those he had seen carried by the knights. The priest handed one to Fides, who felt its weight in his hands and thought to himself that it was just right. The priest grabbed another for himself and then they joined Bill in the passenger compartment.

Bill muttered something when he saw the swords, but neither could understand him. There was an uneasy silence shared between them as the pilot sealed up the passenger compartment and then climbed into the cockpit. The silence continued as the pilot taxied into position. The sound of the engine was loud, but not as loud as Fides thought it would be.

As if to break the tension, the priest volunteered an ice breaker, "Have you ever flown before, Fides?"

Fides laughed. Who has flown in dozens of years? Only the rich and the very powerful, that's who. "Only once, and by accident," Fides joked back. "But it was a distance of only ten feet and my wood pile broke my fall marvelously."

At that, the priest threw his head back in a loud laugh, "That's the spirit! Well, let's pray that you'll have a third flight, eh? Off your roof, now to New Mexico, and then back, right?" But no one had said anything about New Mexico. Fides tried to laugh, but he couldn't conceal the pinch in his gut at this disclosure. Bill interrupted them.

"Don't get his hopes up, friend." Bill's tone was not threatening, but Fides found the remark extremely perplexing. That was not quite the sort of comment he had been expecting. At last, the pilot was ready. He called back to them that they were getting ready to take off. Fides could imagine the looks on his friends' faces when they saw that plane take off so near to them. Frank was going to have the Tall Man's throat when he learned that this is what was involved in the 'transaction.' A moment later, the tone in the cabin had grown somber, but Fides did not perceive the real reasons for the somber atmosphere.

The priest stared at Fides purposefully, "Lift up your window shade, Fides." The way this comment came struck Fides as completely bizarre. It wasn't a suggestion, it wasn't a command. It was almost like what one might hear when called to a tragic accident and asked to identify a loved one. "Do you know this person?" they might say, but you don't want to look. Yet, you know that you need to look. Fides lifted the shade and watched the landscape get smaller and smaller outside his window. He hadn't realized how late in the day it had become. The sun had definitely started its descent towards the western horizon. Strange. He hadn't noticed the passing of time.

All of a sudden there was a dim bulge of light far out on the eastern horizon. A dull, pulsating, shimmering mound of light seemed to rise slowly against the crimson sky. Then there was another one, more to the north. "What was that?" Fides demanded. But the priest was only looking at him with a piercing gaze. Bill grunted.

"What was that?" Fides demanded again. But Fides thought he knew. There was a pregnant pause... "Was that... was that a nuclear explosion?" Bill and the priest remained silent. Fides was getting extremely angry, now. Fides had a tint of red in his hair, and when he got angry his whole head seemed red as blood rushed to his cheeks and ears. Combined with the light thrusting itself into the cabin, Fides knew he was probably radiating anger like nuclear bombs radiate energy. "Was it?" he demanded again.

Father Frederich nodded.

"Not exactly safe in our parts for awhile," Bill muttered sharply.

"How did the two of you know about this?" Fides shouted, thrusting his chin out in righteous anger. But neither of them offered any answer. Fides sat there and stewed in his juices for awhile. His heart was pounding blood into his head so loudly that he couldn't even hear his own breathing. Fides' stomach was suddenly clenched in an iron fist and he doubled over at the recognition, the realization, the sudden specific awareness that that first mound of light had originated from the direction of his own hometown. Oh my God! he shouted inside his skull. My God, my God, my God. He fought back this new emotion. He knew there was really nothing he could do. Nothing he could have done. Nor did he know if it really did come from his hometown. He told himself that the idea was absurd. Terre Haute could not be a target in anyone's book worth wasting a nuclear bomb on. Still, he could not wait until this ridiculous round trip was over so he could join his friends on what he knew would be a hasty journey back home.

Neither Bill nor the priest had yet said anything in reply to Fides loaded question. In fact, Bill had apparently gone to sleep. His eyes were closed, at any rate, and Fides could hear heavy, rhythmic breathing coming from his direction. The priest had apparently been watching Fides throughout Fides' internal arguing. When their eyes at last locked Fides somehow knew that the priest had already realized what the implications of a nuclear blast in a south-easterly direction would be to Fides. There was compassion in the priest's eyes. The priest's piercing gaze seemed to be saying 'be still,' but nothing more. Finally, the priest closed his eyes, and after a moment, he too seemed to have fallen asleep.

Fides stared out the window for quite awhile longer. He did not think it possible that he could sleep. But after awhile, he too fell asleep. He would wake up on occasion throughout the trip and then fall back to sleep. After what seemed like a very long time, Fides felt the plane making its descent. Bill and Father Frederich were both awake. After a surprisingly short amount of time, they were on the ground, and the exhausted pilot was taxiing into yet another hangar. Bill gathered up a few of his items, but as neither the priest nor Fides had anything other than the swords, getting off the plane also was completed quickly.

Bill was waiting for them at the bottom of the stairs. There was a black limo there, with a driver, and a Chinese man with a sidearm on his belt. Bill seemed as though he were in a hurry.

"Alright, let's get this over with. I've had plenty enough fun with you fellahs and I'm ready to part ways. You understand," Bill grumbled.

Fides suddenly realized that he was starting to not feel very well. In fact, he was not feeling very well at all. He made his way over to where Bill and the priest were waiting, but he was feeling quite dizzy. He steadied himself by putting his left arm on the hood of the limo and seemed to regain a bit of his strength. Bill reached up to his neck and fumbled with the necklace for a bit. It unlocked and fell into Bill's hands. Fides was able to see the object clearly for the first time. It seemed to be made of steel and electrodes. Bill walked over to Fides and put the contraption around Fides' neck, clasping it in the front. There was a blinking green light on one side of the necklace, but apart from that the casual observer wouldn't notice anything unique about it. It seemed as though he was wearing a rosary made out of steel and computer parts. He had once seen a rosary a long time ago when he had experimented with becoming a minister.

"That alone won't get you safely home," Bill explained. "I chose this priest out of the lot of them because he seemed like he was an honest fellah and wouldn't compromise his word. You don't know what the necklace does, but that's ok. They know what it does. And they know that something won't work without it. But you need something special to get it off. You need the code. I'm going to give you the code, and by God, you don't tell this guy what it is. You don't tell anyone what it is until you get safely back to Peoria. You understand?" Fides didn't, though. He was starting to see black. His eyes started to hurt because of the light in the hangar, which confused him, because there really wasn't that much light. He felt dizzy. He heard Bill's voice again, "Do you understand?" Then Bill was very close to him, and he could hear him right by his ear, but he could no longer see him. He could hear Bill faintly say, "The code is...."

He couldn't see anything. Black. Things were going black. Dark. All the events of the last few weeks made one final streak through his mind in quick succession as he slowly faded into unconsciousness: the ominous warnings about a killer disease from the east; his argument with his wife; his parting from his family; his journey to Peoria; his observations of the strange people he was working for; his plane-eyed view of a nuclear explosion; and now this one final recollection as the heavy blackness at last conquered him: a brusque voice saying, "The code is...."

== Chapter 2 ==

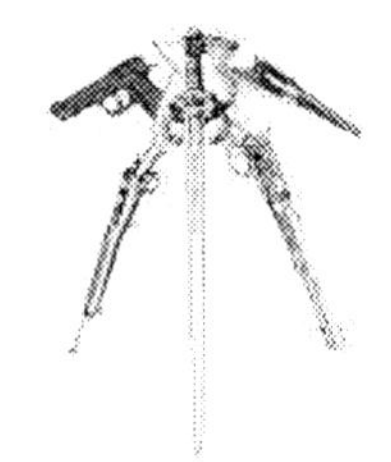

Darkness. The first thing he was aware of was that he was aware only of his own awareness. His senses were reporting no sensations; it was a full sensory black-out. It was as though that which was the real 'him' was clawing up out of a deep cavern towards an entrance it couldn't be sure was there and then a thick blackness would envelope his consciousness again, and there was not even the awareness of any self within his being.

So it went for a time. Each time this dim self-awareness occurred, he would seem to draw closer to the cavern entrance. He started to hear things. He began to see shades of light, or perhaps, reverse shadows. There were smells every now and then. Somewhere someone was cooking. He was conscious of himself for longer periods, too, which did not comfort him, though it should have. It meant he was coming out, but he feared he would wake up and find that he was in a coffin.

Now, voices. A woman's voice. Older. And a man's voice. Adults, definitely. He couldn't distinguish any words. As he progressed, he made up his mind to try to measure the time going on around him. Without any frames of reference, this was as frustrating as his sense of being in a coffin. Nonetheless, he was encouraged and strengthened by the ever increasing quality of the sensory information he was getting. He still couldn't make out any words, but it was definitely lighter around him, and he was quite sure he smelled a baked potato once. He began to feel... comfortably warm.

One day, Fides opened his eyes and he could see. It was as sudden as that. He was lying in a large room. His bed seemed to be situated in the back of the room. He wasn't very far off the ground. The other objects in the room also seemed to be close to the ground. There was something that was clearly a table, but it was very low like everything else. He could look out and see across the plane of the table. There were plates on it, and some utensils. Next to his bed was a short stool. On it was an empty bowl, and next to it, a spoon.

He sensed movement on the far side of the room. He screwed up his eyes a little in the dark and he realized that this was the woman whose voice he had heard. She was not very tall, but he couldn't make out anything else about her because her back was to him. She was busy working in a small kitchen area that was in sight. There was a loud whooshing sound.

Fides looked in the direction of the sound and realized that it was the sound of the wind rushing in as the front door burst open. There was a moment where a man's figure was situated perfectly against the bright, sunny background, and he appeared to be only shadow with substance. Then the man was inside and the door was closed. The man moved quickly to greet the woman, and went to the table. He sat down cross legged at the table and began eating from one of the plates. After a moment, the woman came over with a large pot of something so hot the steam appeared to form small clouds over it. She set it down and was about to sit when she saw Fides studying her.

"Ah. We have company." She was locked in a half-standing, half-sitting position as she noticed his eyes peering out at her. The man had his spoon an inch from his mouth, similarly frozen. She sat down with a self-deprecating thump. "We are so very glad that you have officially joined us, Fides. Very glad." The man completed the transaction between hand and mouth, and commenced regular eating. But now he was also smiling pleasantly as he chewed.

Fides said nothing. Instead, he studied the two individuals eating. There was the smell of incense and some sort of soup. The woman was indeed an older woman. Shriveled might be the appropriate word. She was a shriveled up Chinese woman, who nonetheless seemed filled with energy, bounce, and joy. She beamed at him. The man was at least his age, possibly older. He couldn't tell because the man seemed, for lack of a better word, weathered, which may have given an exaggerated appearance of older age. The man was still smiling at him, but he also remained very interested in his soup.

Fides continued to let his eyes roam around the room. It dawned on him at last that there was only one room to the whole residence. Two cots were lined up against the wall on one side. On another side were the stove and a sink. On another side there was a desk with a number of books heaped up on it. In the middle was the table that the two were dining at. He only saw one door, and he knew already that it lead only to the outdoors. Finally his eyes returned to the Chinese woman and this weathered cowboy and he discovered that they were still watching him. He made an attempt to sit up and the woman frowned.

"No. Don't you be sitting up now. You haven't sat up in... oh, it's been more than a year, I'd say. No, lay back down." She was beside him now. She had entered into 'mothering-mode' and he couldn't do anything other than obey. She called over to the man. "Dietrich, come over here and help me raise this cot." The cowboy put down his spoon and joined them. They appeared to be working together on some mechanism underneath his bed, and finally there was a creak (she exclaimed "Slowly, Dietrich!") and the side of the bed where his head was resting began to elevate. The woman beamed, "Old hospital bed. Dietrich stripped it out and adapted it for you." Fides was sitting up with his back against the tilted bed.

Dietrich cleared off the stool, removing the bowl and spoon that had been there and replaced them with a glass of water.

"See if you have the strength to take some water," he said.

Fides reached out and took the glass to his lips. His arm shook a bit as he was bringing it up but the woman helped his arm up. "He's still got to regain some strength, I'd say. These muscles haven't properly worked in a long time. You've come through a hard spot, Fides." She brought a napkin to his lip. Not all the water made it into his mouth. Dietrich appeared to be taking measure of him, but it was the woman who issued the verdict: "You're going to rest, Fides. We'll move you around the house, some. Get your blood going."

She noticed Fides looking at her, inquiringly. "Me? Oh, call me Corrie. Why not? Everyone does. Not my real name, of course. No one can say my real name properly, not even Dietrich." Dietrich appeared to blush, but it was really too dark in the room to know that for sure. "You've been gone for more than a year. You got left for dead, you did. A man brought you to us, and we agreed to take you in. Didn't know what we were getting into, though, did we Dietrich?"

Dietrich nodded and seemed to be very pleased that their efforts had paid off. Fides really had no idea what kind of effort had been involved in sustaining him. But Corrie kept talking. "You'll be embarrassed to know it- but don't be, you had no control- you had blood coming out all your openings if you can guess my meaning and we had to clean it up. We didn't know if taking you in might be our own deaths really, but it was the right thing to do, and living for you was better living than the living we had been doing anyway." Dietrich again nodded his assent. "But we never did get sick, and you never did die. You just got all pale as though you might run out of blood for sure. But then you stopped bleeding- we thank God for that, I'll tell you. Some of my sheets... oh never mind that... but then you just lay there this whole time. Feeding you soup and water. Soup and water. All it seemed like you could take. Broth really." The woman was obviously very pleased that it had not all been in vain. But Fides was still not really happy with the explanation. He had to ask.

"You're Chinese," he whispered. He expected to see her face darken, and perhaps there was a hint of that, but she only chuckled and leaned in a bit.

"Look at my face, Fides." She brought her face close to his. "You think I'm old enough to have been here in this country before the great southern invasion? Oh yes. Ol' Corrie would never walk away from the things she knew was right. Everyone knows that. I'm as American as they come. Even when I went over to the other side everyone here knew I was just working them. Listen to me talk. Don't hear an accent, do you? It so happens I can speak both Chinese and English perfectly."

Fides knew very well at this point that here was an extremely trustworthy woman. Whatever she put her word to, she did. She'd stick to her guns. Her being Chinese, or of Chinese descent, had little to do with her identity. Her being was derived from her principles and values. Learning that she had been involved in the great southern invasion suddenly grabbed hold of his curiosity. An actual participant? That had to be forty or fifty years ago. After the American defeat, there had been a virtual withdrawal of the victorious foreigners. As Fides understood it, right now hundreds of thousands of Chinese troops were in control of the United States-Mexican border, making sure that nobody gets out of the US and nothing gets in. Reliable information was so hard to come by he never really knew what the current state of things was down on the southern border and he'd never had a credible person to ask. It's not that it mattered. He was just interested. But Corrie wouldn't let him speak again to ask her. After taking care of him a little longer, she crouched over his face and told him to go back to sleep.

He realized that he had grown extremely exhausted. He had probably only been sustained this long because of the novelty of the situation. He obeyed her command, allowed his eyelids to fall shut like heavy quilts resting on a bed and fell into a deep and dreamless sleep.

When he woke up the next morning there was a great deal more light in the house. Some windows had been opened. Corrie and Dietrich were nowhere to be seen. He had been left to sleep in the reclined position, but he used his elbows to prop himself up more so that he was in a sitting position. His stomach muscles immediately protested, but he thought it was probably good to start moving his limbs about. Now that it was lighter in the house, he realized that there wasn't anything more to see than what he had seen while it was darker. The residence was fairly sparse, actually. He thought about throwing his legs around the edge of the bed so that he could have his feet on the floor in anticipation of a 'stand' command, but his legs seemed unusually heavy. He wiggled his toes and verified by smaller commands that everything was still functional. He saw that he wasn't going to be able to rush anything.

Within about thirty minutes Corrie came in. "Ah, you're awake!" she exclaimed, exultant. You slept for a full day my friend. Oh yes, you did. Don't worry, though, you're coming out of it just fine." She set to work at the stove and kitchen counter. Whatever it was that she was cooking smelled fantastic. After a few more minutes, Dietrich came in. He had a pile of vegetation which Fides took to be food of some kind. Corrie took the greens and started chopping them. He could hear her whistling a happy tune. Dietrich sat down at the short table.

"A lot has changed since you went under," he started.

"Hush, Dietrich. He doesn't need to hear any of that right now," Corrie interjected, with her back turned still, working on the food. Fides struggled to find his tongue and spoke.

"No, actually, I want to know," he smiled. "I feel like I've been stuck in an empty box." Dietrich implored Corrie with his eyes.

Finally, Corrie relented. "Oh alright, but don't get him worked up." Dietrich smirked, victorious.

Dietrich walked across to a pantry and removed some water from it, poured it into three glasses, and brought one over for Fides, and another for himself. Then he pulled over the short stool that had apparently served as his bedside table for a year and sat down on it. He could see Dietrich with greater detail but he still couldn't guess an age. Dietrich appeared very eager to tell some stories and after taking a gulp of the water he had poured for himself, he began.

"Of course, we don't know all the details, but we know enough to know that everything has changed. Here are two things that we do know. Last year, right about the time that you came to New Mexico, there was some sort of nuclear attack against the United States. But we think that there were actually nuclear attacks all over the world, because the southern invaders have completely left. They've gone home." Dietrich appeared to be nearly giddy about this news.

"The Chinese have left North America?" Fides asked, filled with incredulity.

"Yessir. Now, we don't know if it's only because of nuclear attacks, though. You see, the disease that brought you down- it kept coming and coming. Even though millions died in the nuclear attacks, all told (I'm guessing) that disease killed tens and tens of millions. We think it got into the Chinese. Pretty sure, in fact. And boy, if they took that home with them, we can only imagine what they are dealing with!" Fides noted that he didn't seem to be one bit sympathetic to whatever plight he was imagining was facing those in China. Not that he could blame him. It was a bit of a humiliation to have had a good chunk of the southern part of the US captured by a mass of Chinese and Mexican troops, only to be given back under not so agreeable terms. Then the border was manned as though the US was some sort of prison. Naturally, his knowledge of this scenario was gleaned from the many rumors he had heard, and these events happened when he was very young. He had never been in a position to know what the real truth of things was.

Dietrich was continuing without him. Were those scars on his arms? "Well, I think the disease has pretty much run its course in our country by now. Between nuclear and biological holocausts, I think it's safe to say that our country has maybe only five percent of the population that it had about a year ago. And if we're right in thinking that this has happened globally- well you can imagine the situation. Everyone is back to square one."

Corrie bustled over to set some bowls. "Square one, indeed," she snapped. "We both know it's only a matter of time before some that still have access to technology try to assert themselves." Dietrich ignored her.

"We're only a hundred miles from the border. Nobody coming up that way has any talk about any Chinese or even that many Mexicans wandering around. Whoever let loose that scourge I bet has come to regret letting it go. That's my opinion. No armies forming up down there, that's for sure. And if ever we were ripe for being conquered again, it's now, I say. But nothing from the south."

Corrie brought over some more place settings. "Sounds great, except for the billions that probably died to make it possible. Even better, right, when we think of what we're left with, eh Dietrich?" she concluded sarcastically.

Dietrich smirked again. "She's a happy cynic. She knows full well that we are free again." He got serious, "But there are still lots of small towns and villages that aren't letting anyone travel to them or through them. Like I said, I think the disease has run its course, but I could be wrong. A lot of people aren't taking chances. Also, from what we learned while there were still some travelers, a lot of American cities are just completely gone. Not only that, but there were some strange explosions high up in the atmosphere for a couple of days after the attacks- in fact, that was the first we knew of things, because obviously news travels by foot, but we could see with our own eyes one of them explosions- these explosions wrecked almost all of our electrical stuff. A lot of the left over cars from the old days don't work one bit. The guy who dropped you off complained about his plane not working anymore."

"The guy who dropped me off?" Fides wondered aloud.

"A priest, I think. He begged us to look after you. Said you were mighty important and that you hold the very key to success for our nation. Didn't believe him, of course, and you were already starting to... uh..." Dietrich trailed off.

"Let's not talk about those details!" Corrie admonished Dietrich over a hissing pot of stew.

"Well anyway, we didn't believe him. But he showed us that necklace you've got there..." This was the first time that Fides remembered some of the strange events leading up to arrival in New Mexico. His hands went up to the thick strand of strange metallic objects threaded around his neck. He felt around for the center, where there was some sort of keypad. He suddenly remembered, dimly and in a fog, a voice talking about a code. Dietrich let Fides rediscover the necklace, and then returned to his story telling. He thought he could hear Corrie muttering, or chuckling under her breath, but her back remained turned to them.

"That necklace was like nothing we'd ever seen before, and the day before we had seen that bright explosion way off in the distance- over El Paso, we reckon- so we knew something was going on. So we took you in and took care of you. Now we're hoping you can tell us what that necklace is all about!" Dietrich said, almost greedily.

"I really don't know," Fides apologized. "I can't even... I'm not even sure I remember. I can't recall." Dietrich appeared to be somewhat deflated. Corrie came to the rescue carrying a big pot of some very good smelling soup or stew. She ladled up some for everyone. She told him to try feeding himself again, but again, Fides needed help because he was so unsteady.

"Now, what Dietrich hasn't said yet," she continued for Dietrich, as Dietrich began to eat, "Is that the people coming through our parts are talking about there basically being anarchy all over (not that they know what that word means in order to use it) and there are already rumors of some terrible tyrants gathering up little armies for themselves. We've got nothing like that here, so I don't know what the truth of it is, but I'd say it's inevitable. You just have got to plan on that happening. I've tried to talk to some of the local folks about it but they don't seem to want to listen. Don't want to get very close to me to listen, either, on account of them knowing we are taking care of you. The time is coming where the power vacuum is going to be filled, and if we don't fill it rightly and purposely, it's going to fill itself up with whatever happens to be naturally around. And since we already know what man can do, since what man did has put us in this spot, we also know what happens to be naturally around." She seemed to be arguing with someone, but whoever it was, they were not present in the room with them.

In the next breath she informed him, "You are too weak to do anything for a long time so I don't want you to even try. You understand?" Fides allowed himself to smile at being mothered by this woman half his size and twice his age. "You look tired. Why don't you take another rest? We'll talk more, of course. Get your rest."

Fides did not protest. He'd only been awake for a little over an hour and he was already exhausted.

Each day he was awake for longer and longer periods and he was able to do more and more. After about a month he was wandering around the small house. Seeing as there wasn't much to the place, he found that the desk covered in books was the only destination of any interest. He had never considered himself much of a reader, so he only thumbed through them. They were all very old. They had interesting titles. Corrie would encourage him to read them, but he would nonchalantly dismiss these suggestions. He was interested in reading them, if only so he could have something to do, but he was too embarrassed to admit that he would need help.

He also began a daily fight against consuming guilt. He had been away from his family for more than a year. He had left them despite his wife's insistent pleas. Things had gone wrong in the world. Terribly wrong. They had been left to face events on their own. Worse, rather than being only a week's journey from them, he was now apparently months and months away, and he would not have the strength to make such a journey for as far as he could see into the near future. His mind invented horrible possibilities. Perhaps they had been overcome by the disease. Perhaps they were alive, but his home had been confiscated by bandits, leaving them to wander the countryside as beggars. He suddenly recalled the incident with his son at their shed. Fides was certain that if he had been there when these new troubles had descended, he could have protected them. If he would not have been able to, he would have died alongside of them. Naturally, he didn't know anything about his family's situation, but that didn't stop him from imagining the worst. He took to sulking.

Corrie and Dietrich could see him lapse into these funeral moments and would try to talk him out of them because they could last for hours, otherwise. They had correctly guessed what was going on inside of him, but they didn't talk about their guesses with him. Corrie found that telling him stories of the great southern invasion would take him out of his despondency. Of course, the conclusion of that particular war wasn't exactly America's finest moment, so it brought with it its own depression. This was mitigated, of course, by the fact that the invaders had apparently gone all the way home. The Disease was America's Divine Wind.

Corrie also increasingly prodded him to read some of the books she had. "It will take your mind off your mind," she would say. He always gently declined these attempts, but he was quite confident that Corrie was compensating for his refusal to read them by summarizing them for him in their conversations. At dinner one day, he would hear about utopian societies and their fatal flaw, and how it was this fatal flaw that came to undermine everything, everywhere. On another day, she would pine for the days when the US constitution had been the law of the land. She bitterly recalled the war to disarm the United States, and snidely remarked (again, to someone not even present) that the world had reaped fruit of its own sowing. Other days, she would launch into long rambles about good and evil and man's place in the universe.

Conversations of this sort were making him more and more uncomfortable. He had applied to be a minister in the state-approved church when he was younger and had been on his way to becoming part of the educated class. He grew disenchanted almost immediately, however. It wasn't because of the banal message he was reduced to sharing, but because events all around him warred against any notion that God was Good. If there was a god, that is. Though atheists filled the state church, he was uncomfortable being in their number. His own integrity wouldn't allow it. However, here in New Mexico he now experienced a severe form of survivor's guilt. He blamed God, whom he did not believe existed, for allowing him to depart from his family at such a critical time. He blamed God for letting him live through a disease that he had heard everyone else always died from. Of course, this was completely irrational.

Interestingly, in contrast to Fides' own conclusion from the evil in the world, Corrie was confident of God's goodness. She was as confident of God's goodness as she was of man's badness, and she cursed Man for being so bad and stupid to underestimate just how bad and stupid Man was. She denounced the powers that had reduced the world to rubble. Vitriol unbecoming an aged Chinese woman was reserved for the people that had allowed those powers to have the ability to ruin the world in the first place. "If the right thing is not done in the small things, it will be impossible to do it when come the big things," she would say. Or, similarly, "If you never do a little exercise, you shouldn't hope to jump over any mountains." Another: "You can't save the world if you won't save the man lying on your doorstep." Fides assumed these things were platitudes recorded in those books. He considered them carefully, but whenever they found their way back into any talk of the divine, he'd darken his heart. Sometimes he'd kick himself for not putting such wisdom into action in regards to his own family a little over a year ago. There was lurking in all these conversations a sense that if there was a God, whether good or bad, this God would never tolerate abandoning one's family in the time of its severest need.

After a handful of months, his strength had returned well enough that he was able to help Dietrich tend to the plot of land that they owned. Actually, calling it a plot of land didn't quite do it justice. It was a very large ranch. Dietrich taught Fides how to ride a horse, and the two of them would patrol the property. Since all the guns had been confiscated in the Humiliation, Dietrich was armed with a bow and quiver of arrows. After a short time, Dietrich had constructed a bow for Fides, as well. It took him a good month to gain the power to pull it back, but once he did Fides felt... well, manly. Sending those arrows out across the sagebrush at various targets filled him with a sense of his own strength. The arrow was an extension of his will and a representation of willed vengeance. The only problem was that at this point in time, he felt that any revenge to be exacted ought to be exacted from him.

While out on these rides, Fides had occasion to see other people. These folks would also be riding horses out on patrol. They never came very close, however. Often, Dietrich and Fides would pull up and stop when they saw someone else and they would see their counter parts doing the same thing. They would stand in place for five or ten minutes, neither side moving, separated by four or five hundred yards, and then both groups would continue on their way. Fides thought this was very un-neighborly. Dietrich explained that he was sure that his neighbors were still concerned about Fides' presence and that once they all became convinced that he was entirely healthy, they'd probably find the neighbors narrowing the distance between them.

What Dietrich said was true enough, but neither of them expected it to take as long as it did. You could say that Fides had plenty of time to regain his strength. Nearly four years passed before, on one of their patrols, they saw that one of the neighbors caught sight of them and was coming toward them. It appeared to be a father and his son, but as they got closer Fides saw that both appeared to be every bit as weathered as Dietrich did. The father had a thick scar across his cheek and was missing part of his right ear. Fides did not stare.

"Dietrich!" the older man called out.

"Howard, how very nice to speak to you again," Dietrich said coolly. The man seemed only moderately affected by this.

"We had our reasons, as you well know," Howard asserted, giving a slight nod towards Fides.

"It's been almost five years, Howard." Dietrich flatly stated. It hadn't really dawned on Fides before how much anger may have been lurking behind Dietrich's demeanor during this time. He certainly had never expressed it to him. Fides felt a pang of guilt as he realized that Corrie and Dietrich had given up much to care for him.

"Well, those were some pretty bad years, friend. We think that just in the last year the Disease has finally run itself out," Howard offered in his own defense.

"Well, I'm glad that you didn't hurry over to me too soon, then. Are you sure you shouldn't have waited for two years to pass before talking to us, just to make sure? It's not as though you haven't seen me on the ranch with him healthy as one can be for the last three years." Dietrich was not to be satisfied so easily.

Howard ignored this, but seemed desperate to change the subject. "I don't suppose you know about much that has happened in the last year."

"You'd be surprised at what we've managed to learn," Dietrich slyly remarked, and chuckled. Howard didn't seem to think much of this, but the younger man that Fides assumed was Howard's son squirmed a little in the saddle.

"Well, the news I've got right now concerns the man sitting next to you more than it concerns you, I reckon."

"Oh?" Dietrich cocked his head at him. Fides shifted his eyes from the son to Howard.

"Well, I'm sure by your various means you know that the whole country has disintegrated. You know that lots of cities were destroyed by nuclear weapons. You know, obviously, that a lot died on account of that disease," Howard rambled on. Fides could sense that Dietrich was getting impatient.

"Yes, we knew all of that. Didn't have to pay anything to find that out, either," he said pointedly. Now it was the father's turn to squirm.

"Well, I'll cut to it. Because of all the scattering and the like, they've set up a place up in Illinois for families and friends to find each other again. I'm sure that this man here will want to see to it that he finds his family again. People go and post their names and kin and where they live. Then everyone sorta looks out for everyone else to try to match people up again. We heard that this man was with that priest originally. That priest came from that area, so I'm assuming your friend might have interests in that area, too."

"Well, Howard, we sure do appreciate you telling us this. I hope that you'll tell the other folks that this man- his name is Fides, by the way- is alive and well, and our ranch can be taken out of quarantine." Fides had realized over the last couple of years that the sacrifices made to save his life went deeper than he had imagined initially. It wasn't only that he had been taken in and cared for at great personal effort. When they took him in, they were cut off. This had been a source of personal discomfort for Fides, but both Corrie and Dietrich had made pained efforts to assure Fides that they had no regrets. Nonetheless, it was times like these that Fides could not avoid feeling some guilt.

"Now you know we had to do it-" Howard began, but Dietrich cut him off.

"I'm not angry, I don't hate anyone. I think I'm the right amount of hurt. My friends and neighbors don't talk to me for five years and won't even allow an exchange of notes or supplies. I suppose I would have done the same thing. Its just going to take me a bit to heal is all, and I hope you can understand."

"Alright then, Diet. I know where you are coming from. I'll make sure I help smooth things over as best as I can so we can get that healing done properly." Fides realized that there had probably been a time when Howard and Dietrich were very close. In fact, it wouldn't surprise him to learn that they had fought together in the last war. Only a half moment after that Fides arrived at yet another conclusion. He had to go back to Illinois. He could not delay any longer. They were bringing families back together and he needed to bring his own family back together.

Corrie reacted in an unexpected way when he announced his intentions to them that night at dinner. Instead of trying to persuade him to get stronger first, or consider the risks, or some other approach he thought the motherly sort might take, she got a steely look in her eye. "That sounds just right. It's time you went on a quest. It's time for you to receive the dignity you feel has been robbed from you. Can't get it by asking, either. You've got to go out there and take it back from whomever it is that robbed you."

The next week was spent in making preparations. Now that Dietrich and Corrie were allowed to access the rest of the population, it was easy to get supplies. Their steady diet of soup was mixed up with other tasty choices. For the first time he found out that Dietrich and Corrie weren't married. Throughout his time with them, he couldn't see it even being possible for them to be married given the disparity in their ages, but he hadn't known what else to think. They had never talked about it and he didn't think it was polite to ask. Some of the townspeople alluded to their regret at having to quarantine the Dietrich ranch. "Especially since that woman was such a hero in her time. No surprise that she would save one more," they would say. This didn't exactly tell him what Dietrich and Corrie were all about, but he felt confident that it had something very much to do with the great southern invasion. However, as Dietrich was often with him at the time, he didn't explore this folklore.

Dietrich obtained a map for Fides and Fides discovered that he was on the outskirts of Las Cruces, not very far from the Mexican border and El Paso. Further inquiry informed them that the family reunion center was in Bloomington, Illinois. There was talk among some in the region of starting up a center like the one in Illinois but in the southwest somewhere. This was not relevant to Fides, of course. He opened up the map so he could see the entire country. He had an extremely long journey ahead of him. He learned that it was almost certainly going to be completely on foot. He'd make his way up old I-25 to Albuquerque where he hoped that he would learn otherwise. Dietrich reminded him that after the last round of nuclear attacks, most of the vehicles no longer worked even though they weren't around any blast. There were theories as to why that was, of course, but one knew they were all shots in the dark. At any rate, Fides very much hoped that he would not have to walk all the way back to Indiana.

While out gathering supplies and information, Dietrich and Fides passed by an airfield. Dietrich informed him that this was where he had flown in, and the airplane was actually still in one of the hangars. It still didn't work. This prompted him to inquire more about how he had come to be in Corrie and Dietrich's care.

"Well, it's simple," Dietrich said. "This priest was going from bar to bar and store to store telling people right out that he had someone in his care that had the Disease and that this person needed long term dedicated care. Of course no one would take him (you) in, but he found out somewhere that Corrie has never turned down an opportunity to do the right thing. So, he bundled you up and found someone to drive the two of you out-" Dietrich laughed out loud- "Ha! Ol' Jessup would never have done that had he known. Last thing he'd have done. Would have liked to have seen his face!" Dietrich regained his composure. "Anyway, this feller brought you to our doorstep. Jessup tore off cursing. We found you a place to lie down, and the priest told us over some tea that you were critical to the future success to the country, if not the world. We thought that was pretty far out there, but he made us look at that strange necklace," Fides instinctively reached up to feel it again, "and we realized there may be something to it. Not that it would have mattered. Corrie would have taken you in anyway."

Fides suddenly remembered hearing a bit of this story once before. The success of the country, if not the world?

But Dietrich continued. "So, later on we saw that bright light flash in the skies over Texas. Not much longer after that, we heard that a lot of our cities had been lost. Of course we'd already heard about the Disease. But about a year or so after that the Chinese army stationed at the border disappeared, leaving a whole lot of dead soldiers who had somehow caught the Disease. This is just rumor, but I think it's probably safe to say that the I.F. is gone, now, too."

Fides gave a little gasp of amazement with that news. There had been plenty of talk with Corrie and Dietrich about the Chinese and Mexicans, but never anything about any other foreign armies. "If the International Force is gone, and the Chinese and their Mexican allies are gone, that means the United States can become what it was a hundred years ago!" he exclaimed.

Dietrich nodded, but frowned. "That's true. There is great potential. But remember, a hundred years ago people didn't see the writing on the wall and the terrible things of this last century are the result of their lack of predictive vision."

"I don't really know much about things before my time. I only know what my father has told me, and of course even he wasn't alive yet when Washington D.C. was destroyed."

"Well, if you'd have read some of the books that Corrie has been pushing on ya, you'd not only know some of the history of this last century, but you'd know better about how we got here in the first place," Dietrich rebuked him. Fides had no answer to that, but by this time they had arrived at the ranch and found that supper was ready.

Dietrich was set to leave the very next morning, so Corrie had the finest meal possible ready for them. The conversation was good, the food was good, and when it was complete the three of them sat quietly, contemplating what had come before and what was soon to come for Fides. Finally, Corrie went to her bed and pulled out a thick leather package. She presented it to Fides. Fides unwrapped it slowly, revealing a hefty book. The cover read: "The Holy Bible."

Fides was awe-struck. When he found his tongue, he forced it to speak, "Is this the real thing?" He started thumbing through the pages and knew the answer for himself immediately. He also saw at once that this was Corrie's personal copy. She had notations and highlighting throughout the book, and a lot of loose pages had been glued in or taped in, or even sewed back in. Fides spoke again. "I thought that all the Bibles had been destroyed, along with all the other books sacred to religions."

"Over my dead body," Corrie said curtly.

"When I applied to be a minister, they were going to let me see one of the official edited versions, but I never had a chance."

"Well, that one is not edited by any 'official' state power," Corrie remarked sharply, "And I'm giving it to you, Fides."

"Oh, no, Corrie. I couldn't possibly take this. I know that they are perfectly legal now, but this has to be incredibly precious to you," Fides protested.

"Don't you worry, Fides. I have got it all memorized."

Fides couldn't believe that, but he knew that there was not going to be an argument about this matter. Corrie wasn't quite done, though.

"I wish you and I would have had a chance to discuss some of these things. Well, I suppose we had plenty of chance, didn't we," she said with only a hint of rebuke in her voice. "I know you probably don't believe anything in that book right now, and that's ok. There are many other books I have that probably could have helped you better for what you are going to face in the very near future, but you'd need to take all of them. Well, this one book will be enough, but you'll have to draw the lessons for yourself now. I know you can read well enough to work your way through it. Don't try to tell me otherwise."

Fides was deeply touched by the gift. That night he organized his supplies one more time. He looked at some of the worn pages in the Bible and wondered if the book would make it through the journey. Naturally, Corrie was right about everything. He had never read anything right out of an un-edited Bible anyway, but from what he had learned about what was in it he was sure that he wouldn't buy into any of it. He couldn't dispute the fact that he really had a one in a million gift in his hands, though.

The next morning there was a hefty breakfast prepared for him. Howard and his son, Steve, also came to see him off. He gathered up his supplies and threw them over his back. "Remember, Fides," Dietrich reminded him, "You'll find it better to walk in the cool of the early morning or the cool of the evening. Its better to settle into a place of your choosing while you still have your energy than to push on and find that you will have to sleep exposed to the elements." Fides nodded in understanding. Now it was Corrie's turn.

"It's been an honor, Fides. You don't owe us a thing. You go find your family, but I sure hope you find yourself, first. And as soon as you get the chance, I want you to read one particular part of that old Bible, and I want you to remember it." She reached up and grabbed his shirt, pulling him down so that they were more at eye level. "They've come back, Fides. They're here. The Nephilim are back. Book-ends, mind you. Be watchful. I wrote the passage down on a piece of paper and stuck it in the front. Genesis six, Fides. Prepare yourself." Fides had never heard the word 'Nephilim' before and didn't know that he would be face to face with one sooner rather than later.

With her last cryptic words to him, Corrie slapped him on his back and disappeared into the house. The door shut. He was on his own already and he was not more than a foot away from the house he had been living in for five years. He left the ranch with one last long look back, giving himself a few moments to reflect on the good that Corrie and Dietrich had done for him. Then, he turned toward the road to Las Cruces and didn't look back again. Within a few hours he put a foot down on old I-25, and for the first time, he really felt as though he were on his way.

Dietrich and Corrie had given Fides plenty of advice for his journey and Fides did his best to follow it. They had advised that he travel in the early part of the morning and the late part of the evening, or even the dead of night, so that he could avoid the oppressive and dry New Mexican heat. As he walked, he considered Corrie's last words, but he could not make any sense of them. He spent a little time pondering why Dietrich did not accompany him for at least a little while. Dietrich had said something about 'having business to attend to' and exchanged glances with Corrie and said nothing more. To compensate for not going along with Fides, Dietrich heaped advice and tips on desert travel on him.

Fides was trekking up I-25 towards Albuquerque, a more or less barren route with small towns here and there along it. There were ranches butting up against the interstate on each side in many areas heading north, but Dietrich told him he really wouldn't ever see anyone on them. The road, however, would have enough traffic to warrant his interest and caution. Dietrich advised Fides to use the road judiciously.

Fides settled into a pattern. In the evenings he would journey until he found a safe for a place to stop and rest. He'd rest until about two a.m. in the morning, at which time he'd get up and start walking again in the deep cool of the night. After the sun started to come up, he would begin looking for another safe place to sleep the day off. It was hard work to find a suitable place because it had to allow him seclusion, shade, and the ability to see potential threats before they saw him. Dietrich had advised him to walk parallel to the road, about fifty yards out from it. Most of his fellow travelers were using the road and that is where they would camp for the night. Dietrich suggested that these travelers would have their attention directed on the road, so by camping and traveling well off of it, Fides would be able to largely avoid having to interact with people all the way up to Albuquerque. The trade-off was that avoiding the road would mean slow going. And it was slow going. Fides made only about ten miles a day. It would end up taking him a good three weeks to make it to Albuquerque.

He had other routines he maintained, as well. Every day, a great amount of time was invested in anxious consideration of what would await him on this long journey. This lead to a common self-rebuke: It was his next destination he would need to worry about first. Dietrich had always said, "Don't worry about the things you can't control. Prepare for the things you can. Leave the rest to God and your good character." This would turn him to new worries about Albuquerque, successfully focusing on the challenge before him and not the unknown beyond that, but forgetting the whole point of not worrying!

After contemplating a half dozen worst-case scenarios about his travels after Albuquerque and another half dozen about his experiences in Albuquerque itself, he'd remind himself what he was doing and why he was going. He would remember his wife. He would remember his children. A bitter lump would form in his throat. Sometimes he would have to stop and weep. Having wept, the dark chasm of separation he felt within him would become hidden again. No sooner did he overcome his sense of grief, he would grovel in his shame. He would remember his role in fomenting the separation in the first place, and he'd spend another long while in bitter self-recriminations. He had hope that after all these years, she would forgive him. He repeated this psychological cycle a couple of times each day.

The groove of depression could deepen when he reminded himself of how many years had passed. Five, at least, though he had given up on determining an accurate accounting of his time away. A lot can happen in five years. She may have re-located. She may have had to flee. She may still be home, safe and sound in the house he had built for them. Their children would be older now: the youngest, either eleven or twelve. The oldest, eighteen or nineteen. In five years, they could have found themselves endangered many times. They may... have been... among other terrible things, murdered. Or, they may have been overcome by the Disease.

At that possibility, a shudder would go through Fides' body, followed by a stinging sense of guilt, and rage (at whom he did not know), and perhaps more tears. At sometime during this vicious cycle, he would compel himself- by sheer force of will- to stop thinking those terrible thoughts. True, some terrible scenario may have played out. However, it may very well be that they were alright. Why should he entertain only the scenarios that reduced him to despair? Why not entertain those that strengthened his legs for the journey? If he could choose which set of thoughts to think upon, and there was equal basis that either may correspond to reality, why not choose then to ponder the more hopeful scenario rather than the grim one? As hard as it was, eventually he would shake off the morbid thoughts and resolve that the only thing he could do is go to Bloomington, Illinois, and find out which scenarios were right.

Each morning after he'd found his day shelter, he would open up the old copy of the Christian scriptures that Corrie had given him. As he was not a Christian, the scriptures were only significant to him for a small set of reasons. One, he was still terribly honored that Corrie had given him this book. Only after a week's reading did he realize it was actually a collection of books. Fides knew that Corrie would have had to have played a risky game in order to keep a copy of it. Such things had been confiscated and destroyed a long time ago. Secondly, there was something about her warning that lit a fire in his soul. However, no matter how many times he read Genesis six, he couldn't quite fathom what she had meant. Thirdly, he was just plain bored by it. He couldn't read very well, as he often reminded himself, but learning to read better using a text such as this was one of the best ways he could think to do so constructively. So, he'd read a bit, eat, and then observe the road for a time. Then he would try to get some rest.

Seeking safe havens, engaging in cycles of despair and hope, and reading Corrie's bible, formed the pattern of existence for Fides on his travels to Albuquerque. Finally, he thought he saw a glow on the horizon. He knew this must be the city, but he didn't know what was causing the glow. After another solid day of travel Fides arrived on the outskirts of town and realized with surprise that Albuquerque had electricity. Las Cruces did not have electricity, but Corrie told him that in the past, when it did, there was nothing more magnificent then coming up on it in the dead of night from the west. It looked- so she told him- like you had stumbled onto an immense patch of fallen stars in the middle of a black blanket.

These days, Las Cruces was dark, but Albuquerque had light. His awe faded, however. The street lights were all burnt out and only some of the buildings seemed to have power. The glow appeared to actually come from a number of large search lights that had been modified in order to act as street lights. You did not dare stare at them at night because you would surely be blinded, but they did allow for safe travel in a fairly large swath of the city. He realized immediately that safety was a prime consideration for people in this town. During his brief stay in the city, he never found out where the electricity was being created, or how.

He entered the town in the cool of the day and immediately sought out to find a safe place to stay. By noon he was growing pretty tired. This was to be expected, as his schedule had been such that he had normally picked up a good four hour nap every day in the coolest spot he could find, so that by noon he was usually either finally laying down or well asleep. His frustration grew as he struggled to find appropriate lodging.

In his searching, he quickly determined that there were many more people in Albuquerque than in Las Cruces. He tried to remember back to his visits to Indianapolis but couldn't remember if he'd seen this many people there, even before the Disease. He decided that there really had to have been, but most of his visits had been when he was younger and with his father. In his adult life, his trips to Indianapolis had taken him only to the western edges. However, since he saw so much refugee traffic coming through his own town that had come from or through Indianapolis, he realized that he had probably never appreciated the full scope of how many people had lived there at one time.

The popularity of Albuquerque was immediately obvious. For one thing, there was electrical power for those who could afford it. There was more to it then that, however. As a crossroads for I-40 and I-25, there were also many travelers passing through the town and it welcomed them with warm hospitality. Some travelers would continue down I-25 to Las Cruces and on into El Paso, but most of the traffic seemed to be on the east-west axis. At some point he learned that the main population consisted of refugees from the environs of Denver. It had been decimated in the nuclear assault that had occurred about five years ago, and those that could get away went in any direction that was immediately available to them. Albuquerque was the solution for many of those escapees. He realized, too, that Denver had probably been lost on the same night that he had witnessed the bright flashes while he was traveling by airplane.

There were signs that the city was still very much on edge. The Disease had burned itself out, but he found that long-term residents were very apprehensive about mingling with those passing through. In fact, whole communities appeared to exist where the residents had gathered together in the height of the Disease, essentially self-quarantining themselves. These communities remained intact. The brave within those communities made a living offering services to the travelers.

Having gained all this information, Fides finally found a place to lay his head. There had been plenty of places that had available rooms, but none of them were willing to give him a room in exchange for some of the small knives that Dietrich had given him for purposes of bartering. He scribbled his name down on a piece of paper and reached for the key.

"How do you say that?" the manager wondered of him.

"First name or last name?" Fides smiled.
"First," the manager returned.
"Feye-dehs," Fides answered helpfully.
"Alright, thanks much. You have a good night, Mr. Ranthem," the manager said, pushing the key across the counter to Fides' waiting hands. Beat tired, Fides went directly to his small room and fell into the dusty bed. He slept through the afternoon and through the night, only waking up the following morning.
Fides began to explore the populated areas of the city. There was a steady flow of travelers heading in all directions. Old buildings from yesteryear had been brought into operation to service the travelers. Fides went from one building to the next, trying to gain information that could help him when he finally set out east on I-40.
These old buildings all really had the same basic function nowadays. They provided liquid refreshment, mainly of the alcoholic sort, and a place to sleep. Many of the travelers he encountered seemed to be seeking information just as he was. He came to the assessment that Dietrich had been right in telling him that there would be enough travelers in Albuquerque that he could very easily select a larger group to travel with. He hadn't made any actual efforts to choose a group yet, but he already had it in his mind to do just that. He discovered that plenty of the folks around him were ones he didn't want any kind of long-term association with. He made up his mind select his fellow travelers carefully.
On his fifth night in town, Fides had worked through several of the town's traveler's dens before arriving at a certain "Jed's Tavern." Like some of the other places, this establishment had been an old fuel station for cars and trucks. The innards had been gutted and tables had been created out of all sorts of crazy objects. There was a bar on one end that really did seem pretty professional, however, and Fides couldn't help but be impressed. Some places he'd been to had just thrown boards over large empty oil cans. Jed's Tavern did lack electricity, however. This was compensated for by the fact that someone (presumably Jed?) had managed to manufacture working indoor plumbing. A toilet he could flush? That was enough in itself to prompt Fides to plunk down a small piece of silver that Dietrich and Corrie had told him would pass for currency in Albuquerque. It successfully fetched him a healthy shot of the worst whiskey he'd ever had.
The indoor plumbing seemed to have many admirers. Unlike many of the other places which seemed to serve travelers, this one had a healthy population of locals in attendance. Since the place was lit by lamps rather than overhead light bulbs, there was a country feel about the place. His first sip of the whiskey convinced him that the lamps and the people were being given the same thing to drink. He choked down the liquid with a sardonic chuckle. Fides scanned the shadowy environment, deciding to strike up a conversation with a fellow sitting near him.

"What do you know about the place in Bloomington, Illinois?" Fides asked the friendly looking stranger. The stranger turned out to be as friendly as he looked.

"I couldn't tell you, actually," the man replied. "I lived in Texas before the sneak attack. Houston and Dallas were both wiped off the map. But I lived far enough away that it didn't affect me, except for the fact that I couldn't get supplies anymore for the ranch I managed. Food was a big problem. I heard that Albuquerque hadn't been attacked and had actively been storing up food because of the Disease..." but Fides interrupted him.

"Sneak attack?" Fides inquired.

"Well, we don't know really what happened. I don't care who you ask, either. Nobody knows what went down, or why. But we do know that Denver was nuked. Houston was nuked. The Dallas-Ft. Worth area was nuked. Los Angeles was nuked. And I heard that St. Louis was nuked, but I don't know about that one, myself. Plenty of people come here from the west or the north, either from California, Utah, or Colorado, so I'm pretty confident about the cities in those directions. A lot of those people that head east don't come back, though, and the west bound travelers coming across the country pass south of St. Louis to get here. We don't get that many folks from that direction, to tell you the truth," the man answered, gagging down his own drink.

Fides suddenly realized that St. Louis was probably right on his way home. If St. Louis had been destroyed in a nuclear attack, he would certainly have to go around it. This trip might take longer than he realized. He was very uncertain of the geography, though. He would just have to feel his way across the country as best as he could. "Do you know if St. Louis is on the way to Bloomington, Illinois?" he asked the stranger. The stranger did not know.

"I would suggest going to Oklahoma City and asking that question. It's about a month's journey. I hear that they've actually got motorized transport out of Oklahoma City, too. So it may be very well worth your time to go there, anyway. That could just be another rumor, though. You never know what to believe, anymore. I'm sure someone there would have to know, though," the stranger explained, and then ordered another shot of 'whiskey.'

The doors to the store suddenly flew open. Five dangerous looking men and one nasty looking woman strutted in. The local residents seemed to know these people as many of them turned back to their drinks with scowls on their faces. The bartender had a frown flash across his face, which he promptly replaced with something more neutral looking. The bartender, it turns out, also seemed to have a little courage. He confronted the group. "Jack," the bartender stated matter-of-factly, "I thought we worked it out with the Resident's Council that you were going to keep out of the traveler's taverns."

"Well, this isn't really a traveler's tavern, is it?" Jack shot back, eyeing the many local residents that were present.

The bartender was not to be rebuffed, though, "I suppose a lot of them are here because you've soiled up their favorite drinking holes, Jack."

One of the men with Jack turned his nose up at that remark and muttered something dark. Fides noticed that there was a long iron pipe in that man's hand, and Fides knew the man had used it in combat before.

"Franklin," the brave bartender said, coolly addressing this other man, "You know very well that if you cause any trouble, Jed will wake up and then you're going to have your hands quite full. You know it's not a lead pipe that *he* carries." The bartender jerked his thumb back towards a doorway where Fides supposed that Jed lived.

Franklin did not seem overtly intimidated, but the pipe seemed to drop lower in his grasp. Jack decided to take a different tact.

"Alright, we'll cause no trouble then. We've got silver. It's good everywhere in town, including here. Fact is, we can't find anywhere that has enough spirits for the six of us, and we know that Jed keeps a good supply. He won't turn down our silver if we behave, will he?"

"Let's see what you got," the bartender said noncommittally. Jack threw a bag up on the counter, brusquely pushing aside the stranger that Fides had been talking to. The stranger slid over, eager not to involve himself. This meant, of course, that Fides would have to move over, too. The bartender examined the contents of the bag and appeared to be satisfied. "I know very well what you guys are like when you've had too much whiskey. I'll give you three bottles for this bag, but you've got to take it out of here. I don't want you drinking in here. And I don't want you coming back in for more, either, because you've only got enough for three bottles, and that's not going to change just because you come back to argue about it. Unless you have more silver?" Jack shook his head, and the bartender deftly threw the bag into a chest, which he locked, and slammed down the three bottles.

Jack and his crew took the bottles and left singing a drinking song in such a way Fides knew that they were trying to intimidate the other guests. They seemed to be saying that they didn't really care if Jed woke up. Finally, they were gone.

"Louts," the bartender asserted matter-of-factly.

The friendly stranger nodded grimly but said nothing about them. Fides suspected there was probably some great set of circumstances lurking underneath all of this, but didn't feel it was his place to ask about them. The locals themselves didn't offer anything on the subject, so Fides changed the subject back to areas that would keep him out of trouble. He began asking questions about places to stay moving east, and the stranger obliged him as best as he could. The bartender would sometimes add details, too.

A couple of hours later, having consumed two shots of lantern fuel and some water, Fides decided it was time to make use of the fine indoor plumbing. He excused himself. He took the opportunity to do more than his business. He washed his hands and his face in the sink and soaked his hair, too. The motel he was staying at did not have running water, so this was a real luxury.

After what had been a rather long time, Fides exited the bathroom and to his surprise found that Jack and his crew had re-entered the tavern and were gathered near the bar again.

"Leave'em alone," the bartender was growling. Jack and the rest of them were poking and prodding a man who had taken over Fides' chair.

"Tell me I'm misbehaving," Jack said, taunting the man. "Might makes right. So you don't have any right to tell me what to do. You got that?" Franklin was saying things of the same sort, and the woman was cackling something in the man's ear, but he couldn't tell what she was saying.

The man himself seemed unmoved. He sat on his bench with his back to Fides. A long black cloak hung off him, nearly touching the ground. He had long, somewhat scraggly hair, hanging in a pony tail off of his head. This was all he could see of the man. Unsure about what to do, Fides remained in his spot. He couldn't leave because he had left his travel bag in the care of the bartender and stranger. He couldn't leave without getting it, first. There was this little problem of a gang of miscreants blocking his way, however. He would have to wait for the scene to play out.

"You know it's all your sort's fault," Jack said, escalating the tone of his voice. "You jolly God believers are what put this world the way it is. I think I should have some revenge."

"Jed!" snapped the bartender over his shoulder. Jack paused for only a moment, and hearing nothing from the back, resumed his tirade.

"Yeah, that's right. Where is your God, anyway? Nuclear bombs fall from the sky like rain. A disease guts our country. Where is he? I say your God-belief is the disease. I say religion is to blame for it all. For all your self-righteous patting of your back, no God-idiot like you ever did anyone no good."

Well, at this point Fides hadn't realized that he had come very close to Jack. He was uncontrollably angry. His aversion for situations where violence might occur had been overcome without much reflection on what he was doing. The ironic thing was that on a different day, he could have found himself saying the same things that Jack was saying, but he knew that Dietrich and Corrie believed in God and they had saved his life. He owed them. It was to uphold their honor that he did the unthinkable. He tapped Jack on the shoulder.

"What?" sniped Jack, surprised by the touch.

"I don't think it's right for you to talk that way," Fides said slowly. The bartender appeared to be gone, and the friendly stranger was nowhere to be seen, either. Other guests were still in the room, but just sitting quietly. Several slyly put distance between themselves and Fides and the black-cloaked man.

"I don't think it's your job to tell me what's right and what's wrong, fellah. If you know what's good for you, you'll walk out of here before we pay some attention to you." Jack glared menacingly at Fides, but Fides was not moved. In his building contracting days he had kept in pretty good shape, both in regards to strength and stamina. The disease had sapped much of both from him, but working the ranch for a couple of years had generally restored him. Over the years, he'd had his share of tangles, even if they were always on the defensive. If anyone deserved to be tangled with, Fides reasoned, it was this man here.

The man at the center of all this attention turned his head towards Fides, "If you ignore them, they'll just go away." Fides now noticed the clerical collar around the man's neck. He couldn't see this from the back. From the back it was just the black cloak, hanging like a thick cape to the floor. The man peeked up at Fides from underneath hanging gray hair and then turned back to his drink, completely unconcerned with the menaces at his back.

"The priest knows what's good for you," Franklin heaped onto Jack's contempt, interpreting the priest's behavior as weakness.

"I'll decide for myself what's good for me," Fides declared.

With that, Franklin swung his lead pipe towards Fides' head but Fides was ready. He ducked and brought both fists deep into Franklin's gut. It was only a second before everyone else reacted, but it was just enough time for Fides to step back into a better fighting position. Franklin fell to the ground, stunned. He was slowly rising. Before he was up, the woman and the other three men were after Fides. Fides caught one on the chin right away and yanked the woman's hair, causing her to yelp, but the another man had produced a bottle and smashed it over his head. Except it didn't break; it may as well have been a club. Fides felt himself fall backwards, dragging the woman with him since he still had her hair. He regained his composure and stood up as Franklin and the one he'd hit in the chin reached him. He kicked Franklin in the knee and cracked another man in the nose. But now a fourth guy and Jack were there, and Fides was on the ground. Jack pinned Fides down, hovering over him, his breath reeking whiskey.

"I think you're going to die, my friend," Jack said viciously. Jack produced a long knife in his hand and let it hang over Fides' chest.

"I wouldn't do that, if I were you," said a voice from behind the bar. It was Jed, at last.

Franklin looked up at Jed, and turned to Jack, "He ain't got no gun, Jack. Go ahead and do him."

"It's not me you need to be afraid of," Jed muttered loudly, grumpy at having been woken up.

"Oh yeah? Who, then?" Jack had the knife to Fides throat now. Two men were standing on his arms, Jack had him straddled, and the woman was sitting on his legs. Fides was completely immobile.

"This one didn't take a vow of non-violence," Jed informed Jack, nodding towards the priest. The priest was still sitting in his chair with his back to the scene playing out behind him.

"Him?" Franklin laughed uproariously.

"Now, what is this?" Jack exclaimed, catching sight of Fides' necklace. It had revealed itself from out from under his shirt in the scuffle. "You wear computer chips for a necklace?" Jack scoffed, returning his attention to the knife in his hand. "Might makes right, kid. Don't you forget it."

Unseen to Jack, the priest was now on his feet. The black cloak twisted in the air as the priest abruptly turned to face them all. A long sword was in the priest's hand and he assumed a fighting position. Jack sensed the movement, turned his head, and saw the danger. He paused.

"Do him, Jack. That priest can't get here in time," Franklin cackled, raising his lead pipe as though it were a sword as well. Still, everyone was caught off guard by this strange sight. Jack hesitated from delivering the death blow. Fides' eyes were wide as he strained to see what was going on.

"You're right. I won't be able to stop you in time with this," the priest said, re-sheathing the sword. Instead, he raised both of his arms so that his hands were turned out away from him, his palms directed towards Jack and his cohorts.

A glow instantly emanated from between the hands and abruptly the priest was holding in his bare hands what looked to be a fireball. Instead of hurling it as a man might throw a ball, the fireball shot out like a laser, propelled by some unseen force. There was a bright flash that filled the room and the fireball caught the two men and Jack and engulfed them all together, knocking them back into the stunned Franklin. The woman's hair caught on fire and the sounds of her shrieking could be heard even outdoors after she ran out of the tavern. Droplets of light seemed to cling to the walls and objects in the room. The priest had his sword in his hand again.

He strode over to where Jack was lying on the ground. Franklin was also lying down, nearby. The priest brought the sword point to Jack's neck, and he turned to Fides. "What do you think, Fides? Should I- how did they say it- do him?"

Fides was getting to his feet. He was in as much shock as everyone else was in the room. Except for Jed; Jed appeared to be quite unimpressed. Or, at least he was not surprised.

"No, really, it's not worth it." Fides clambered into a chair. "What... what was that? Who are you?"

The priest gazed fiercely into Fides' eyes. "Don't you know, Fides? Don't you recognize me? You should at least have a guess. You were warned. The Nephilim have returned."

The priest grabbed Fides by his shirt muttering something about Jack having more friends, slung Fides' traveling bag into his arms, and then pulled him out the door. Jack and his friends were strewn unceremoniously throughout the room, but except for the burned hair of the woman, there didn't seem to be any outward sign of damage to their bodies.

"Where are we going?" Fides asked, somewhat fearfully.

"We're going to get your stuff. Then we are going to go get my stuff. Then we are going to leave," the priest responded curtly.

"Leave?"

"Yes, we're going to go to Oklahoma City. For one thing, you were going there anyway so sooner is as good as later. But Jack has plenty of friends around town and I think we both just made ourselves pretty unwelcome yet easy to spot targets." The priest was hurrying Fides along. He moved pretty well for being an older man. Interestingly, the more Fides studied the man, the less convinced he was that the man was old. Fides chalked it up to the gray hair alone conveying the impression of age. Apart from the hair, he seemed younger than Fides. Indeed, Fides thought the man looked as though he were in his mid-twenties, maybe fifteen years younger than himself.

"Are you a Nephilim?" Fides inquired as they rushed past evening travelers.

"Yes, I am among their number," the man replied, pushing his hair out of his face to glance at Fides.

"Are you what Corrie meant when she said that 'they' are here again?" Fides pressed.

"It is," the priest replied tersely, clearly eager to postpone the conversation until after they were either safely hidden or well on their way.

"I saw the word in the book that I was given, but I do not know what the significance is that you are a Nephilim or that they are here again," Fides plied him, still being tugged along.

"You will have to wait a time to have your explanations, and even then I suspect you will have questions that remain unanswered." The Nephilim priest pointed at a building ahead, "We are drawing near to where your possessions are." For the first time it dawned on Fides how curious it was that the priest knew that Fides 'had been warned.' In no time at all, Fides was in his room. He gathered up his belongings and settled accounts with the manager and then the priest was again hurrying him along. He soon found himself in an area that he had not yet explored, but he realized that it was only a road adjacent to the road that Jed's Tavern had been on. It was too dark now to properly see that they were in fact in the back of a large parking lot that had a good number of old semi-tractor trailers. The priest led him to one of these old trailers. Windows had been cut out of the metal sides of the trailer, but there were several doors on it that appeared to have been part of the original design. Most of these seemed to have been permanently shut, bound up with chains and pad locks and one that looked like it was welded. But the priest took him around to the other side where there was another row of doors and windows. In front of one of the doors was a set of stairs, which they rapidly ascended.

"Home," the priest said. The priest twisted a key inside a massive padlock that secured the door and at last they were inside. It was a little stuffy, but the priest went around opening several of the windows wider than they had been. In short order there was a breeze blowing through the trailer. Fides still couldn't see anything. "Now, light!" the man exclaimed. Moving deftly in the near dark, the priest lit several lamps that very much resembled the lamps in Jed's Tavern. Fides strongly suspected that they used the same 'whiskey' as fuel, as well.

Given how much space there was in the trailer, Fides was surprised to see how scant the furnishings were. There was a make-shift bed, a table, a shelf underneath a long opening in the metal of the trailer at one far end, a trunk, and that was really about it. On top of that shelf he saw what looked like a gas grill of some kind. The opening, he suspected, was for ventilation. On top of the bed was a good sized rucksack. The priest grabbed it and moved towards the chest.

"My name is Fides," Fides said. "What is your name?"

"You can call me Fermion," the priest replied. Fides thought that was a strange name but he wasn't going to say that aloud. Fermion grabbed the rucksack and moved brusquely to the chest. The top opened with a loud creaking noise and he handed Fides a long, narrow object, wrapped in thick cloth. Fides unwrapped it, knowing he would find a sword in it.

To his surprise, this sword was very familiar to him. Abruptly, he felt that his eyes had been opened. He had held this sword before. His head jerked up to take another look at Fermion.

"Father Frederich?"

"Yes, I went by that name once."

"Is Fermion your first name?" Fides wondered.

"Not exactly. It is a rough equivalent to my real name."

"You won't tell me your real name?"

"It is not for you to know, my friend," Fermion explained kindly. "I did not always know it myself. And it is only understandable to some, and knowable by fewer than that."

"That makes far less sense than you might think it does," Fides replied, turning the sword over in his hand. A distant event tugged at his memory, but he couldn't put his finger on it. Fides continued his questioning, "Are you saying that you have a Christian name now that you are a priest?"

"Oh, no. Not at all," Fermion said, finally ready to leave.

"And why would that be?" Fides asked.

"Because I am not now, nor was I ever, a priest."

Fides was slowly deciding that he didn't really know what was going on and that asking questions was really only deepening his ignorance. This was an uncomfortable feeling he thought he could eliminate by asking no more questions. Fermion handed him a sheath for his sword and showed him how to strap it on.

"You'll need this, too," Fermion added, throwing a cloak over to him. "Naturally, it will be a bit hot to wear in the daytime, but your fall season is coming and we are heading north, ultimately, anyway. But people are a bit uncomfortable seeing swords hanging by people's sides."

Fides thought that people would be more comfortable seeing a sword in a man's hands than witnessing a ball of flames emerging from out of them, but he didn't say anything. The sword was now secured at his waist and he had pulled the cloak over his shoulders. Fermion quickly sorted through Fides' belongings, throwing some things out ("You won't need this...") and leaving some other items ("We need to travel light," he explained). Fermion took no apparent interest in Corrie's Bible, but left it in the 'keep' pile. Finally, Fermion threw Fides' own bag back to him and wordlessly went outside. Fides took this as the cue that they were leaving. Fermion was waiting for him in the dark outside the trailer. Once

Fides was out, he replaced the padlock. Motioning to Fides to follow him, they officially began their journey together.

It was twilight as they passed by Jed's Tavern. It turned out that Fermion's residence had been situated on the same piece of property. It was a still night. After about an hour of silent travel together Fides realized that he was getting tired. It had been quite a long day, and besides that, he was really starting to feel the bruising he had received earlier in the evening. Shortly after Fides felt the oncoming exhaustion, Fermion came to a stop.

"We'll stop here for the night," he said, ignoring Fides' grunt of approval. "We are not far from an area that travelers use as a staging area to travel together to Oklahoma City. We'll go there tomorrow morning, early, and join up with a group. You go ahead and sleep. I'll keep watch."

Fides felt no reason to protest. After getting as comfortable as he could on his bedroll, he fell asleep instantly.

== Chapter 3 ==

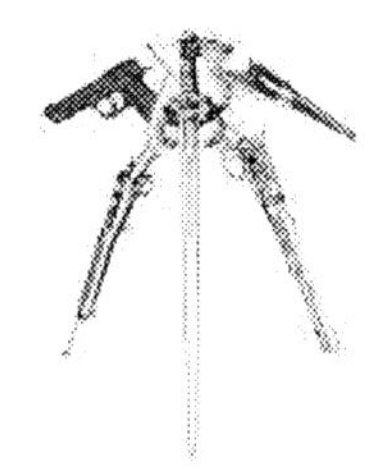

The sun came up in glorious feathers the next morning and Fides opened his eyes to find Fermion cooking over a small fire. Fides received a piece of fried bread and drank a hot cup of coffee. Last night he had been too exhausted to press his inquisition, but as he now pondered making a trip back to Illinois with the very man who had escorted him to New Mexico in the first place- and this time on foot- he thought maybe he needed more information. Now that there was better light, he judged that he truly could not say that Fermion was an older man. In fact, he shared only some of the characteristics he remembered Father Frederich having. The silver hair no longer seemed like the hair of an older person, either. It was not grey, it was not white. There seemed to be a liquid quality to it. Fides thought it best to stop staring, but Fermion never noticed.

"How did you… I can't think of a good word… disable Jack and his friends?" All Fides could remember clearly was a knife at his throat, Jack's loathing eyes, his immense feeling of helplessness, and a sudden flash of cold light.

"Oh, you may very well come to understand such things better as time goes on."

"I beg your pardon, sir, but frankly it makes me a little nervous to travel with someone who can conjure light on demand," Fides bravely argued.

"Conjure. That's an interesting word. I can see how it would seem that way from your perspective," Fermion said, cleaning up the cooking utensils. "Was it magic? Was it technology? Wouldn't you like to know? What if I told you that the answer depends on your perspective and what you mean in both cases? So, from one person's perspective it is magic and from another its technology. For others, the answer would be 'both.'"

"I really have no idea what you are talking about," Fides replied. But Fides was smiling, because he had the real sense that Fermion was actually telling him the truth, even if he couldn't understand it. Fermion caught the smile and smiled himself. Fides continued, "Perhaps you can tell me what it is from your perspective."

"Easy. Neither." Fermion stowed everything away and stood up. "Do you accept that answer?" Fermion asked him.

"You don't seem prepared to tell me more, so what choice do I have?" Fides replied.

"Choice. That is an interesting word to have used. You trust me now because you have no choice but to trust me. When you do have a choice, will you still trust me?" Fermion probed. They were about ready to start walking now, but Fermion hesitated.

"I suppose if I have good reason to trust you, then yea," Fides returned, confused.

"There will come a day when I ask you to do something, and you must trust me and do what I say on that day. No matter how perplexing it seems to you, I'm asking you to trust me at that time and just do what I request," Fermion told him, locking eyes with Fides.

Fides felt uncomfortable. "Trusting people has got me into a lot of trouble," he finally said.

"Yet people have helped you when you had no choice but to be helped. I am asking you to allow yourself to be helped when the choice is before you," Fermion gazed at him.

"I don't suppose you can share more details on the matter?" Fides said, a little annoyed.

"I'm sorry, I don't know much more than that," Fermion replied.

"And yet you know enough to request my trust? On what grounds?" Fides parried.

"On the grounds that you ought to trust who I trust, if I have proved to you that I myself am trustworthy," Fermion replied. Fides thought that was about as cryptic as you could get, but Fermion would not elaborate any more. Fermion nodded towards the east, and they set out.

They climbed a nearby hill and after cresting it saw old I-40 stretched out beneath them racing for the horizon. There was an overpass within a short walk. Next to it was another retired truck stop similar to Jed's Tavern, but bigger. There were quite a few people milling about the parking lot, and there were quite obviously even more around too. That was the only explanation for a large store and restaurant that seemed to be doing brisk business. As they got closer, it became obvious why the place was doing well. It had gone out of its way to make sure that travelers had everything they needed. Tents were erected throughout the large lot and merchants were circulating throughout offering wares. Even as they approached from the west, others were arriving at the travel stop. In the distance, Fides and Fermion could see people coming in from the east. What would be their port of departure would be these travelers' port of entry.

There was loud yelling and shouting coming from a shaded area on the eastern edge of the property. The closer they got, the more they could make out that people were trying to arrange traveling parties. One man would shout, "Leaving in a week, meet in the south lot!" Another would shout, "Leaving in three days, form up at the large tree on the north side!" They listened for their call. At last they heard it: "Leaving today, grove of trees, north side!" Gathering their belongings, they fell in line with a large number of people heading towards the grove of trees to the north.

Once they had arrived at their own rallying point, they noticed that there were several men already standing there. Fermion explained that these were men who worked for the new Albuquerque as highway security officers. The small group of men that were already there were soon joined by another ten. Fermion explained that their group would be escorted about a day's journey by these men, but after that, the group would be on their own. Fides noticed for the first time that in some of the groups arriving from the direction of Oklahoma City there were men in similar dress, apparently escorting inbound travelers. The men were armed mainly with clubs, but two of them had sturdy cross bows.

Fides glanced briefly at the people around them, but Fermion was actively scrutinizing them. Nearby was a short, stocky man with an unnaturally round head. He could not have been more than four feet tall, and had a nasty look about him. Fides saw someone nod towards the man and whisper something about 'radiation' but since it was rude to stare, Fides was already looking elsewhere. There were at least fifty people in the group, not counting the armed escorts. He saw men, women, children, teenagers, and one old man. Everyone was clumped together under the trees, so it wasn't easy to tell who was traveling with whom.

As they were waiting patiently for some sort of cue that they were ready to begin, they observed other groups coming in. They looked tired and worn out, and very much ready to rest. Employees of the travel center greeted them and offered water and food and tried to guide them towards the main buildings. This was actually high salesmanship. The employees, Fides determined, were probably all members of the same extended family. They were heaping hospitality and soft words on the weary travelers in hopes that they could get some to commit to staying with them for awhile. Fides reasoned that inside those buildings were all sorts of things for which travelers might be willing to exchange whatever valuables they had. Things like hot meals, lodging, showers- maybe some hard liquor- would all be things that people coming in from a long journey might decide are worth giving up a bag of silver for. The fact that these employees were attractive young women could only help the overall success of the operation.

After Fides and Fermion had loitered for nearly an hour, the young women started attending to Fides' group. They rolled out a cart filled with fruit, vegetables, salted meats, and canteens filled with water. There were other items, as well. Long wooden sticks apparently were designed to be both walking sticks and weapons if it came to it. There were a handful of lead pipes and sling shots. There were paper boxes filled with assorted food items. Boots, socks, and roughly made cloaks were heaped up in the front. The women circulated amongst the group making casual small talk and being genuinely friendly, offering to help the group on its impending journey. They were very good at their jobs. They talked Fermion out of three silver pieces in exchange for a canteen for each of them. Fermion insisted after they were out of ear shot that they really had needed the canteens, but Fides was certain he had noticed Fermion's cheeks flush slightly red as they 'bartered.'

For himself, Fides had experienced a sharp pang of anguish and a deep sense of longing to once again be with his wife and children.

Now fully equipped with four canteens, they waited for the group leader to arrive. Fides had gleaned that besides being escorted by armed men, they would be led by a person who would actually be taking them the whole way. What Fides still hadn't figured out yet was what danger lurked out there that required a guide and a band of armed escorts.

Fermion nudged Fides. Fides looked in the direction Fermion had indicated and saw that Jack and his cohorts were on their way towards the travel center. "I think we'll be seeing them again, Fides. And look, they've brought some more friends with them, too."

The guide came at last, and not too soon in Fides' opinion. With Jack and his band in the area, reinforced, he thought it best to be moving on as soon as possible. The guide was rugged and lanky. She was probably in her fifties and by the looks of her she had been leading such groups since the day of her birth. He would have sooner expected one of these armed escorts to be their guide rather than this woman, but he had the good sense to recognize that she probably knew what she was doing. She called for the travelers' attention and began issuing announcements. After informing everyone that she would be giving more instructions later on at lunch and then again in the evening, she motioned for them to follow her.

The group moved quickly to follow her lead, but after not more than an hour it had dispersed into a long string of people along the road. He was surprised to have a nice pine forest greet them, but by mid-afternoon the terrain gave way to sage brush again. The guide told them matter-of-factly to get used to it. Fermion and Fides walked together in relative silence for the early part of the day. They found that they were well ahead of the entire group by the time that it was too hot to travel anymore. They had been told about a stopping point just a little beyond them where the travel center stocked water and had some tents erected. Fides marveled at how well the travel center they had left behind worked to provide for their needs. He didn't know if he'd ever come back this way, but if he did, he'd find a way to repay them with interest.

They reached the way station before everyone else. As they enjoyed a drink from their ample canteen supply, they watched the rest of the group far off in the distance slowly trudging their way towards them. Fides was in the mood for conversation.

"Alright, Fermion," Fides began. "Tell me about the Nephilim."

"Wow, right into it, eh?" Fermion replied, drawing in the sand. Fides merely shrugged and waited for Fermion to explain himself. Fermion stopped writing in the sand and instead pulled out a blanket from his pack. He motioned to Fides to give him his sword, and he placed both of the swords under the blanket. "Let's take these cloaks off, shall we?" This seemed a good idea to Fides. He took it off, laid it down, and stared at Fermion expectantly.

"Ok, ok," Fermion smiled. "Well. There's not much that I can tell you right now that you'd believe, let alone understand. You once thought of yourself as a spiritual man, but now you think you are a man of the world, and you think that's the right way to be. To understand the Nephilim you've got to be open-minded. I don't mean to offend you, but I think you're pretty set in your ways."

"Why don't you try me?" Fides responded graciously.

"Oh no, it's not that easy. Sometimes knowledge is like medicine. Take it before you're ready for it, and it can just make things worse. If I give it to you and you aren't ready for the side effects, I'd have done you a disservice," Fermion said patiently.

Fides thought about that. He felt the answer to be fully inadequate, but knew that Fermion was telling him the most honest answer he could give him. Fides decided to take a new tact. He'd been thinking about this necklace around his neck for years now and never expected to be able to talk to anyone about it who might actually know something about it.

"What can you tell me about this necklace?" Fides inquired.

"Well, that necklace was really a stroke of genius. I actually don't know everything there is to know about that necklace. You remember Bill Huxley, of course, right? The general contractor on that project where we first met. I do know that what he was contracted to build cannot be accessed without that necklace. I know that self-destruct mechanisms were put in place to destroy that whole facility if someone tried to go around the security system. Bill started getting nervous there at the end. Frankly, I don't blame him. He wanted out of the situation while he had some leverage to make it happen. That necklace is a sophisticated key and he held onto it for dear life. He also was the only person who knew the code that operates the necklace-key. This naturally made some of my peers uncomfortable. So, waiting to give the code to you until he was safe was Bill's way of making sure that both he and you remained alive. "Oh," Fermion noticed Fides' startled look. "You have nothing to fear from me. My selection was not by accident, nor was it their design."

"It's not that."

"What then?"

"I don't know the code," Fides moaned.

"Well, that is a problem, isn't it? Bill refused to give it to me, as I had implored him to do so. You became very sick very suddenly, just as it was reported by others that had seen the Disease strike. Bill may have been self-seeking, but he played this card right. It seemed certain that you were going to die and the code would be lost. He thought I was a priest so he trusted that I wouldn't actually try to torture it out of him. He told me that if we wanted that code, I'd better do my best to keep you alive. I swear to you I would have done nothing less, but Bill could not have known this was in my heart. Everything would have worked out perfectly if you had not become sick. Well, there was that little thing about some sort of limited nuclear strike on the United States. That night there was a bright flash in the far off sky, and a funny feeling in the air, and then the airplane wouldn't work. It looks like we would have been stuck in New Mexico no matter what. We can only trust that it is Providence that has forced us to wait these many years to finally start our journey back."

"Where is Bill now?"

"I don't know. California, maybe. Mexico, perhaps. Bill had a good sense of what was coming, and what is still to come, and he didn't want to be around to experience it."

"What is coming?" Fides wondered. "And how do you know that it is coming?"

"Some things have been given to me to know. But not everything. And not everything I know is for you or anyone else to know. We..."

"So there are more of you?" Fides pounced. In that very moment, Fides remembered the beautiful woman who saved him when he was a young boy fleeing for his life. The incident in the clearing not far from his home came back to him in startling clarity. The strange thing was that the moment he recalled the incident anew, details he remembered now that he had dismissed at the time as being the products of hallucination and disorientation from being struck were actually the most vivid of all of his memories of the incident. Fermion studied him.

"We know some things that everyone can know if they just think clearly," Fermion finally replied. "But your race has always refused to think clearly. Each of us has a very specific set of goals. Mine is to escort you back to Illinois. After I deliver you safely to your family and to the place that necklace belongs, my time here will be coming to an end."

"My family? Do you know, is my family ok?" Fides asked hopefully. Fermion frowned, however.

"I'm sorry, Fides. That is something that I don't know." There was a flash of despair on Fides' countenance but another question percolated out of him in short order.

"So, are you an alien? Are you human?" Fides smirked as he asked the question. If it weren't for seeing the man wield a fireball, he would have openly scoffed at himself for asking the question. But he smirked because he was convinced that Fermion was probably nothing more than a magician. More likely, these Nephilim possessed some special technology- no more, no less. A fireball alone could not convince him of the extraordinary claim that Fermion was an alien. Fermion noted the smirk, but answered honestly anyway.

"I am an alien in the sense of being a guest on this planet. But I am definitely human. Indeed, I am more human than you are, and more human than any of your fellows currently at large. And some of the humans we will encounter lost their humanity a long time ago."

"Where is your planet, then? Can you point it out at me tonight? Is it Mars?" Fides played along.

"I sense sarcasm. Surely you can't so easily dismiss what you have perceived with your own senses?" Fermion replied. Fermion pondered for a moment and offered his own answer, "Well, of course. That is what you have been taught: to demand real world evidence for everything but then to always claim it is never enough when the conclusion challenges your preconceptions. Indeed, you have not been simply taught this, but you have been drenched in it. I pray that you will not need to see another such demonstration."

Fides was humbled. Fides knew that the fireball was not the first time he had been a direct witness to something remarkable. Perhaps of more concern was the mysterious woman's claim that an angel was even more terrible than a Nephilim, yet she and Fermion alike terrified him quite enough. Fides knew that in the face of these two startling incidents, he was being unreasonably snide with Fermion. Fermion was studying him as he tried to piece together his memories of the incident. He had suppressed or dismissed most of the details for most of his entire life, beginning even at the incident itself. But Fermion's impressive display meant that he needed to reevaluate. Perhaps he hadn't been hallucinating at all.

"You've seen something else, haven't you?" Fermion probed. He seemed curious to learn more. Fides was hesitant to answer, so Fermion said, "I won't make fun of you or mock you. I am open to evaluate any and all claims. Why don't you just tell me the story?"

So Fides did, including the fantastic details.

\+ + + + +

Away. He was running away. His mother had yelled, "Run!" and he did. Fides was only ten or eleven years old. There were two men not far behind him. He could hear them crashing through the branches. Fides was moving silently because he had the advantage of knowing the woods and also because he was able to duck the low branches. He knew that if he got to the shed, tucked away in a small clearing not too far into the woods, he stood a chance of being able to barricade himself inside.

The men were catching up.

Fides emerged into the clearing, in sight of the shed, and promptly fell down. If he had only fallen once, he might have gotten away. He slipped again, however, on some leaves. He slid head first, arms outstretched. As he climbed to his feet, two heavy hands fell on his shoulders and he found his face stuffed back into the vegetation. The two men were not happy.

"Think you're faster than us, boy?" one of the men sneered.

"Made us run! You're going to pay for that!" the other man gasped, out of breath. Fides found himself pulled to his feet, but only for a moment. The first man slapped him so hard he fell backwards onto his back and had the wind knocked out of him. He tasted blood and wondered if he was going to die. The man hauled Fides to standing again, but this time took him by the arm and threw him across the clearing. He rolled awkwardly over his arm and yelped in pain. The two men laughed. Fides knew how a mouse felt after the cat had gotten hold of it. In theory, he was far enough away he could try to make another dash for the shed, but now there was a sharp pain in his arm hindering him. Fides couldn't think of anything else to do, so despite the pain, he started to crawl away. The men were standing over him now, guffawing.

"Come on, finish him. We want to get back and see mom, right?" one said to the other. Fides didn't know what that meant, but he knew it couldn't be good. There was a spark of righteous rage, too. He wanted to protect his mother. On the other hand, he knew his rage could have no outlet. One of the men now had a firm grip on him, and he couldn't move. He heard a knife being pulled out of a sheath. He bent his head and waited for the blow.

"Picking on a boy? Is that the new mark of a real man?" a silky voice washed over the clearing. Fides was shoved roughly to the ground. He rolled over to try to locate the speaker. The two men were trying to do the same thing. Fides struggled to determine the gender of the voice, but concluded it was probably a woman's voice.

"Who are you? Where are you? Come out and I'll show you the mark of a real man!" one of the fiends declared.

"Oh, I believe that. Why slay a boy when you can slay a woman!" the silk voice replied.

"Oh, you won't get off that easy, my dear," the other man snarled. The two were patrolling the inside of the clearing, peering into the woods around them in an attempt to find the origin of the voice. Fides was peering, too. "Show yourself, or show yourself a coward!" the man dared.

Suddenly, there was a loud crack and the first man went hurtling through the air. The other man's mouth opened in shock, but another cracking noise followed on the heels of the first one and the man found himself knocked to the ground. Fides' eyes were wide open: he saw nothing except for men flying through the air.

The first man rolled over, holding his head. He scanned the clearing to try to find his assailant. Seeing no one, he deduced that he must have been struck by a rock. "Are you just going to throw things at us? We'll find you soon enough, and I doubt your aim will be so good with my hands around your neck."

"Big talker," the voice said smoothly. The men had both found their feet again and were advancing in the direction (so they thought) of the voice. Fides thought he could hear a lilting whistle on the wind. Like the men, though, he could not identify the source. The men started to get a little nervous, now. It was one thing to face a woman hiding in the trees. It was another to face a woman- or anyone- hiding in the wind. The men exchanged nervous looks.

The first man gathered up his courage, "Yea, that's right. I'm a big talker. Give me a chance to show you I'm bigger than talk and you'll regret it."

"Or," countered the voice, "you could let the boy go and simply walk away." The men snickered in response and maintained their slow patrol of the clearing.

"We'll find you. It is just a matter of time," the first man answered her. "You go finish off the boy and I'll find the woman," he told his friend. His friend turned toward Fides, who grimaced. His grimace evolved into awe, however. Fides could see the man approaching him, but the air between them began to quiver. It was as though it had become liquid in nature, but this was only a passing state. The liquid took on a definite form, and no sooner had it done so, it also took on color. Glistening electric blue flames marked the outline of a woman's body. The blue flames alternated with crimson flares spinning out of her being like solar flares from the sun. The man could not yet see what Fides could see. He kept striding toward Fides while the other man examined the low bushes around the edge of the clearing. Fides now saw that the form had produced a sword of the same quality and nature as itself. At last, the man could see something. The form continued to take on definite shapes and features. The man made a gurgling noise which served as a call of alarm that his friend heard.

The three of them- the two men and Fides- watched the liquid fire become a human being before their very eyes. When the transformation was complete, a beautiful woman stood between the men and Fides. She had a sword (a sword!) but it was angled away from her with the tip of it ahead of her and resting on the earth. She had her other hand on her hip. Her hair fell about her shoulders, shimmering under an unseen light. Her clothing was not anything remarkable, and yet it did not seem normal, either. Fides could not see her eyes. If he could, he would have noticed that they were like small suns. Or was it more like a single sun was shining out of each eye? At any rate, for some reason the men didn't notice this remarkable sight. Instead, they advanced on her as though she posed no threat to them at all.

"Oh, she's fine," one man said to the other. The other chortled greedily.

"Let's get some," the other replied.

"Yes," she replied coyly, "come get some."

The men threw themselves upon her but could not hold her. Their arms fell on her like heavy logs but she mysteriously emerged from their grasping as though it was the easiest thing in the world for her to do. Surprised, they turned around and found her facing them calmly. Infuriated, they rushed at her again. This time, she left her blade standing upright in the grass while she moved to engage them. She grabbed one by the shoulder and he spun around. She caught his arm with both her hands and then... there was a loud snap. The arm was broken. He howled in pain and rage. He fell to the ground, writhing. The other man had turned around to see his friend fall to the ground, but did not see the cause. He had his knife out.

She looked at the knife curiously. "Shall we have a battle of blades, then?" she asked him softly. She had her sword in her hand, now. This was the first time the man had noticed it. He appeared determined to not be intimidated by a woman, though. He mustered up whatever contempt he had left in his body and lunged at her. From Fides' perspective, she did not appear to move at all. It was as though the man simply threw himself onto her blade. He made a final noise and gave a last gasp and fell to the ground, dead. The other man was still in agony but stood up, furious. He reached for her, but only briefly. He met a slashing blow and he too fell to the ground, finished. The woman looked down on the men with sadness. Fides gazed at her. Finally, their eyes met.

"Go home, Fides," she said soothingly. Fides suddenly remembered that his mother was still in danger. At the same time, he realized he'd be no match for the men that remained. The woman felt his fear. "All is well at home. Go home, Fides." Then, she melted into the wind the way she had emerged from it. She was gone. Or was she? Fides could hear a melody on the wind. He couldn't see anything, but he was suddenly certain she was still present.

"Are you an angel?" Fides asked, testing his suspicion that she was still present.

Indeed, she was still there... somewhere... She laughed, "Not at all! Pray that you never see an angel! Terrible! Terrible to behold!" Fides heard her voice all around him.

"Then what are you?" Fides cried into the air. He thought that she had been terrible to behold. If an angel was even more terrible, he thought she was probably right that he didn't want to see one.

But the woman only laughed, "I am human, just like you."

"You may be human, ma'am, but if you are, then I must not be," Fides said slowly.

"I can see how you would think that," she agreed. "Realize that there is more to Man than the eye can see."

"I don't think there is anything more of me to see. I don't think there is more than a disgraceful little boy," Fides moaned, thinking again of his flight from danger.

"Sometimes we must defer judgment to those who are in a better position to know. You are certainly more than a disgraceful little boy. You can put your faith in that," she encouraged him.

"Are you magical?" Fides persisted. The woman smiled and laughed playfully.

"Your race always treats as magic what it does not at first understand. When it finally understands a matter, it heaps contempt on it as though it were something always self-evident to intelligent, sophisticated people. Yet, the wondrous does not cease to be wondrous just because one knows what made it wondrous or 'magical' in the first place," she explained to him patiently. She continued, "Your race then takes it to the other extreme, reducing the wondrous to the banal, thus failing at the end to understand in the slightest the very thing it understood- at least in part- at the beginning."

Fides contemplated these words. She talked to him as though he could understand what she was saying. Though he could not understand, her thinking he could encouraged him. There was a change on the wind. Though he could not see her, he could tell that she was preparing for a final departure. Fides struggled to find words that might prompt her to linger. He very much liked her even though he would be hard put to explain why, as besides being beautiful, she had been awful at the same time

"What... what is your name?" he stammered at last.

She laughed again. It wasn't a mocking laugh. It was innocently mirthful. "My name cannot be translated into your tongue. Maybe someday you will know the language by which it is understood, and you will know me. Peace, boy. Go home, Fides."

Fides felt her hands on his face, stroking his hair. She wiped the blood from his eyes, and his sight and his awareness sharpened briefly. He could see her again! She was beautiful. She drew even closer to him so that he could feel her warm breath on his cheek and ear. Her eyes were unnaturally bright and she looked deep into his eyes; he thought she was examining his soul.

"It is bright in there," she said. Then, he could see her no more. The breeze lost its song and Fides was sure he was alone. He felt completely at peace, and rested right there on the grass.

+ + + + +

"When I woke up, I went home and found my mother safe, and all four of the men who had remained to attack her lying dead. I always thought that she must have been saved as I had, but we never talked about it," Fides said.

"This is a very interesting story," Fermion told him.

"Was it real? Did it really happen?" Fides asked him.

"Yes, I think it's safe to say it did. You have a trouble believing your own eyes, don't you?" Fermion asked him. Fides didn't really want to respond to that, so he asked another question.

"Was she a Nephilim?" Fides asked.

"No, actually, I don't think so," Fermion replied, with a look in his eye that was hard to interpret. It was stern, and formidable, and compassionate, and affectionate.

"But she said that she was a human, and she materialized out of thin air, and she said she wasn't an angel, too," Fides persisted.

"Exactly. She was a human and materialized out of thin air. This is something that as far as I know, a Nephilim cannot do. But if she was not an angel, our options are limited," Fermion replied cryptically.

"Do you know what she was?" Fides pushed him.

"Yes, I think I do," Fermion answered him.

"Are you not going to tell me?" Fides was getting annoyed.

"Will you tell me why you refuse to trust and believe me and your senses even though you have sufficient grounds to trust both?" Fermion challenged Fides. "I think you left something out of your story," he added.

That was true. Fides hadn't said anything about the fact that he fled the men when he should have stood, fought, and died for his mother. Fides looked for a graceful way to change the subject. He saw a group of travelers with the guide drawing near, "It looks like the guide has almost made it to us."

"That sounds like a very good reason to talk about other things to me, too," Fermion agreed, respecting Fides' desire to talk about other matters for the time being.

Fides peppered Fermion with questions throughout the journey. They were now traveling alone and well ahead of the main part of the group. The guide had informed the group that it would be unlikely for them all to stay together for the entire trip. Some people could do the trip in three or four weeks, but others would take months. There was no sense in holding back the faster people, but the guide explained the obvious risks involved in leaving the main group. She gave each individual a map of the route marking various places people could stop and get water and supplies. Initially, Fides and Fermion had had no intention of permanently leaving the group. However, several days into the journey they spied the forms of Jack and his band in the distance behind them. They mutually decided that pressing forward as fast as they could was the wisest strategy. Traveling by themselves without worrying about people overhearing talk about strange matters allowed Fides to ask more and more questions.

Fermion deflected many of Fides' questions before he could form them with his lips. It became a bit of a game for Fides to try to trick Fermion into revealing something more about his identity than he wanted to. Despite Fermion's parrying of Fides' many solicitations, Fides managed to learn a great deal.

"The Disease, if you can believe it, as terrible as it was, may have accomplished a tremendous good. You do not realize how close this country was to utter absorption by rival nations of the world," Fermion was telling Fides. "And after that..."

"Are you suggesting that the Disease was a good thing, like something from God?" Fides responded, surprised.

"Heavens no," Fermion shook his head vigorously. "I am a student of your world's history from its very beginning until the present, but up until a relatively short time ago, I had an access to that history you would not believe. The Disease was a project in development for decades. I was not able to see who the final owner of the project was, or who finally deployed it. I have inferred from what I learned in the American southwest that the Disease went beyond its intended target and washed over the entire world. The Chinese had maintained an iron border to the south with the Mexicans, but both have withdrawn. I am certain that their own homelands have been decimated, and those in power needed what healthy soldiers they could get in order to maintain said power. I would not be surprised to learn, when I have a wider vision once again, that the nuclear attack on the United States was not confined to the United States at all. Both the Disease and the limited nuclear strike that we suffered here I believe was suffered by countries throughout the world."

"Corrie and Dietrich offered similar theories," Fides told Fermion.

"I doubt they have considered the width and breadth of the matter. No, the Disease was not good, but it may yet be worked to the good. I only know the details of my own mission, but I think it is safe to say that every country and every place has been reduced to rubble. Yes, that's terrible," Fermion continued, "but it provides the opportunity for each nation to re-think where it has been and how it arrived in the place it is now in. For the first time, I suspect that I am not alone..."

"What makes you think you know these things, Fermion?" Fides was flabbergasted. "That there were Chinese armies on our southern border I always took to be true, but it isn't as though I ever hoped to think I could verify it or know otherwise. You are talking about conditions across the oceans!"

"Some of it follows from what I already know. Some of it I have only inferred, but I suspect my inferences are correct. In fact, I will go further and say that I am quite certain that the United Nations organization..."

"United Nations?" Fides inquired.

"They eventually became the 'International Force,'" Fermion explained.

"That's right. I think I knew that," Fides said, allowing Fermion to carry on.

Fermion continued, "The UN, who once fought alongside the Chinese to subdue this great nation, disarm it, and remove its sources of knowledge, has also been eliminated. I am certain of this. I believe that the world has been reduced to much the way it was thousands of years ago. It is a great opportunity because the previous course that the world was on I suspect was close to bringing about the final calamities."

Much of this was material that Fides had heard from Corrie and Dietrich, but not all of it. Tricking Fermion into subtly revealing that somehow he had first hand observation of the earth's history, for example, was obviously new. The idea was to keep Fermion talking. "As I understand it, Fermion," Fides maintained the interrogation, "you have been in New Mexico near me these few years. How could you know anything about what was happening on our east coast? After all, the Disease, I am told, was still running throughout the country and a lot of cities and towns sealed themselves off. How could you get information about the UN?"

"The Indians, of course," Fermion explained matter-of-factly. "Realize that the American Indian population in this country is in the middle of making a grand decision. Cherokees, Apaches, Sioux- all of them. There is no Federal government any more to push them around. They are debating as to whether or not they should take advantage of circumstances and re-assert themselves in this country. Some tribes, as you learned from our guide when you asked her about this, have already made up their minds. The Indian tribes of America sealed themselves off much sooner than the average village did. The Indians did not suffer the terrible purging of the Disease. They are at nearly full strength, and it is rumored that they still possess actual firearms. There have already been raids reported to have occurred throughout the Southwest and West. But other tribes consider themselves as American as you consider yourself to be. They are not so sure it is right to do to the white man what the white man did to them. At any rate, seeds planted long ago are soon going to bear a bitter fruit."

Fides thought about this for awhile and decided he hadn't really heard much in what Fermion said that he didn't already know to some extent on his own. He slowly formed the question, "What does this have to do with the UN?"

Fermion continued to lay out the national situation for Fides, "There must be a terrible power vacuum in this country if the American Indians believe that they can re-claim the country as their own. I suspect that they have reliable information to the effect that the UN is no more, or significantly weakened. Remember, only the UN and the Chinese armies were believed to still possess firearms. The Indians fought right alongside many Americans not too long ago when the war to disarm this country and suppress its knowledge began. They suffered loss as much as anybody else. They would not be foolishly debating the morality of 'reacquiring' their own land if they thought the UN was at full strength. No doubt, they probably learned a great deal from their neighbors to the south as the Chinese withdrew. No, I think it's safe to say that the Disease has returned the whole world back to starting positions. It was a tragic thing that certainly killed billions, but in killing billions, it only accomplished what was on the horizon anyway. Yet it spared many from a more final conclusion that was otherwise on its way."

"That is all very interesting," Fides replied somewhat skeptically. It all seemed like a lot of conjecture to him, but it was true that the guide had told them that certain factions of Indian tribes in the region had already decided to make war against the 'white man.' It was only firm resistance from within the greater Indian population that had prevented something more full scale. Nonetheless, besides the normal problems associated with travels these days, they had been clearly warned that there was a real risk that a large Indian raiding party might cross their paths.

"It will be getting far more interesting, I'm sure. In such a vacuum, there are many forces that rush into the void. The Indians are just one group of people suitably poised to exploit the vacuum. I predict that when we get to Oklahoma City we will learn about other groups of people trying to do the same thing. Nothing less than the future of this country, and possibly the world, is at stake. Humanity must learn from its mistakes this time around and establish a government that will adequately prevent what you yourself have witnessed from happening again. Weeds must be uprooted and good seed planted. There will be great battles throughout the world. Some of them will be fought with sticks, clubs, swords, and perhaps guns. Many of them will be fought simply by individuals deciding to do the right thing that is hard rather than the wrong thing that is easy or merely gratifying. Do not be deceived, Fides. This is a time of great opportunity but also a time of great danger. I know for a fact that there is much bloodshed ahead of us, and we will be in the middle of it. I worry about what we will find in Illinois," Fermion said slowly.

Thinking again of Illinois reminded Fides of his reason for traveling. His wife, Melody, vividly broke into his mind. Her long hazel colored hair, her crystal blue eyes, and her stunning smile, all paraded in turn in his imagination. Yet, for some reason the totality of what she looked like seemed to be obscure. Could he not remember what his own wife looked like? It had been more than five years since he had seen her, but he had lived with her for fifteen. How could he forget what she looked like?

And what about his children? There could be no doubt that after five years each of them would look considerably different. Would he recognize them? His oldest, son, Milton. What was he now? Was he twenty-two? Older? Probably, but in his agony he couldn't piece it together in his head. He had been unconscious for more than a year and that had been.. four years ago? Milton had been strong and noble. What would he be like now? His daughters, Suzanne and Mary, what about them? They had only started to make their parents' lives miserable as they both earned the title of 'teenager.' Fides realized that he'd take that misery now in a heartbeat and call it joy. Finally, young Keane. When he left his blond-haired youngest son behind, it required every ounce of discipline that he had. Young Keane was a 'daddy's boy.' Keane would follow him around and imitate him in everything. Unlike his other children, Keane seemed to be enthralled with becoming like his father. The flattery won Keane a special place in Fides' heart.

Fides had by now drifted into a quiet reverie that Fermion wisely perceived and treated with respectful silence. Fides' thoughts were again filled with alternating guilt and hope as he replayed the various possibilities that lay ahead of him in Illinois. Would his family's name be listed there in Bloomington? Should he go there first? Or should he go home first? Are they alive at all? A vision of his youngest son wearing one of his tool belts wrapped around his waist twice appeared in his mind and Fides couldn't keep a single salty tear from gathering in his eye. Only by pure force of will did he keep that tear from descending down his face. His children were now so much older. There was at least a five year gap in their lives. Could it be more? Keane was probably fifteen. His daughters were now women in actuality rather than their self-perception, and his oldest was old enough to take on the world. And his wife...

The longing was too much, but he could not break down in front of this strange man he'd only known for a week. He forced himself to think of something else. He turned his attention to the rock formations far off the road and Fermion willingly engaged in a trivial conversation about them.

In their third week of traveling they had the frightening experience of having to fight off wild dogs during the night. Fermion informed Fides the next morning that it was time for Fides to begin training in how to use that sword that hung at his waist. Fides felt very manly with that heavy object strapped to his leg, but he didn't feel very manly thinking he would need training.

Beginning that following evening, however, Fermion effectively demonstrated the need for practice. After some initial hesitation, Fides dove into the training whenever Fermion was willing to provide it. They managed to practice every day in the early evening, though if it was a cloud covered day and cool enough they might spend an hour at midday.

The curious thing is that the more he handled the sword the more he felt like a warrior. He had never thought of himself in this way before. The sword had helped elicit from his being a latent aspect of his personality that he had not known he had. He had a sense that he was no longer powerless. The more he felt that way, the harder he trained. Fermion was clearly pleased with his progress as the weeks went on. However, as his skill with the sword increased, a question grew on his mind. Could he actually use the sword? Could he kill a man? Fermion knew that this question was growing on Fides, and one day after going through the practice steps, Fermion raised the issue in the curious way Fermion was ought to raise issues.

Having finished that day's lessons, the two were resting on boulders, gazing upon the setting sun. Fermion began speaking as though reciting the lyrics of a song, "There is a time for everything, and a season for every activity under heaven: a time to be born and a time to die, a time to plant and a time to uproot, a time to kill and a time to heal, a time to tear down and a time to build, a time to weep and a time to laugh, a time to mourn and a time to dance, a time to scatter stones and a time to gather them, a time to embrace and a time to refrain, a time to search and a time to give up, a time to keep and a time to throw away, a time to tear and a time to mend, a time to be silent, and a time to speak, a time to love and a time to hate, a time for war and a time for peace."

"What is that?" Fides asked him.

"You can find that in Corrie's book. One of the great displays of nonviolence forms the basis of that book, and yet it is still acknowledged within that same book that there is a 'time to kill and a time to heal,' a 'time for war and a time for peace.' You see what the problem is? How do you know which time it is? Wisdom is required. But see what this means: if it is the right time for war, than 'peace' will not do. If it is the right time for 'peace,' than war is for naught. Your race has the curious habit of doing the opposite of whatever it is that needs to be done. Thus, whether at 'war' or at 'peace,' it carries out much evil," Fermion muttered darkly. He continued, "Whether planting or uprooting, your race does the wrong thing at the wrong time. It weeps when it should laugh and laughs when it should weep. It tears down when it should mend and mends when it should tear down," Fermion concluded.

"Many of the world's religions argue that the highest ethic is to respond to violence with non-violence. I do not know much history, that is true, but I know that great things have been done by those who have turned the other cheek," Fides challenged Fermion.

"You misunderstand me," Fermion objected. "There certainly is a time and place when responding with mildness and meekness, or nonviolence, at any rate, is not merely justified, but the absolute right course of action." Fides said nothing, so Fermion continued, "If your wife was being raped, what do you think you ought to do?"

"I should stop the man," Fides did not hesitate to say.

"But what if he would not stop?" Fermion pressed.

"I... I would have to pull him away..."

"And if he would not be pulled away?" Fermion persisted.

"I suppose that what you mean is that situations exist where it is not merely a lesser evil to inflict violence, but it is in fact the right thing to do," Fides concluded.

"Yes, exactly. This is a broken world peopled with a broken people. This fact cannot be avoided. No sincere sentiments about the good of man can change that bitter fact. Only recently, terrible seeds wrought terrible fruits upon your world. Now, that world is in a vulnerable position, ripe for exploitation- for raping. Yes, some in this particular generation have noble intentions. Others, however, seek to take advantage of the world's vulnerability. They seek to rape, to dominate, to oppress, to take by violence what they could not get by persuasion. Yes, it lacks the visceral rage one might have in response to stumbling upon the rape of his own wife, but rape of another person- or all people- ought to be no less enraging. Furthermore, people in this mindset are not going to stop merely because you ask them to," Fermion explained.

"But how do I know what the right thing is in all of this, or even if there is a right thing?" Fides returned.

"It calls for wisdom. And knowledge. The key is to think about such things in advance. Once you're in the situations, it will be too late. Work out these questions in your own mind to the best of your ability. However, there are limits to all types of moral calculations. At some point you can only submit yourself to Grace," Fermion replied.

"So what time is it now?" Fides asked Fermion, knowing full well what Fermion would say.

"War, I am afraid," Fermion sighed. "Previous generations had the luxury of winning peace by nonviolence. There very well could be perfectly appropriate applications of such behavior even in this day and age, don't get me wrong. Nonetheless, it is written in bright letters for all to see: Violent men see a void, and wish to fill it. They must be stopped, yet they won't be persuaded by words. They won't be persuaded by purposeful nonviolence. Indeed, they welcome that response, and would encourage as much of it as they can."

"War ahead, eh?" Fides said, frowning.

Fermion looked at Fides with compassion, "The morality of killing is not the only thing on your mind, is it?"

Fides knew that it wasn't. He thought again of incident in the wood when he was young. Even though his parents had assured him that he had done right, and even to some extent agreed with them now that he was a parent as well, he knew without need of a moral authority that using violence to defend the innocent is sometimes the right thing to do. The real question in his mind was whether or not he would use violence if the moment was upon him. Could he do it? Here he was, spending an hour a day swinging a sword, but could he bring himself to connect steel with flesh, even if he was convinced it was the right thing to do? Tied into this whole question, he knew, was the notion that being able to stand and fight in that manner in that moment meant exposing himself to possible pain, injury, and death. Was it only his disgust with violence that held him back, or was it also his fear of possibly getting hurt?

"When I was a boy..." Fides began.

"Hold it right there," Fermion stopped him. "You were only a child, then. Now you are a man, think like one. You are a man among men. No one is superior to you, now. Everyone is in the same position. Everyone sees but a poor reflection of themselves. A day will come when you will see clearly, and you will be clearly seen. I have faith that you will not be seen as a coward. You do not believe me?"

"Thanks for that, I think," Fides sighed, "I do not know that I will be brave, though."

"Now you know in part. A day will come, I pray, when you shall know fully. Fermion studied Fides for a moment, "Sometimes we must admit our ignorance and defer to those in a better position to know. Your knowledge is incomplete, but you are fully known by others. If you do not know who you are, content yourself with knowing whose you are, and who knows you."

"I don't want to sound like a weakling, here," Fides replied, "I have had to fight before, but I've never had to... kill."

Fermion exclaimed, "By God, I tell you that if that prospect did not unnerve you, that should tell you and I both that you are a cold-hearted, violent man! All good men have no desire to kill, and abhor it. But all good men have no desire to allow the slaughter of innocents, either. I have faith in you, Fides. If you do not have faith in yourself, content yourself in my faith in you." Fermion continued, "I assure you, you may fail a hundred times but there will be a day when you stand up. I believe it. After all, you did try to come to my defense back in Albuquerque."

Fides thought carefully about these words, but could not perceive the source of Fermion's confidence. Setting aside the incident in Albuquerque, he didn't feel tested. He was prepared to give and take a few lumps in that instance, but he did not consider that there had been much chance at the time of killing or being killed, even though he nearly was. The matter was left lingering in his mind, but the conversation came to a close.

By the fourth week of traveling together they had made it about two thirds of the way to Oklahoma City. Throughout their journey, they had seen many other travelers. Some were going the same way as them, but slower, and they carefully passed by these people. On occasion, they would pass a larger group with a guide under the employ of the travel center that had treated them with such hospitality. They also encountered people traveling from the opposite direction. The closer they got to their destination, the more common it was to come upon west-bound travelers. As they didn't trust anyone, they remained extremely cautious whenever they encountered someone, whether they were coming or going. They would not have to worry about any of these travelers, however.

The fifth week, though, revealed that there were some travelers they needed to mind. It was the middle of the night and Fides was taking his turn keeping watch. At first, he thought he might be imagining things, but at last realized he was hearing the sounds of travelers coming up on them from the west. He quietly roused Fermion, and the two of them quickly but quietly concealed themselves better behind some large boulders that they had camped behind. It was not at all rare to see and hear other travelers, but it was very rare for them to be passed by anyone behind them. Fermion and Fides had been out-pacing everyone. It was even more singular to get passed in the middle of the night.

As the sounds of the travelers got closer they heard a woman's voice which they recognized distinctly as belonging to the woman in Jack's goon squad. She wasn't alone, though. She was speaking with two other men whom they assumed were part of Jack's reinforcements. Fides thought it strange that Jack would get this close to them and then blunder by revealing their proximity. The answer became clear, however, as they were able to hear more of the conversation. The three people were obviously drunk.

"Good Lord," Fermion whispered. "Their whole group must not be that far behind us."

"What do you think we should do?" Fides replied in an appropriately hushed tone. Fides could see Fermion's face creased with a frown in the moonlight.

"If we go on ahead, they'll probably catch up to us unless we actually plan on running the rest of the trip. If we wait until they pass us, they may think we are still ahead of them. Our only risk in that scenario is that they may stumble upon us anyway while we wait for them to pass us. Well, there is also the chance that they figure it out and try to ambush us."

After a few minutes of reflection and quiet discussion, they decided it was wisest to try to keep Jack as far behind them as they could, even if it did mean running. Because of the desolate nature of the countryside, it would be hard for either group to hide from the other. However, if Jack got ahead of them, with his superior numbers he could easily block their advance. They quietly gathered their belongings and went out much further from the road than they normally did and jogged until Fides was too tired to jog anymore. Then they took a break, and then they jogged some more. They continued this pattern all night. They never did see or hear the woman and the two men again. As the sun came up, Fermion encouraged Fides to keep moving. "They'll be moving at their normal rate, probably, and they've obviously caught up to us. Our only hope is to put some extra space between us before they realize how close they are."

That day, they forced themselves to move very quickly even during the hot parts of the day. As the sun was slowly making its descent, they climbed a high, rocky hill, to see if they could spot anyone behind them. They appeared to be alone in the world. Relieved, and utterly exhausted, they went to bed. Fermion had Fides up before the sun made even a hint of an awakening, however, and they put in yet another day of hurried travel. Much to Fides' relief, they saw a sign that said "Oklahoma City- 100 miles." They were four-fifths of the way there. The landscape also seemed to have been changing around them. There were far more grassy fields around them than there were before, although there will still wide patches of desolate sandy wilderness and large gatherings of stoic boulders. On the third day since their fortuitous encounter with the drunken members of Jack's gang, Fermion goaded Fides into double-time hiking for only part of the day. That night they examined the road behind them and again they saw no trace of any pursuers.

Oklahoma City was less than a week's journey ahead of them and they estimated they were a full day ahead of any trouble. Their conversations resumed and there was considerably less tension accompanying them as though a third burdensome member of their traveling company was no longer with them.

The next morning, they awoke to the sound of a growling in the distance. Fides rolled over in the direction of the noise and rubbed his eyes. Fermion was already on his feet and straining his eyes westward. Fides stood up and looked in the same direction. The sun had only just started coming up, so it seemed as though it were the night itself muttering at them. The sound seemed very familiar to Fides, but he couldn't place it.

"It's a vehicle," Fides realized.

"I agree," Fermion replied. The two of them gathered their belongings together in preparation for whatever might be coming down the road. Once they had their affairs in order they waited expectantly. The engine noise continued to increase as they waited. It had an interesting pitch to it, and Fides thought it almost seemed to be coming to him in harmony.

"Those are motorcycles," Fides ventured.

"I think you're right," Fermion again concurred. Fides saw that Fermion had his hand on the hilt of his sword so Fides reached for his sword, as well. A few moments later they could see a speck on the western horizon, accompanied by the swelling sound of racing motorcycle engines. It was at this moment that Fides realized that they were not in a well-concealed position. In fact, there was no place to hide within fifty yards. They both seemed to have realized this at the same time because when Fides dropped low to the ground he saw that Fermion had done the same.

The motorcycles were growing bigger both in perceived size and volume of sound. They could tell now that the machines were towing something, and had attached compartments. Each vehicle had two people on it, one at the handle bars and one in the attached side compartment. They were now only two hundred yards away. Fides crouched as still as he could. It was too little, too late.

Both the motorcycles slowed down abruptly, as though they were people being caught by surprise. Re-gaining their composure, the motorcycles left the road and veered toward them, bouncing along the hard terrain in a way that was surely uncomfortable for the side compartment passengers. Fides and Fermion drew their swords and assumed fighting stances. The cycles dove at them in an attempt to ram them but both Fides and Fermion were able to jump aside in time. Fermion was able to slash at the motorcycle that had charged him, but didn't make any contact. The cycles drove on about fifty yards from them and stopped. The riders were obviously in consultation.

"I think in the motorcycle that came at me was two of the men that I dealt with on your behalf back in Albuquerque," Fermion said, warily watching the assailants.

"Well, we've got nowhere to hide," Fides reflected. "They can stay in front of us and hold us back until the rest of the gang get here, if they want to."

This was indeed a valid concern, but it seemed that the two men that Fermion had identified wanted revenge. Within a mere moment, the two motorcycles were again bearing down on them. This time all four of the assailants had clubs out and were ready to swipe at Fides and Fermion if they tried to jump aside again. The riders were heading towards them at a high rate of speed, but it was clear that they were having trouble steering straight on the bumpy soil.

The moment of collision came quickly: Fides again managed to escape impact and dove into the dust. He could hear the sound of contemptuous cackling as the riders sped around. Fermion, on the other hand, had leapt upward rather than to the side, fitting just above and inside the narrow gap between the driver and the passenger. The butt of his sword caught the driver in the back and the motorcycle took a nose-dive into the dirt about twenty feet away. Passenger and driver alike rolled for another twenty feet but quickly recovered and were advancing on them. The other motorcycle discovered that it was alone and made its way back towards them.

Fermion did not wait for the two men he had dethroned to reach him. He quickly closed the distance between him and the two men, with Fides close behind. Fermion quickly dispatched one of the men with very little effort. Fides had his own sword out as the other man charged at him, but he only held it in front of him. Fermion pondered aiding Fides, but instead marched out towards the other motorcycle, leaving Fides and the man alone. The man swung his club towards Fides, but Fides only blocked it. Fides used his free hand to push at the man and hold him at bay. The man was unaffected by this. Instead, the man caught Fides by surprise by bringing the club over his head so hard that even though Fides again blocked the blow, he was knocked backwards onto his butt. The other motorcycle had circled away from Fermion's advance and was coming in from the other direction. Fermion calmly returned to where Fides and the man were in mortal combat.

The man was raining blows onto Fides, but Fides could not bring himself to slash with his sword. Fides kept scooting back in the sand and the rock and the man kept coming at him. Fermion grabbed the man's shoulder, earning his attention immediately. The man swung his club wildly at Fermion, but with one smooth stroke, Fermion rendered him dead. Fermion looked at Fides with questioning eyes. Fides looked away.

The oncoming motorcycle veered off away from them as it witnessed their second friend's death. From a safe distance away, the motorcycle turned so that driver and passenger could reassess the situation. After a moment, the vehicle sped back to the west, its riders certainly intending to inform their friends about these events as well as alert them to Fides and Fermion's location. Fermion was not waiting around. He quickly strode over to the other motorcycle. The trailer had come off, but the side compartment was intact.

Fides joined him and pried off the cover to the trailer. Inside was food and water and a full gasoline can. Fermion whistled when he saw what Fides had found. "They managed to come up with some vehicles and the gasoline to power them right in the middle of the desert. I wonder how they managed that. Can you ride a motorcycle, Fides?" Fermion asked.

"Yes, I sure can. Let's fill this thing up and see if it can get us out of here," Fides said.

They poured as much of the gasoline into the tank as it could hold, stuffed some of the food in their shirts, and refreshed their canteens. It was clear that the riders were only scouts. There was enough fuel available for some good exploration and then a return to where they had originated. It was unfortunate that the trailer was no longer connected to the bike. They spent a few minutes trying to connect it, but it was badly mangled, having twisted off when the bike had rolled. They abandoned their effort and decided it would be wise to move along as quickly as possible.

As Fides gunned the engine and pulled onto the road with Fermion sitting next to him in the side-compartment, he couldn't help but thank God for their surprising good fortune. Naturally, it had been a stressful experience and the outcome could have been very different. Nonetheless, they were now poised to be in Oklahoma City that very day. In fact, they could be there in mere hours. Rather than another arduous week of traveling on foot with Jack and his band lurking behind them in close pursuit, they'd be at their destination, if everything continued to work in their favor, before lunch.

Fides was kicking himself for not dealing with his assailant on his own. He fought back a terrible feeling of disgrace and humiliation. Something told Fides that this was still not a very good test, though. He had only been concerned for himself. If he had been called to defend the defenseless, he had a sense he would have behaved differently. Still, it was embarrassing. He could not help feeling slightly better as he sped down the road with the wind slapping at his face and body. It was even better when he saw that Fermion was not enjoying the ride. It was nice to be able to show Fermion, the mighty Nephilim and warrior, that here was something he could stomach that Fermion could not. Fides only just managed to contain his smirk when Fermion turned fully green and would clearly have left his breakfast spread out over a hundred feet of old highway I-40, if only he would have had time to eat it this morning. Still, this was only some consolation. The mere ability to ride a motorcycle without getting ill is a small measure of a man's character, and Fides knew it.

== Chapter 4 ==

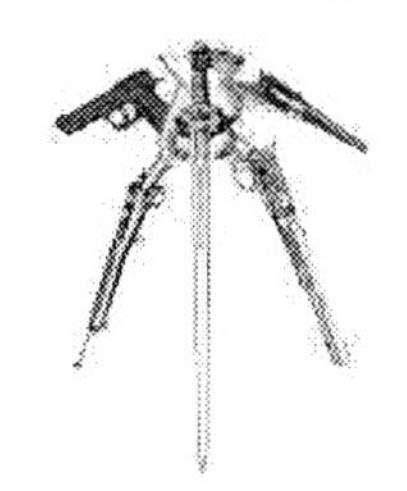

Fides couldn't believe his good fortune in cutting a week to ten days off of the journey to Oklahoma City, even if it had meant having a confrontation with Jack's associates. That confrontation, though stressful and a bit humiliating for Fides, ended decidedly in their favor. Fermion probably would have been happy about the same thing except motorcycle rides didn't seem to be his bag. Fides thought that it may have been a different story if they could have been riding on the interstate when it was new. After all these years, however, it was filled with various sized potholes and large cracks. While the roads here were in better condition than the roads north, where winter caused much more damage, there was still enough damage here to force them to ride carefully. Riding was definitely quicker than walking or running, but clearly it had its own hazards. After a couple of hours of riding they saw the city slowly rising in the horizon.

Oklahoma City had an entirely different look and atmosphere than Albuquerque. The old suburb section had been razed to the ground, appearing to be nothing more than a uninhabitable wasteland, now. There were numerous reinforced outposts spread along the perimeter of the city, clearly composed of materials scavenged from the old residential section. The outposts were filled with stern looking men who eyed them suspiciously as they made their way closer and closer to the city proper. When they did actually come to the city limits they found that a wall had been created around the city for as far as they could see. The wall appeared to be composed mainly of old semi-truck tractors and trailers and piles of junked cars, buses, and vans. The wall was at least eight feet tall throughout.

Where the interstate punched through the wall, the wall was solely composed of over-turned tractor trailers. There were holes cut out of the wall here and there and he could see that there were men armed with cross bows peering out of them. Because they had been tipped over, the tops of the trailers were now the sides of the wall. For about one hundred yards in both directions, solid looking shacks appeared to be stocked with men armed with bows, clubs, and spears. He couldn't tell just how fortified the wall was because it curved around and away from him, presumably to envelop the city.

Standing in the middle of the road, blocking their entrance to the city, were three sturdy looking men who plainly meant business.

Fides and Fermion stopped the motorcycle, turned off the engine, and then walked the bike the remaining fifty feet to where the men were waiting patiently. Dressed in beige garments with red sashes serving as a belt, they looked pretty sharp. It took Fides a second look to see that both the tops and the sashes were salvaged from other garments. Perhaps the garments were cut out from old cloth burlap bags- he couldn't tell. Nonetheless, they had been fixed up very professionally, and they looked very proper.

The center man was in charge of the gate. "A motorcycle?" he inquired.

Fermion spoke for the two of them, "Yes, sir, a motorcycle."

"Where did you come from that was close enough to get by on a single tank of gas?" the head gatekeeper asked, continuing the interview.

"We were attacked on the road, sir, by four men on two motorcycles. We were able to resist two of them, and we took their vehicle. We do not know where they themselves got the motorcycles," Fermion patiently explained.

"These men you took the motorcycles from... will they tell the same story?"

Fermion did not blink as he replied, "The men who once rode on this particular bike are in no position to walk, let alone, ride. They are dead- I killed them. Their friends, however, are certainly going to be coming down the road in due time. They have been chasing us since Albuquerque, but only recently does it seem they have acquired motorcycles and the gasoline to operate them. We have not seen the other pair, or the group that was with them, since this morning."

The two men standing on either side of the head gatekeeper seemed to think this was somewhat discomforting news, but the head gatekeeper himself didn't show any reaction. His next question came as though such incidents were commonplace and he was just giving a routine interview.

"So you killed some of these people, did you? I'm sure you'd describe them as bandits of some sort..." the gatekeeper left it as an open question.

"Criminals from Albuquerque, actually," Fermion corrected him, "and I'm sure you could find some people from Albuquerque that could verify what we say about them. I know the name of the ringleader and can produce it, if you so desire."

"Criminals, then. And how is it that you came to kill them when they were the ones with the motorcycles?"

"I knocked them off their vehicle," Fermion said matter-of-factly.

"I suppose I'm not really being clear. What was your weapon? A rock? A club?" This seemed to be the gatekeeper's chief concern and Fermion appeared to have known that from the beginning.

Fermion maintained his cool composure: "It doesn't matter, really, does it?"

The gatekeeper's eyes formed somewhat narrow slits as he also replied coolly, "Produce your weapon, sir."

Fermion sighed, and moved aside his cloak, deftly unsheathing his blade and stabbing it into the road so that it stood at attention before the three men. The three guards jumped back, startled. "Let's have yours out, too, Fides," Fermion nodded towards Fides.

Fides took out his own sword, but held onto it. Fermion nodded reassuringly to Fides, so Fides took a cautious step forward and leaned hard to push his sword into the ground next to Fermion's. It took him far more effort to make the tip penetrate the crippled pavement than it seemed to have taken Fermion. Fides then followed Fermion's example and stepped back a few feet from the blades. As it was obvious that the two did not pose a threat, distancing themselves from their own weapons, the gatekeeper and guards relaxed from their defensive posture. That did not mean they were comfortable.

"These look like actual swords. I confess, they are beautiful, but I cannot figure how two travelers from Albuquerque managed to acquire them as well as a motorcycle," the guard said.

"We told you about the motorcycle, but the swords are our business alone," Fermion replied.

The guard gave no indication of being put off by this answer. It seemed there was something else on his mind, though. "Are you an Indian?" he asked Fermion, staring right into his eyes.

"The long gray hair, is that it? No, I am not an Indian."

"That is good, because if you were we'd have to extend this process." The gatekeeper turned his attention to Fides finally, and immediately caught sight of Fide's bizarre looking necklace. "What is that?" The guard asked.

"That would also be none of your business," Fermion again replied coolly.

The guard was not deterred. Still fixing his eyes on Fides, he said, "Where are you going? What is your final destination?"

Fides replied this time. "We are on our way to Bloomington, Illinois, to consult the family registry that they are creating there. I am looking for my family." There was no contesting Fides' genuineness. The gatekeeper's gaze softened some, but it was clear this was the oddest entrance interview that he had conducted in a long time. The gatekeeper spied a wrapped bundle underneath Fides' cloak.

"What is that?" the man said, turning his attention to Fides.

Fides had to look to see what was being referenced. "That is a book."

"A book? Can you read?" the head guard pressed.

"I can. Not very well, but I'm getting better," Fides offered in his defense.

"What book is that?" the head gate keeper pressed further. Fides moved around uncomfortably. It's true that book banning and burning had not been an American policy, but rather an international policy imposed on America, but afterwards there were many that attached a stigma to learning, intellect, and religious thought and materials in particular. Many people seemed to think that if the international community thought it important to remove Bibles and other religious material from the US (and later, large swaths of the world), they probably had good reason. Experts can't be wrong, can they? Fides could see no way to avoid being truthful, though, so he answered honestly.

"It's a Bible," Fides said slowly. At that, the three guards laughed uproariously.

"A Bible! That is a good one. Fine, then. Don't tell me," the head gatekeeper continued guffawing. The three settled into sporadic chuckling. Finally, the head man returned to his serious tone, "Well, you are certainly the strangest pair I've seen come or go to this city, but I can't keep you. I also cannot take your swords, since in this city everyone has the right to defend themselves. However, because of the obvious lethality of your weapons, you need to present yourself and your weapons at the president's manor. I suspect they'll say you need the president's express permission to retain a weapon that I suspect is the better of any instrument here."

"The president's manor?" Fermion asked.

"Yes, I will send Gus and Splint to escort you there, directly. You'll need a written pass or else patrolmen will harass you indefinitely." With that, the head guard nodded, and the other two men- Gus and Splint, apparently- motioned towards Fides and Fermion, who retrieved their swords, re-sheathed them, fetched their bike, and followed. They made their way slowly through the streets, which increasingly got more and more crowded as they went. Many people would stop, point, and stare, especially at Fermion. Fermion explained to Fides that they were staring for the same reason the head gatekeeper had been concerned: he looked a bit like an Indian.

Gus jumped in on this and explained the situation. "We are in the area of the Cherokee tribe. They were displaced from their original homeland hundreds of years ago. There is a big debate among various tribes right now about whether or not they should re-claim their lands. Of course, the Cherokees originally came from the east coast area, so even some of those who want to take the land disagree on which land to take. The original land before the US moved them? The land they've got right now that has non-Indians on it? They can't decide. But there are still bands out there that have decided the only good non-Indian is a dead non-Indian, and they have been slaughtering or raiding traveling parties for about a year. It's been random, though. It's not a full campaign. Last month, though, some Indians attacked the north wall. They killed some people, but we think they were just testing our defenses," Gus explained.

Gus continued talking as they wound their way through streets that became progressively more and more crowded. "Right now it just so happens that the Cherokee chief's second-in-command and a large delegation is in town right now, discussing such things. We think the Cherokee Nation does not want any harm to us. We think the chief in particular considers himself fully American. It's hard for him to control all of his people, though, especially since many of the Indians have real honest-to-god guns. If the Indians ever did want to re-take the country, I think they've got a good shot, if you pardon the pun."

They took a right turn.

"Of course, we don't know how many guns they've got. They certainly have some. You've come at an interesting time, though, because the Indians are not the only people of interest here," Gus continued.

Fermion's interest was suddenly aroused, "Oh?"

"Yep," Gus rambled on, "The Pledge have a delegation here, too." Gus apparently thought that would mean something but Fermion and Fides only returned blank stares. "The Pledge. You know, the Pledge? Hmmm. Well, maybe news hasn't gotten to Albuquerque yet. The Pledge is an army from the southeast somewhere. They say that they know best how to rebuild the country and want to take all of the land in the country, and all of the resources, and then distribute them equally to everyone. They also think that the average worker should have a larger say in the country's decisions. They don't like the idea of Oklahoma City having a president, that's for sure, but I bet they haven't said that."

"They're here?" Fermion asked.

"Well, a delegation of them, yeah. They are trying to convince the president to turn over the city to the protection of the Pledge."

"Lord, when will they learn?" sighed Fermion.

"Eh?" Gus intoned.

"Don't you know your history?" Fermion asked him. "It sounds to me like the Pledge is just an old philosophy in new dressing. We can only pray that they do not get their way."

Gus shrugged, "They sound good to me. Especially if the Indians want to make a go of things, we'll need to stand together."

Fides interjected: "But you said the Indians have guns."

Gus smiled slyly, "Well, the rumor is that the Pledge does, too. Obviously, I don't know. But I think it must be true because it sounds like the Pledge have a pretty good army formed up. They must be big enough and powerful enough that they can send delegations off to the intact cities to try to get other leaders to join them."

"Your memory has been carved out, my friend," Fermion said wearily. "Be wary for things that sound good but aren't." Gus looked as though he was going to respond, but they were at the gate of the president's manor. There were two men armed with crossbows standing along the wrought iron fence.

"What's up, Gus?" one of them asked.

"These two have got swords, Ged," Gus explained.

"Swords? Really? Let's see!" Fides and Fermion pulled their cloaks back well enough for the two guards to see the scabbards. That wasn't enough to satisfy them. They had to pull their swords out so the men could ooh and ah.

The other guard noticed the motorcycle. "A motorcycle? Does it work?"

Splint muttered something, making a noise for the first time. The manor guards seemed to note this. "Well, ok, we'll take it from here." The guards escorted them up to a large white building that looked to be both the offices and residence of the president of the city. They were brought to a spacious office, filled with busy looking people. In the back of this room, there were other offices. Fides was surprised to see that they were using electric light. The guards brought them to one of the back offices, knocked, and nudged Fermion and Fides in. A short, pudgy, bald man appraised the situation.

One of the guards simply pointed at Fermion and Fides and said, "They've got swords." They looked like they were going to linger on to hear more of the conversation, but a stern look from the man directed them back to their posts.

"Well, let's see them," the man instructed.

Fermion and Fides both withdrew their swords, and at the man's beckoning, laid them on the desk. The man carefully inspected the swords, giving a low whistle as he studied the ornamental engravings around the base of the sword and their hilts. He ran his finger along the sharp edge of both swords. His eyes got wider and wider as he examined the swords. The longer he studied them the more he was impressed.

"Well, these appear to be the real deal," the man said quietly.

"You have seen swords like this before?" Fermion asked him.

"Hmmmm. Not swords, but a shorter blade of similar craftsmanship," the man replied, noting Fermion's interest. "In fact, I saw one very recently."

"Oh?" queried Fermion.

"Yes, today in fact. And it and its owner currently are in the building," the man answered shrewdly.

"Why, that is interesting," Fermion answered cautiously. Fides thought the man might be trying to extort a bribe or something, but Fermion didn't appear to care to go that far. Fermion could not contain his interest fully, though, and so asked, "Might I have a chance to speak with the owner?"

"You might, but it won't be because I permit it," the man replied gruffly. "That won't be any of your business, will it? Obviously, if they choose to show it to you, that's one thing. But I won't say who it is, and you won't be going around asking people, will you?"

"No, I don't think so," Fermion agreed.

"Well, then," the man said, standing up. "Take your swords back. I can't give you the authorization to take these into the city. You'll need to speak to the president directly. You can call him President Neff. He's very busy today, as you may have heard, but our laws are clear. So, on we go."

They followed the man out of the office area into a long hallway. It opened up into a lavish foyer, and then narrowed down into another hallway. As they continued, they could hear voices shouting and arguing. They finally came to what appeared to be the president's main office area. A conference room nearby appeared to be the source of the arguing. A handful of armed officers of Oklahoma City were stationed outside the conference room. The man went to the door of the conference room, knocked on it, and opened it. They heard the substance of some passionate words before the speaker was distracted by the door opening: "We keep our word: If not by choice, than by force!"

"My apologies, sir, but there are two men here who need a right to a lethality permit..." the man's words became muffled as the man got further from the door, from which Fermion and Fides were standing a respectful distance.

"Swords?" came an exclamation.

After a moment, the bald man came to the door and nodded to them. "President Neff would like to see your swords," the man told them.

Fermion and Fides entered the room. To their surprise, it wasn't a small room, but rather a very large room filled with long tables and a platform at the end which had other tables on it. The room was crowded with people. It was a strange sight to behold.

The president and a number of advisors were standing on the floor just off of the platform. There were more armed officers that answered to the President standing near him and in other parts of the room. To Fides' left were about twenty people that were clearly either Indians, or with the Indians. To the right were another twenty people that Fides inferred were members of the Pledge delegation. These two groups were staring at each other, looking very tense. President Neff looked weary, but apparently interested in swords. That, or glad to have a break.

Fermion and Fides walked up to the center area, which was open. They couldn't help but look around them as they made the short trip. It was amazing the differences that seemed to emanate from the groups merely by observation. To Fides' surprise, the Indians seemed to project honor, bravery, and pride. With all the talk about the danger of Indians ambushing them on their way to Oklahoma City, Fides expected to see shifty warriors. These people, however, had kind faces and bright eyes. To the extent that they looked angry, their stern looks seemed to reflect righteous indignation. The Pledge, on the other hand, seemed to project greed and conspiracy. Some of them were wearing old-style suits and ties. Their leader had slicked-back black hair. He had the look of a salesman about him, but Fides sensed that there was violence glistening behind his shrewd eyes.

"Alright, let's see what the fuss is all about," ordered President Neff as he motioned to Fermion and Fides. They withdrew their swords and held them out to him, handles out. The president selected Fides' to examine first. Fermion put the tip of his sword down into the worn carpet, holding it away from him in a non-aggressive posture. Fides noticed that Fermion was examining both sides of the room for any response to the blades. Fides also discreetly tried to detect the owner of a similar blade, but there was murmuring on all sides of the room. Hoping to find this other person (Fides wondered- another Nephilim?) based on reaction was not going to work.

"A fine specimen. I've only seen one like it, myself. And that was today," the president said whimsically.

A speaker from the Pledge side of the room interrupted them, "No offense President Neff, but there are things of more importance than swords, and all in all, there are more fearsome weapons in the world, as you well know."

Without missing a beat, the Cherokee chief's second-in-command and head of the Indian delegation, answered, "Yes, we all know the rumors that the Pledge has firearms. I'm sure you are also aware of the rumors that the Indians have firearms."

"Actually," sneered the Pledge spokesman, "we have it on good authority that this is no rumor. It is truth."

"You say it is so. It does not seem wise for this city to base their decision based on the rumors about your capabilities against the facts of our capabilities, then, don't you think?" the chief retorted. "Why not be plain about your threats rather than rely on insinuations?"

The Pledge spokesman's demeanor soured, and he went silent. During this exchange, Fides looked more carefully at both sides of the room. Fermion, however, tensed his body during the exchange and kept his eye only on the Pledge spokesman. The Pledge spokesman was accompanied by about fifteen comrades. Not all of them were as well-dressed as the spokesman, however. Some had clearly dressed themselves by scavenging fabric. Though they hadn't done a bad job of assembling their outfits, they still didn't look as smart as the Oklahoma City gate guards did in their scavenged outfits. The Pledge delegation appeared to be attended by a small group of tiny men, very much like the man he had seen at the Albuquerque staging ground. These little men looked like adults that had been severely stunted. They were mainly hairless, and shriveled, and seemingly completely passive as they waited on the Pledge delegation.

On the other side were the Indians, but Fides noted that not all of them possessed the physical features he expected Indians to have, but perhaps he was not in a position to have derived realistic expectations. The group was dressed in modern looking clothing. It did not look as though they had scavenged anything. Some of them wore pants or tops that were made of tanned leather, but most used this more distinctive Indian dress as nothing more than accessories. Several of the men were younger and clearly warriors. They even had knives and hatchets hanging from their belts. There were some women, as well. The four or five women appeared to be as brave as the rest of them and remained more or less silent. One of the women was standing next to one of the young braves as though she were associated with him. She looked well for her age. He examined the rest of the group, noticing that there were several older men who were pronounced in their Indian features. Finally, the chief's second-in-command was an ancient looking man who gave every indication of having spent every moment of every day of his entire life under the sun. Fides thought that if the chief's second-in-command was so old, then the chief must be practically a fossil.

There was a stony silence after the exchange. At last, President Neff returned attention to the two men in the middle with swords. Fides and Fermion didn't mind getting matters settled so they could withdraw from this tense situation.

"What is your purpose in Oklahoma City, gentlemen?" President Neff asked them.

"We are only passing through, sir," Fides replied. "We are going to Bloomington, Illinois, to try to find my family."

"Oh yes, they have some sort of a project there, don't they? The Disease and the nuclear incidents were devastating. People got trapped all over the place. This project is supposed to be a central location to try to reconnect families and friends. I do hope you find your family and that they are well," the president said compassionately. It gave Fides confidence hearing that others had heard of the project as well and that it wasn't just one more rumor.

"Thank you," Fides responded graciously.

"I am concerned that people will be nervous with you in the city, however," President Neff continued. "It's true that there are more potent weapons in the world, but not in this city- at least not legally. How long were you thinking of staying here?"

Fermion answered this question: "We are ready to leave at once. Just give us a day or two to collect additional supplies and we'll be off."

"Pardon me," interjected a voice from the Indian delegation. All heads turned to see who was talking. It was the young man who seemed to be attached somehow to the older, withered lady with young eyes. "Who is permitted to go to this project in Illinois?"

"As far as I know, it's open to anyone in the country that is trying to reconnect with loved ones. I've heard that other places may start up projects like this in the future, too," President Neff explained.

The young man turned to the woman and to the head of the Indian delegation. "Ramaen, you know that I came to you from that area. Tasha brought me to your people and I have been very thankful for that. She saved my life. But I don't know what happened to my family, either. I would like to go to Bloomington, Illinois, too."

Ramaen, the Cherokee leader representing the real chief and a number of other tribes and their chiefs, tilted his head towards the young man in a clear sign of respect. "King, you have done well as an adopted member of our Nation. Your fighting spirit will be missed, even when we saw it as mischief. You know I cannot keep you here."

"I would like to go with these men, Ramaen. And if Tasha would like to return with me, I would appreciate her company, as she has been a mother to me," King continued.

"That is not for me to say, but you can leave with or without them whenever you like. I give you leave. And Tasha, you are released from any obligations you may feel, as well," Ramaen said.

"A new adventure seems appropriate," Tasha replied.

Fermion now interjected his own approval, "King and Tasha are more than welcome to journey with us. We hear there are evil things afoot in that direction..." There was snickering out of some members of the Pledge. "And the more people we have the better we will be."

"Splendid," President Neff said jovially. "Now we can return to some other matters that perhaps may be more critical for us today," he sighed. "We need to find a way to appease the nationalistic Indian groups and keep them from slaughtering our travelers, and we need to decidedly reject so-called offers to join the Pledge. You are dismissed," the president said, handing Fermion and Fides each a piece of paper authorizing them to retain their swords. The Pledge spokesman snarled at the president's words, but the president ignored him, "Take up to three days, but I would suggest you leave as soon as you can. The people are nervous, and we must not make things worse."

Fermion nodded in agreement and acceptance. They once again retrieved their swords, but this time left as a group of four. They were escorted back to the gate entrance, where the two guards were goggling at the motorcycle. The guards' eyes lit up when Fermion made it clear he was leaving the bike temporarily in their care. The four of them walked to the Indian delegation's lodging and rested there for the remainder of the day, becoming acquainted with each other. When the delegation returned in the early evening, they were ominously silent, leaving the four of them to gather up materials and supplies as though they were alone.

Fides, Fermion, Tasha, and King spent the following morning discussing what provisions they would need and where they could be obtained. As Tasha and King had been in the city for several days already, they had had an opportunity to explore some of the market places and it quickly became a matter of deciding what would be brought with them and who would carry it.

The Indian delegates had left in the morning for the next conference before the rest of them had gotten up, but there were plenty of others that remained in the camp. Fides found them to be an extremely friendly group of people and he couldn't understand how any of them might have aspirations for reclaiming any land. Fides quickly made friends with two men about his own age named Charlie and Marty. They were Indians, but they looked like any other American citizen. It was perhaps this melting of the populations that made the Cherokee Chief resistant to trying to assert themselves over people who were, after all, in many respects just like them. Fermion explained in a later conversation that it was this very fact that served to be a rallying point for the more nationalistic Indians of various tribes who longed for the 'pure' days.

Charlie was a witty man with a good sense of humor, and Marty was good with his hands the way that Fides was. Fides was pleased to be with someone that was a lot like him. These men were much like the men in his work crew, and the good-natured banter and fellowship that came from such an association was something he had missed. By contrast, he had been traveling with a silver haired man who said he was of the Nephilim and could produce fire from his hands. There was very little banter with Fermion, as nice as he was. Fides could do without the cryptic and occasionally condescending (sounding) comments.

Fermion spent more of his time talking with Tasha and King. He learned that Tasha had saved King's life many years ago during one of the nuclear strikes. Tasha seemed to have no real concept of geography, however, and could not say where it was that the rescue had happened, and King had been too young at the time to know, either. They discussed how they would resolve this issue once they got to Bloomington, and King grew increasingly excited at even the mere prospect of finding his family, while Tasha became more pensive in proportion to King's rising enthusiasm. Tasha had fled with King into the upper Midwest, finally turning south and being taken in first by one Indian tribe in Iowa, and then by the Cherokees in Oklahoma. It was with the Cherokees that King began to grow into a young man, and both Tasha and King shared how they had already had occasion to fight in small battles. These battles had mainly consisted of fighting off small bands of non-Indian people trying to take over some Indian property, but on a couple of occasions they had fought against fellow Indian tribes. Both had proven their worth in battle, and first won the confidence and respect of Ramaen, and then Chief Thunderfist. It helped that King had become a friend to the chief's own son, who had not come with the delegation and instead had remained behind with his father.

At around noon, the delegation returned to the camp and enjoyed a massive lunch that had been prepared for them by the other members of the party. Ramaen had instructed that the best food be made in honor of Tasha and King's departure, and Fides, at least, could not remember the last time he had a meal such as this one. But there was only a short time for conversation with the delegation, as they once again adorned their faces with scowls and returned to the talks with the president and the Pledge. This left the four of them to finally head into the market place to buy provisions.

Ramaen had given them a substantial gift of gold, silver, and other items that might have value in a bartering situation, so they were now in a position to acquire just about anything that they might find, let alone need. Charlie and Marty accompanied them. In fact, they were the ones left to carry the weight of the valuable gift, which they did without complaining. They picked their way through the market looking for salted meats, water purification tablets, new boots, and other essentials.

As Fermion predicted, they did catch the eye of people in the city. Wearing their long dark cloaks, Fermion and Fides together projected a certain intimidating air, but Fermion's long silver-like hair made people visibly draw back. Since their new friends were all wearing different types of Indian-style clothing, it was easy to infer that Fermion and Fides were among them. Though people were often taken aback by the presence of this fearsome looking group, they were generally well received by the population. It especially helped when they began producing gold, silver, or other wares in exchange for whatever it was that the businessman was offering.

They saw a city patrolman only once, but as their swords were tucked discreetly within their cloaks, they did not have to produce their authorization letter. They walked for several hours and were returning back to the camp, satisfied that they had obtained all that they would need to get them at least to Tulsa, and perhaps even to Carthage, Missouri. Close to the camp they heard a loud voice calling out over a crowd in one of the market places. It wasn't exactly on their way, but Fermion led the group over to listen. It was a member of the Pledge, though not one that they had noticed as present when Fides and Fermion had received authorization for their weapons from the president.

"Look at what government has done!" he was saying. "Democracy brought us the nuclear bomb. It brought us a terrible disease. Look at our fractured world! Today, the citizens of Oklahoma City live in a place that is protected by a wall of over-turned semi-truck trailers. Is that a good thing? That is what our Republic has come to- grown men and women hiding behind ugly tipped over trailers! We have seen the fruit of history, and we are the ones tasting it and dealing with its poison. Why would we do the same thing over again? Why would we repeat the same mistakes of the past? We have a chance now to do right, right from the start, and so save ourselves- and more importantly- our children- from having to live in a world like this for generations. We can build a nation where the individual is the most important unit, not the government, not society, but the person. Only when individuals band together and recognize that they are brothers-"

"And sisters!" a woman shouted from the crowd.

"And sisters!" the man laughed, "Only when we realize this can we understand that each person is their own law and there is no need for any authorities above or beyond any person. It's time to live like free men and women. We can be free to be, and that means we don't have to strive for status the way people had to in the past. Why have ten chickens when you only need three? Is that not just status? Show that you are not bound by greed and avarice and give your brother a chicken, for God's sake. Why have a million gold coins when you only need ten? What kind of free man withholds that kind of wealth- which they don't even need- from their needy neighbor's family? Why have twenty acres of land when you only need five? We should not be slaves any more to our wants. We should each acknowledge our needs, and in freedom take what we need, and no more. And if everyone does this, we will finally live in a free country."

"The Pledge," the man paused dramatically, "The Pledge recognizes that not everyone thinks this way. These people are slaves- slaves to their own passions. Animals, really, muzzled with their own muzzles, doing as they are told without thinking on their own. The Pledge is assembling free thinkers from wherever they can, and already we have many that are willing to lay down their lives for freedom, if it comes to that. We are here in this city of yours right now, offering to your president the same vision for our country that we have offered to other men in other cities. We are ready, if it comes to it, to bring freedom to the land by force if necessary. That is our pledge. And those who survive- my brothers- they will receive their equal reward. They won't have to worry about government conspiracies or corrupt senators or power hungry presidents. We'll just divide it all up equally, and it's as easy as that. You need to tell your President that Oklahoma City and its surrounding areas want to be free! If your city stands against freedom and clear thought, there will some day be a battle. You need to be on the side of your human brothers, not on the side of the enslaved beasts."

"What about the Indians?" called out a man.

"The Indians have no unified view. We invite them to join our march for freedom. Some will join us and some will fight us, even as some are fighting with each other. But if they insist on taking more than what they need- which retaking the country, as some Indians are calling for, obviously is- then the Pledge will match them, stone for stone, knife for knife, arms for arms," the man replied boldly.

"Does the Pledge have guns?" yelled out another voice.

"Guns were confiscated by the International Force. How would we have guns? We have power, might, and we are right. We will prevail because our cause is just..."

Fermion was leading them away through the crowd, visibly disgusted with what he had heard. Fides thought that there were some good things in what the man said, but having seen the delegation of the Pledge with his own eyes, he felt that he could not trust any of them. They seemed a very disreputable lot.

"They've got a few men like that scattered throughout the city," Charlie explained to them.

Fermion opened his mouth to reply, but they suddenly found their way blocked by ten men. One in the middle was sneering. "As far as I'm concerned," the man said, directing his comments at Fermion. "We can never trust the Indians, even if they did want to join the Pledge. We know both the Pledge and the Indians have guns. You're both liars."

Fides and Fermion and the rest of the group looked around at each other. Four of the six were not Indian at all, and the two that were didn't even look it. "We don't want any trouble," Fides said.

"Well, you've got trouble, my friend. I don't trust you, and I need to, you understand. I only trust the dead, see?" Fides noticed that the men had pulled pieces of sharpened metal out of places of hiding on their body and some had clubs at the ready.

"You've got to be kidding me," Charlie laughed. "Are you planning on fighting us in the middle of a busy market? You think Neff is going to allow our slaughter to go unpunished?"

Marty chimed in as well, "Not that you're going to slaughter us, mind you. We're just trying to make the point that you've got nothing to gain by standing in our way. Now step aside or someone is going to get hurt."

The Sneering Man continued to sneer, and men on each side of him started inching their way forward. The marketplace had grown quiet and people were backing away from the argument while still staring at it in curiosity. Fides' group held its ground, but their aggressors were now within five feet. All of them had tortured smiles on their faces, as though the smiles represented no joy or pleasure at all, but were only masks for something else.

The Sneering Man opened his mouth, "Alright boys, get..."

"Oh, what's this?" Charlie asked as though surprised at what was suddenly in his hand.

"Why Charlie, that looks like a gun to me," Marty explained nonchalantly. "I guess the man was right."

Charlie had deftly pulled his firearm out from hiding and the barrel was now pointed directly between the Sneering Man's sneering eyes. The Sneering man was pulled up short by the move. He was only a few inches away from feeling the cold metal on his skin.

"You don't suppose anybody else in our group has guns, do ya, buddy? Does it really seem wise to attack a group you've just accused of possessing weapons? Did you not believe your own accusation, or was it perhaps just pretext?" Charlie asked the man, whose eyes had become wide with fear. The man trembled, and Charlie continued, "Look, I have an idea. How about you tell your henchmen to get out of our way, and to do it quickly? Then, we are going to be on our way, thankful that we live where civilization is still real and honors lives, rather than locked inside a city with scoundrels like you. What do you say?"

The Sniveling Man nodded obediently, and his thug friends moved out of their way. Finally, Charlie waved the gun off in the same direction, and the man skirted away somewhat defiantly and disappeared into the crowd.

"Do you think it was wise to show your weapon?" Fermion asked Charlie as they once again made their way towards the camp.

"Actually, it's part of our strategy," Charlie explained.

"Part of your strategy?" Fides asked.

"Yes, we want there to be strong rumor mixed with fact that the Indians really do have guns. There are plenty of people in this city who think they ought to raise an army and go out and bring down the Cherokee, and it's only because the population has a pretty good idea that we are better armed than they are that they haven't done it yet. But you've got to keep in mind, too, that it's for their own good. Chief Thunderfist would likely not choose to use the weapons. But other tribal members, and other tribes, would have no hesitation."

"So, it is true? The Indians retained their weapons despite the efforts of the International Force?" Fermion asked them.

Marty winked, "I'd answer that, but then I'd have to kill ya. You understand."

Fermion allowed a smile to cross his own face and decided he had received as much of an answer as he was likely going to get. The answer was more or less as he expected, anyway. They finally arrived at the camp where Charlie and Marty left to find Ramaen to update him on what had just happened. While they were gone, King explained to Fides and Fermion that President Neff knew that at least some of the Indians had weapons, and that furthermore their party had brought some along with them for personal security purposes.

It occurred to Fides suddenly that Charlie and Marty, besides being very friendly, may have been sent deliberately as guards for them while they remained in the city. He kept this suspicion to himself, however. To find out this was the case might take the wind out of his new friendship. It was better not to know.

The next morning was when they were planning to leave the city. That night the Indian delegation stayed up late, circled around a roaring fire, talking and laughing and otherwise saying goodbye to Tasha and King. Fermion and Fides let members of the delegation inspect their impressively crafted swords, and Ramaen delighted them with tales of some of the mischief that King had gotten himself into while living with them. Charlie shared a story about a battle against Domasi, a renegade Cherokee leading a band of followers who believed in re-conquering. Tasha and King both figured highly in this tale, and Fides marveled that a man as young as King and a woman as old as Tasha could have performed so well against a band of armed men.

Ramaen caught everyone's attention with a loud clap, interrupting Charlie's tales, "Alright, Tsahli, that is enough storytelling for tonight. Our friends must leave early tomorrow and they will need their rest. I want to use this as a chance to say that we gained more than Tasha and King did in our friendship with them. As a token of our thanks, we have decided to let you all ride on horses as far as Tulsa. Tasha knows who to take them to once there. Then, in order to hasten you in your journey- which we hope will be fruitful- we will pay out of Cherokee wealth the cost for Chummy's Transport as far as he is willing to take you. Now, off to sleep for everyone!"

"Chummy's Transport?" Fermion inquired of Tasha as people began slipping away to their tents.

"He calls himself 'Chummy.' He is a man who lives in Tulsa that has found a way to create fuel. He operates a small fleet of cars and small trucks, taking travelers to various places. I know that he runs some routes down into Texas, but I don't know what he does to the east. But what Ramaen just said, basically, is that he will make it worth Chummy's while to take us as far east as Chummy is willing to go. We can hope it is all the way to Bloomington!" Tasha explained.

"Indeed. That is a remarkable gift, then," Fermion said gratefully.

"The more so when you see how greedy Chummy is!" Tasha exclaimed ruefully.

The party dispersed slowly. Fond farewells were exchanged with Tasha and King by members of the delegation who would not be able to see them off the next morning. Polite goodbyes were shared also with Fermion and Fides. Charlie and Marty joked loudly with Fides, and then turned serious in wishing him the best as he sought his wife and family. Ramaen and Fermion shared a moment of private conversation, the result of which appeared to be that Ramaen had declined Fermion's offer to take possession of the motorcycle they had commandeered. Presumably, the motorcycle was going to be given to President Neff, instead. Finally, everyone made it to bed.

In the morning, the foursome gathered their belongings together and made their way to the makeshift stables where the Cherokee had been housing their horses. They spent a short time organizing their belongings, and finally mounted up. Fides had trouble getting his leg over, but only King cracked a hint of a smile. Even Marty didn't make any smart comments as he helped shove Fides up.

"I can ride a horse, honest," Fides laughed. It was true, too, thanks to his time on Corrie and Dietrich's ranch. One clumsy mistake was all that was needed for his new friends to tease him for a few minutes. Fermion, of course, looked as though he had been born atop a moving horse. His long black cloak flowed down the sides of the horse and his shimmering hair flowed down the back of the cloak. His sword was visible for all to see in its sheath. Fides couldn't help but think that Fermion seemed, well, regal. He wasn't the only one thinking that, either. Bystanders and Indians alike gazed at Fermion.

They left the stable area and their friends behind as they proceeded towards the eastern gates of Oklahoma City. The city was starting to wake up. Some people poked their heads out to see who was out riding this early. Those who did were rewarded with a sight right out of medieval times. After an hour of quiet travel, they saw the ramp up to the old highway, which meant that they could see the east gate out of town.

As they rounded the corner, they were confronted yet again with the same group that had accosted them in the market place. They were about fifty feet away, blocking the entrance to the ramp. They appeared to be reinforced, but no better armed. Fermion gave a grunt and set his horse at a faster trot, his sword out and held forward like a javelin.

"What are you doing?" exclaimed Fides.

Tasha silenced him, "Don't worry about him, Fides."

Fermion was now in a full gallop and the Sneering Man's eyes once again boggled with surprise and fear. In less than an instant the horse was barreling into the group. Men jumped every which way, but none remained on their feet. Fermion wheeled back around, pulling back the reins, causing his horse's front legs to claw the air above the Sneering Man, who waited for the terrible crushing weight to fall on his skull. But Fermion turned the horse again until he was positioned over the once again Sniveling Man, with his sword hovering only several feet above the man's throat.

"Clarence," Fermion began firmly, "If I have to deal with you and your cohorts again it will be with utmost finality. Do you understand?"

Clarence appeared to understand perfectly. He and the rest crawled away and finally scampered completely out of sight. Fides wondered how Fermion had known the man's name, but did not ask. The way to the ramp was now wide open. The four guided their horses up the ramp and onto the freeway. The gate was a mile down the road but within sight, clearly delineated by a line of truck trailers forming a wall as far as the eye could see both to the north and the south. Fides breathed a sigh of relief. There was something in that city that just didn't seem right.

== Chapter 5 ==

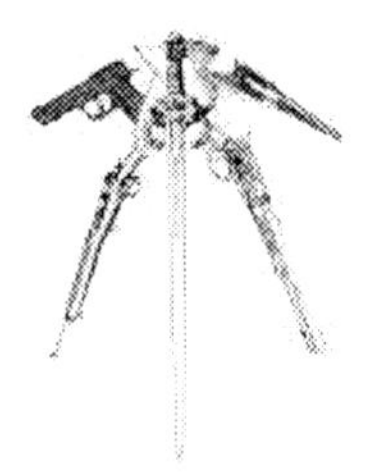

Melody was reaching out for him. The woods exhaled a wintry breath as he fell into her warm arms. They clung to each other for a moment and collapsed into sobs of joy. A moment later the door to his house burst open and his children were running for him. They huddled together in an embrace, alternating in sobs and laughter as their long absence resolved into renewed fellowship. The wind turned ominous, however, and Fides realized that none of the members of his family had faces. He fell backwards in shock and within his dream he realized it was a dream and he willed himself awake. His eyes opened and everything was black outside. Finally, though, dots of light poked through the fabric of the night and he remembered he was sleeping about a ten hour ride, by horse, from Oklahoma City. The starlight helped him regain a sense of joyful life, but he was disturbed to think again that he could not remember what his own family looked like. Would he recognize them? Would they recognize him?

Fides was trembling slightly as he rolled out of his blanket, but it wasn't because he was cold. The sun didn't seem to be close to coming up yet but he didn't really feel like sleeping. He made his way to where the fire glowed and threw in some sticks, stoking up a small flame. Staring at the growing flame helped take his mind off his angst. He heard one of his company rolling over in their blankets nearby, but he did not wake up. A short time later, he had a pretty decent fire going, and he decided that he hadn't read any of Corrie's book in a long time. There was enough light, and anything was better than thinking about the status of his family, so he sat down to read some of it.

In doing so, he remembered Corries's warning about the Nephilim being back on the land and the fact that Fermion apparently was one such person. He couldn't remember where the passage was that talked about the Nephilim so he just started from the beginning. The old pages seemed to radiate the old mythology contained within them. The first chapters he read seemed to speak to the planet's current situation, and unexpectedly he found the reference to the Nephilim near the sixth chapter of the first book, Genesis:

"When the men began to increase in number on the earth and daughters were born to them, the sons of God saw that the daughters of men were beautiful, and they married any of them they chose. Then the LORD said, 'My Spirit will not contend with man forever, for he is corrupt; his days will be a hundred and twenty years.' The Nephilim were on the earth in those days- and also afterward- when the sons of God went to the daughters of men and had children by them. They were heroes of old, men of renown."

The passage didn't help Fides understand much about who the Nephilim were or how Fermion was described there, though if anyone seemed like a 'hero of old,' it was Fermion. Fides decided to broach the subject again with him, hoping that he wouldn't mind talking about it with Tasha and King around. He read a bit more of Genesis and found himself bored and flipped through the big old book, randomly reading passages as he landed on them. He noticed a hint of orange on the horizon, alerting him to the impending sunrise. He also noticed that his mind had been settled. He closed Corrie's book and climbed back under his blankets, sleeping peacefully for another hour before he woke up to the smell of cooking potatoes.

Tasha was cooking and Fermion was gathering wood. King rolled out of bed at about the same time that Fides did. King mumbled a good morning to them both and disappeared for awhile in search of a moment's privacy. Fides was rubbing his eyes when Fermion returned with a pile of wood. Fermion left Fides to tend the fire and then went and tended to the horses. That meant that Fides got the first helping of fried potatoes.

King returned and devoured what was offered to him and looked for seconds, but Tasha scolded him and told him he had to wait for Fermion to have 'firsts' before anyone was getting another serving. King smiled slyly and speared a tasty chunk when Tasha wasn't looking (but Fides could see she wasn't fooled) and began packing up his bedding.

Horses were a nice change of pace for Fides. Traveling on foot was very tedious work, and the motorcycle, though much quicker, was hard on his rump due to the disrepair of the roads they were traveling over. Horseback riding seemed to be a good compromise, but he couldn't deny that he had a different sort of soreness today, a day into the ride.

The journey had gotten progressively greener as they had traveled from Las Cruces, but it was now at least October, so the green was coming at the expense of increasingly chillier nights and a corresponding changing of colors in the leaves. By the time that they might arrive at a place where the green was truly lush, winter might be upon them and they might have to wait several months to enjoy the change of scenery. Fides found himself missing his Indiana forest almost as much as he missed his wife, children, and friends.

Together, the four of them put out the fire, finished packing their belongings, and continued the journey at a pace just above a walk. At this pace, Tasha told them they could be in Tulsa by late evening the next day. As they went, they talked.

"How did you come to be together?" Fides inquired of Tasha and King.

"I was young at the time," King answered, "and I don't remember much of it now. But I remember that there was a huge flash of light in the sky far away, but not as far as I thought. It got very windy, and then there was a rumbling, and then it was like a wave of heat hit us and the building we were standing just inside of. The building collapsed, but I felt swept away. That was Tasha grabbing me and pulling me away from where the building was falling."

"I had been fleeing the Disease," Tasha explained. "I was passing through the town, is all. There was a flash behind me. I felt the wave coming and I saw King standing alone under the awning of a building. I was pretty close. I yanked him away as the building was coming down. Then we fell into a ditch and waited for the wave to fully pass. King was very scared. He must have only been eight or nine. He was scared silent. I asked him where his family was and he could just point to the building." Tasha became silent for a moment, and then continued, "There was no way anyone was alive in that building. So I took King as my own and we've been together since."

Upon the completion of this dramatic story, the group traveled in uneasy silence. King especially seemed to be entrenched in thought, and everyone could understand why. As if knowing that everyone was honoring his grief with their silence, he gave them permission to talk by continuing the story. "I didn't talk for a year," he said. "It was like I had been thrown into shock. I knew my family was gone and it changed me somehow. But Tasha took care of me. She became my new mother. At some point I realized I had to move on. I miss them, though."

"We are born to joy but are destined for sorrow. It is wise not to let the sorrow be your master, so that you can stand again to experience joy," Fermion said tenderly. "You were wise to move on. You will always love and miss your family, but they would not want you to cling so hard to their memories that you do not make new ones. You are wiser than your years."

King nodded deferentially, "If that is so, it is because Tasha has made me so."

Tasha blushed slightly at this compliment but said nothing. Fermion studied them both carefully. If King was wiser than his years, Tasha was wise beyond her generation. Fermion said nothing about that, though, and inquired more about their travels after that. The two had traveled together into Wisconsin, then Minnesota, then Iowa, and finally into Oklahoma. They had passed through Indiana and Illinois, but as quickly as they could.

"What family do you hope to find if you think your immediate family is no more," Fides asked King.

"I can't say for sure, to be honest. I'm sure that I must have some other relations, though. Besides, you know, maybe they got out. We'll find out," King said.

For awhile, no one said anything more, but then Fermion took the initiative and shared portions of his and Fides' story. He subtly shared how he had first met Fides in Illinois but had become reacquainted again in New Mexico. He didn't explain how they got from one place to the other. He explained that he posed as a priest for a number of years in Las Cruces and Albuquerque because priests, despite the underlying contempt that existed towards religious people in the US since the great American Wars, still carried a certain amount of respect. He abandoned that guise when it came time to travel, if only for the reason that with two people in the party, he no longer needed the psychological advantage.

"But what about your swords?" King probed curiously.

Fermion laughed. "They are wonderful specimens, aren't they? Would you believe I raided them from a museum?"

"I wouldn't," Tasha replied cynically. Fermion only chuckled but would say no more. Fides was reminded of his decision that early morning to ask Fermion more questions about the Nephilim. Now that he saw Fermion avoiding direct mention of the odd circumstances that brought them together, he thought it might be unwise to ask about it with King and Tasha present. At least, he thought he should let Fermion be prepared for the possibility he might bring it up. The conversation drifted into more superficial areas, though, and only small talk remained until they stopped for lunch.

Their first location for lunch was a brief stop, because when they dismounted they discovered the grisly remains of a number of people. Tasha, who had apparently seen some people with the Disease, thought that these had probably died from it while traveling. There were a number of piles of bones that had been picked over by animals, but they were wrapped in tattered rags. Tasha explained with a shudder that as people's skin and body parts started falling off them while they still lived, they'd simply wrap themselves up- or someone else would if they were too weak- and wait for death. This way, at least, they'd be all in one place when it came time for burial. These people, however, had never received a burial, obviously.

This struck Fides as terribly tragic. His eyes welled up and he declared that they should be buried. The other three immediately concurred. They spent about an hour digging a shallow grave for all of the bodies. Fermion said a few words befitting a man who had posed as a priest and they got back on their way to try to find a different location for lunch. It didn't seem right to eat near the graves of those poor souls.

Journeying about a mile further, they found a patch of grass and a nice big tree to tie up the horses to and someone else's fire pit. Tasha cooked up some more potatoes. King found a small creek nearby and took the horses to it to drink, returning at last to have some water himself. Fermion and Fides scouted out the area ahead of them on foot. This was fine in Fides' opinion because he wanted to talk to Fermion, alone.

"I want to know more about the Nephilim, Fermion. What does it mean that you are a Nephilim?" Fides asked Fermion as they walked ahead to see what awaited them.

Fermion seemed to be perfectly at ease with the question, yet pretty unhelpful in his answers. "I'm afraid you still aren't yet prepared to know about the Nephilim, my friend," Fermion said kindly. "Trust me, I know. I've had such conversations before," Fermion patiently explained.

"So, there are people who know what the Nephilim are?" Fides asked.

"Absolutely," Fermion asserted.

"Is there anything you can tell me that will help me in the future to understand?" Fides pushed, trying not to be offended by the purposeful distance Fermion was maintaining on the subject. There was a long delay before Fermion answered.

"At one time, you studied to be a pastor in the state church, didn't you?" Fermion finally responded. "What happened to that?"

"Well, when I was young, naïve, and stupid, I was very interested in matters that some people might call 'spiritual.' So, I went to the training schools." This was not the whole truth, but it was true as far as it went. In fact, Fides had been possessed by a sense of the 'other' after being saved by the mysterious woman of the wood as a child, and this, together with encouragement by his mother, had pushed him to consider a religious line of work. Fides continued, "When I got to the training school, I found out that we don't really know anything. They told us that religion, faith, and God were all just things that people have made up. We could decide to take any belief system we liked, and so long as we stayed within their guidelines, we could become officials of that belief system. But once I found out that it was all a fraud, really, I didn't see any point in going further," Fides explained.

"So, you just believed them?" Fermion pressed.

"Well, they controlled all the available information. If there had been something more, I'm sure it would have been made available."

Fermion chuckled at that, but then continued his questions. "So what options were there for you to choose from?"

"I could have done anything. Hinduism, Christianity, Islam. You name it."

"Well, after they told you that these were all just cultural expressions of a deeper set of universal truths that humans had really invented on their own, did they give you an opportunity to read their sacred documents for yourself? Did you get a chance to examine their historical foundations, to see for yourself which of them, if any, were true?" Fermion probed.

Fides looked confused. "Well, none of the documents really exist anymore, do they?" Fides replied at last. Fermion looked on him kindly.

"Well, what is it that you think you've been carrying around with you for the last month or more?" Fermion said, pointing out the obvious.

"Uh," Fides managed to sputter. "Well, it's in English, so it can't be the original Christian and Jewish documents, because those would have been in Greek and Hebrew," Fides countered, trying to rebound from the appearance that he was, well, dense.

Fermion seemed to appreciate that answer. "That's fair enough," he said. "Still, it's better than what you had at your school, isn't it? It may still not be enough to provide you with a sure enough footing for you to think it true, or true to the exclusion of other possibilities, but at least you can acquaint yourself with it directly instead of learning about it only through intermediaries."

Fides nodded in agreement, but he had doubts. "So, ok, Corrie gave me a copy of her old Bible, and copies of Bibles are rare. So rare, in fact, I might have the only one left. It's the only one I've ever come upon anyway. But that won't help me evaluate any of the other beliefs," Fides protested.

"Ok, you're right. But you've got to start somewhere," Fermion said, motioning to Fides to turn around and return to camp.

"But what's the point?" Fides continued. "And what does this have to do with the Nephilim?"

"Let's just say at this point that something is better than nothing, and if you want any hope of understanding the Nephilim, you'll need to at least acquaint yourself with the Christian Bible a little bit more. And even then, it's one thing to understand what I'm telling you, and quite another to accept it. To accept it, I suggest you re-think whether what you see in this world is really all there is."

"But obviously it is," Fides replied. "That was something they really spent time showing at the school of religious ministries."

"It's always a good idea, my friend, to think for yourself whenever it is practical to do so. Surely at the very least, you have seen something in regards to me that could prompt you to at least consider the possibility of unseen realities?" Fermion gently suggested.

"That's a pretty big request," Fides answered somewhat sarcastically. "That was only one incident, really. I need more than one or two strange incidents to justify belief in something extraordinary. Against your curious exhibition, let's place against it terrible diseases, nuclear warfare, and evil people, and death, death, death. None of these things seem to be consistent with anything other than a brutal and base world. What we see is what we get. That's what I think. That's how I lived, and I did fine. I live in the real world, and if there is anything besides what we can see, I have to be honest, I don't feel I can respect it for what it allows."

Fermion looked at him sadly. "I suppose that feeling will only deepen over time. I don't necessarily blame you for having that feeling, but realize that it was you who asked me about the Nephilim. To understand and accept the Nephilim, you'll need to think differently. Perhaps you can understand now why I said you are not yet in a position for a straight, direct answer?"

"Not really, but you haven't let me down yet. One question, though," Fides said.

"Yes?" Fermion replied.

"Why did you not talk about you being a Nephilim with Tasha and King? For that matter, why not tell the full story of our meeting? They're going to notice my necklace eventually, anyway," Fides wondered.

"When they notice the necklace you may feel free to share with them whatever you like. I trust these two, though I do not yet know if they would be receptive to an in depth description of my nature. But feel free to tell them anything you want. If they believe you and don't laugh in your face, we'll be on to something!" Fermion chuckled.

Fides realized that he might have to wing it when the subject came up. The strange looking device around his neck might give substance to his tale, but if they hadn't seen Fermion hurl a fireball from his bare hands, they might not be able to swallow their incredulity. If Fides couldn't swallow his own incredulity, and he was a witness, how would it fare for them merely receiving a report? Fides really had seen Fermion hurl a fireball from out of his bare hands and he still had doubts. He argued with himself, "Don't extraordinary claims require extraordinary evidence? Isn't observation only ordinary evidence?" Fides knew he wasn't being reasonable, but couldn't put his finger on where his logic was going wrong. Fides determined that he would make a better effort to keep the necklace hidden so as to not have to explain the circumstances around it.

They finally returned to the cooking fire that Tasha had been tending to. King was back from his chores, too, so Fermion reported to them that the road looked clear on up ahead. They ate their fill of canned vegetables and salted meat, and quickly broke camp. They were eager to use the available daylight to their advantage. Once again on the aging freeway, they turned their faces to the east and set out.

About three in the afternoon they saw some westbound travelers who were also on horseback. They seemed kindly enough. The two parties waved, and passed each other. About five in the afternoon they glimpsed that up ahead was a much larger party going in the same direction as they were, but on foot. Fermion stopped to consider the situation.

"Well, we know that the westbound party had no troubles when they passed this group, so I think we're probably safe to pass them, too. Does anyone have any thoughts?" Fermion asked them.

"There is nothing saying that we can't break out to one side and pass them on one of the flanks," King suggested.

"We've probably only got another two hours of good light, though. By the time we catch up to them to pass them we may very well be just running out of good travel time. Maybe it would be a good idea just to set up camp here and pass them in the morning," Fides threw in.

"Does it seem as though they've noticed us?" asked Tasha. "We wouldn't want them doubling back on us tonight if they are up to no good, or have some among them that aren't."

"No, I don't think they've seen us. But look- they are going to be going up that high hill. If I were them, or even when it is our turn,

I'd want to see what is over that hill before I brought the full party along. I don't think we can pass them and properly scout ahead of us in the available daylight. I think perhaps we should put all of the ideas together," Fermion suggested. "Let's head out a decent distance from the road, set up camp for the night and tomorrow morning pass them on the flank." Fermion paused. "Agree?"

Everyone agreed. Another short conversation later they had selected a campsite about two hundred yards off the road just inside a large grove of trees. The grove had been left standing by some farmer a hundred years earlier to fight erosion but certainly the farmer had not been aware of the service he would provide to others decades later. It did appear that others had put it to similar use, as well, but it was far enough off the road that it looked as though only a few groups over the years had ever decided to come and camp there. Someone had done them the favor of building a nice fire pit, though, even to the extent of erecting stone towers on opposite sides of the pit and laying an iron rod across them to use for roasting any small animal that one might find. On seeing this, King had spent a little more time evaluating when the campsite had last been used to make sure it wasn't likely that its owner might return yet that night. All appearances were that it had not been used for months, though, so they immediately set to work making it their own.

Tasha once again prepared a supper for them. Fides took a turn at collecting the firewood and tending to the horses, while King and Fermion took their own horses on a short trot to scout out the lay of the land and get one last look at the party ahead of them. They wanted to make sure that the group had stopped and would not be coming back in their direction. Tasha and Fides shared light-hearted conversation together. Fides once again thought that Tasha's spirit burned brighter than her body, for despite her apparent age, she seemed youthful in every other respect. By the time King and Fermion returned, the food was already done. The two took a few minutes to feed and water their horses and then joined them around the fire.

"Everything looks fine. The other party has set up camp. They know about us now, though. They sent out scouts, too, and we saw each other from a distance, and waved. They seemed really friendly, so we met them. Apparently there are about one hundred of them. We told them that our party was smaller, but didn't say how much smaller. I assured them that we were no threat to them, and they seemed to believe us," Fermion explained.

"They really seemed like good people. Just solid, down to earth, good people," King added. The four of them talked for awhile around the fire and decided that despite the apparent goodness of at least some members of the group ahead of them, it might be wise to set a guard. King volunteered to take the first watch. Fermion would take the second, and Fides would take the third. Tasha, as she had cooked for them the entire trip, would be free from any duties and permitted to sleep soundly.

As the light of the fire got smaller and smaller, the air got colder and colder just as one might expect in the middle of the fall season. This prompted the very natural decision by the three who were not on watch to retreat to their warm blankets. After the normal routines associated with bedding down, King was alone by the fire, at watch. Fides fell asleep immediately.

As quickly as Fides was asleep, he was awakened by the sounds of King's frantic shouting.

"Get up! The other party is being attacked!" King was shouting. Fides could hear distant yelling and whips cracking. After a moment he realized that it was not the sound of whips cracking, at all, but gunshots. Fermion was already on his feet and Tasha was meeting him with the reins of all four horses. Fides quickly dressed, threw on his boots, his cloak, and his sword, and climbed on top of his horse. Tasha was the last to be ready, but it wasn't very long before they were ready to ride.

It was not discussed, it was not suggested, it was not debated. It was known without saying that they would ride to assist the other party. Fermion slapped the rear of his horse and the four rode off into the dark night towards the sounds of yelling and shouting. They crested a small hill and saw the camp beneath them. There were a large number of fire pits belonging to the campers, and some tents were also on fire, too. There was plenty of light to see what awaited them inside the camp perimeter. The travelers were fighting desperately against men on horseback. Except for the dress of the riders, it was like a scene from the old west. The attackers were clearly members of some Indian tribe. There were a number of them charging back and forth through the campsite while others circled the perimeter, beating back those trying to escape.

It appeared as though the goal was full-scale slaughter. As they crested the hill, Fides saw a bandit standing over a man laying on the ground, clearly wounded. The bandit shot the man point blank in cold blood before moving on to grapple with someone else. Fides felt an emotion he had never felt before.

Fermion let out a blood-curdling yell as they descended the hill, and King and Tasha joined him. Fides was surprised to hear his voice issuing the same threatening yell, and something swelled up inside him much like the sense of righteous indignation that had prompted him to try to rescue Fermion only a few weeks ago. Fermion's sword was out, Tasha had a long dagger in her hand, and King had a long wooden staff. Fides' own sword was out, swinging loosely at his side. Some of the training Fermion had put him through seemed now to come naturally out of him, even though he had never been trained to fight on horseback. Fides turned his horse in the direction of the merciless bandit.

The ruthless man was working along the outside, using a knife to injure and then his gun to slay. He had just dispatched another victim when he looked up and saw Fides atop his horse, next in line. Fides stared at the man with angry, incredulous eyes. The Indian bandit met Fides' gaze stubbornly and even mockingly. Fides dismounted, perfectly willing to engage the man. The sounds of the battle clattered around them. The bandit looked around, already thinking about who his next target was. Fides, on the other hand, could hear nothing. Nor could he see anything except this cocky, murderous fiend. The battle was on, but it was brief.

The bandit lunged with his knife, but hadn't noticed that Fides was armed with a sword. A sword has a bit of a longer reach. Fides was swinging his blade even as the man was lunging, and caught the man in the arm. Fides did not appreciate the impact of what he was doing. The man screamed in agony and also in fury, using his unharmed arm to reach for his gun. He was in the process of aiming it at Fides when Fides' blade fell deep across his shoulder and chest. With startled eyes, the bandit fell, dead. The sounds of the surrounding battle now rushed upon Fides. At the very moment he became aware of what he had just did he knew that he could not take the time to reflect on it. He quickly appraised the situation, and located Tasha. He fought his way in her direction.

Meanwhile, the assaulted travelers still alive in the camp were not by any means out of the battle. With their attacker's attention suddenly turned towards the west, the travelers were able to see to it that some of the Indians were rapidly disabled. Fermion had barreled through the circling Indians to face the attackers making mayhem inside the camp itself, but Tasha and King engaged the Indians that had been trying to hem in the travelers around the perimeter.

Tasha dismounted, but King remained on his horse. He proved to be particularly effective with his staff, throwing every Indian he met off his horse, either by solid blows to the attacker or swats at the horses themselves. Once King had de-horsed a man, Tasha and fighting travelers moved in. Soon, Fides was helping. It was a bloody melee as some thirty bodies clashed on the western edge of the perimeter. Shots were fired by some of the Indians but they were quickly targeted and received priority bludgeoning.

Meanwhile, Fermion was darting in and out of tents and horsemen, slashing and thrusting, and wreaking mayhem on the surprised attackers. It took several dead Indian horsemen before the attackers figured out that not all of the people riding a horse were on their side. Fermion's long hair probably perpetuated the illusion, as in the dark he looked much like the attackers themselves, except for the fact that he swung a magnificent and mighty sword, which many noticed too late.

The attackers had probably numbered a hundred in their own right when the attack began, but the surprise entry of a counterattack of an unknown strength had thrown them into disorganization. Indian warriors were no longer pressing the attack, but kept looking over their shoulders seeking a way to regroup or escape altogether. In the midst of the cracks of gunfire and grunts as blows were delivered, there was a steady moaning from the wounded and the dying.

The perimeter battle was a bloody scrum. By now, no one was still on his horse, and the attackers were fighting as though they were cornered animals. In a very real sense, they were. Without the advantage of the high ground and intimidation, the attackers found themselves met by men encouraged by the parity of position and emboldened by their desire to protect their loved ones. These two different inspirations sparked fierce self-defense in the half-lit edges of the camp.

Fides felt like something inside him had been unleashed. It was not merely primal instincts given expression. He fought without compromise, without intellectual ambiguity. He intuitively sensed that even if he died, he felt that the good story about it would precede him to the grave.

King and Tasha were grappling with assailants to his right and there was a tumult of unidentified men to his left, ahead, and behind him, distinguished only by the clear Indian markings on some of them. He caught a glimpse of King cracking a man across the jaw as he heard a shrill scream of panic behind him. Whirling around, he saw an Indian warrior straddling a squirming man. Turning abruptly from the man he was currently engaging, Fides charged over and tackled the brave, falling headlong over the man the Indian had been trying to kill and whose life Fides' had just saved.

The Indian brave rolled over and came to his knees, exhibiting fierce anger and indignation at this unexpected challenge to his dominance. Fides rolled to his knees and then to his feet. His sword, which had fallen out of his hands, had been recovered instinctively and now was in his hand. The fierce anger of the Indian paled in comparison to the resolute glare that Fides laid upon the brave. The Indian appeared momentarily to wilt, and then in order to counter the changing momentum, lunged at Fides with a howl.

Fides was ready for him, and his month of training, though certainly not exhaustive, kicked in again. He sensed something stout stand up within him. Though he had never met this side of himself, he knew at once it belonged and should not be suppressed. Fides brought the handle of the blade crashing into the brave's jaw while deftly stepping to the side. The Indian brave fell to the ground, stunned. He remained there only an instant and was on his feet ready to try again. He had lost his knife and had produced another.

The sight the Indian beheld, however, stopped him in his tracks. Fide's back was up against the burning camp and the Indian was standing half in and half out of the dark. Superimposed against the bright fire light behind him, Fides appeared to the brave as only a sharply outlined shadow. His cloak hung down behind him and his sword glinted as he let it hang down at an angle away from him. Despite being confronted with a shadow warrior, the brave could yet see a burning in his opponent's eyes, and a cold fear began to fill up the man's body, beginning with his feet. Fides took a fearsome step toward the man. As suddenly chilled as he was, the Indian brave was made of stronger stuff. He mastered his fear, gathered up his courage, and rushed again at Fides, though this time with a little more caution.

All the brave had as a weapon was a long knife, though, so before he could close the distance to employ it, he found he needed to dive away from Fide's anticipatory thrust. Another step forward and the brave would have plunged himself into the waiting spike. Fides was still standing in a stout, thrusting position, daring the man with his eyes to try it again. The two men stood still, and it slowly dawned on both of them that no one else was fighting. The Indian brave was alone. Tasha and King stood nearby along with a number of other armed men. The ground was littered with bodies. Apparently, the travelers had carried the day. The black shadow that was Fides dared the man to continue the battle. Not only was this Indian warrior brave, he was smart as well. He stepped backwards, put his knife in its sheath, and with as much dignity as he could muster, disappeared into the darkness behind him.

"We must tend to the wounded," Tasha announced immediately. All those that were still in good health turned their attention to the fallen. A good portion of those on the ground were dead, but they found plenty who were still alive, too. There was a short debate about what to do with some of the injured Indians, but Tasha settled that quickly enough by coldly daring any man to try to kill off one of them. One look told them that they ought to obey, but she couldn't stop them from being a little rougher than she would have insisted on. She couldn't be everywhere and do everything, after all.

Fermion was now on foot as well, and he brought his report. "A lot of them got away on horseback. I saw them checking their wounded, too, and taking some with them. I guess at least thirty riders got away. I didn't see how many got away on foot. It's too dark to give a good estimate."

"I make them to be Sioux braves," King said. "If I'm right, and we may find out soon enough by asking some of these, it's probably Thomas Lighter Jones. He leads a very large group of Sioux who are for re-conquering. This seems further south for them than I expected, but they move around a lot."

"We'll find out in due time, at any rate," Fermion said. Fermion nodded approvingly towards Fides, "Fides! You put your training to good use today." Fides could only nod back in response. His strength suddenly dissipated and his hands started shaking. Fermion leaned into him- Fides could smell the blood on him- and said softly, "This part is normal. Don't let it trouble you too much- let it trouble you the proper amount. I'd like to say such battles will be rare as I have said, I'm afraid many such battles are ahead," Fermion paused, "I knew you would stand when the moment came. Well done, Fides."

"Enough talk," Tasha snapped. "Tend to that man," she said, pointing to a wounded man nearby. But Fides could not move, for he now found his legs embraced by the man whose life he had saved. The man was weeping and kissing Fides' shoes, making Fides extremely uncomfortable. Fermion put his hand on the man's shoulder, and when this did nothing, he leaned over and grabbed the man under his armpits and pulled him to standing.

"Friend, this man was only doing his duty. I'm sure he would say not to think anything of it," Fermion patiently said to the man.

But the man turned around to face Fermion, revealing the source of his gratitude. He had in his hands a long knife, and he was holding it by the blade. Blood was flowing out from both of his gashed hands. The man spoke: "That Indian was driving this knife into my chest and I used all my strength to hold it from going in. I was losing strength. I owe this man my life. I- I am bound to him by blood, my own blood and future scars will serve to make the commitment real."

Fermion grew silent as Fides tried to soak in what the man was saying. Tasha had come over and had removed the knife from the man's hands and was bandaging them. They were badly slashed. The man spoke again, saying, "I will be your servant until my debt is re-paid, even if it is to a violent death, or else you die of old age."

Fides shook his head violently, "I want no such thing."

"I have said it and I am a man of my word," the man proudly protested. Fides looked to Fermion for help, but Fermion appeared to have none to offer.

"Has honor returned to this land?" Fermion asked thoughtfully. "This man offers himself to your service freely, Fides. He comes on his own free will, not coerced. Your act of instinctive courage has inspired a courageous commitment that has been missing from this planet for hundreds of years. I do not think you can release him, even if you wanted to. He is bound by his own word and will, not by yours."

"I don't know what this means," Fides said in exasperation. Fermion only smiled wearily.

"Alright then, that's settled," Tasha said bluntly, "Now help with the wounded."

The dawn brought more clarity to the scene than the night had allowed, but with the diminishing of adrenalin since the battle, people were tired and their exhaustion brought its own confusion. The wounded had been placed into tents for care. Sioux wounded, and they discovered it was in fact Lighter Sioux, were also placed into tents, but first were bound. Tasha made sure that the bindings were not cruel. There were some who were nervous allowing the captives to live. Tasha told them that if they wanted an extra level of security, they could post a guard. Again seeing in her an unbending will, this is what they decided to do.

There was intense discussion among the rescued travelers about their next steps, and finally Fermion suggested to them that they were too tired to make rational decisions. Though this wasn't well received, about nine in the morning, with the bickering persisting with nothing yet accomplished, Tasha sternly commanded everyone to speak no more about pending decisions. Instead, they worked to bury their fallen fellow travelers and some of the Lighter Sioux bodies that had not been taken away by their tribesmen. Among the dead travelers were several married couples and one whole family. The cruelty of the attack was a stench in everyone's nostrils.

While the travelers buried their dead, Fermion, Fides, and King were joined by the scouts they had met the night before, Felix and Chester, to ensure that they were not still in danger. These two were brothers who had worked ranchland in Texas and knew how to live off the land. They were among those trusted by the group to make important decisions. The five of them crested the hill, and tried to track the fleeing Indians as well as they could. They ranged far and wide, and only succeeded in finding the staging ground for the attack. It had been a very well planned ambush. The staging area would have been easily overlooked unless you were specifically looking for such locations, and Felix and Chester lamented that they had only looked for signs of ambush right on their route. The staging area was a good mile from the road.

However, the fleeing Indian braves did not flee to any one spot and did not seem to be anywhere in the vicinity. This was a cause for concern, however, as it could very well mean that they had fled to get more warriors. This could be important information to consider in deciding what to do next. They returned to the camp as people were finishing their burial duties, and Tasha was distributing lunch. Fides was not eager to get back to the camp, however, as the man he'd saved, Jonathan, was constantly trying to attend to him. Fides felt very awkward about the whole matter.

Tempers flared up while eating stew over whether to go forward, or back, or to Fermion's deep dismay, to the Pledge. Then there was the matter about what to do with the wounded Indians. Felix and Chester calmed down their fellows by telling them that everyone should get rest, and sleep. Indeed, being awakened in the dark hours of the night, fighting a violent battle, and the gruesome clean-up in the morning, had all served to exhaust people to the point of being senseless. The camp gradually became silent as people heeded the counsel of their guides. Fermion and Fides volunteered to mount a day watch, and they took their steeds to the top of the hill ahead of them so that they could have a good view of the topography around them. After a while of stillness, Fermion spoke to Fides. Apparently, Fermion had some things on his mind to discuss with Fides.

"That was quite the show you put on last night, Fides," Fermion said, eyeing Fides with a steely look. Fides didn't know if this was complimentary language or not, and remained silent. Fides, for his own part, had been thinking about his role in last evening's events and was as surprised as anyone else might be at how they played out. Fermion continued. "I wonder, when King said that the traveling group was under attack, we came to their side without any argument amongst ourselves. How do you explain that?"

"I don't really know what you mean," Fides said, knowing full well what Fermion meant.

"Well, you stepped in on my behalf once, too. What makes you willing to risk your life for people you don't even know? You killed people tonight. How did you know that you were right to do so?" Fermion inquired.

Fides felt a little annoyed by the line of questioning. It seemed like Fermion was playing a little game of 'I told you so,' which bothered Fides, but he knew the question was worth considering. "I can't really say," Fides finally stammered. "I just knew that it was wrong to waylay travelers. In your case, I had no idea you could defend yourself. Sticking up for you was like sticking up for someone who couldn't fight for himself."

"But these travelers were not your wife or your children. You had never laid eyes on them," Fermion prodded him along. "When I saw you near the end of the battle, if I didn't know better, I'd say you had become filled with something 'other,' what do you think?" Fides pondered this new perspective. He remembered the liquid rage that filled his veins, both when he first heard King's call, and when he saw Jonathan on the ground about to be killed. Rage was not even the right word for it. It was as though his very innards had been stirred for battle, but not directed randomly, as one might expect rage to express itself, but very narrowly focused. Fides tried to put this into words for Fermion, who nodded appropriately, and waited until Fides was finished before saying anything else.

"Is that the type of feeling you expected in a world where nothing else matters except protecting your own wife and children so that your genes can be passed on?" Fermion asked.

"I don't know what you mean," Fides said in exasperation. Fermion appeared to be trying to teach him an entirely new lesson.

"Come on, man. If it had been your wife and children you would have no doubt fought to the death to provide them safety. There is nothing remarkable about that. Anyone would do that. But you stepped in to save people who were not your kin. You were stirred to action to protect people who very well may one day be threats to your kin. How does their business concern you? And yet you acted, and your soul was fired. You could have been killed."

"Is there supposed to be some important conclusion from this?" Fides responded, annoyed. "There is no soul. You're right, I acted foolishly-"

Fermion cut him off abruptly, "No, you acted nobly, valiantly, heroically. You need not look any further than the man, Jonathan, for evidence of the most accurate characterization of your deed. You did not enslave him, but he has enslaved himself for a time for you. In what kind of world do such events make sense?"

"Perhaps in the future I will not be so brash!" exclaimed Fides.

"I know something about you that you do not, Fides," Fermion said, softly.

"And what would that be?" Fides snapped back.

"In the future you will continue to be valiant, because it is in your nature to be valiant, and the world has not been successful in stomping it out of you. In fact, the world can only do so much to any man. There is always something that remains after the world has done its worst. This part, even if it is not much, remains through it all. Yet it is still not safe, even then. The man himself can squeeze out that little bit at the very last, if he is not diligent. Beware."

"You always speak in riddles," Fides sighed, relenting somewhat.

"I'm not done, Fides," Fermion continued. "I know something else, too. Not about you, but about me."

"Oh?"

"Yes, that righteous anger you felt when you saw the defenseless under assault is what I feel when even a child steals an apple, or a man curses his wife, or a government diminishes, even in the slightest, the freedoms of men."

"That's absurd," Fides exclaimed. "Are you telling me you would draw your sword if you saw a child steal an apple? No doubt he stole because he was starving in these days!"

Fermion hastily explained, "No, not at all. My point is that I do not need the blatantly easy and obvious injustice to alert my principles that something is amiss. You rose up to defend the waylaid, as well you should, because defending the waylaid is a very easy moral calculation to make, even for those who have had most of their morality pressed out of them. In order to save this country, and this world, from what is coming, it is the small and seemingly harmless moral deviations that need to be opposed, in the way appropriate for each, not just the obvious deviations."

Fides stared at him with his eyes wide open, "Sometimes I can't say I understand a word you are saying."

Fermion smiled kindly, "Let me put it this way, if two hundred years ago people would have recognized the destructive consequences of seemingly benign policies of a certain United Nations, this country would not have been disarmed when peril was obvious for everyone to see- and was already on their doorstep. Who knows whether you could have thrown off the invaders or not? This is just one example. There are many. I could give you a million more examples of bitter seeds planted by this country, but I constrain myself to this country only because it is the one you belong to and are familiar with. What I am saying can be said of all nations, back to the very beginning of your race. We all reap the fruit of seeds that were sown generations earlier. Indeed, you are harvesting the fruit of the first bitter seed that was planted. Do not be deceived, a particular seed always bears the fruit particular to it. The smallest seeds can still bear plenty of the most bitter fruit. It is easy to identify the larger seeds, because we can see them better. We must not pat ourselves on the back because we were able to confront an obvious evil. Whether we succeed or not is irrelevant. Ours is not to know the success of our efforts, only to make the right efforts, even in the little affairs, as often as we can."

"Do you think you could boil it down to one sentence?" Fides cried out, frustrated.

"Sure: Do the right things, even in the small, and you will likely not have to do the right things in the big, at all, because those circumstances will be kept from coming about in the first place." Fermion explained.

Fides let this soak in for a little while and at last replied. "So, you are saying that my anger upon hearing about the defenseless being attacked shows that there is this sense that I have that has been… deadened… but its appearance in this case shows that it is not completely dead at all. Besides that, it cannot be explained by invoking survival of the fittest. Furthermore, I should not be too happy, because this particular moral travesty was easy to spot. I need to be on guard for the ones that are not so easy to spot, as well. Is that the idea?"

"Oh ho! He can be taught! Very well said, Fides. And in that light, you can hone and develop that sense of indignation so that you know how to respond appropriately in different circumstances. In a world like this one, it is rarely easy to know how to do that. But despite the great violence that is sure to surround us that is easy to recognize and respond to in the future, there are other more troubling things that deserve equally indignant responses that are ultimately more dangerous and frankly, are harder to spot. Do you understand?" Fermion asked.

"I think so. I think it has something to do with your distrust for the Pledge. I'm sure it has something to do with the history of this country…"

Fermion interrupted, "The whole world, Fides."

"…Something to do with the history of this world and how it has come to be this way. You seem to think that even worse things could be ahead. Does that sound right?" Fides asked.

"Yes, that is quite right. Once again, we are faced with the fact that you are robbed of a solid knowledge of your own history. Not just yours, but all of humanity's. Something lies ahead of you that I only have glimpses of. It is imperative that we get you to your wife and children, and then back to Peoria, where that necklace can serve the good it was meant to serve," Fermion said.

"This is all well and good," Fides said slowly, "but, what should I do about Jonathan? I can't have this man following me around, can I? Can't I release him? And why does it so impress you?"

"I think it goes without saying that there are honorable people around today and that there have been throughout all time. But honor and its cousin, loyalty, hasn't carried the day. To a large degree, it is specifically because your people forgot about honor that it is in the predicament it is in today. When a man makes a pledge, it's only his own sense of integrity that compels him both to make the pledge and to keep it. It was noteworthy that he could even perceive that a debt existed between the two of you. The willingness of people to make pledges and their integrity in really carrying them out has fallen away over the last centuries, and when you can't trust the word of the man next to you, you are left to your own devices. To trust a man who is dishonorable is to ask for trouble, after all. But our lot is dire indeed when there is no man we can trust," Fermion explained.

"I know a lot of people who are good to their word," Fides countered.

"Oh, I'm sure you do. Keep in mind that it's easy when it's your own friends and family, though. For a stranger, it's a little more difficult. However, the treachery of man accumulates in a society so that, acting nationally, it betrays internationally, and internationally, is betrayed. That is why seeing that honorable response heartens me so," Fermion replied.

"Betrays internationally?" Fides asked.

"Absolutely. Let us again use an example from your own country's history. For example, what your country did to the Taiwanese," Fermion said matter-of-factly.

"The Taiwanese?" Fides wondered.

Fermion grunted disapprovingly, "You have been robbed of your geography, as well? You do know who the Taiwanese are, don't you?"

"I know that they are somehow related to the Chinese," Fides replied, gingerly.

"Well, about two hundred years ago China and Taiwan were at odds with each other, and the United States pledged to support Taiwan against China in the event of a Chinese invasion. The United States maintained that pledge over and over again for a hundred years. The day finally came when China did invade Taiwan. Instead of coming to their defense, however, the United States looked the other way. Consequently, Taiwan was China's Poland, except China did not make the same mistakes that Germany made in World War Two," Fermion explained. "You have heard of World War Two, haven't you?"

"Yes, that much I have heard, though I do not know much about it. I do not know what you mean by 'Poland,' for example," Fides said.

"Well, very simply, Germany invaded Poland, and the Europeans, instead of standing up to Germany, decided to let Germany have Poland in exchange for peace. Germany interpreted that, rightly, as a sign of weakness, and gobbled up as much as they could after that. When the United States allowed Taiwan to be taken by the Chinese, the United States lost their credibility in the eyes of other countries that had depended on the honor of the United States. These countries turned in on themselves when what they really needed to do was to strengthen links with other nations. Ultimately, when China began doing their own gobbling up, the betrayal of the Taiwanese would come back to haunt the United States. The United States trusted Mexico, but Mexico did not trust the United States, so when Mexico calculated based on its own interests, Mexico betrayed the United States. It is hard to blame them. Finally, Mexico threw its lot in with the Chinese. It was all very predictable, even if some of the finer points couldn't have been foreseen. It's disturbing that the human race fails to learn lessons taught to them so vividly, so often."

"I feel badly about what we did to the Taiwanese," Fides said, annoyed about this stain on America's record. For some reason he had always perceived that his country was, generally speaking, an innocent victim.

"It's only one illustration. It happens to be one that figures highly in the later history of this country and your world, but the point is that the honor principle works from the bottom up. Let's face it, it was not the country at large that abandoned Taiwan, but this country's president and congress. Men and women sold their honor for 'peace.' So, when I see an honorable man in these days, I am encouraged, and have hope for the future. If honor is indeed loose on the land, there might come a day when the citizens of this country can atone for their traitorous deeds. But first we will have to see what kind of country these formerly united states will become. That is very much in doubt right now. If I didn't know better, you and I will play a part in deciding that question," Fermion said, the tone of his voice heavy with sadness.

The two of them remained on the hill for several more hours, conversing every now and then, but largely remaining quiet, keeping watch. After awhile, King rode up to them and told them that he was relieving them so that they could eat dinner. Fides and Fermion returned to the camp, which was enjoying a fine dinner. At least, those who were awake were. Many still slept. It was amazing what Tasha could do with a pot, a fire, and basic traveling staples.

Felix and Chester were among those eating, as was Jonathan. They were discussing what to do. Chester, the brown haired, stocky scout was saying, "We are only twenty to twenty-five miles away. That's not very far. We could do it in three days if we really wanted to."

"This group is not going to travel that fast. If we left behind our gear, perhaps. Some people are carrying all of their worldly possessions. I don't know that they will want to leave them," Felix replied. Felix was a taller man, but not lanky. He was very well built. He wore a cowboy hat and definitely was not the sort of man you'd want to cross. On the other hand, he very much seemed the sort of man you'd want on your side. Fides could see why Fermion and King had so rapidly concluded when they had met the night before that the pair of them were good people, and Fides was glad in his heart that he had risked his life to save them.

"What do you think? Fermion? Fides? You've had a look again. What kind of danger do you think we face ahead of us?" Chester asked.

"Let's face it, if the Sioux are still out there, if you decide to go back to Oklahoma City, they'll still come after you. There is no changing that. At least going ahead, you stand a chance of coming to your destination. If you go back," Fermion pondered, "you'll have to risk the trip at some point, anyway, or be stuck there. In my opinion, you're already more than half way to Tulsa. It would be foolish to go back, now, even if the Sioux were ahead of you."

"Will you come with us?" Felix asked.

"That is something we have not discussed, and we would have to discuss it privately. I cannot say what my mind is on the matter, and I won't try to speak for them. Let us think about it tonight, and we'll be able to let you know," Fermion replied.

"There are some who think we should turn south and try to meet the Pledge's delegation, and join them. What do you say to that?" Felix wondered to Fermion. Fides chuckled, having some sense of what was coming.

Fermion seemed roused. "I would say that would be a terrible idea. No matter what sweet words they give, or how sincere they are now, their efforts can only end in calamity if they are allowed to succeed."

"I do not doubt your sincerity or your wisdom, but we have seen what happened in this country when we decided to be a democratic country. Does it not seem that it's worth trying something new?" Felix asked.

"New? Is the modern inherently superior to the ancient? Does human nature change over time?" Fermion studied Felix for a moment, seeking for the right words. "Modern masters of science are much impressed with the need of beginning all inquiry with a fact. The ancient masters of religion and philosophy were quite equally impressed with that necessity. They began with the fact that humans were corrupted- a fact as practical as potatoes. Whether or no man could be washed in miraculous waters, there was no doubt at any rate that he wanted washing. But then there came a time when the scientists, the philosophers, the religious leaders, the materialists, the skeptics, went beyond denying the highly disputable water, but denied the indisputable dirt. Some religious people admitted divine sinlessness, which they cannot see even in their dreams, but they deny human corruption, which they can see in the street. Several generations of your world's population has been forced to experience the consequences of this philosophy."

"I'm not sure I'm following you," Felix said, his eyes squinted in concentration.

"I'm with you," Chester told Fermion.

Fermion smiled, "I thought you might be."

"Explain it to me," Felix pleaded with his brother.

"Basically, he's saying that the strongest saints and the strongest skeptics alike took positive evil as their starting point," Chester told him. Felix looked only moderately helped.

"That is correct," Fermion affirmed him. "I am saying that the human race is at its core, very sick. It cannot be healed on its own power. It can only be healed by the Doctor. But what if someone refuses to admit that they are sick? Then they will not seek medical treatment, will they? When a bunch of people who don't acknowledge that they are sick get together and try to advance their best intentions, you can be sure about what will follow. The Pledge fails in its philosophy to account for the corruption of man. The results are predictable, and terrible."

"However, it would seem from what you're saying," Felix said, seeming to catch on, then, that it could be argued that the political system is irrelevant. It could be used for ill, or it could be used for good."

Fermion smiled, "Now you are talking with some sense. If it is true that any system can be used for ill or for good, then let us be wary of systems that have no checks on the certain abuse that will follow. It is humanity itself that has the capacity to behave wickedly or honorably, and it carries this capacity into its systems. All systems."

"That is a cynical point of view," Felix smirked. Fermion looked at him.

"It is your history," Fermion replied, unfazed by Felix's dismissive remark.

"What do you mean 'your'? Don't you mean 'our'?" Chester asked him. Fermion looked as though he were kicking himself for the lapse in language.

"Of course. It is our history," Fermion corrected himself.

At this point Tasha interrupted and assigned chores to the men. They all scattered to do as they had been told, but later on Felix and Chester cornered Fermion again to talk about the Pledge and the future of the country. Fides decided he'd heard enough of such talk, though, and took a nap. Fides learned later that the Pledge delegation from Oklahoma City had advertised that they would be traveling back to their home city, in Little Rock, Arkansas, and would tarry in Henryetta, Oklahoma, so that anyone in the region who wanted to join them could find them. Henryetta was south of Tulsa, and by turning south at any point on the trip there was apparently a good chance that they might be able to intercept the Pledge delegation on their way to that city. The prospect of doing so is what prompted Felix and Chester and others to discuss the matter, and were glad at least to hear a different perspective.

Jonathan, who had been traveling alone, made it clear that in order to fulfill his pledge he would have to stay by Fides' side and that he was prepared to follow wherever Fides went until it was satisfied. Of course, Fides remained uncomfortable with the whole affair, but he had resigned himself to the arrangement. Jonathan was clearly a stout man who did not go down easily in a fight. He had probably been quite surprised to find himself nearly killed despite his great strength. The Sioux Indian that had bested him must have been a fearsome warrior in his own right. Fides thought that having Jonathan at his side was having a real asset on hand. The only problem is that Jonathan had nothing for a weapon other than an old hammer, and though a blow of that hammer was no doubt a painful prospect indeed, it wasn't exactly the sort of weapon that could be trusted to support a man in the types of melees they were likely to find themselves in. Fides made up his mind to find something more potent for him in Tulsa.

That night, Fides, Fermion, King, Tasha, and now Jonathan, discussed together whether they would stay with the travelers or not. It was quickly decided that they certainly would not accompany them if they decided to return to Oklahoma City, and though clearly going to Henryetta was inconsistent with their own goal of Bloomington, Illinois, the prospect of coming anywhere close to elements of the Pledge struck them all as unacceptable, though each had his own reasons. All that was left to be decided was whether they would go on to Tulsa with or without waiting for the travelers.

This point was a little more difficult because they could be in Tulsa as early as the next day if they traveled alone, but with the group, it could take as long as a full week. It also seemed difficult to imagine how they would be able to realistically serve any real purpose if they came under attack again. Fermion pointed out that the Indians were not likely to make the same mistake twice, and would come with significant force. King, who of all of them felt the most strongly that they should escort the group, argued that it was unlikely that the Indians knew the strength of those who had come to the travelers' rescue. Fides reluctantly agreed with Fermion that the Indians were going to make sure that they were very certain about their true strength, and in particular whether or not there were more hidden in the hills, before attacking again. This all presumed that the Indians were returning. It seemed as though the best course, though still not without risk, was for their own five-some to move hastily to Tulsa and see if there was help that could be sent back for the travelers. This was their tentative conclusion, though none of them felt exactly right leaving behind the travelers. Nonetheless, as it seemed to provide the best hope for everyone's survival they resigned themselves to it and hoped that Chester and Felix would understand.

The next morning, however, Chester and Felix had their own news to share that saved them from having to reveal their own difficult decision. Apparently the remaining travelers had come to many of the same conclusions, and did not have the same resistance at the idea of joining with the Pledge. Felix, in fact, was going to lead the majority of the travelers south to link up with the Pledge delegation. Knowing Fermion's views, Felix explained that he wasn't planning on joining the Pledge, but that they really needed the security, and for those of them that still needed to go to Tulsa, there was nothing from keeping them from doing so once they got to Henryetta. Fermion abided this wordlessly.

Chester, however, was going on to Tulsa with a handful of people who had an interest in getting to Tulsa, or beyond. As he explained, many of them were violently opposed to being near the Pledge even one little bit. This smaller group numbered only about ten and apparently some negotiation had taken place where the smaller group was given almost all of the horses left behind by the Sioux in their thwarted attack in exchange for almost all of the provisions that this smaller group had at hand. As those riding on horseback would not be traveling very long and those heading south added a least another four or five days to their journey, if not more, the deal seemed to work out well. The only regret was that there were not more horses altogether, or else Fermion would have tried madly to convince them all to ride to Tulsa.

This made the situation from the perspective of Fides and his gang very easy. They would ride together with this smaller band and arrive in Tulsa sometime the next day. Everybody had been packing since the sun had first come up, so after only a short time discussing these issues, the two groups parted. Felix and Chester exchanged warm farewells, vowing to reunite as soon as they were able. The two groups soon disappeared from each other's sight.

The riders made good time that day and experienced no incidents. Indeed, that night when they made camp they thought they could see the glow of Tulsa in the distance. They set a guard, but the night passed without event. Late in the afternoon the next day, the city limits of Tulsa greeted them.

Like Oklahoma City, there was a ring of defenses set around the city. Here, however, there was little scrutiny given to visitors, and they entered the town unchallenged. Chester, along with the other travelers that had joined him, bid them farewell. Fides and his fellows found a place to pitch their tents for the night and gave food and water to the horses. The next morning they'd deposit their horses and look for the one they called 'Chummy.'

== Chapter 6 ==

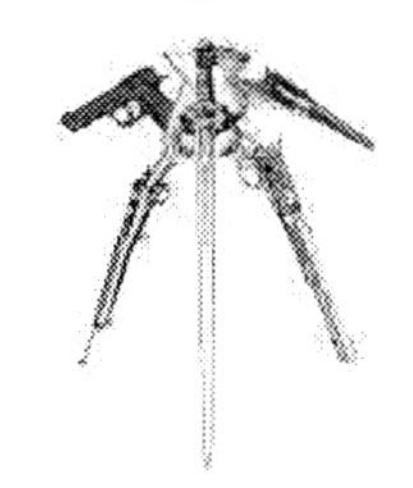

Tulsa was much smaller than Oklahoma City in almost every respect, but it became immediately evident that in the final analysis, it saw many more people. There were hundreds upon hundreds of people passing through on their way to other places, facilitated apparently by the services of a certain man who went by the name of 'Chummy.' The situation here in Tulsa was much as Fides had experienced at Albuquerque. Great effort was expended to help travelers form groups for safer travel and help them be as well equipped as they could afford.

As they explored the city in the morning, they found it to literally be humming. In the distance they could hear the sounds of engines. They could distinctly make out car engines, motorcycle engines, and truck engines. Their first task, however, was to deliver the horses that the Cherokee in Oklahoma City had let them use to their fellow Cherokee that were residing in Tulsa. King and Tasha knew right where to go and promptly led them all to a section of houses on the north side of town. The houses were surrounded by two separate fences, one set inside the other, and both of equal and great height. Other than this somewhat uneasy detail, the layout of the houses evoked a sense of neighborhood. They numbered about fifteen and were definitely a well preserved remnant of a middle class neighborhood block from a long time ago. White picket fences were set around many of the yards, and there were actually children playing in the yards. The scene was almost idyllic. This tranquil scene was given a new context when one noticed guard shacks at the corners and on both sides of the city block, and armed men, presumably husbands, fathers, and sons, patrolling the streets and the outer fences.

King and Tasha were welcomed immediately at the gate. As Fides was discovering, King and Tasha were already quite familiar with the whole area. Their time with the Cherokee had allowed them to do a fair bit of traveling and they had gained respect wherever they had gone, and had become adopted into the tribe. In fact, word spread through the neighborhood of their arrival and many people came to greet them. Fides noticed that a very attractive young lady had greeted King, and the two of them spent a moment in quiet conversation before they were interrupted by a gaggle of teenage girls clamoring to relieve them of their horses.

In due time, an older gentlemen by the name of Philip came out to greet them. Tasha introduced Philip to Fermion, Fides, and

Jonathan, and explained that Philip was the head of the Tulsa Cherokee council. Philip had short gray hair and was dressed in a nice shirt and tie, which was completely out of the ordinary in this day and age. Fides couldn't even recall the last time he had seen someone wear a tie. Such a sight created the illusion that he had gone back in time and was merely traveling through a normal neighborhood before the troubles began in America. But this was only a passing illusion: it could not survive the reality that this was only an oasis in the midst of bubbling anarchy.

Relieved of their horses and newly acquainted with Philip and some other older men and women, they made their way to a house that appeared to be an old farm house. To their surprise, there was actually a barn behind one of the houses, and it was to this barn that the horses were led to. Next to the barn was a large white shed. A young man sat outside it, seemingly whittling out a flute. Next to him, however, wrapped somewhat in a cloth, was a quiver of arrows and next to it, a bow. The young man looked up at them and immediately looked away as though wholly uninterested, but Fides was certain that young man was not simply passing time outside that shed. He was a guard.

They walked past the shed and were escorted into the house. They were offered tall glasses of water at a large dining room table, and in no time they found themselves surrounded by the entire crew. Settled in at last, Tasha produced a piece of paper, and pushed it over to Philip, who appeared to be expecting it.

"Chief Ramaen has asked that you provide the funds to allow myself, King, Fermion and Fides to travel using Chummy's transportation services," Tasha explained. "Jonathan is a new to our party, but we trust him, and hope that you can allow for him, as well." Philip examined the document that Tasha had provided her, nodding approvingly.

"Absolutely. No question. This document authorizes funding for as far as Chummy is willing to take you. I am not quite sure what that means," Philip replied.

"We have heard that in Bloomington, Illinois, a registry is being created allowing divided families to attempt to find each other and re-unite," Tasha explained. "I myself have no family in that region, but King might, as well as our new friend, Fides. What Chief Ramaen is authorizing is a payment to Chummy sufficient even to pay for motor travel as far as Bloomington, if Chummy is willing to go that far."

"That is very far. If Chummy were willing to provide such transport, it would certainly cost a great deal," Philip replied. There was nothing in his tone of voice to indicate that he was displeased with the idea, but it was clear that he was skeptical that Chummy would be willing to do such a thing. At this time, another person, Mary, spoke.

"Right now," Mary explained, "Chummy runs Tulsa as a hub, serving Wichita, Kansas City, Springfield, and Little Rock. There is no doubt he would take you to Springfield, of course." Mary was a middle-aged, pleasant looking woman. After some time, Fides realized that she was Philip's wife.

Bill, a friend of Philip's and another member of the Tulsa Council, spoke up: "I have traveled to Illinois before. And I mean long before. It was well before the Disease and before the nuclear attacks. I know where Bloomington is, and I know that the most direct route would be through St. Louis. As that is not possible, they would have to go to Cairo, first, and then many miles north."

Fides' curiosity was piqued. "Why is it not possible to go through St. Louis?"

"It was one of the cities destroyed by nuclear attack," Philip grumbled sadly.

"So," concluded Mary, "Chummy would have to go to Springfield as normal, and then to Cairo, and then to Bloomington. As I understand it, that is altogether three times longer than his normal run to Springfield, and he will of course want to be compensated for his trip back."

"We can only know if he's willing to do it if we ask. The question is whether or not we have anything to offer him that'd he'd take as payment," Bill mused.

Philip explained some of the considerations that were involved. As they lived in Tulsa, they had many opportunities to deal with Chummy. Chummy was a tall, pudgy man. Apparently he had been an engineer at one time, but before that he had grown up on the farm. Adjoining that farm, owned by him and his father (now deceased) was an old junk yard filled with all sorts of ancient vehicles. Chummy's skill as a mechanic proved to be very profitable for him, which was good, because by all appearances, Chummy enjoyed profit. He had brought a number of vehicles into working order and had somehow managed to procure enough fuel to keep his fleet in action. The source of his fuel was unknown. In exchange for motor transportation, people were willing to give over many of the valuable items that they had. People got tired of walking from place to place, and as times were getting more and more dangerous, the sooner they were at their destination, the better. Chummy was not likely to give them transport to Bloomington out of the goodness of his heart, but a trip that far would require far more than just room for passengers and their gear. It would require additional vehicles and therefore more drivers to bring the fuel with them to get there and back. Chummy would also want to send along some of his security forces to protect his assets. All in all, they'd have to provide a great deal of incentive to convince Chummy to make such a trip.

For a time they sat in silence, prompting Fides to fidget somewhat uncomfortably. At last, though, King spoke up. "It seems that there is something being left out. Isn't it easy enough to ask him what it would take and then see if it is available?" This question was greeted with silence, too.

Philip nodded towards Fides and Fermion, "I apologize for our discomfort in this matter. It is not meant to be rude. The problem is that we already know what Chummy will want, and we are not so sure..."

"I assure you that Fides and Fermion are completely trustworthy," Tasha hastened to say. "In fact," she continued, "I give you my word that you can speak of anything in front of them that you could say in front of me and King." At this, Tasha told them all about the mighty battle that they had had with members of the Lighter Sioux and in particular, Fermion and Fides' conduct in the battle. Convincing them that Jonathan was likewise trustworthy was much more of a challenge, but when the circumstances were explained, and Fermion vouched for him, Philip finally acquiesced. At that point, naturally, the men in the room wanted to see their weapons, which Fides was glad to do because he much more preferred that the attention be on their blades than on his supposedly valiant fighting. He did not feel valiant. He merely did what seemed natural at the time.

As they marveled at the fine swords, Philip suddenly gasped in recognition of some fact. He smiled slyly, but all he said was, "I do believe that we received word of your battle, actually." But he would not elaborate, though it was clear that the other Tulsa residents slowly realized what he was referring to. The most critical point, however, was settled. They could all be trusted, so Philip was going to lay the situation bare. Apparently, though, a full explanation required a trip to the shed, so that is where they went.

The young man outside the shed greeted them with a friendly smile. Philip and the young man shook hands, and then they all went inside the shed. For all intents and purposes, the shed appeared to be nothing more than a normal machine shed. There were all sorts of shelves filled with supplies or assorted machine parts. In the corner, there was what appeared to be a little office. A large metal contraption was in the middle of the shed. They paused around it and talked about it very briefly, almost as though it were part of an act. After pointing out several features of the machine, Philip led the way to the office. He opened the door to the office, moved a cabinet that was on tiny coasters, and revealed a staircase descending into blackness. He gave a nod, and they all followed him down into the dark. There was the sound of fumbling, and then the sound of a switch being thrown and they were suddenly immersed in electric light.

Before their eyes was revealed rack upon rack of military issue weaponry. There had to be hundreds of guns and boxes and boxes of ammunition. Besides this, there appeared to be all sorts of military supplies stacked around, as well.

"This," Philip explained, "is what Chummy will want in compensation."

"But does he know you have such weapons?" King asked, in awe of the sight. Fides, too, was in awe. It was quite an arsenal. Fermion appeared to be completely unsurprised and even uninterested.

"Chummy and his family grew up in this area," Bill said. "His family and our families all know each other very well. These weapons came here on his trucks a decade or more ago. Though we made a great effort to make sure that they were not seen, that very effort fueled his suspicions. On occasion, he has subtly suggested payment in arms for transport when we have asked for it, and naturally we laughed as though he were joking. He has been satisfied with normal payments of goods prior to this. But there is no doubt that if we seek transport as far as Bloomington, he will want weapons as payment."

"In all the times we visited here, we never knew of such things," Tasha said. "What are they all for?"

"I can tell you a couple of reasons. Obviously, with attempts by foreign authorities to fully disarm the citizens of this country, we realized we had to retain arms. They were to be used only when it would seem as though it would make a difference. Now they remain here in Tulsa for several important strategic reasons. For one thing, in event of a need to muster an army, we know that we can at last resort use these weapons to purchase Chummy's entire fleet- or even commandeer it, if necessary. For another, we can make use of Chummy's vehicles to rally quickly and deploy quickly, too. In the event of any kind of invading force trying to commandeer Chummy's fleet- something that is a real threat- we also will want to be able to repel that force. If an army gained Chummy's fleet, they would have a real strategic advantage," Philip said, laying the situation out for them. "We know that many of Chummy's drivers at least have handguns. Now, the Pledge is based out of Little Rock, and Chummy provides transportation to Little Rock. So, we know that the Pledge is aware of this strategic asset not too far away from them. The Pledge is not likely to be deterred by a few armed drivers. Chummy, we think, is well aware of the threat. We think, too, that the Pledge knows that we have so many Cherokee here in Tulsa for the specific purpose of protecting Chummy and his fleet. However, if the Pledge knew that there were military weapons floating around Tulsa, rather than be deterred, they'd find the temptation overwhelming. Naturally, we have enough guns to repel them, but we would not by any means have enough men to bear them."

"What strength do you make them out to be?" Fermion inquired.

"They have at least five thousand warriors, according to our spies," Philip replied gravely. "Come, let us go. We don't like to talk about these weapons in our houses, even with the security we have. Now you know. We have put great confidence in you and your ability to preserve our secret." Philip led the way up the stairs. Once they were all out, he moved the cabinet back into place. Once again they congregated around the machine in the middle of the shed, and Philip said, "If anyone asks you what you did in this shed, you tell them about this nifty machine that I am so proud of!"

They exited the shed, nodded towards the young man, and made their way back to the house. Fides noticed for the first time that there were other young men about, seemingly preoccupied with simple tasks like the man resting by the shed. Once back at the house, they found themselves back in the dining room where Mary served them a fine breakfast.

King left them after their late breakfast to chat with the black-haired young woman that had greeted them as they entered the compound, leaving the rest to try to make some decisions on their own with Philip and Bill. The rest of the Cherokee left them as well, trusting Philip and Bill to make the best decisions from the perspective of the Cherokee community. After significant discussion, a decision was made. They would offer to Chummy a large piece of property that Bill's family owned outside of Tulsa. Fides protested the generosity, but Bill waved him off.

While not as enticing as guns, of course, a large tract of land would be a significant payment, especially since the land in question had several structures on it and good natural resources, like water and woods. There were also several dozen acres of tillable land, and as it was known that Chummy still liked to work the land, it was thought that this might tip the balance. All that was left was to talk to Chummy.

It was decided that the following day would be the day that they would approach Chummy. They each enjoyed the comforts of civilization that afternoon and evening, but King was nowhere to be seen that day. Indeed, it was only the following morning that King was at last spotted, and that was in his bed, exhausted. As is sadly the case, good, comfortable times do not inspire events worth dwelling on, whereas the troubling times do. So, there was little to say about their day of peace and rehabilitation. It passed, and the only thing worth adding is that they were strengthened by it.

The next morning a festive breakfast was had. Many visitors dropped in while they were eating and said a few words before going on with their day's activities. These folks were good folks, and Fides thought to himself that if he did not have a family of his own to seek, he'd seek to become part of this family. They all had their fill of breakfast, and then a little mid-morning slumber. In the meantime, King finally rolled out of bed in the mid-morning and ate a meal by himself. Around lunch time, the five of them, along with Philip, made their way to the eastern edge of Tulsa, with Chummy's garages their ultimate destination.

Though the rest of Tulsa hardly compared with the tranquility of the Cherokee complex, the static residents appeared to have a very good life. Philip explained that everyone benefited from Chummy's success, ultimately. Chummy had so much wealth- and wealth was not merely measured anymore in pieces of paper and coin- that problems of proper storage arose. He couldn't help but share liberally with the rest of Tulsa's inhabitants.

Most of the travelers had little reason to travel through the town proper since Chummy's garages, located on the eastern edge of town, were the center of attention for those using his services. Consequently, other than the constant engine noise (that was growing louder as they got closer to his operations), the town was very quiet. In this respect, there was a dramatic difference between Tulsa and Oklahoma City. There were a lot of travelers in Oklahoma City, too, but the whole town was used for transit, so it was always crowded in every part.

At last they arrived at the center of Chummy's operation. It was past the lunch hour, and drivers were getting ready to take passengers to their various destinations. There were a dozen large warehouses with garage doors cut into them, and inside were vehicles getting worked on and vehicles getting loaded. There were a number of other buildings throughout the complex, too.

One of these buildings stood out as certainly being Chummy's office. Before they got close to entering the complex, though, they were stopped by some of his security officials. Though there was no fence, there were dozens of men patrolling the grounds in bright orange outfits designating them as security guards. These men not only screened those entering the complex, but they also helped travelers find the right garage. Off about one hundred yards from the complex was a massive tent city. Here, Philip explained, travelers stayed and were served while they made arrangements for a ride, or to meet others who would be traveling on foot to the same destination.

Philip was recognized immediately by the security officials that stopped them and they were pointed in the direction of Chummy's office. Philip, of course, did not need directions. They made their way across the open area that was in the middle of all these garages, dodging a couple of cars and wading their way through a number of people, presumably travelers, going to one part of the complex or another. Philip led the way to Chummy's office.

Inside the small, single story building that served as his office, there was only a conference room, a secretary's area, and Chummy's own office. Apparently, most of the transacting and coordinating happened elsewhere. It was clear from the start that Chummy and Philip were very familiar with each other. Chummy was just as Philip had described him. He was a very tall man, wearing overalls. He looked like a farmer that had been fed high-powered corn for much of his life. He was a little overweight, but his sunburned arms showed all that he possessed farmer-strength, and was not to be underestimated. He was definitely doing well for himself.

"Chummy, we need a private place to discuss a customized trip. Is now a good time to have such a discussion, and do you have such a place?" Philip asked him.

Chummy's eyes narrowed, eagerly looking forward to a negotiation. "Now is perfectly fine. As you know, my conference room is private," he replied. Philip shifted his eyes to Chummy's secretary briefly and then back to Chummy, and he asked him again if there was any truly private place to talk. Chummy took the hint this time, and the unsuspecting secretary was given another hour's worth of lunch. He led the way to the conference room. The six of them sat down, but Chummy leaned on an old lectern. "So," he said, "what's this all about?"

"This is Tasha and King. You might remember them from a few years back. This is Fermion and his friends, Fides and Jonathan. These three have won our affection. The five of them would like to speedily arrive at their ultimate destination. It is a little further, I'm afraid, then your normal routes," Philip explained.

"We can certainly handle a little further, especially for an old friend like you, Philip," Chummy replied. "Somehow, I think that you have something a little different in mind."

"Have you heard of the efforts in Illinois to help re-unify families broken apart because of the Disease and the nuclear attack?" Philip inquired.

"Yes, we get many people through here looking to get there. We help them all along to Springfield, Missouri, and then they walk to Cairo, Illinois, because of the desolation in St. Louis. I suppose you want me to take them all the way to Cairo, eh?" Chummy responded. There was a glint of delight in his eyes.

"Actually, we had something more along the lines of a direct passage to Bloomington itself," Philip returned.

Chummy was not quite expecting that. There was a moment of thought, and then the glint returned. Fides thought that maybe this wasn't a 'glint of delight' so much as a glint of greed. "Bloomington is quite a trip, Philip. I have been trying for months to establish a route back to Oklahoma City, and even Albuquerque, and that makes much more sense then wasting resources on a trip to Bloomington."

Fermion's interest was piqued, and he had a thought he decided he needed to put into the form of a question: "Trying to establish a route to Oklahoma City and Albuquerque? Did you recently send motorcycles in that direction?"

Chummy was again surprised, "Yes, actually, we did. I sent out two motorcycles and four men, but I have not seen my bikes nor my men since. I am afraid that tells me about my prospects, but it's seriously hurting our business to not be able to at least have a route back to Oklahoma City. What do you know?"

"I believe your men were waylaid by a band of men in Albuquerque who wanted to deal violently with Fides and myself," Fermion explained. "We were attacked by some members of that band of men, and they were on motorcycles. I am very aware of the region around Albuquerque, so I know they did not get their rides from that area."

"And my men?" Chummy wondered.

"I cannot say. If we assume the worst, I can assure you that I have given you some measure of revenge. Two of the renegade riders are no more. And I thank you for the ride. We used your motorcycle to get to Oklahoma City, and you can likely re-claim it from the President of the city himself," Fermion said, while Philip beamed. Philip was happy, because this sort of news was likely to soften Chummy, and information on where to obtain one of his vehicles could very well serve as payment to some degree, itself.

"Those were good men," Chummy said. "I'd rather have them than the bikes. But now that I know something, I will send a much larger group of men to Oklahoma City to see what can be learned. The problem, as Philip here certainly understands, is that it is not safe even to travel between here and Oklahoma City. Various groups are active. There are rebel Indian tribes and Pledge scouting parties, not to mention ordinary bandits. It would be nice to secure that road. I wonder if some arrangement can be made?"

Philip smiled, knowing that the conversation would turn this way. "Naturally, if we could help in that regards, we would." Chummy grunted, unpleased that this particular game was still going on. He decided to up the ante.

Chummy leaned forward on his lectern and said, "You know, a trip to Bloomington... that's a nasty ride. Of course we've been to Cairo on occasion, but none of my drivers are familiar with anything further. For the five of you, I could provide no protection. But I think for the five of you to go that far we'd need at least three vehicles. I think a van might serve for the passengers. We'd need a truck to carry the fuel. We'd need an escort vehicle. And we'd need between ten and fifteen men to operate the vehicles and provide the security. Not for you, of course, but for my property. I don't know what you have to offer to compensate for such a great expense."

"Bill Samuelson has agreed to part with his one hundred acre parcel outside of town. I think you are aware of it?" Philip replied. "That is significantly more than any traveler is likely to ever offer you, and I think it will well compensate you for your troubles."

"I am aware of that land. These folks must be very important to you if Bill is willing to part with such a nice morsel. Still, let us be plain. We are speaking in private, so I think you knew I was going to say this. I have land. I have vehicles. I have many loyal friends and family that work for me. I have many interesting contraptions that travelers have parted with in order to use my services. I have gold, silver, and jewels. But I have no way to protect any of this, or the people I care about. Philip, by God, you know that the Pledge is not all that far away and my fleet would help them. You know that I would never do business with them, but how could I stop them if they decided to take things into their own hands?"

For the first time, Chummy did not seem to be acting only according to greed. He seemed genuinely interested not only in his possessions, but those around him. Chummy was not quite yet finished, though. "Philip, I know what you had in those blankets and boxes all those years back. I know you have guns. Lot's of them. And I bet they are high quality. If ever there were an appropriate time for a reasonable transaction involving just a few of those guns, it's now."

Philip sighed. The room was quiet for a time. Finally, Philip spoke, "Look, friend. If the Pledge knew that this city was as well armed as it was, I think you know that it would promptly come up here and sacrifice as many men as they thought were necessary in order to procure those arms. As much as I agree with you, on nearly every level, you can understand how if it suddenly became known that you had such weapons, even just a few, we'd quickly have the Pledge Army at our doorstep."

"Perhaps you speak the truth," Chummy said. "Still, as the incident about my riders out to Albuquerque shows, it is dangerous in this time to travel. Surely you heard about how even the Lighter Sioux were routed by yet another new group of bandits? We are constantly in danger, both close to home and far from it. Perhaps if our men and your men were combined, and armed, we could repel whatever the Pledge threw at us. As it is, at least as far as we are concerned, right now we risk being cut off piece by piece. I'd rather have it all out in a single battle then die from a thousand cuts."

"We have heard that the Pledge have at least five thousand followers. How can the thousand men of Tulsa resist such a force?" Philip rejoined.

"Surely you have more than five thousand rounds of ammunition! Do you suggest that you have a thousand weapons?" Chummy blurted out in amazement.

"Oh, heavens no," Philip hastily said. Fides knew that Philip was probably telling the truth. For as many guns as he saw in that underground shed, it certainly came nowhere close to a thousand. "We certainly have more than five thousand rounds of ammunition, but if we could arm the entire city, I would probably agree with you and simply risk standing up to whatever force came. I cannot tell you exactly how much of either we have, except to say that the Cherokee in Tulsa are well accommodated."

"So, that's really it?" Chummy impatiently snarled.

"I'm afraid so," Philip said sadly.

"I will have to consider your offer. You are right about that parcel of land. It is truly a good offer, in general, even though I am up to my ears in land, if you will pardon the pun," Chummy said.

"Excuse me?" Philip asked, confused.

"Never mind," Chummy said, chuckling. "Point is, I don't actually need any land, nor does anyone else that works for me. It'd be nice if you could offer me something I don't have. I have to admit, it's a bit annoying that you not only have something I don't have, but something I truly need."

"You see the wisdom in it, though?" Philip asked.

"Yes, I'm afraid I do. Doesn't make things any better, though, does it?" Chummy replied. Philip said nothing. They heard the door to the building open, and they realized that the secretary had returned. Chummy told them again that he would consider the offer and send a messenger back with his decision. At that, the six of them returned again to Philip's home to await Chummy's messenger.

They would not have to wait long.

The six had barely arrived back at Philip's house when a young man from the complex's guard shack informed them that a messenger had come on behalf of Chummy. Chummy was on his way, personally, and asked if they would please remain at Philip's residence. Philip accepted the message, and told the guard to send Bill to him immediately. They were settling in when Bill arrived and Philip and he had a private conversation.

"I suspect that they are going to have a few more guards on hand and send out some spies to make sure Chummy is not coming in force," Fermion suggested to Fides. He was probably close to the truth; Bill hastily left the residence and Philip returned to them looking slightly perplexed. Fides realized that though Chummy seemed like a good man, even if a little ambitious (in the bad sense), once he had some reasonable assurance that there really was something of immense value in the Cherokee complex, he might see fit to try to take it without asking. At any rate, Chummy's coming to them appeared to take Philip and Bill by surprise.

But Chummy came alone. He was escorted to Philip's residence, and came into the living room, where everyone, including Mary and Bill as well now, were relaxing with some hot coffee. Chummy had appeared to be a large man when he was in his own office, with high ceilings, and lots of open space. Here, though, he filled up whole corners at a time. He was positively massive. On his face, though, was a very peculiar expression that Fides realized was sincere concern. As Chummy knew everyone in the room, there were no introductions or similar pleasantries, and he didn't seem quite in the mood for them, anyway.

"Look," he began, "Philip, you and I go ways back. Our families have known each other for at least a hundred years, and our fathers went together to the war in the south and shared the same fate. Through thick and thin, that's us. Right?" Philip nodded to Chummy, who continued, "Alright, I know that you have..."

"We don't say the words, even here," Philip interrupted.

"Alright, well you know what I'm talking about," Chummy continued. "But we can bet that the Pledge have got their hands on some, too, and besides, if you've got them, we can be sure other Indian tribes have them too- there certainly have been enough murders out in the wild to prove that- and you know that all of my vehicles would be very tempting for any of them. My workers report more and more problems. It's only a matter of time, I think, before they come here to take over my operations. I understand that they would be here sooner than later if they also knew... Well, you know... so you won't let me have any. Fine, I get that. Here is the deal I will offer you."

He stopped for a minute to enjoy a drink from a tall glass of water that Tasha brought him. He wiped his mouth on his oversized coat sleeve, and continued. "I'll agree to have some of my men take these five as far as Bloomington. I would say that I'd decline Bill's land altogether, but I think those men who take you will need something like that for compensation. So, it'd be for them, really. I hope you understand."

"Well, I was already prepared to let it go, Chummy, so it's all the same to me," Bill replied.

"You know, Chummy, I should at least ask you whether or not you might just be willing to sell the vehicles and fuel," Philip joined in.

"Oh no, that's out of the question unless, you know, we really had the type of transaction that I desire in mind. I need all my vehicles. I've assembled all the intact vehicles I can. I've only got enough extra to serve Oklahoma City if I could ever secure the route," Chummy countered.

"Well, it was worth asking," Philip said.

"No problem," Chummy said, brushing aside any notion he was offended. "So, here is what I'm going to ask. I'll send the men and vehicles out with you in exchange for that parcel, but also for your assurance that if there is an attempt on me and my fleet, you will help defend us, even if it means bringing out your treasure." Now that it was out on the table, Chummy was quiet. He had nothing more to add.

There was quite a pause after that. Philip and Bill just stared at Chummy with a look that Chummy could make no sense of. He started to squirm just a little bit, and it was really clear to all that Chummy apparently possessed information about how precarious his situation was that had been held close to the vest and hadn't made its way out into the community. But what Philip and Bill were thinking was that they were already prepared to do just what Chummy was asking, and in fact, the only reason why the arsenal remained in Tulsa at all was because of Chummy's massive fleet. Obviously, this was a good turn of events for them, but Philip could not let on, or Chummy would up the ante some more.

"Of course we will have to consider this offer of yours. It is a very modest proposal you have compared to what it could have been, but as you are asking us and the rest of the tribe to possibly die for you and your business operations- and of course the people who help you- I cannot make such a decision without first clearing it with the Cherokee Council. But I will not hesitate in calling a meeting of the council. In fact, I will call a meeting as soon as you leave and I will send word to you no later than supper time tonight about our decision," Philip countered.

"I understand. Incidentally, when would you like to depart?" Chummy asked.

"Fermion?" Philip redirected the question to him.

"We want to go as soon as possible, but recognizing the preparations that might be involved on your end, I would say we could allow at least two days," Fermion pondered aloud.

"I think we can probably do it in one day. Would that work?" Chummy replied. King looked somewhat disappointed with this number, but Fermion nodded and indicated that that would be just fine. With that, Chummy gathered up his being, and left.

After he was well out of sight, Philip smiled and said, "Well! Who would have thought we'd get something more out of our willingness to protect that man?" Everyone agreed, and general conversation followed, but finally people dismissed themselves from the company. Fides took a nap. Jonathan took a tour of the city. Tasha helped Mary in the kitchen. King went for a walk somewhere. Fermion and Philip were left alone to discuss arrangements or whatever else it might be that was pressing on their minds.

The next days were very restful. The day after the bargaining session, Chummy had sent word that one day had been overly optimistic, and indeed the departure would have to be on the second day. This suited everyone well, actually, as they were able to enjoy each other's company a little longer. At the same time, the whole Cherokee community worked together to make sure that the travelers had all that they needed. Chummy had sent word that he was sending a fourth vehicle because there was not room enough for fuel and provisions, otherwise. This made packing much easier. They put together enough food for the journey by vehicle and plenty of extra if they had to end up going on foot.

The night before they were supposed to leave, Philip prepared a mighty feast with entertainment besides. Fermion surprised them all by dancing in some of the ritual dances, leading many of the tribe to decide that though he had denied being an Indian despite looking like one in some respects, he must surely have some good blood in him anyway. That's the way that they put it to each other.

Tasha, occasionally joined by King throughout the night, also participated in some of the dancing. King was elusive, though, and sometimes could not be found to dance with. This disappointed the young girls who had welcomed them originally and expressed such interest in their horses. Maybe it wasn't the horses they had been interested in, really. But the night passed, and it was soon morning.

The sounds of engines in the Cherokee complex stirred them all from their breakfast and a great crowd of people came to watch as they loaded up their supplies. Chummy had not come to see them off- too busy, no doubt- but the men he had sent seemed very capable. There were more of them then he expected, too. The foreman, a man named Tom, informed Philip that the rumors were that the Pledge was on the move north from Little Rock, though not towards Tulsa. That, of course, was the very direction they were going, so they had decided on sending a few extra men. It turned out that the men were more easily convinced to go than Chummy had indicated they would be: Bloomington was a nice adventure, well beyond their normal route, and the promise of a few of Bill's acres was just bonus.

Altogether, Chummy was sending along ten men to operate and accompany the vehicles. One of the vehicles was an old jeep that had been cleaned up pretty well. Closer inspection revealed it to be an old military vehicle and where there had once been mounted a machine gun, there now was a pretty impressive looking crossbow. The jeep carried three men who had the sole purpose of protecting the rest, though the whole crew could take care of themselves and operate that crossbow if they had to.

It did not take long to get loaded as both parties were well organized. After no more than an hour, the four vehicles rolled out of the complex. The caravan weaved itself through the city streets and finally found the open road towards Springfield, Missouri. In the front was the jeep. As it was winter time, though yet a mild one, it would have been pretty cold for those in the jeep except they had been doing this for so long that they knew how to keep the heat in and even make some more right inside the vehicle.

Next was one of the passenger vans. It had some of their supplies, and carried two of Chummy's men, Fides and Fermion, and of course Jonathan, who refused to be too far from the man he had vowed to protect. Next was a small flatbed truck, loaded with some boxes of tools, parts, and other supplies, as well as quite a few barrels of what they presumed to be gasoline. Finally, in the rear was another passenger van carrying Tasha and King and some more of Chummy's men. Though the roads were bumpy from disrepair, they were still able to speed along at forty to fifty miles an hour.

Because of the fact that winter was starting to get underway, there were fewer travelers along side of the road. Most had arrived at their destinations or were stopping at various waypoints to wait until the spring time. At any point the weather might turn dramatically and drastically cold, and no one wanted to be out in such weather. In fact, in another four weeks, Chummy would shut down his fleets for the winter months. Aside from a few groups of travelers, all they saw as they drove was an old station wagon going the other direction. The driver was of course another one of Chummy's employees, and they knew each other. They didn't stop to chat, but Tasha saw him gawking at their caravan as he passed by it. Apparently Chummy didn't often send out four vehicles at a time.

Though the trip from Tulsa to Springfield would have taken quite a long time on foot, when you are traveling at forty-five miles an hour, you are only looking at a three to four hour trip. If things went well, they could easily be in Bloomington, Illinois, late the next night, especially because they were prepared to drive nearly non-stop. Once they got past Springfield, their knowledge about the conditions of the road or the mental states of the natives would become less and less sure.

They did not want to stop for very long anywhere since they didn't know what the circumstances around them would be. On the other hand, though they were confident that the roads would be at least as they were used to on their normal routes, during the darkest portions of the night they would send the jeep ahead to scout out the road before the other three vehicles would follow. They would slow the caravan down to no slower than only twenty miles an hour, even then.

Tom explained this all to the three travelers in his van as they bumped along. For their own part, they shared with Tom some of their own story, naturally leaving out all of the truly interesting parts, and what they hoped to find in Bloomington. In the end, the trip to Springfield was accomplished very rapidly, and they didn't see much of the city at all.

The caravan stopped at Chummy's garage there to get more fuel, thus conserving the fuel that they were carrying. They shared some conversation with the mechanics and drivers that were based out of Springfield, specifically looking for any information about anything of interest to the east. There wasn't anything more than what they had already learned, so after a quick hot meal, they bundled back into their vehicles and were driving again.

Having spent the preceding parts of their journey on horseback, Fides enjoyed the little effort required of him at this point. To think this could all have been on foot! Fides tried to remember the events that led to him being deposited so far away from his family so long ago. The details were fading. It bothered him that he could not remember his wife's face, or his children's. He could more easily remember the months of rehabilitation back in New Mexico. He was weak for so long, and the process to regain his strength had been so very painful to begin with that it was hard to forget. One other memory that remained vivid was the sight of Fermion tossing a ball of flame over his head. That was something.

The road got a little rougher after Springfield. Because of the radioactive destruction of St. Louis, they would not be able to use the direct route with the nicer highway. A smaller state road would have to do. Route 60 was their path to Cairo, Illinois, and it was bumpier by far then the interstate. That did not stop most of the passengers from falling asleep, though. In fact, it may have helped it. It had started to get dark, and as often happens on long trips, conversation had become exhausted, and people drifted first into their own thoughts, and then into their dreams.

Sometime in the late evening they stopped and switched drivers. Fides cracked his eyes open for the event, and remained awake long enough to observe them get started again, but was lulled back to sleep. Again, in the early morning, just before the sun was up, the caravan stopped again. Everyone crawled out of their vehicles to stretch out. It had been a long ride.

They were in an old park picnic area. There was a sign that said "Mark Twain National Forest" prompting Fides to ask aloud who Mark Twain was and Fermion to sigh and merely mutter something in return about Fides not reading when he had the chance. Perhaps everyone was a little grumpy. Compared to walking, it was obviously a much better alternative. Still, driving was revealing its own issues.

The sun fully came up while they walked around, stretching. Clearly, at one time, this park had been well maintained. It still maintained some of its former glory and beauty. After a short time, they realized that the old buildings had actually been commandeered as residences. Some of the people who lived there came out to greet them. These seemed to be somewhat simple, but nonetheless very good people.

A little later, they were joined by travelers who were on their way on foot to Springfield from Cairo. Some of these had come from Tennessee, and they were informed for the first time that Memphis had been one of the cities destroyed several years back in the nuclear attack. Chummy's men knew that already, of course, but it was the first that Fides and Fermion heard it.

"So, really," Fermion had observed, "Cairo is really the best way through the heart of the country."

Came the reply, "It's basically the only way."

That made Fermion quiet for a little while, but after a nice hot breakfast he returned to normal. Tasha had gone on a walk on the trails after breakfast. When she returned, they all jumped back into their vehicles. They said their farewells to the good people at the national forest's picnic area, and were off. They had hopes to be in Cairo before noon, and then in Bloomington by late evening, unless they decided to spend some time exploring Cairo, as none of them had ever been there and had heard it was an exciting place to be.

That was not to be, however.

== Chapter 7 ==

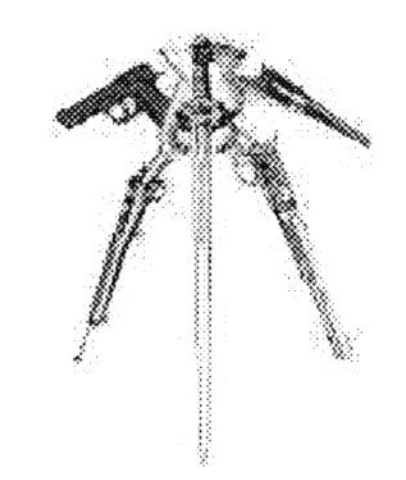

It seemed as though everything was going according to plan. Their ride since Springfield, Missouri, had been relatively swift, even if it had been bumpy. They made it all the way through to a town named Poplar Bluff without incident. However, about an hour's ride after Poplar Bluff, they were suddenly confronted with their advance vehicle, the jeep, coming back towards them at full speed, flashing it's headlights at them. The other three vehicles screeched to a halt right there in the middle of the road. The man arming the crossbow jumped out of the jeep and ran over to the window of Tom's van. Tom rolled down the window.

"What's going on?" Tom demanded to know.

"There is an army in front of us! It's the Pledge, for sure! It looks to be moving on Cairo, right now!" the man blurted out.

Tom swore. "Did they see you?"

"Absolutely. They've got a rear guard. It looks like they have a couple of vehicles in there, too, but I think we caught them pulling up their tents, and there are definitely too many to be carried in the number of vehicles we saw."

"Those vehicles are for dealing with people just like us, I bet. We'll have them on us soon. How many vehicles?" Tom pressed him.

"I saw about ten. Nothing armed, I think. Trucks and vans. They'll be able to move some people quickly, anyway."

"How many total?" Tom asked. The man's face had gone pale.

"I would say there are at least a thousand, but I don't know if I am a good judge. There is not less then a thousand, I'll tell you that," the man blurted out.

"Let's pull off the road. I think we can make it to those trees over there. It's an obvious place to look, but they won't know how far you've gone. Tell the others to follow me!" Tom pulled the van off the road and drove it towards the trees. Fortunately, there was a rise in the land, and he was able to park the van behind it. The other vehicles soon joined them. They were safe from observation from the east, but from the west they stuck out like a sore thumb. They shut off the engines and slunk up the little rise, keeping care to stay in the low bushes of the forest outcropping, so as to not be seen. Sure enough, they could hear engines in the distance, though they couldn't make out if they were moving towards them or not.

"Hearing that Cairo was the primary way through the country here I realized it had some obvious strategic advantage," Fermion said. "I bet that Cairo is not at all prepared for a Pledge waging war. The Pledge's time of diplomacy and verbal persuasion must be over. We must warn them."

At that, Chummy's men, normally nice and decent men, began to swear. Tom settled them down and spoke on their behalf, "We didn't agree to get caught in a fight with the Pledge army. We'd be willing to hide for a time, if it were possible, or maybe see if there are any other bridges across the Mississippi and try them, but we're not going to tangle with something like this. I think the guys are right to protest."

"Are there other bridges across the river?" Fermion asked.

"We've got a bunch of old maps. They've got the places where the roads used to cross the river. There aren't many, but there are some we could try, and we'd have to go around this group. Maybe on the other side of the river we could dash down and warn the city," Tom replied.

"Let's see that map," Fermion said. Tom had it right on hand and they all gathered around it as well as they could. It's not easy for fifteen people to surround a little piece of paper, but they all tried. They studied it for a time, talking about the various ways of dealing with the issue. The proposal that surfaced first as a possibility was to go back toward Poplar Bluff and pick up what appeared to be a small county road that went north a ways and then picked up a road that went east. They'd be able to take that around the Pledge army altogether, and rejoin the state highway ahead of them. This is what they had decided to do when King interrupted them.

"I went and listened to their engines. They haven't come any closer, but I'm sure that they have moved north. Do you think we are very close to this road here, going north?" King asked, pointing to a road on the map. Sure enough, there was between them and the Pledge army a road that went north and joined the road east that they were thinking of using to make their way around.

"So, they've got some maps, too. They have anticipated what we might do, and they are putting out a blocking party. I'd wager they've done the same thing south," Fermion mused.

"They probably don't expect us to go all the way around. They probably are thinking we'd try to find a way to cut across the countryside, off the road, to try to get around them. They might not go all the way north. And by the time we retreat that far and go around, I bet they are all well along," Tom suggested.

"We'll need to decide soon," Tasha said urgently.

"If I were them," Fides said hesitantly, "I would not rest until we were hunted down completely. It's obvious that we were on our way to Cairo. They'd know we'd want to warn them or get ahead of them. I bet we'll soon see some coming our way, and they'll follow us right around if they have to. We'd have to completely evade them, or make them think we've completely retreated, or something like that, or they'll relentlessly pursue us to keep us from spilling the beans."

"You might very well be right," Fermion said. "Quick, let's have a decision. Are you and your men willing to try going around to the north by taking this county road up from Poplar Bluff?"

Tom was getting ready to say that he was when it became too late to really do anything. The sounds of engines started getting louder and louder as Fermion was asking his question, and some of their group was making their way to the top of the rise during that time to see what there was to see. After no more than a moment or two, three pick-up trucks came into sight. In the back of each were a good half dozen men who appeared to be well armed, even if only armed with clubs.

"Well, we're out numbered by this lot, but not by much," King whispered. He had no reason to whisper, but it seemed like he should. "Maybe we should try to take them?"

Tom gasped, "We are not weaklings, but we are not soldiers, either."

"But if we did defeat them, that would give us time to get away," Fides replied. But a couple of the other men swore at them. What they didn't realize was that they were not quite as hidden as they thought they were and the pick-ups had suddenly veered off of the road heading in their direction.

"Well, this is a beast," Tom cursed.

"Well this is the moment, really. Retreat is not an option. We can either take them on right here on foot, or we can try to take them on in our vehicles," Fermion declared, taking out his sword. Fides took out his, as well. This was the first that their escorts had seen these weapons. The sight of them appeared to give Chummy's workers some nerve and the hesitancy went out of them. They made some fast decisions. The jeep-men got back into their vehicle and manned the crossbow. They left the fuel truck where it was, and the rest climbed into the vans. They peeled out of there and were only some fifty yards away from their hiding spot when the vehicles met.

They had decided as they climbed into the vans that they would not overly risk the vehicles, but they would make use of the fact that they were in closed vehicles while they were faced with pick-up trucks. Much to the surprise of the Pledge drivers, the vans did not slow down at all as the vehicles got closer. If anything, they sped up as though it were a game of chicken. Surprised, the trucks turned to get out of the way, sending some of the more eager soldiers, who had been leaning out ready to jump when all the vehicles came to a stop, tumbling out. They did not quickly get to their feet. But they were better off then those who remained in the trucks, because both vans managed to smash into the rear ends of the trucks as they turned away and it spun one of the trucks out, sending Pledge soldiers flying through the sky. Those men did not get up at all. The other truck had only been smashed in the back corner and kept going forward a little further. One poor man, if we can feel any pity on him at all knowing what kinds of things he had done, was badly injured at the impact and passed up and over the roof of the van as it passed by. They might have just kept driving back and forth crashing into trucks and soldiers except at least one of them had a gun. He stumbled out of the back of the truck that hadn't been hit at all, and got a shot off at the van that Tom was driving.

Tom nearly lost control of the vehicle at that point and had to slow it down to nearly a stop in order to regain control. In that time, the truck had pulled out to hem the van in. The gunman fired another shot at the van, which was now fully stopped, and things were looking pretty grim for a moment until the jeep zipped by. One of the steel arrows loaded into the crossbow zipped through the air and stuck the gunman dead. The jeep kept going, meaning to circle back around with another arrow loaded.

In the stunned moment where the gun lay on the ground, flung out as the man collapsed, everyone in the vicinity stood still. The shock wore off, however, as Fides flung the van door open and charged out, his sword high in the air. This produced it's own shock, which would have been very fleeting had Fermion not immediately followed. Fides, Fermion, Jonathan, Tom, and two of Chummy's workers named Neil and Patrick emptied out and charged towards the six men (one now quite dead) that had jumped out of the unscathed pickup truck.

The odds were much better now than they were only a few moments before. Instead of twenty-five to thirty against fifteen, it was closer to twenty, and of those, some were slow to collect their wits after being tossed off of their steeds. Already, though, a good ten of them were rushing towards the stopped van and for the gun, which was more than the Bloomington travelers had on the ground yet. The swords helped balance it out, though. Seeing that the fight had moved to the ground, the other van pulled up and stopped. Out poured Tasha, King, and four of Chummy's workers. Each group was getting a little bigger each moment. By the time the jeep swung back and unleashed another bolt, both sides were at full strength. Or, as full as they each were going to get, for at least five soldiers of the Pledge were laying on the ground after getting thrown from their respective vehicles. The incapacitation of the gunman helped even up the odds, too.

A brutal melee followed. Fermion and Fides stood in the middle of it all, slashing violently at their lesser armed opponents. Jonathan was nearby with the long knife he had cut his hands on in the battle against the Lighter Sioux, but he could not handle it well because his wounds were not yet healed. Instead, he tackled and wrestled people away from Fides' back, fulfilling, in some small way, his oath. Tasha and King were off on a flank doing quite well. Unfortunately, the gun had been successfully re-claimed by a member of the Pledge, and he had discharged it completely into the body of one of Chummy's men. Out of ammo, he was tackled and beaten to death by two of the fallen man's enraged friends. The tide was clearly turning fast in favor of the members of the caravan, when at last the five left standing retreated rapidly to one of the trucks before they could be stopped. They drove off towards Poplar Bluff.

The battle over, the travelers took a moment to catch their breath and tend to their own wounded. Except for Luke, their fallen friend, anyone else that was hurt only had relatively minor cuts and scratches. Tom confiscated the gun, and searched the body of the gunman for ammunition, and put it in his pocket. He was all business when he called them all to attention.

"Friends, we just can't go on ahead and face more of this. We have brought you fairly close to Cairo, and you should have better luck sneaking by that army on foot than we would with a vehicle. But if you want, you can have the jeep," Tom told Fermion and his friends. Fermion waited a respectful moment before answering, because they were placing the body of their friend, Luke, into one of the vans. But part of the pause had to do with Fermion's calculation that a jeep that was designed to hold four probably wouldn't be a comfortable ride for five.

"Let us put a little distance between the army and ourselves," Fermion suggested. "Let's all go back to Poplar Bluff. There were lot's of abandoned homes there that we can find shelter in for the night if need be. But at least we can find a warm place to talk." Tom was fine with that, so they climbed back into their respective vehicles and drove back to the fuel truck. Two men jumped into the fuel truck, and they started their short drive back to Poplar Bluff.

They were moving at a pretty fast speed in order to get further away from the Pledge when Fides tugged at Fermion's sleeves. "That truck. It didn't go back to the Pledge army. It went back towards Poplar Bluff."

Fermion's mouth dropped open, "Fides, you're right. That must mean-"

But he didn't get the words out. What it plainly meant was that the pick-up truck had a reason to go towards Poplar Bluff. At that moment they rounded a bend and saw in the open area ahead of them thousands and thousands of men marching in their direction. The truck that had scurried in that direction had parked near some other vehicles but both sides appeared to be just as surprised to see the other. They saw two men jump on top of one of the vehicles, and Fides blurted out, "I think there is a gun on top of that strange truck!"

The first rounds were already coming towards them. Loud popping noises and puffs of smoke made it clear that they were being fired upon, but what really made it evident was the big hole that opened up in the windshield.

"Dammit!" Tom exclaimed, trying to turn the vehicle around as quickly as possible without tipping it over. The other vehicles in their caravan were also trying to turn around at high speed. For a moment they were in as much danger from rolling over or hitting each other as they were from bullets from a machine gun. Everyone braced themselves inside the vehicles as the inertia from the turn pulled at them. At last they were all turned around and headed in the opposite direction. They were on their way back towards what they thought had been the Pledge army but which they now knew to be only the advance elements of the real army. Fides looked out of the back windows as they drove away.

"If there are a thousand men ahead of us," Fides exclaimed, "There are ten thousand men behind us!"

"Our only hope is to break through the forward guard's lines and get to Cairo as soon as we can," Fermion declared from the passenger seat.

"Break through the line? What on earth are you talking about?" shouted Tom. Tom was no coward, but he was no idiot, either.

"Pull over. Over there! Take that dirt road into the trees," instructed Fermion. It wasn't a dirt road, exactly. It was an old over-run driveway. The house set inside the trees was run-down and uninhabitable. Once they were stopped everyone jumped out.

"Neil is dead!" wailed someone from King and Tasha's van. They were pulling out the body of a young man who had been caught in the path of one of the bullets. The young man named Patrick was weeping.

"We have no time to give him a proper burial," Fermion said firmly but compassionately. "Listen to me. We need to park the truck and the jeep here behind this house, back in the woods. We can try to find an appropriate place to leave your friend's body while we do that. But then we need to get into this van and we need to drive as fast as we possibly can toward Cairo. The enemy in front of us is not likely to know about what has happened to their friends yet, so we'll have the element of surprise. We'll drive through their camp at fifty miles an hour, and if they move, they move. If they don't, they're dead."

Tom scratched his head. "But aren't they likely to have guns, too?"

"They surely might, but they aren't likely to have them trained back behind them. It's risky, but we can be sure that the main army is going to be coming to look for us, and if we don't hurry, they'll get a message through to the forward guard for sure. We're trapped. We can go back in the direction where our presence is known and even expected, or we can go ahead where we are not known or expected. And there are less men. We must do it now-right now!" Fermion argued.

"Alright, it's settled. Patrick, get a grip. Take Steve and find a place for Luke and Neil's body. Chris and Manny, go park the jeep and the truck back there in the trees. We'll try to get back to it sometime. Then hurry back! Five minutes! Go!" ordered Tom.

And in five minutes everything was indeed done. They climbed into the vans and pulled onto the road just as they saw behind them the truck and the armed vehicle coming in their direction.

"Step on it!" shouted Fermion. And Tom did.

They were soon up to sixty miles an hour, sometimes more when the road would allow it. The vehicles chasing them were traveling fast, too, but clearly not trying to over take them. After only a few minutes, they were at the point where their jeep had first spotted the forward elements. "Keep the foot on the gas," Fermion said. "No matter what happens."

Tom floored it. As they crested the slight hill concealing the camp, they saw before them a horde of individuals armed with clubs and spears. Sure enough, initially the soldiers thought nothing of the vans hurtling towards them. By the time that they figured out that these were not their own vehicles, the vans were already within the camp. They charged right through the camp with Tasha and King's van right behind them. Amazingly, most of the Pledge warriors were able to jump out of the way. Those that got hit were only grazed. This, of course, would have still been quite painful and even life threatening, but at least no human served as a speed bump that day.

It took less than sixty seconds to emerge on the other side of the camp but it felt like twenty minutes. Fides looked back through the windows as they fled the army and saw that the armed vehicle and the truck that had been chasing them had stopped in the camp. He informed Fermion and Tom of this reality, and Fermion grunted something about hoping that this did not mean there was yet another element of the Pledge army ahead of them.

It turns out that there was, in fact, an army ahead of them. But it was not the Army of the Pledge.

The five travelers to Bloomington and their escorts, now slightly diminished in number, were celebrating as they careened towards Cairo just as fast as they could. There were high-fives and also a bit of nervous shaking all around. Even Fermion abandoned his normal serious demeanor to smile as accolades were heaped on him for providing the winning plan. In the rear van, there was just as much relief, but obviously they could not applaud Fermion in person. For this reason, the reaction there was more subdued as Chummy's men considered their losses, too. It helped everyone that the roads had greatly improved.

They had only just passed the intersection of I-55, where Route 60 turns into I-57, when they caught sight of something that made them bring their vehicles to a screeching halt. It will take some explaining to convey what it was that they saw. In short, stretched for a good thousand yards, both to the north and to the south, was a line of cavalry men and soldiers. There were ranks upon ranks of men and beasts stretching back as far as they eye could see from ground level. If they could have seen it from on high, they would have seen that it was forty men deep, loosely packed, and then a break, followed by another twenty men lined up in reserves. To each side, behind the front ranks, was a large bank of men and horse. All told, there appeared before them a massive army numbering close to ten thousand.

Though this was a stunning thing to encounter after having only just recently escaped the clutches of another army, there was much about this one that was unique. It looked as though it were a scene from a Revolutionary War battlefield, or an old European one, perhaps. There were flags and banners waving all up and down the line, and they were waving even now as units communicated with each other. The men were not dressed like modern military men, but not quite like what one might expect from medieval soldiers, either. Many of them had a silvery-looking, but obviously thin, armor on their bodies, and even on the war horses. Crests of different colors were overlaid over the silvery armor, clearly indicating different units.

There was a large gap right in the middle of the army, right along the middle of the road, which is why they had not spotted the army in front of them as they raced up the road. The earthworks of the old highway system had concealed the army from their sight. Into that gap now rode about forty men on stout horses. They spread out into the gap, and five of them trotted a little further forward from the others and appeared to be waiting for the occupants of the van to come forward.

"I don't know who these are," Tom said slowly, "but they ain't no Pledge." He opened up his door and got out, his hands up and palms facing the army. Everyone else followed suit, except for Fermion and Tasha, who did not raise their hands. The travelers looked at each other, and Tom said, "Well, let's go. Fermion, you do the talking!"

The twelve of them walked slowly towards the center emissaries. As they drew closer, they were able to make out the details of the army facing them a little bit better. There were several ranks of archers that they could see that some of the horsemen had lances, though most had long broadswords. In the third and fourth rows there looked to be men armed only with sticks and clubs. These looked nervous and even somewhat timid.

As Fides came even closer, he saw that those with swords, horses, and bows were some of the most beautiful people he'd ever seen. They had a timeless look about them, just as Fermion did. By comparison, the men armed with sticks and clubs looked like frail shadows, and Fides quickly realized that the Beautiful people were likely to be Fermion's sort, while the frail shadows were people just like him. "Do I look that dismal?" Fides thought to himself.

He didn't have much time to ponder that question because as they were now within thirty feet of the five emissaries riding out to meet them, he now turned his attention to them. If he had thought that some of the men to his left and right were awe-inspiring, these five, and the thirty or so behind them, were overwhelmingly so. Their armor seemed to shimmer like waves on a silver pond, and the colors of their crests were vivid, almost unworldly. They had helmets but they did not cover their faces. Though they too were covered in the strange armor, these warriors had been colored in darker tones.

The five dismounted as they finally came within speaking distance. Now it became evident that there were not only men in this army, but also women. One of the emissaries was a woman of profound beauty. Now aware of the possibility of women in the army, Fides noticed that on both sides there were several other women, as well. Fides had little time to reflect on that, though, because the tall man spoke.

"Your weapons, if you please," he said. Tom and his men flashed weak smiles, because they really didn't have all that much to show. The men threw forward their thick clubs that they were accustomed to traveling with and Tom at last remembered he had a gun, which he threw at their feet. Jonathan gently tossed his long knife ahead of him. King produced the two parts of his staff (it had broken over the head of one of the Pledge soldiers). Tasha threw her dagger into the middle of the road, and it twinkled in the light as though it was studded with diamonds though, of course, no diamonds could be seen on it. Fermion turned toward her in surprise.

"That is a fine weapon you have been carrying all this time," Fermion said to her, moving his cloak aside and pulling out his own magnificent sword. He nodded towards Fides to pull his own weapon out, and the two of them placed their swords next to the broken staff, the dagger, and Jonathan's short sword. Fermion looked at Tasha out of the corner of his eye and muttered, not disrespectfully, "Fine craftsmanship. Only seen a few like it." Tasha only smiled slyly.

"My Lord," gasped one of the emissaries, addressing the tall man, "I believe those three weapons are from my own stores." The emissary was pointing at Fermion's, Fides', and Tasha's weapons.

"Interesting. We'll have to hear the story of how they have acquired them," the taller man said. This man turned his attention to the people, now. "Are you with the Pledge?" he demanded to know.

"The Pledge are our sworn enemy, my Lord," Fermion said, bowing slightly. "In fact, we have only just escaped their armies. They are coming now to Cairo with a force that will at least match what you have here. We have fought with some of them and lost some friends, but we are here now and will fight alongside of you if you will grant us the honor."

The beautiful woman now spoke, "A force to match what we have here? Our scouts tell us their force is much smaller than ours."

"Indeed, my Lady. We know the force that you speak of," Fermion replied. "At first, we thought that was the extent of their army as well, but when we were trying to retreat and hopefully get around them so that we could warn the city of Cairo, we fell against a much larger force just coming into the city called Poplar Bluff. That force alone has as many soldiers as I see here. I should add, too, that they have guns as weapons- I don't know how many- and I see that you have no guns nor armor that could repel bullets. They fired a machine gun that sent a round through the side of the van over there and killed one of our comrades. The first army must only be a forward element, perhaps a probe, or perhaps even something meant ultimately for diversionary purposes."

The tall man's demeanor soured slightly, "This requires new consultation, if it be true. But how to know if you are speaking the truth and not just a scouting party for the forward element? I believe we might be able to find out the answer to that question depending on the quality of your account of how you came to possess these weapons. They, at least, are not what we expect to see in the Pledge." They heard suddenly the sound of hooves coming in their direction. The tall man saw them, and before they arrived nodded to Fermion, "These are my advanced scouts finally returning to report. Tell me, truthfully, can we expect an attack by the force that you consider the 'forward element' today, as we expect?"

Fermion did not miss a beat, but said, "No. Though the forward element has a handful of vehicles, they have no horses to ride and appeared to be traveling mainly on foot. They are at least twenty miles from us, and still encamped. They might march double-time though, and try to attack you in the morning if they know you are here. But if they have no idea of your presence, I submit to you that you won't see them until the morning of the day after tomorrow."

"Alright, it is not much- after all, if you were the Pledge we'd expect you to know perhaps that much- but it is something. Let us see," the noble man replied, beckoning for his scouts who had finally arrived but had waited patiently for Fermion to finish. "Well, you heard him. What do you say?"

"Sir, he is quite right. We have heard from our forward scouts through the signal flags that the army has only now begun to pull up their tents and make their way towards us, and at no great speed. We appear to have arrived with plenty of time to spare," the man said.

"And an army behind the army?" the tall man inquired further.

"Sir?"

"You weren't here for that. Right. This one says that beyond the army that we know about is another army that is our match in size, and has guns as arms. Do you know anything about that?"

The man's face, though as profoundly other-worldly as some of the others around them, went pale white. "Sir? No, sir. We know of no such force. I will signal ahead and dispatch some of our best men to find out. How much further behind?"

The tall man nodded towards Fermion, who replied, "Not more than five or ten miles, my Lord. It was very near Poplar Bluff when we encountered it and that was not more than forty-five minutes ago."

"Such advantages one has when they have mechanical vehicles," the tall man said. "Well, you may be a Pledge spy, but if so, not a very bright one to tell us such information. I will hear your story and decide your fate." He turned to a person on his left who had not yet spoken. "Apparently we do not fight, today. Dismiss the ranks but put out a large guard."

"Yes sir," the man replied and promptly left to give out the orders. The flash of flags giving out the signal all along the ranks was a sight to see. You have not seen such silent precision wrapped in choreographed dance. The movement of so many people could not be done completely silently, though. The sound of men moving to obey the orders, and horses neighing, and armor clinking was wonderful in its own right. Meanwhile, the tall man motioned to the captives to come with him. He wanted to hear a story.

The soldiers slowly disassembled as they followed the tall man and his men (and women) to the rear of the lines. Off to the right side, behind a hill, lay a huge tent city. To the left side, further back, was another tent city, and it was in that direction that the poorly armed men that they had previously observed went to, though not of course, alone. Even as they were all returning to their tents, a good five hundred noble looking archers and swordsmen on horseback trotted out in the direction of the Pledge armies to serve as a watch, and if necessary, an obstacle if the Pledge army did in fact try to march on them soon. Fides gathered that this number would have been smaller had they not been informed of the second army behind the first.

After a long walk, more or less in silence, they arrived in the center of the tent city. There, a very large meeting tent was waiting for them. Maps of the entire region, from Illinois to Kentucky to Missouri to Tennessee to Arkansas, were erected on the inside of the walls of the tent. A large table in the middle of the tent had even more maps laid out on it. It was clearly a war room. They heard their vans being driven up somewhere out of their sight. It was about this time that the man given the orders to disperse the army arrived at the tent. Fides and his friends waited for whatever was next. The swords and Tasha's dagger were placed on the table. The tall man gave an order, and chairs were brought in for the guests to sit in.

Fermion, however, remained standing. The tall man gave a gesture to Fermion, who said, "The story that I have to tell cannot be told in its entirety for reasons I hope my Lord will allow me to keep private. However, I shall tell you what I can here in public, but perhaps I could share more in private."

"We'll see if that is warranted. Please tell your 'public' story," the man answered him.

"Many years ago now, I volunteered for and was dispatched on a very important mission by my own Lord. As part of that mission, I worked with a group of people protecting a very valuable treasure, the worth of which surpasses all anyone might imagine. It is a treasure one might sell everything to obtain. It cannot be measured in any currency now in existence on this planet. Part of my mission was to help secure that treasure, and in the course of that business, my friend here- Fides- was sent as a construction worker to help. In the course of events, the man who possessed the sole key to access the treasure became nervous with rumors of the times. It was after the Disease had been unleashed, but before it had arrived in our parts. So, he took Fides as a ransom, and me as a mediator, and he used an airplane to carry us all the way to New Mexico. I suspect that he has now fled south into Mexico. However, those entrusted to protect the treasure had access to many weapons even though we were few in number. I chose these two swords from what was available, knowing that they might be of use for us. When we arrived in New Mexico, it was not without any weapon.

"However, Fides was struck immediately with the Disease even as we got off the plane. Knowing nobody in the area, I found finally a good and decent man in the town, who possessed a deep good, and a willingness to risk all for that good, who agreed to care for Fides until he was either well, or dead. At great personal risk, to his own being and that of his wife's, he cared for Fides. I remained in the area, roaming to and fro, and received word on occasion of Fides' health. I eventually learned that he had indeed survived the illness, so I awaited his inevitable journey home. Fate was with us as we found each other in a tavern near my home. Fides showed great courage in defending me against bent men. Since then, we have been journeying together towards Bloomington, Illinois, where we hear that there is a repository of information to help families reunite.

"Though I have no family of my own, Fides does. He left his family to work on the project I was associated with, and it was on the very same night that this country was attacked by nuclear weapons that we landed in New Mexico. The only machinery that has worked since, as you well know, are purely mechanical devices that do not rely on electronics. Fortunately, we were not affected by the atmospheric event that caused that, since we were already on the ground. Nonetheless, we could not fly back.

"Along the way, we were escorted to see the president of Oklahoma City, also on account of these weapons, and it was there that we met King and Tasha, who also had fled the Disease at one time and had become welcome in the Cherokee community. King apparently is in a similar position, having family in the Illinois region. They sought leave to join us in our journey, and we welcomed them. They have helped us both against rebel Indians that wish to reclaim the country they believe- with reason- was robbed of them many centuries ago, and then again against Pledge scouts. This man, Jonathan, was saved from death by Fides, and now in gratitude travels with us in order to repay his debt. I should say that these men over here are hired men who have agreed to drive us to Bloomington. Hired or not, they have shown great bravery in helping to defeat the Pledge scouts, and of all of us it is they that have endured the burden of cost, having lost two of their friends in the ordeal."

The tall man spoke again. "That is a fine tale, filled with courage and honor. These are themes we well appreciate. It explains how you came to possess these swords, but not how they came to be accessible to you in the first place. Also, as you indicate that this Tasha only more recently joined you, it does not account for her dagger."

"I cannot speak to that, my Lord," Fermion replied. The tall man nodded towards Tasha.

"My Lord, I am afraid there is no interesting story behind my acquisition of this fine weapon. I found it many years ago, in the woods. I considered it at the time a gift from God, and hope it may yet be returned to me," Tasha said.

"Found it in the woods, eh? Well, Nagro, how do these stories sound to you?" the tall man asked the one who had made a claim to them earlier.

"These blades have a curious look about them that would be more at home back in the light of my own homeland. I know of no one from our party that brought them, so I cannot say that they must belong to me. I only argue that they are not of this land. I believe there are some among our party that might know the lore behind them, though I don't, myself," Nagro replied.

"Oh, so they are not really yours?" the tall man replied.

"Well... I think they are, but they don't seem the same, either. I am certain at least that they did come from my land," Nagro returned.

"And yet this is the public story," the tall man pondered. "There is more to tell, is there? Still, you seem sincere, and genuine. Frankly put, you are just the sort of men and women I'd expect with such weapons, and I am inclined to trust you and believe you, and even to admit you into our army with high rank. What say you?" the tall man asked his friends.

The woman replied first. "I do believe that I'd want to still hear what he has to say in private before bestowing such honors. And, I am thinking that I would want the counsel of Gongral and Dolam first. I am thinking we will want it anyway in light of the news of a coming larger army."

Nagro agreed, "I, too, would like to hear the more private words, and I also would like to submit these weapons to the examination of Falda and Leredo. Like Henryetta, I think that counsel is required at any rate in light of the changing facts on the ground." The tall man accepted these words, and turned his attention back to Fermion.

"How small of a party is required to ensure that the privacy you desire is maintained?" he asked Fermion.

Fermion replied, "It is no insult to my friends who have agreed to take us to Bloomington, but I would only want Fides, Jonathan, Tasha, and King to be allowed to hear the other things I might say. Of your own party, I see that there are five of you that govern this army, and that you seek counsel only from an additional four. So, I would be comfortable speaking with my friends and you and your counselors- just the fourteen of us, then."

"Let it be so," the tall man said. "We will go to the tent of Falda and Leredo. Henryetta, please go and ask Gongral and Dolam to meet us there in an hour. Let us in the meantime provide a meal for these men, both for this one..."

"Fermion, my Lord," Fermion said, offering his name for the first time.

"For Fermion, and for his friends and those hired to escort them," the tall man said. "You will have my name in an hour." At this, guards were set around the tent and food was brought to them, but the tall man and his counselors and those with them left. They ate in relative silence because there was plenty to listen to, anyway.

There was singing coming up from some of the nearby tents. It was beautiful and melodic. There were rich harmonies and not a single voice out of key. Every voice was superb, and the timbre of the whole was such that despite there obviously being many, many voices, it sounded as though there were only one person singing the different parts. And they were singing:

One breath is all it takes
One mighty breath to come
and makes the stone arms move
and gives the shadow form
It lives, it lives, it lives, he lives.

It was a lovely song to listen to, but also militant; like a romance where the lover's coming is thwarted by a foe and must be overcome before the lover can at last arrive. Fermion leaned forward and said to Fides, "Now, that is a song worth hearing." Fides couldn't agree more, but he did not want to spoil it all by talking, so he kept eating. Tom and his co-workers also listened, and were soothed by it.

After a little while, glorious looking people arrived to escort them. The men of Tulsa were left behind. They were taken to the tent of Falda and Leredo, while their hired escorts were taken to tents that had been vacated so that they might rest. Their weapons- the swords, the dagger, and the gun- were brought with them.

The tent of Falda and Leredo was something to behold. It was brightly colored, and looked like a wigwam. From the top of it there spun out wisps of smoke. Not smoke as from a fire, but smoke as from pipes. Indeed, pipe smell was what greeted them as they entered the tent.

One man was saying to another as they came in, "I do say, Falda, that you were quite right. There are things worth smoking here, after all. This is fine, fine indeed, oh!" he exclaimed, for he had just noticed that company had arrived. Seated around the circular tent were the five that they had already seen, and in the middle, opposite the entrance, were four very odd looking people.

Fides could not help but stare as they were directed to sit down. The one apparently named Falda was dressed in a long white robe. He had long, grey hair coming down both from his hair and his chin. Around his neck was a thick necklace of gold. In his hands, however, was a pipe and a flint for lighting it. The other man sitting next to Falda greatly resembled Falda, except he wore a long black robe but no jewelry. He was puffing on his pipe and staring at Fides who in return was staring at him. At that man's side was an older woman. Dressed in a dark forest green, she seemed stern, but friendly. She declined the offer of the pipe that was handed to her. At the side of the Falda was a young looking man. He was not wearing a robe, but rather garments made from very nice looking leather. He was wearing a vest made of the same silvery material Fides had noticed that much of the army was wearing.

The five that Fides had already met were also seated close by. The tall man sat next to the man adorned in leather and silver.

The one called Henryetta was next to him, and next to her was a very proud looking man. He looked absolutely regal. On the other side was the one that had been ordered to dismiss the troops. Next to him was the one they had heard was named Nagro. All of them were stunningly handsome, or beautiful, if either word could really convey the profound depth of pristine appearance that they possessed. Even the three older people in the middle were wearing robes cut from marvelous cloth. Every eye had a light in it that Fides had seen only on occasion in his life's experience. These days he saw that light mainly in his friends Fermion, Tasha, and King, though Corrie and Dietrich had had it too. Fides wondered if his eyes had such a twinkle, or if they were dim like so many other eyes he had seen recently.

The tall man began his introductions. "Starting from where Fermion is, are people you have already met. That is Peder, Henryetta, and my name is Yuri, Yuri Ryson. Next to me here is Leredo, and next to him is Falda. Helping him to cloud up our meeting with their incessant smoking is Dolam," Falda and Dolam's eye's twinkled at the rebuke. "Next to Dolam is Gongral. Leredo, Falda, Dolam, and Gongral are our most trusted advisors. Next to Gongral is Calvin, our master-at-arms. And finally, Nagro, whom I shall add is so valiant that though he deserved to rule this lot, and really ought to do so even now, has deferred leadership to me. I am not worthy to lead them. Indeed, even when I come to those who are my own it will not be mine to lead them."

"We call ourselves the Shadowmen, and we ask that we be spoken of by that name, too," Yuri added. Fides thought that this was a very strange thing for these people to call themselves or be called. They were not shadowy, at all. They were vibrant, brilliant, and shiny. It was as if their outlines against reality were better defined. Their figures starkly contrasted against the background they moved against. This 'background' was reality as Fides thought he knew it. At any rate, however much their name didn't match their obvious nature, what they chose to be called was their own prerogative.

Yuri spoke now to his friends and counselors, "Next to Peder is a man named Fermion. As I understand it, this is his friend, Fides. These are the two in possession of the fine swords. Then Jonathan, the faithful friend. Then it is Tasha, who had the dagger. Finally, King."

"Nagro tells me that he thinks the weapons came from our land. May I see them?" Falda asked. Peder handed all of them over to Falda for inspection. Falda and Leredo looked at each weapon very carefully, with a hint of recognition, and some gasps, and some appropriate expressions of appreciation of the quality of the craftsmanship. At last Falda delivered his verdict, "If they are from our land, they look different than they ought. They do not seem to belong here, either, so I suspect there really is more to them then we can see. Still, I do not think we can lay claim to them in any way. We should return them, I think, to their apparent owners." Peder took the weapons and handed them back to them.

"Now then," Yuri said, "Let us hear what you wanted to say in private."

Fermion appeared to be brimming with a desire to share his secret. "I am of the Nephilim," he declared. "I have been tasked to protect a treasure that surpasses all worldly estimation. It is important that I escort my friend, Fides, to Bloomington. He must find his family, but then he must go with me so that I can accomplish my task. He possesses the only key."

Fides had grown so used to the odd necklace around his neck, and kept it hidden so discreetly, that he had forgotten it. But under Fermion's direction, he brought it out from under his shirt. This was of interest to his three friends, who had not known about it, but of very little interest to the counsel, who were more interested in Fermion's `Nephilim' declaration.

"What is this... `Nephilim' ... you speak of?" Dolam said aloud.

"I have not heard this term before," Peder said.

"Nor I," Nagro said. Around the circle it went, with no one having heard the term before, except Fides, of course. It must be admitted that Fermion had also seen the wonderful appearance of these people and he had assumed it possible, if not probable, that they too were of the Nephilim. Clearly, Fermion thought he was speaking to his own kind.

His disappointment was displayed on his face when finally someone said, "I think I have heard of the Nephilim." It was Yuri, and he had a very reflective look on his face. "But I must confess that I do not know very much about them. But I have heard of them, from my readings." Fermion's face now brightened considerably.

"Fides," Fermion said quickly, "Show us your book." Fides had not had much time to read from Corrie's book in all this time but had not quite forgotten it. Mainly he noticed it only long enough to move it around his pack to make room for other things that had become more important to him as time had gone on. He slid the book out, and handed it to Fermion, who handed it to Yuri. "Did you read about the Nephilim in a book like this, my Lord?"

"Yes, I believe I did. I am surprised this book exists. I had heard they had all been destroyed many decades ago now. Even so, I don't recall much about the Nephilim in it," Yuri said, thumbing his fingers through the book. "This Bible was much loved at one time." At that, Fides felt a little ashamed, because it was not his love that Yuri was detecting, and though he thought it would not matter at all to him, for some reason it did, anyway. Fermion had determined that he had miscalculated the situation and tried to make some sort of connection with these beings that he perceived belonged to this reality as much- or as little- as he did.

"Suffice it to say that I am not of this world, my Lord," Fermion said. "But I have been studying this world from its beginning, in preparation for this day, and my duty in it. I have been sent to do the task set before me and then to do good as I have opportunity, besides. I have but a few orders given to me from my own Lord, and I must do them in the order of priority and importance. I confess, then, that though I would desire to join you in your army, my duty first is to see that the treasure is protected, and then to move on to my next task."

"I wonder," Yuri pondered, "if we do not in fact serve the same Lord."

"If so," Fermion offered carefully, "it might follow that neither are you from this world." By this time, Fides, Tasha, and King were all well out of the realm of possibly understanding what the talk was about. To some degree, though, the rest of the group did not seem at all confused by the course of the conversation. Fermion thought a little longer, and said, "But if you are not from this world, neither apparently are you of the Nephilim, as you are not aware of the term..." The question of where the Shadowmen were from was allowed to hang like one of Falda or Dolam's smoke rings.

"You are right, of course, in some ways. We are not of the Nephilim, but I am not so sure it can be said we are not from this world. We have our own tasks given to us, but we are not permitted to speak of them with others, and I am afraid- I mean you no insult- that I do not think we are permitted to speak with them to you, even though I am certain we are in the same army," Yuri explained.

"I certainly understand," Fermion replied.

"For my part, I believe every word he has said," Nagro said. Peder concurred, and in turn everyone did as well. If anyone appeared to have any doubt, it was King, who was shaking his head in bemused confusion.

"If it pleases you, sir, I ask leave to go on with my friends. I hope you might also give us back the vans and our escorts. We will go and warn Cairo of the impending battle, and then go to Bloomington, where I will fulfill my oaths, and then I may return to you- or we may all return to you- for I know that there is much warfare to follow for a long time still," Fermion suggested.

"We have already warned Cairo. Indeed, you probably saw many of their men in our ranks. We have been accumulating noble men as we can. We purposely determined ourselves to resist the Pledge and those like them and learned not too long ago of their plans for Cairo. The men of Cairo have joined us on the battlefield to await the coming battle," Yuri informed Fermion.

Nagro spoke up, here, "Join us this evening for food and fellowship, friends. And then in the morning, my vote is that we see you on your way. If you wait too long, the battle will be upon us, so we need to get you gone while you still can. That is my vote." There were nods of affirmation from the rest of the counsel.

"Let it be so," Yuri commanded. "Our counsel has much to talk about. We believe you, and believe that our scouts will confirm what you have said about the greater army coming. If you will pardon us, we still need to have considerations. Please ask the guard outside- his name is Redemptus- to take you to some tents where you can receive refreshment. Then, join us for dinner and fellowship."

Fermion hesitated. "My Lord," he said, "I am very concerned that you are not prepared to deal with the weapons that the Pledge have."

"You mean guns, I suppose?" Yuri asked, not overtly concerned.

"Yes. The days of lining up in ranks, as impressive and formidable as it seems, ended a long time ago. Perhaps they could return in some situations if the extent of the lethality of the guns employed were more limited. However, we encountered a machine gun that sent rounds clear through the panels of our van and killed a man. If they have enough ammunition, they will be able to kill all of you, especially with you grouped so nicely together." Fermion seemed uncomfortable to have to share this news with them. It was almost as though he was disappointed that he even needed to.

"We believe our armor is sufficient to stop a bullet from a gun," Nagro informed Fermion. At this, there was a collective gasp from Fermion and his companions.

"It is lovely to look at," Fides blurted out, "But you can't believe it can stop a bullet round?"

"Here is a gun," Yuri said. "How about a demonstration?" At this Nagro stood up and invited Fermion to shoot him in the armor but Fermion adamantly resisted, and his friends with him. Finally, they agreed to the demonstration, but only if Nagro's silvery armor was placed over a wooden beam. Everyone exited the tent together and someone quickly procured a large wooden beam and placed Nagro's armor over it.

Fermion took the gun that had been previously owned by a Pledge scout but more lately handled by Tom. He carefully aimed the weapon, which was not by any means the most powerful handgun in existence, and fired. The armor, impressively, did not let the bullet pass. At first Nagro beamed at the success of the armor, but when Fermion had to dig the armor and bullet out of the wood where it had become embedded a look of concern came over all of the beautiful faces.

"The weapons, or at least one of them, that are coming to you are much more powerful then this one," Fermion said, showing the indentation in the wood. "I admit, I am amazed that your armor kept the bullet from going through. It is a remarkable thing. Yet, I do not think you need only be concerned with keeping it from going through, if you see what I mean."

There was a cloud of dark contemplation that hung over them all as they absorbed this demonstration. At last, Yuri told them that, given this new information, they may want to speak with them some more. Fermion of course said he'd be available, and they were at last dismissed into the hands of a certain Redemptus.

== Chapter 8 ==

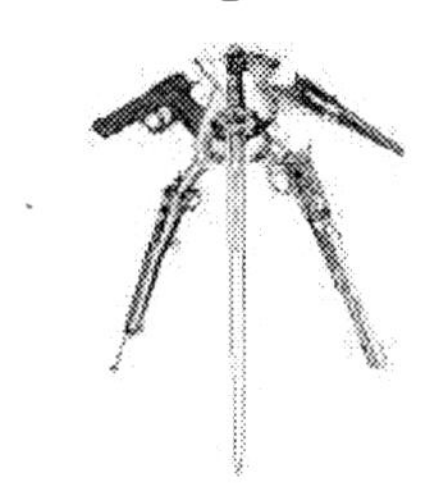

They were led through the camp by a young man in a thick, black, hooded coat. They only had a sense that it was a young man by the build and a passing glimpse at his face. This was Redemptus, apparently, and he took them to a large tent that was to be their's for the time being. Redemptus pulled back the large flap to allow them to enter and told them that someone would be along to refresh them. Fides was last into the tent. He turned to say thank you to Redemptus and happened to see all of the man's face. Everyone else Fides had seen who were not men of Cairo were gorgeous human specimens. Redemptus, on the other hand, was hideous. There was no disfigurement or anything of that sort. It was simple ugliness, framed by blond hair, yet the same light that he saw twinkling in the eyes of the glorified-people he saw in the eyes of Redemptus. Fides was visibly startled, but the man did not notice, for the man had already turned and departed. Thoughtful, Fides entered the room to find his comrades reclining on light sofas, eating from a table that had dried fruits and other snacks on it. A conversation was already well under way.

"I always thought you were holding out on us with something, Fermion," King was saying. "But to learn that it was something that no one has ever heard of, anyway, I have to say… well, I don't really know what to say. What is the Nephilim?" Fermion was munching on nuts he had found on the snack table. He seemed to take little notice of the somewhat annoyed attitude that King had adopted. When Fermion didn't say anything, King rounded on Fides, "What about you? Did you know he was a Nephilim? And are you one, as well?"

"Yes, actually I did," Fides admitted. "But I am definitely not of the Nephilim."

"Well, then, can you tell us what it means to be `of the Nephilim?'" King insisted. Tasha and Jonathan were observing the conversation, obviously interested, but appropriately distanced.

"Well, I wish I could. Other then knowing that the Nephilim are not to be trifled with, I can't say much more. Well, there are some things I could add, but it seems to me like Fermion ought to answer them, not I. To tell you the truth, I am mainly in the dark on the matter," Fides confessed.

Fermion spoke at last, "Fides, bring out your book." Fides produced Corries's ancient Bible, which Fermion took from him. He waved it at King. "Do you know what a Bible is?"

"I have heard of Bibles. I know my father was interested in them at one time. Obviously, I've never seen one before," King said.

"Did your father ever teach you anything about what the main message of this book is, or anything else about it?" pressed Fermion, tossing the book back to Fides.

"No, not that I can recall. I don't recall much about my father anyway. I was much younger, then," King explained.

"Well, as I have been trying to explain to Fides for many months, now, it will be very hard to understand what the Nephilim is without taking the time to at least acquaint oneself with this book's contents," Fermion said, tossing the book into King's lap. "Can you read?"

"Tasha taught me how to read a little, but mainly just sounding out words so we could read the old signs we saw," King replied. Fides thumbed through the pages as the conversation progressed.

Fermion turned his attention to Tasha, "So, can you read?" Tasha nodded. "Can you teach him more, so he can read this book?" Fermion asked.

Before Tasha could answer, King objected. "Now, wait just a minute. First of all, I'm sure there were some very good reasons for destroying this book. I think it likely that it must mean everything in it is all rot, for one thing. Second of all, that is a huge book. When am I going to read it even if I could read?"

Fermion sighed deeply. "Perhaps you do think it rot. Assume it is, even. I assure you, unless you at least have some knowledge of the contents of that book, what I have to say will be simply unbelievable. I wish it could be otherwise, but it isn't. But, ok. Let me ask all of you a question, and perhaps we can give you a hint. What do you think will happen to you when you die?"

The question hung in the air as the other four people sized it up in their own ways. The question was not congruent with the times they lived in. A question as esoteric as this one didn't belong, it seemed, in a world where hour by hour living was dangerous and risky. Deep philosophy was alien. On the other hand, was it really? Living by the seat of your pants from moment to moment, constantly fighting for survival, surely invites one to ask what the point of survival is, and why death is to be avoided. So, the question was not in fact such a foreign invader into the world of hard knocks, after all. Indeed, considering the question at all might be a true mark of distinction between men and animals. Nonetheless, it was obvious that at least some in the room had never really thought about it before. Perhaps they'd just never had the leisure time to consider it.

Fides had paused in his skimming of the book in a section titled "Jeremiah." He read: "'I know the plans I have for you,' declares the Lord, 'plans to prosper you and not to harm you, plans to give you hope and a future.'" Fides suddenly felt that everything would work out. He'd make it home. His family would be well and healthy, and would welcome them. But the pause from Fermion's question was still lingering.

Finally, Jonathan offered an answer, "I suppose that there are only a few basic options. The obvious one would be simply that we cease to exist, and our body returns to dirt. But the other option is that one of the old superstitions is right, and we will continue to exist in some form or another. Given how many of the superstitions speak of heaven for those who do right and hell for those who do wrong, I'd say the odds are good that perhaps there is a reason for that, and that goes right along with the belief in an afterlife, too."

"Well summarized," Fermion said. "And the Bible obviously has its own views, and a more particular set of positions on the matter. Pretend for a moment that the Bible is right about what it says. Do you know enough to know what the Bible says about the afterlife?"

Fides piped up, "Well, eternal life in heaven for those who do good, and eternal life in hell for those who don't. I know that much."

"You forget faith, Fides. And grace," Fermion said. "But that's good enough for now. Keep that in your mind, and assume, if you will, that something like that is truly the reality. Have you any thoughts about what a person might do with eternity?"

There was again a hanging silence, and Jonathan, still pensive, ventured, "That is a very interesting question. I suppose I had always imagined one simply sat in a massive church on a much softer pew, and instead of listening to a preacher, one gazed upon God. That was the impression I always had growing up, and I must confess that it never seemed all that appealing to me. I never really took it seriously, because to tell you the truth, it was hard to imagine how a heaven like that was any different then hell." At that, Tasha made a snorting noise, but said nothing. Instead, Fermion clapped his hands and smiled. Confused, Jonathan continued, "I suppose from what you are trying to get at, that you think that heaven is something different, something more than that?"

Fermion laughed heartily, "Indeed I am! Absolutely!"

"This is all well and good," King interjected, "but it still helps little in understanding what you mean when you think you are a Nephilim. Although it makes me wonder if you are not a little nutty."

"Well, now we are really getting into areas where you would have to acquaint yourself with the material in that book," Fermion countered. "I am not going to throw my pearls to pigs."

"There is no reason to be insulting," Fides chastised Fermion, who only sighed again.

"Alright," Jonathan mused aloud, "let me see if I understand the basic premise of your hinting."

"Go ahead," Fermion invited.

"You claim to know what is on the other side of death, and what we do with eternity. In other words, you are saying you are some sort of eternal being," Jonathan offered.

"Sure. Although I had a beginning, I'll have no end. But you've got the gist."

"Ok, for what purpose have you come to us, then?" Jonathan inquired further.

"You heard me explain it to those people," Fermion said. "I am here to do my master's bidding. I have several objectives, and then my time is done. And no, I won't tell you more of that purpose than I've already revealed," he added, anticipating Jonathan's next question.

"Hogwash!" King exclaimed.

"I wish it was," Fides said quietly. Fides then went on to tell them the story of how he had first met Fermion, and the amazing phenomena he had witnessed. When the tale was over, King was ready with his next challenge.

"I insist on a demonstration," King argued.

"I am afraid it is not as simple as that, my friend," Fermion cautioned him.

"So, you can't reproduce it? It was merely a miraculous event, and we will have to simply believe you and Fides?" Jonathan continued the inquisition.

"I'll say this about it, and no more for now. A man may disbelieve another man when he claims that he can deploy a nuclear weapon, but we would not want too many demonstrations before we gave in and believed it. And the man with such a weapon might be mature enough to know he does not parade his arsenal merely because others doubt it, if only because for that reason it is perceived as weakness in that man, as though another's cynicism is enough to force him to do what he knows ought not be done at that time," Fermion explained.

"I wish I understood a word of that," King sighed.

"I get it," Jonathan said.

"I do too," Fides added. "But you are leaving out a lot, aren't you?"

"Yes, I am. I have already shared with you more than I thought you could conceptualize, and I admit, you have got on admirably. To go further would be foolhardy. The rest of you will have to simply decide whether or not I look like a lunatic to you, or if I have a habit of lying, or else, failing these, perhaps it is reasonable to believe that I am telling the truth," Fermion concluded.

Satisfied for the time being with the scant morsels of explanation that had been tossed to them, Fides asked Fermion, "So now what?"

"Well, I admit I am perplexed. I know who you are. I know who the Nephilim are. But these people around us are neither the Nephilim, or of your own world- I am sure of it. But for the life of me, I don't know who they are!" Fermion slapped his knee and laughed, "Boy, let me just say that He likes to throw curve balls when He gets the chance! But to not know the power of Adam's guns? To think a sheet of silver would be enough? Who are these noble, but foolish people?"

"Is it important to know the answer to that?" Tasha inquired.

"No, you're right, Tasha. It is none of my business," Fermion agreed. "I have my orders. They have theirs. My orders are not their business, and their orders are not mine. I know what I need to know, and what I need to know concerns getting that necklace around Fides' neck to Peoria, Illinois, just as fast as I can."

Just then the tent flap was pulled aside, and Redemptus thrust his head through the opening. Now everyone had a glimpse of the man's wholly unattractive features, and they were each as taken aback as Fides had been. The man pointed towards Fermion, "Your services are desired, sir." Fermion tossed the Bible back into King's lap and followed Redemptus out of the tent.

"Well, I'll say I don't buy this whole Nephilim business, but Fermion strikes me as the most honorable man I've ever met," Jonathan said, once Fermion was well out of earshot.

"I think he might say the same about you because of your pledge to me," Fides said.

"If you would have seen the way you fought the night you saved my life, you'd understand why I'd sooner think you were from a different world than I would Fermion. On the other hand, you didn't have flames burst out of your hands," Jonathan replied. "I'm not sure I believe you on that, my friend, but I have made my vow, and even if it's to a lunatic, I'll keep it," he winked.

"Go on!" Fides exclaimed, chucking a dried chunk of some fruit at Jonathan, who laughed as he evaded the toss. At that moment they could hear singing again from somewhere in the camp:

The old stick bears a leaf
The rock bigger than the biggest can move
Is in my pocket and the
Sword is in its sheath.

Though they did not know what this meant, it was sung with such passion and lucidity that they could feel what it meant. Something stirred in each of them that none of them had ever noticed before. It's a bit like how after a lot of physical labor muscles you didn't know you had, or forgot you had, ache and proclaim their existence. That was what this song did to them, but what it was that was stirred in them was unknown to them.

As the verse was ending, Fermion came into the tent, and they forgot about the song. In fact, the singing abruptly ended right about then, and they could hear trumpets and horns immediately followed by the sounds of the camp awakened into action.

"What's going on?" Tasha asked.

"They asked me for my counsel, and I gave it to them," Fermion replied.

"What was your counsel?" Fides wondered.

"I told them that they're going to get a lot of people killed with their camp out in the open like this, for one. Secondly, I told them that they need to consider guerilla warfare rather than their current approach. Thirdly, I implored them to respect the power of the weaponry they are facing, and fourthly, they should deploy immediately and not delay."

"From the sounds of the camp," Jonathan said, "They have certainly moved on the fourth suggestion."

"Yes. Though they did not think guerilla warfare was a very honorable way to fight, they saw the wisdom of it. They were giving out the orders even as I was on my way back. By the way, our weapons are outside the door. King, they have given you a new staff. Jonathan, if you like, they have offered a sword from their stores. I suspect Tasha is content with her weapon." Fermion was rattling this off while pushing them out the door. "Our escorts have already been led to the vans, and we are to go to them, now, and be on our way."

"But what about the feast?" King asked.

"No feasting tonight. They are going to fall back towards Cairo to some positions that might give them a chance to hold the city, even against a few heavy machine guns if they play it right." Fermion was walking quickly, and they all struggled to keep up.

At last they had arrived at the vans, where Tom and the rest were ready to go. They had been given spiked clubs instead of the plain ones that they had before, as well as some smaller, hand-held crossbows.

"Good to see you guys," Tom said, shaking Fides' hand.

"Hope you've been well fed?" Fermion asked him.

"Absolutely. Crazy crew, these ones. But good food," Tom said, shaking his head in amusement.

"Well, let's get going. When I told them that in theory they could have those machine guns here in under an hour, I think I put the fear of God into them, and to tell you the truth, I put the fear of God into myself, because I'd nearly lost sight of that reality, myself," Fermion explained. With that, they climbed into the vans, and threaded their way through the camp as it was breaking up and pulling back and towards the woods. Finally, they were back out on the old freeway and destined for Cairo, Illinois.

The ride to Cairo was pretty straightforward. There were no diversions, or incidents, or events. Most of them seemed to have plenty on their mind, however. Fides pondered the fact that a mighty army was on its way to his very location. Standing in its way was another mighty army that was filled with odd, yet wonderful, people. He was on his way to Bloomington, hopefully to find his wife and children. This hope had been strengthened when he came across a passage in Corrie's book, though he didn't know if he should really trust it. Nonetheless, the idea that 'God' wanted to 'prosper' him gave him a certain comfort. Against all this was a key of some sort around his neck, apparently unlocking a bunker. That bunker had been built by another group of odd people. Fides felt the necklace around his neck with his fingers and wondered what was ahead for him.

Others were thinking deep thoughts, as well. Everyone, that is, except Fermion, who had a funny smile on his face and was humming a tune that Fides was quite sure had been heard while they were in the camp. They were rolling into Cairo as the sun set behind them. As they turned to go over the bridge into town, they saw the signs referring to Fort Defiance, but little could be seen as they drove past where it was supposed to be.

They were not challenged by anyone to gain entrance into the town. It was pretty desolate, in fact. Until they reached the downtown area, they were not sure that there was even anyone in the town at all. But once they pulled their vans to a stop, they saw people walking the streets in the dusky light. There were older men, and women, and children. Obviously, the fighting men were west and that explained their absence from the town's population. Fides and company quickly gathered a crowd around them. Working vehicles were pretty rare things to see in these days. However, everyone knew what was brewing to the west, so beyond the novelty of the vehicles, many of the inhabitants wanted news. The local bars soon heard about their arrival and people were soon peeking out the windows and even coming out to see what could be seen.

They quickly learned that it had been no more than a week earlier that the Shadowmen had come and set up camp south of the city and sent in a delegation to meet the leaders of the city. This was the first time that the people of Cairo had learned that they faced any kind of threat at all, though obviously rumors about the Pledge had been around for some time. Indeed, some of their own people had joined the Pledge. It took some convincing, but the Shadowmen were very persuasive and very earnest. Once persuaded, the men had assembled and journeyed west in order to defend the city. When King asked why they had no defense set up at the city itself, the people only shrugged and said that if the Pledge arrived at their city it meant that their men had been killed and they saw little reason to live on if those they loved were killed. After all, they added, they were all too young, too old, or too weak to fight, anyway. Fides later told Fermion that this was the most disheartening thing he'd heard up until that point. It was enough to convince them that Cairo would be no more than a temporary residence. It was too depressing.

There was a serious problem standing in the way of moving on, however: Fuel. These old vans got very poor mileage, and despite the fact that they had very large gas tanks, there was little point in denying that taking the vans all the way to Bloomington without their fuel truck with them was simply not possible. They regretted not bringing the fuel truck along, but Fermion pointed out that the presence of the fuel truck probably would have encouraged the Pledge to keep pursuing them. It was determined that there might possibly be enough gas in the tanks for the escorts to get back to their fuel truck. Obviously, though, if they wanted to do that there was a significant obstacle standing in their way. That is, there was the ten thousand men in the Pledge army.

The situation was not positive, then. There wasn't enough gasoline to go on, the city they were in was undefended, indefensible, and demoralized, and they couldn't get back to their fuel truck right then if they wanted to, anyway. This made Tom and his friends quite a bit annoyed, but as they couldn't do much about it at the moment, they left all decisions un-made and sought and found lodging for the night. Cairo was a peninsula, and in the old days there were bridges coming in from all directions, but now there appeared to be only two to the south. The one they'd have preferred, the one bleeding into I-57, was out, as they had discovered earlier.

Fides went for a walk through the abandoned streets that night. The stars sparkled brilliantly over his head. The stillness of the night was deceptively out of place, for he knew that there was danger all around and bloodshed was just around the corner. He could hear the sound of rushing water, which he followed. At last, the banks of the Ohio River were in sight in the dark. Off the road there was an old wayside park of some sort where there were some benches. He sat on one of them and watched the water move under the star light.

The sound of a gentle breeze rustling the tree leaves and the rumbling river were the only sounds to break into his thoughts. His wife and children were chief on his mind as water rolled by. He had been months on the road in an attempt to bridge the years apart from them. His heart burned as he realized he could not recall in his mind what any of them looked like anymore. Though he could remember flashes of the old times, where his family's faces were there were now just the pleasant emotions that he recalled when he remembered them individually. He desperately hoped that he would recognize them when he saw them, and he felt a sense of shame, as though his lack of recollection was some sort of sign that his love for them had failed. He rebuked himself even as he entertained the thought. If his love had failed he would not be making the journey home right now. Against his self-recriminations he also set the comforting words of a certain 'Jeremiah.'

How much time passed, he did not know, but at last he felt physically spent, as though he had been weeping. He hadn't been, actually, but that was how he felt. He stood up to walk back to the inn that they had found lodging in. As he found the road, a voice broke into the silence. It was Tasha.

"Hello, Fides," she said, gently.

"Tasha, so you are out as well?" Fides replied in kind.

"The sound of rushing water is like music in my ears. Each river has its own sound. I wanted to listen to the song of this river while I had the chance," she explained. She came along side Fides, and took his hand. "It is very honorable for you to be making this journey back to your family."

"I wonder how you knew I was thinking of them."

"What else would you have to think about? It would be them, or the danger at our backs," she said. They walked together in silence for a time. "What are you thinking about, now?" she asked.

Fides laughed, embarrassed. "I was actually thinking how long it has been since I've held hands with a woman. I had forgotten how pleasant it is."

"Well, I'm much too old for you, Fides," she said sternly, though he knew in the dark she was smiling.

"My dear, I'm taken already, so don't get your hopes up about a younger man," Fides grinned in return.

"Fides unfaithful? I couldn't believe such an absurd thing," she returned. Their inn was in sight now, in the distance, lit up by a single globe by the door. "Fides, I want to tell you something."

"Go ahead, Tasha."

"Neither you or King know what you'll find in Bloomington. I pray for both of you that you find your families alive and well. I truly do. I mean that. You are looking for, among other things, a son. And King is looking for, among other things, a father. You can each be that for each other right now," she said. There was a pleading note in her voice.

"But what about my real family?" Fides said.

"Love has the capacity to include infinite people within it without replacing any one of them. You need each other right now, I know it. I trust that when you find what is to be found in Bloomington, even if you both find your families and great joy, there will still be room enough for each other as friends into the future. And why not? That is very nearly what you have the makings of right now, isn't it?" Tasha was winding up her exhortation as they drew near at last to the door to the inn. "Consider it," she said as they went in.

"I will," Fides replied. They each went to their respective rooms and to their own thoughts, but sleep came upon both before too long.

They were awakened by Jonathan, shaking them each in turn and saying, "Come quick! There is action to the south! Fermion is on the roof to see and insists that you come as soon as you are able." By the time that Fides made it onto the roof, everyone else was already there. Fides had brought his sword instinctively, but of course there was little use for it on the roof. On the south facing edge of the flat roof of the two story inn, they could see down to the road to the bridge they had crossed the night before. The people looked like tiny stick figures from this distance. They couldn't see the bridge itself because the road bent away into a narrow forest.

"Look!" Fermion was pointing. At that moment, too, Fides realized he was hearing gunfire cracking in the distance. Down the road they could see men dressed in dark brown and green clothes, appearing a little like soldiers. They were firing around the corners of buildings, and others were lying down. All were firing at men in white or grey cloaks who were posturing across from them beyond a clearing. The men in robes controlled the road to the bridge, but that was all. Both sides had guns, but from the sounds of the battle it was clear that each side only had old hunting rifles and shotguns, not full blown military gear. "I don't know what those men in dark colors are all about, but I have a sneaking suspicion about the white-cloaked men!"

"Who do you think they are?" King asked.

"A long time ago there was a vicious organization devoted to establishing a so-called pure white race in America. They were dealt some hefty political blows, and pushed underground. I hadn't seen anything about them in my studies of the last century. I could be wrong, but if it is them, then by all means, we side with the men in darker colors," Fermion declared.

Tom and a few of his men had joined them on the roof. "What are we going to do?" Tom asked.

"I think we need to find out what is going on, exactly. This is a very important strategic point. Cairo is at the nexus of the north and south right now. Cities both south and north of any size apparently were destroyed in a nuclear blast. Whether or not there are other bridges to get across these rivers, I don't know, but in any case, we know about this one. We would not want this city to fall into enemy hands if we could help it," Fermion explained.

"Isn't your business north?" Tom inquired nervously, looking for a reason to be moving along.

"Indeed it is, but also I am to do good as I have opportunity. If I can stand in the way of evil or stand up for the innocent, I should. If I fall, I am convinced my master has someone ready to carry out the rest of my orders. And my orders include doing good as I have opportunity. Who is with me?" Fermion asked.

"I am with you, absolutely," Tasha declared.

"What are your intentions?" King asked.

"Right now, only to find out the situation in more detail," Fermion explained.

"I think I can certainly go that far," King replied. Fides also indicated that he would go, too, and so of course Jonathan said he was bound to go.

"No offense, fellahs, but we didn't sign on to fight in any wars. We'll stay up here and see how you do. We hope you return, and we can discuss future arrangements if you do. If we don't see you soon, though, we'll decide based on our own preferences," Tom said.

"I don't suppose it has occurred to you that you can only run from the inevitable so long?" Fermion grunted. They were turning to go down the steps when they heard bugles and trumpets off in the distance to the south-west. "Ho! What's this?"

Because of the layout of the land, and the distance that they were at, they couldn't see anything. Nonetheless, they could hear the loud, cacophonous sound of the heavy machine gun that they had heard yesterday (although much closer). Soon, they felt like they could discern several others, too. "I bet anything that Cairo's Shadowmen have arrived again, with the Pledge at its back. Quite the confluence of powers! Let's go find out what is going on!" With that, Fermion was bounding down the stairs into the inn and out the door. Everyone except for Tom and his men were right behind him. Quickly, Fermion and Fides put on their black cloaks and hung their swords at their sides. The other three laid hands on their own weapons as they found their way to the street. Tom called out a 'good luck' for them from the roof, where he was still watching. Their escorts lingered around the vans, clearly thinking that they'd like to be anywhere right then but Cairo.

They trotted south at a jog, staying close to the buildings along main street. After about a ten minute run, they were well within sight of the outskirts of the town, but still not with any hope of truly seeing what was going on. They could see some of the brown and green clothed men lying prone. Their weapons pointed south, and occasional puffs of smoke could be seen and cracking sounds could be heard as the men acquired targets, and fired.

"There!" King shouted, pointing to some towers on a levee. They ran quickly to the top of the levee, and then up the stairs to the tower. When they got to the windowed room, they found it was already occupied.

"You there, stop right there!" a big burly man shouted, surprised, but not so surprised as to not keep his gun leveled in their direction. "Identify yourself!"

"My name is Fermion. I think we are allies!" Fermion hastily explained.

"We have few allies, so I wonder about that," another man snapped at them.

"Who are you fighting, then?" Fermion probed.

The burly man replied, "They call themselves the Copperheads."

"That is a distantly familiar name," Fermion answered. "What do they stand for?"

"They want to make a new country out of the southern states, ruled only by white people," a third man replied.

"Another old power rises to fill up the void," Fermion sighed. "Yes, we are certainly opposed to such people," he told them. "We are also violent enemies of the Pledge, not merely their organization, but their ideology. Not only that, but we oppose also the Indian nations who wish to re-conquer the continent. As far as I know, there are no other groups to ally with or oppose, though I confess that thirty minutes ago I did not know about these 'Copperheads.' If what you say about them is true, we certainly stand against them," Fermion patiently explained.

"Well, you've got all the right enemies, then," the burly man said. "What do you say, Emory?"

"Well, they clearly started out on this side of the skirmish, and he's saying the right things, so let's give them the benefit of the doubt," Emory said. Emory and the other man, whom they learned in short order was named Perry, lowered their weapons and began looking out one of the tower windows again.

"One Simus," the third man said, introducing himself.

"Pleased to meet you. So, what do we have here?" Fermion inquired, gesturing to the skirmish playing out below them.

"We've got about two hundred and fifty men, all armed. The Copperheads number about a thousand. We think they only have as many guns as we do, though. It's hard to say what the situation is," Perry explained.

"Ok, but why are you here?" Fermion pressed him.

"We've come to Cairo to reach what they are calling the Shadowmen. The Copperheads have been racing us the whole way. We lost contact with them a day ago, and apparently they crossed the river somehow. They came up the southern bridge, but we made it across the other bridge that comes across there just ahead of them." Perry continued, "The Copperheads basically want to do what some of the Indian tribes want to do. Too bad we can't just let them fight it out amongst each other!" he said.

"We have spent time with the Shadowmen," Fides offered.

"That's true. Do you wish to join them in their fight against the Pledge?" Fermion asked.

The three men glanced at each other. Emory answered, "You could say that. But no offense to you all, but I have no reason yet to trust you more than to leave it at that. It is important that we find them before the Pledge finds them."

"Do you hear those horns?" Fermion asked.

"Sure do," Perry replied, gruffly. "Can't figure out what the blazes that's all about, either."

"Worse than the horns is that other sound we hear," Simus said. "We're quite confident that we can hear heavy machine gunfire in that direction."

"Those horns are the Shadowmen and the heavy machine gunfire is the Pledge," Jonathan explained.

Fermion very hastily explained to the three that they had spent some time running from the Pledge on their way to Bloomington and in doing so, had run into the lines of the Shadowmen. The three listened to this with interest, and not a little concern.

"We can't hold those bridges against heavy machine gunfire," Perry muttered. "We can't even hold them against the Copperheads."

"They are about to get squeezed," Fermion pointed out. "The Shadowmen have a good ten thousand people. They don't have guns but they do have bows and arrows and a lot of brave men. They're coming for Cairo because they know they've got to hold it or the Pledge will be able to control one of the primary north-south gateways. If the Copperheads are in between you and them, they are in for a nasty surprise."

"That may be. But we were just getting across our bridge when they started shooting at us from the ruins of Fort Defiance. It looks like we managed to both arrive here at about the same time. Down that road are a thousand men, many of them armed. I think if anyone is going to get squeezed, it's going to be the Shadowmen. It won't take many snipers to pin down that bridge long enough for the machine guns to come and finish them off," Emory said.

"For future reference, does your force have a name?" Fermion asked.

"They call us the Rangers, and we take the name gladly. We're just a large group of average Americans whose folks never gave up their guns. Now we only wish we had better than hunting rifles. We have been pestering both the Copperheads and the Pledge for a decent while now, but we can see things are coming to a head. We have been trying to rally people to us as much as possible, but except for a handful here or there, people are reluctant to take a side," Emory lamented.

"Apathy sucks," Simus growled.

"They'll be roused of it soon enough if the Pledge gets its way, but it will be a long time to throw off the burden placed on them," Fermion said. "But take heart! Your immediate concern are the Copperheads, and if we can, we want to make sure it's they that gets sandwiched and not the Shadowmen."

"It's the Shadowmen we are here to find anyway, so I guess you're right. I guess our only choice is to try to make the effort to push them back across the bridge," Perry said, looking eager to go after them.

"Think of it this way," Fermion pointed out, "if you're engaging their whole force, perhaps they won't even notice the army sweeping in behind them."

"That's a fat chance, but it's worth the effort. Simus," Emory instructed, "Go pass the word. Let's send forty men out into that open area to the west and try to flank them. Let everyone else know that once I give the cue, we're going to do an aggressive push. Tell them that the Shadowmen need us to draw the Copperheads away from the bridge. We're going to threaten them so much that they bring to bear all that they got, and then when I give the cue, we're all going to retreat into the city to try to suck the Copperheads in even further. Go!"

That was the plan, but things went a little differently. The flanking maneuver and the rush south towards the bridge succeeded in pulling up more of their foe, but not as expected. As it turned out, the Copperheads had been grouping for a rush of their own. When suddenly the Rangers opened up on their flanks and they saw two hundred men crazily charging into them, they were caught completely by surprise. Indeed, dozens were dead in the first volley. One of these was one of their leaders, so rather than a feint with a deliberate retreat, the Rangers routed. The Copperheads' glaring advantage was numbers: their glaring weakness was the lack of weapons for all. Now without a leader, many of the lightly armed Copperheads looked to protect their own skins, and retreated. As they fell backwards before the advancing Rangers, the Rangers felt obligated to pursue them.

Meanwhile, the sounds of trumpets and horns had grown a little louder. The machine gun, too, had gotten louder. Perry and Emory's men were running down the road towards the old Fort, firing as they went. The men dispatched to snipe from the flank had sprinted ahead over some open land and passed the large mass of Copperheads. They sniped the retreating men as they passed from left to right in front of them, and though the trees absorbed a great deal of the lead fired by them, many were killed or wounded. They were just too exposed.

At last, the Copperhead lines managed to reform and those with weapons had hunkered down and were firing on their pursuers. They were still some distance from Fort Defiance, which was at the tip of the peninsula. They were right near the mouth of the bridge that crossed the Ohio River to the east that the Rangers had first crossed coming into Cairo. From this line, a blistering defense was established, and the Rangers began to hunker down themselves in the woods and in the ditches along the road.

Throughout all of this, Fides and the rest had kept pace with the Rangers, but of course they did not have guns, and could not get too far ahead. They had remained close by Simus, who seemed to be a superb military commander. They hid behind some thick tree trunks while Simus issued commands to the men around him. Even Emory and Perry appeared to defer to him on the battlefield, proper. Everyone was panting heavily as they caught their breaths. It had been a one mile sprint.

After thirty minutes of exchanging light gun fire, they heard trumpets again. This time, the horns rang clear and close. They thought they could hear a low rumble. The Copperheads all suddenly jumped up out of their positions and began running for the eastern bridge.

"No doubt, the Shadowmen have arrived," Fermion declared. The grey cloaked warriors were beating a hasty retreat to the east even as they spoke, and the Rangers were looking at each other in confusion.

"Well," Perry said, "let's go meet'em."

== Chapter 9 ==

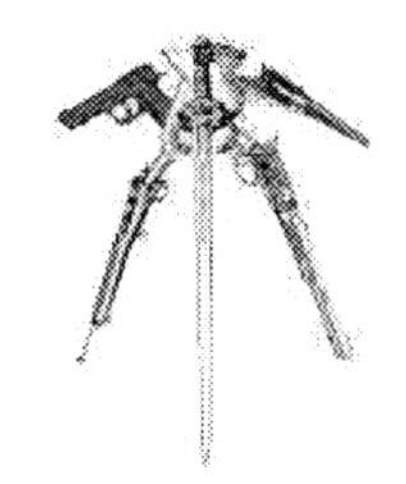

The Rangers slowly followed the initiative of their leaders, cautiously approaching the spearhead of the Shadowmen's force. That spearhead consisted of five hundred horsemen that had bounded across the bridge, many of which were hauling store wagons behind them. These were dumping out dozens of men from within them and turning back around and heading across the bridge. But two hundred very fearsome looking riders remained, and were glaring ominously at the approaching Rangers. In the background, they could hear more trumpets and horns and the staccato heavy machine gun. The riders formed a line. Behind them, four or five hundred soldiers were getting their bearings. They had apparently had quite a ride and had been jostled thoroughly. Fides calculated that the store wagons were on their way back to get another load of men. From where he was at he could see even more wagons coming across the bridge towards them, and alongside them, men jogging.

While this was going on, four riders formed up in the middle of the line of cavalrymen and trotted out in their direction. Fides thought they looked like kings. To his surprise, on further examination they were each only slightly taller than an average boy. Clearly, though, were men. Stout men. They each had a man's look in their eyes and were clearly among the Shadowmen, for all of the Shadowmen seem to have a royal air about them. The four closed the distance in good time and greeted the Rangers walking out to meet them.

"Hail! Friend or foe?" called out one of the ones in the middle.

"Friend, and at your service, sir," Emory shouted out to them as they drew even closer. Now they were within normal speaking range. Perry and Emory stepped forward. "You must be among the Shadowmen, and we have come to bring a message to your leaders, and help you in your struggles to the best of our abilities," Emory continued.

"We will see that you at least see Nagro, and if your message is worthy, he will decide and refer you to Yuri Ryson, our leader," the stocky prince said. "Right now, we are all in great danger. The Pledge is tied up just a little ways from here with some of our archers, but we expect them to get here with significant fire power. I trust you hear the machine gun."

"Yes, we do. How can we be of service?" Emory replied.

"My recommendation would be for you to get away from here as soon as you are able. We do not have the capability to resist their weaponry. Already many men have been killed and wounded," he said solemnly. "We have killed only a few the enemy in return. Nonetheless, we have been on the march since last night in hopes of getting here in time to properly account for that demonic gun. We have had to make up the difference by ferrying our foot soldiers in our supply wagons. It is a very dire situation," the man explained.

"I assure you that we don't consider machine guns to be weak weapons," Perry interjected, "but as you can tell, we all have guns. I bet our range is better then the range of your archers, and I bet we can teach the Pledge a lesson in respect!"

"They have guns, Dor!" one called out to their spokesman.

"Heavens," Dor exclaimed, "and you are willing to fight with us?"

"Without being asked," Perry declared.

"Dor," another of the four said, "All we need is something to keep their guns at bay long enough for us to get our people together and across the bridge."

"Agreed, Thamson. Tell me, friend, who were those men in grey cloaks we saw as we came across the bridge? I don't know who was more surprised to see each other, us or them," Dor asked.

"Those are the Copperheads," Emory answered. The four only returned dumb expressions, so Emory added, simply, "Enemies."

"That much we could tell. How many men can you spare?" the one called Dor wondered.

"We can send you one hundred men, each of them with their own rifles. It should be enough to send a nasty surprise to the Pledge. We need the rest to make sure the Copperheads don't try to come back across this other bridge," Emory said.

"More than generous." Dor turned to one of his fellows that hadn't spoken yet, "Greene, get us fifteen to twenty wagons over here immediately to get these marksmen across the bridge. Yuri will know what to do with them."

At the same time Dor was issuing his order, Perry and Emory had turned around and were barking orders to their own men. Simus had immediately been brought forward and was already selecting some of the squads that were to go forward. The hundred men or so that were selected began walking towards the bridge. Greene had turned his mount around and thundered back to the line, which parted for him. Some others from the line peeled off on Greene's command and they were now sending empty wagons back to pick up the Rangers. The amount of people from the Shadowmen's army that had been ferried across numbered a thousand now. Many of these had begun moving towards Fort Defiance. Fort Defiance was the remains of an old fortress that was situated near the bridge. Those that had arrived there had sat down in exhaustion to wait the next move.

Dor turned his attention back to Emory and Perry, "What are you called by?"

"We are called the Rangers," Emory replied. "I'm Emory, and this is my friend Perry."

"It would seem that our meeting is timed perfectly to help each other," Dor said. "I don't think that either Nagro or Yuri will be over soon. They will want to make sure everyone else is across first. In light of that, we should make some arrangements between you and me about any preparations we think we should make."

"Can you tell us what kind of forces the Pledge is bringing?" Emory inquired.

"They have three large vehicles that are each mounted with heavy machine guns. They have four more vehicles that are loaded with men with rifles such as you have. It is embarrassing, but this force of no more than forty or fifty has managed to rout our army of ten thousand. We have good information that behind these is an army of ten to twelve thousand, mainly on foot," Dor informed them.

"I'm pretty sure we don't have twelve thousand rounds," Perry said to Emory.

"I think that is a safe assessment," Emory sadly agreed.

"If we could get their cursed machine guns silenced, we have more then enough manpower and courage to take them hand to hand!" blurted out Thamson.

"By my measure, you have about two hundred riflemen," Dor observed. "That may be just what we need to do just that."

Fides bravely interrupted the conversation, "If the goal is to keep the bridge, shouldn't you want to deploy your guns mostly on the other side, and hold that? Otherwise, won't it end up simply with each side holding one side of the bridge?"

"Right you are," Dor said. "But even that is better than how things are looking now. I am afraid our plans have been thoroughly dashed. If it weren't for some men who shared with us the true extent of the enemy's weaponry, I suppose we would have been all cut down in the open some miles west of here."

"I believe that we were those men," Fermion said. Dor studied them.

"Yes, you do fit their description. Thank you very much. If only we'd have known sooner. Many are wounded, and some fine friends are dead." There was a deep sadness in Dor's eyes. "You were right- our armor does wonders at keeping the rounds from going through, but it's not as though the rounds bounce. We have been on the march since an hour after you left," he recounted. "Not knowing what the enemy's intentions were, we thought it wise to retreat as quickly as possible. And oh the grumbling!"

"How was I to know?" said one of the three.

"Blessed, I certainly don't mean only you," Dor back-pedaled. "The men of Cairo were especially unhappy. First to learn the rumor that they faced heavy machine guns and then to learn that after trotting them out all that way to meet the threat we were going to triple-time it back? If I were them, I'd be upset, too."

"Plans?" Tasha reminded them of their need for action.

"Wisdom, there," Thamson said.

Emory suggested a plan which was immediately accepted. Of the Rangers that remained behind, they would divide the one hundred and forty men (ten had been killed or wounded in the skirmish against the Copperheads) into two parts. The larger of the two parts would set up in firing positions on the bridge to the south, which the Shadowmen and Pledge were racing to. The smaller of the two parts would keep the Copperheads from re-crossing the other bridge, which they had made their escape over. Meanwhile, the Shadowmen that had already made it over the south bridge would assemble their army again in the wide open floodplain that was south of Cairo, near the bridge itself. The Rangers would cover the retreat of the remaining Shadowmen and their own men who would soon be crossing back to Cairo. When Yuri or Nagro finally came over, they would decide what to do from there.

At this, all the parties separated to carry out the plan. Fermion, Fides, Jonathan, King, and Tasha made their way back to the inn to see if Tom had remained or fled. While they conversed together on their way back, they heard the Ranger's rifles cracking in the distance and a sudden silencing of the machine guns, but it was only temporary. Meanwhile, too, the number of soldiers that had made it across the bridge had gotten very close to four thousand. Many of these were men of Cairo, and they were walking back to their city. There were dozens and dozens of wounded being helped back, as well. On seeing the wounded, Tasha left them and began tending to people as she was able.

The walk back to the inn was pleasant enough. They could see that the vans were still there, and that was a great comfort. Tom saw them coming from the top of the roof and came down to greet them. There was amiable conversation. Fermion brought them up to date about events at the bridge. After doing so, and once they had settled in inside the inn's kitchen for a quick meal, Fermion shared with Tom a conclusion that they had reached while walking back to them. Before Tasha had gone to help the wounded, they discussed releasing Tom and his men from their agreement. Sharing this decision with Tom elicited a relieved expression on his face. Though Tom and his men hadn't known what they would do if they were free to do anything, they had been leaning towards returning home. There was no gasoline ahead of them, Tom explained, and perhaps none behind them, either, but if they were going to have to walk, they may as well start out closer to home. It was hard to hold it against them for feeling that way, so they didn't. Still, nothing fundamentally changed since the Pledge blocked the way home.

After settling matters with Tom and replenishing their stores, they said their goodbyes to Tom and his men. They'd see about returning if the situation changed, but to that point, it was understood that Fermion and the rest were on their own. The town had come to life in that last hour. The men of Cairo had come home, many of them wounded or with the wounded. Some of their families were out looking for them or tending to them or mourning for them. Some of the Shadowmen were also in the city. These were on horses and were clearly sizing up the town's defensive infrastructure.

They arrived near the levee where the Copperheads and the Rangers had first squared off, and found that the whole area had been turned into a hospital of sorts. There were at least two hundred men lying on the ground being tended to. Tasha was in the thick of it all. Fides noticed some other women, too. These were about his age, or perhaps a little younger. He kicked himself when he acknowledged in his head that he found them to be quite attractive. Most of the women he had seen on his journey had aged more than they ought to have on account of the circumstances all were facing. These women hadn't- perhaps they were locals. Fides was confident that they were not of the Shadowmen, either. He looked away from them, though, guilty to be thinking about such things while he was on a quest to find his own wife. They passed through the hospital section, unnoticed (or ignored) by Tasha, and followed the wooded road towards the bridge until at last the view opened up and they could see it and the thousands of people that were mingling about the area.

Horsemen were riding to and fro, trying to organize the mess that had accumulated. There seemed to be almost too many men for the amount of space available for them. Fortunately, there wasn't any flooding, or much of the lowland would have been unusable to them. The wagons were still coming across the bridge, but it was clear that they had gotten the sizable part of their army across the bridge. The Ranger's rifles could still be heard engaging the Pledge's heavy machine guns and the Pledge's riflemen.

Tents were going up. Fermion pointed at them, and they decided that they'd have a good chance of finding Perry or Emory or even Yuri, Nagro, or Dor there. They did not, but they were definitely in the presence of a multitude of the Shadowmen. They were adjusting their armor, counting their arrows if they were archers, and otherwise re-grouping and preparing for combat.

Fides saw one clumping of the Shadowmen that inspired awe. They were a mixture of men and women, but among them was what seemed to be a giant of a man. The men were stunningly noble and the women were stunningly beautiful. Fides thought that all of the Shadowmen had aged somewhat, though. They didn't have the same glow that they had had the first time he'd laid eyes on them. Even their horses, which had appeared just as radiant, now looked a little less so. The horses' eyes were sparkling more as they were watered, though.

Emory was situated on their side of the river. Right about when Fides arrived at the tents, Emory's rifles began firing across the river. The final elements of the Shadowmen's army were coming across the bridge and the Rangers were also among them. Apparently the Pledge's gunners had thought about taking advantage of the exposed field of fire down the length of the bridge, but they changed their minds when Emory unleashed a volley of bullets in their direction. It was too far for Emory's guns to be accurate, but it was enough to convince the Pledge to back off. They drove away out of sight.

You have never seen a wearier crew. The hundreds of horsemen that had been pulling wagonloads of fleeing soldiers for the last three hours were tired, but of course, they were not nearly as tired as their horses were. The Rangers and Shadowmen that had served as interference looked extremely harried and haggard, just as one might expect when you've been engaging three mobile heavy machine gun nests and their able support troops. A system had been put in place during this process where those who had been over the bridge for some time were coming and tending to the wounded or watering the horses or otherwise allowing the folks who just got over to have a rest. It took awhile, but finally they could see Yuri and Nagro heading their way. Dor was with them.

Yuri greeted them. "Fermion! We owe you a debt of gratitude. You were right in every respect. Your counsel was right on. If we had tarried even an hour longer the size of our army would have been measured by counting up how many rounds of ammunition the enemy had, and calculating the difference."

"My lord, it was my honor and my obligation," Fermion replied, bowing slightly.

"Well, we need your counsel again, I think. Because we have been here before, we have a pretty good lay of this land, but we are not so certain what to expect from our opponents, and you could be a help on that. To think originally we rode out only to defeat a force of only a thousand!" Yuri bemoaned.

"I would lay odds, my lord," Fermion said, "that the Pledge will not have nearly as much urgency that you and your army had. Plus, you do have many fine horses, while they only have a handful of vehicles, regardless of how well armed they are. The bulk of their force is on foot. They will surely come, and they will surely try to take this bridge, but you have at least until tomorrow. You may even have until the day after next."

"We shall certainly need every last bit of that time. We are in disarray," Nagro sighed.

Perry and Emory joined them right then, and Dor provided introductions. Again, Yuri expressed his deep thanks for the efforts of the Rangers. "Without your rifles," Yuri confessed, "we would very likely have all been cut down."

"Lobi has died, Yuri," Dor said quietly.

Yuri looked at Dor and then the ones who stood with him. "I am very sorry, my son," Yuri replied compassionately. "I hope he has found his breath."

"As do I. I didn't think it would work that way," Dor said, struggling to hold back his emotions.

There was a hanging pause while nobody said anything. Yuri broke the silence: "You have a message for us?"

"Yes, we do," Emory said. "If you don't mind, we'd like to share it in private, no offense to any friends here."

"No offense taken," Fermion said.

Yuri said, "Very well, let's go and hear this message."

"First, sir," Perry interrupted. "I know that all of us have been marching for days straight- I know we have been. If you have some men that can stand by our Rangers at the bridge so that they could get some rest, that'd be greatly appreciated. We'll even teach them how to fire the guns, but likely they won't have to fire them."

"Dor, send for Harold. We'll dispatch his contingent to the bridge," Yuri ordered, and then led Emory and Perry into the tent city that was being thrown up, hoping to find that the meeting tent was set up already. Meanwhile, Dor left to give the order. Fides saw Dor deliver the message to a Shadowman that was skinnier than his fellows. Fides presumed that this was Harold. Harold was standing among a number of other Shadowmen, including, Fides realized, the one he had met named Henryetta. Harold obeyed Dor at once. Henryetta made her way to the meeting tents where she found Fides and his friends waiting while Yuri concluded issuing orders. Like all of the Shadowmen, Henryetta was beautiful and had a beautiful sense about her. Upon seeing her again, Fides decided that she seemed... rather bookish, but not in an overbearing sort of way. She marched right up to Fermion.

"Thank you so very much, Fermion. You've spared us much suffering!" she declared to him, embracing him, and kissing him on the cheek. Fermion smiled and reddened slightly. She let him go, but held onto his hand. "Guns. Horrors!" she added, shaking her head.

"War is a terrible thing, my Lady," Fermion answered.

She shook her head vigorously, "Please, you can stop with the 'lords' and 'ladies' thing. We are not as special as you suppose."

"That cannot be true," Fermion replied, "else you wouldn't exist."

"I don't think you could have said a truer word," another voice joined in. It was Calvin, the man that Yuri trusted to manage the army. Calvin had reddish hair that needed cutting and freckles. His eyes were an oddly bright blue, even for a Shadowman.

"I'm glad you heeded my counsel," Fermion smiled again, shaking Calvin's hand.

"Nasty things, guns," Calvin muttered. "We had hoped that... well, anyway, we didn't expect to see many."

"I am afraid that if it wasn't guns, it would be something else," Fermion argued. "There is no way to break the cycle within this broken world. The change in heart needed within the human race that would do away with guns altogether would at the same time do away with all weapons, but it would need to be a change that extended into every human heart. Even so long as there is one human heart that wishes to do violence, there will be a need to counter that violence, with at least the same measure- or else be overcome."

"So you think we should get us some guns," Calvin winked.

Fermion laughed, "It couldn't hurt!"

"Ah well. I'll keep my eye out for some," Calvin winked again. "I've got to check in with Yuri. Wish us luck. The Pledge will be here soon."

"Peace!" Fermion said. Calvin left them to find Yuri, and was replaced by Nagro.

"Many thanks again!" Nagro exclaimed to Fermion, pumping his hand in gratitude. Nagro looked a little older than the first time they'd seen him, but still looked exceptionally stout and regal.

Fermion was growing tired of the accolades, "Truly, please, don't mention it," he insisted.

"We shall mention it often and think of it even more often. What a blunder we made!" Nagro shook his head sadly. "I am afraid I cannot stay and talk," he informed them. "I have a solemn duty to perform."

"We understand," Fermion assured him.

Nagro gazed at them with his probing eyes, "We will be forming ranks two days from now to meet the Pledge. Yuri has invited you all to fight with us, standing side by side. Will you join us?"

"Most likely, sir," Fermion answered. "We are obviously honored by the invitation. However, we must consult with our friend, Tasha, and also take into consideration our own particular mission," he added, nodding towards Fides.

"That is understood," Nagro replied. "The invitation is open. I must go, now," Nagro said, shaking Fermion's hand again. Fides and his friends were left alone for the time being. After examining the bridge defenses, they decided to go back and see how Tasha was doing.

People were going back and forth along the road. The area was humming with activity, now. They fell in behind three Shadowmen who were threading their way in the same direction. They were having a conversation.

"It all seems very horrid, to me," the princess-looking one was saying.

"What do you mean, sister?" he replied.

"I did not expect to be in retreat. I thought we would be able to resist anything we found here," she complained.

"I don't know why you would have expected anything of the sort. Don't you see we had it easier before?" her brother said to her.

"Truly, Susanna. Don't you see that that is the point?" the other young man said to her.

But Susanna shook her head and said nothing, leaving the two young princes to talk as they went.

"I do say, Hector, that we certainly did not account for the brutality of this place," the brother said.

"No, I think it's fair to say we did not. But Peder won't steer us wrong- or at least, we know he'll do quite his best. And Yuri is not here for no reason at all," Hector replied. But conversation came to a sudden stop, and in fact, people all around them had stopped walking, too. Fides was taller than most, so by standing on his tip toes he could see that people were paying respects to someone or something coming their way. The crowd was parting.

It was Nagro again, but now he was on his way back from the direction of Cairo. Behind him was Falda and Leredo, and behind them was Dor, Greene, Thamson, and Blessed, bearing between them all a stretcher. On that stretcher was a body, but it was covered in a brown blanket. There was clear sorrow etched on the faces of the stretcher-bearers. Now that they were not on their horses anymore, Fides noticed for the first time how short and stocky these men really were. They passed them without giving them any look. Behind them trailed another pair of Shadowmen, but Fides hadn't seen these before. One was fairly tall and slender (nimble was the word that came to Fides' mind) and the other was short again, but not short in the same way as Dor and his friends were. If you came across this one at night, you'd think you had come upon a boulder- until it moved. And then they were past.

"I would say that is Lobi," Hector said. Susanna began crying, and the other man with them consoled her. People began moving again. The road opened up into the clearing that they had become so familiar with. The ground was still strewn with wounded men, and here and there, women. There were many people tending to them. Both Shadowmen and people from Cairo were there. "Look, there is Luce," Hector said. The threesome went in a different direction then Fides and friends, because they saw Tasha working in a different area.

"How do things seem, Tasha?" King asked her when they got close. Tasha was working alongside the older woman that had been in the tent of council. As Fides recalled, her name was Gongral. There were other women helping, too, but Fides recognized the flamboyant looking Dolam in the mix, too. He appeared to be serving more as a priest issuing comfort or last rites, though. It was a depressing scene.

"Well, we simply do not have the supplies we need in order to save many of the worst wounded. Those we have tried to make as comfortable as possible. Many of them could still be saved if we had basic surgical instruments. It is very sad," Tasha replied.

"Is there anything you need? Any way we can help?" Fermion asked her.

"No, we are very well helped. Over there is a woman named Margory. Go and ask her, but as far as I know, we have all the blankets, water, and bandages that we need."

But Margory did have a use for them. They wanted to move people from the field into the houses and old hotels and inns that were in the city proper, so the four of them spent a good part of the morning and afternoon being stretcher bearers. Many of the fallen were men from Cairo. Those of the Shadowmen who had been injured were born away by their own comrades to the tent village that had been erected nearby, not too far from the bridge.

That night, they all slept back in the inn with Tom and his gang. Tom and friends were waiting for the outcome of the battle before deciding what to do. In the middle of the night, there was an exchange of gunfire at the bridge. The Pledge had sent in one of their machine gun vehicles to scout out what was going on in Cairo. The Rangers tried to drive them off, but it was obvious that the scouts had a good look at what awaited them. This prompted Yuri and Nagro to conclude together that perhaps the Pledge army had picked up their pace and were preparing for a morning attack. Yuri dispatched Calvin, the master-at-arms, to make final, hasty, preparations. This included sending a message to Fermion at the inn that they would be forming ranks that morning rather than the next.

While it was still dark, then, Fermion roused them all and they made their way down to the bridge again. Tasha had not returned to the inn that night, but King had visited her to make sure all was well with her. Now, they passed by the building she was sleeping in and followed the road toward the bridge and Fort Defiance. They could increasingly hear the sounds of the camp coming alive and organizing. There was just the hint of light arising in the east, and the air was wintry cold.

They found their way to Yuri's meeting tent, where they were warmly welcomed. The original five (Yuri, Nagro, Peder, Henryetta, and Calvin) that had first greeted Fermion and friends west of Cairo were there. Perry, Emory, and Simus were also on hand. Redemptus stood outside the tent, and Dor was nearby as well. Yuri nodded to Fermion, "Emory, why don't you run your plan by Fermion and see what he thinks?"

"Alright," Emory agreed. "We are working under the premise that we don't stand a real chance keeping those machine guns from coming across. We can unleash a hail of bullets on them, but they've got armored vehicles. It would be a lucky shot indeed. So, we save our ammunition and let them come within our range, which of course is their own range. No need to tell us that. The priority of the Rangers will be to take out the guns so that it's a fair fight for everyone. The problem is that doing this let's them get quite a lot of people over, while it would have been preferred to keep them off the bridge altogether."

Perry continued, "A good length of that bridge is fully exposed to the length of the ruins of Fort Defiance. So, we think with two hundred and forty men firing on it, with some of Yuri's archers in the trees right where the bridge finally turns into the road, we might stand a decent chance of knocking off the guns."

Emory concluded, "We also don't know how many guns they have ultimately. We know what we saw yesterday, which was three heavy machine guns in an armored vehicle, and about thirty rifles. In an army of ten thousand that seems like the tip of the iceberg. But the Copperheads have a thousand men, and they could generate weapons for about a quarter of them."

"Twenty-five percent of ten thousand would be two thousand, five hundred rifles coming down that bridge," Fides pointed out.

Emory shrugged. "We just don't know, really, what they have."

"And what of the rest of the army?" Fermion asked.

"Once we believe the machine guns have been disabled, we will charge," Nagro said.

"That's pretty straight forward," Fermion chuckled skeptically. But there was no more time to try to come up with a new plan. Battle was near.

The sounds of engines coming their way alerted them to the fact that the attack was under way. The Rangers were already in place in and around Fort Defiance, ready to broadside the coming army. (Some of the Rangers were still out of action, watching the bridge that was still up to the east that crossed over to Kentucky, which the Copperheads escaped over.) Fermion, Fides, Jonathan, and King were invited to join the ranks of the Shadowmen. Horses were provided for each of them. Then, they were once again arrayed in an intimidating pattern in the wide open area facing the bridge.

There wasn't a whole lot of room for maneuvering ten thousand soldiers, so some were in reserves back in the city, waiting for their signals. The men of Cairo were interspersed throughout the army, but now that Fides was immersed in the army himself, he could see that the bulk of it was composed of the Shadowmen themselves.

Fides and his friends were in the second rank. To Fides' left and right were spread out the forty men and women that had confronted them on the road to Cairo just a day or so earlier. The five main leaders of the Shadowmen were numbered among the forty. Fides tried to locate each of them in relation to his own place. To his left a little ways was Henryetta and what was clearly her contingent. There were about ten with her, on powerful horses. Dolam, Gongral, and Redemptus stood behind them, providing for their needs as they could. To Fides' immediate left was Peder. His contingent was much smaller, but still clearly demarcated. With Peder were two men. These were the two men that they had followed into town the night before. One was named Hector, but they hadn't learned what the name of the other was. He inferred, though, that it was the brother of the one named Susanna.

To his group's immediate right was Calvin and a small, intelligent looking man. To the right of them was Nagro with his lot. There were about ten of them, too. Dor, Greene, Thamson, and Blessed were people that they had already met. Leredo was another. There were two that Fides hadn't learned a name for, yet. Behind these, Falda was providing encouraging words. Just ahead of them all was Yuri, who was peering unblinkingly towards the bridge.

Fides saw that he was in the tip of the spearhead of the second rank. For, next to them on both sides stacked dozens deep, were various distinct units assembled in a line. Fides could see spears, swords, and shields. There were also several cavalry units in the second rank, and also in the third. There were no men of Cairo in the second rank. In the first rank were intermingled men of Cairo and soldiers of the Shadowmen. Archery units were interspersed in each rank. In another day and age, and perhaps in another place altogether, they would have been well equipped to face any enemy. Now, they desperately needed to silence the fast and powerful weapons of the Pledge before they could truly be formidable.

The sounds of rifle fire snapped the night air in half. Fort Defiance was again earning its name. The Ranger's fusillade went without a response for a moment, but the Pledge's weapons were merely trying to locate their attackers. The sputtering sound of several machine guns erupted from somewhere on the bridge and they could see their flashes. At about the same time the Pledge issued a response, signal men were flashing flags with a message for Yuri: There were men on the bridge and they were coming their way!

There was now rifle fire coming from the bridge, too. From their position, the Rangers had an advantage over those on the bridge. They had well-concealed positions and a clear field of fire on the bridge. This could not keep the Pledge from advancing, however. As the sun came up and it became easier to see, the Pledge began putting firepower on Ranger positions. One could now see that the bridge was thick with men all the way back to the other shore. Some had already started pouring out of the Ranger's end of the bridge, or jumping down the side of the bridge onto the ground if they were far enough along to do so safely.

All signs were that the Ranger's efforts were not being rewarded. Hundreds of men were streaming off the bridge, and many of these were armed with rifles. Though it was still a decent way off, many of these men were firing at the main army, and because of the way they were massed, some of the Shadowmen were bound to get hit. Indeed, a few fell wounded while standing in their ranks. The men jumping off the bridge were protected from the Ranger's rifles because they jumped to the side opposite to them where the earthworks shielded them. It was quickly becoming apparent that their strategy was not working. Hundreds and hundreds of men were safely across the bridge and in the open plain. Besides being safe from the Ranger's rifles, they were also unconcerned about any weapons that the Shadowmen could bring to bear at the moment since they were well out of range of their weapons.

Still other Pledge soldiers were pouring off the bridge and taking cover on the Ranger's side as well as they could. There was a fierce battle near a copse of trees by the bridge. Shadowmen archers had been hidden in that grove because it was felt that even if their arrows couldn't reach far enough on the bridge to do damage of their own, they were in range to protect the flanks of the Ranger riflemen. With enemy soldiers getting clear, however, the archers were finding that they were engaging in close combat. Some of the Rangers had to break out of their cover to run over and provide help. Fewer arrows were falling on the Pledge mass that was accumulating just out of sight of the Ranger rifles.

Despite the Ranger's inability to stop the individual soldiers from getting across, they were able to engage the machine guns and keep them and their drivers from getting a clear view as they tried to roll off the bridge. With the Shadowmen and Rangers engaged in hand to hand combat, two of the vehicles mounted with heavy machine guns managed to get off the bridge and into the plains. One turned right to engage the Rangers, the other turned left and participated in the re-grouping that was being organized out of range of Shadowmen arrows. It did not take long before that gun was pointed in the Shadowmen army's direction, though. Rounds from the weapon were being fired about one every five seconds, apparently in an effort to see if it could be effective from that range.

Yuri wasn't waiting to find out, but there was little he could do. He began issuing orders for a full rush. He reasoned that he might lose two hundred men while crossing the field, but at least he would have men left over to fight. Unfortunately, the third vehicle that they knew had a machine gun had made it across the bridge, too. It had turned to the left, joining its like in sending rounds at the Shadowmen. A quick decision had apparently been made, and the two vehicles began slowly coming in their direction, surrounded by a thousand or more men who had managed to get across in that time. Now, the rounds from the machine gun were really coming in. They could see men in Shadowmen's first rank collapsing, and some in the rear of that rank were starting to fall backwards in fright, and for good reason. Yuri was just going to give the order for the suicide charge when Fermion grabbed hold of his arm.

"Belay that order," Fermion said. It was a command.

"Can you do something as a Nephilim that can remedy this situation?" Yuri hastily asked him, unconscious of the imposition.

"I can try, and you have nothing to lose," Fermion returned, grim faced. Yuri nodded his assent, and Fermion drove his heels into his steed's side, sending it bolting out towards the first rank, and then through it. Fermion was now in the wide open. His sword was pointed at the Pledge, and his cloak flapped behind him in the wind. In his heart, Fides simultaneously cursed Fermion's madness and praised his courage.

The Pledge had a reaction that might have been expected. Initially, they were taken aback. Instinctively, though, they realized that they had to take this man down, for if he were able to taunt them without an answer, he might be able to strengthen the courage of their opponents. Soon, both machine guns were firing in his direction. The hundred or so other men who had rifles also took a knee in an attempt to bring him down. Puffs of flame and smoke erupted in a sphere around Fermion. It wasn't as though the aim of his attackers was off. Their aim was dead on. And normally, bullets did not explode in mid-air. One by one, beginning with the machine gunners, the Pledge soldiers realized that something was not quite right. They could see nothing at all that could stop their bullets, but their bullets were being incinerated by something shortly before they could reach their target.

Fermion pulled within forty yards of the advancing enemy, and dismounted. As he did so, he took his sword and thrust it into the dirt. Then, he stretched his hands into the sky, and a ball of fire appeared between them. It grew in size, even as both sides watched. Even the Rangers and the men on the bridge could see the light and both sides stopped firing, in awe. It was now the size of one of the passenger vans that had brought them to Cairo in the first place. It was not a fire like one might see at a campsite. It was a fire like one might imagine star-fire to be like. Rolling currents of amber colors percolated along the exterior. Indeed, it seemed as though Fermion had Sol in his hands.

And then, all at once, there was a strange green flash, and the tiny star between his hands disappeared. A green sphere now appeared around Fermion, but it was in fact only a wave of some kind, and it rapidly spread out in a circle from him, first encompassing the Pledge army, which was closest, but quickly enveloping the army of the Shadowmen, too. And then it was gone, zipping out into space behind them all. Fermion collapsed to the ground next to his sword. His horse turned around and trotted back to the first rank. Both armies faced each other in stunned silence, staring at the fallen figure between them.

Nobody knew what had been accomplished other than being treated to a marvelous and mysterious light show. A series of shouts came out of the Pledge ranks: they were renewed orders to press the attack. Once the Pledge soldiers begin rumbling slowly forward, the Shadowmen observed that a wave of panic had overtaken their enemies. The vehicles were not moving. The weapons, as a whole, were not firing. Members of the Pledge who had rifles were checking their weapons' mechanisms. Some were able to fire, but most could not. Even some of the Ranger's guns had failed. Most importantly, the heavy machine guns were not firing. Yuri realized the significance of this fact before the Pledge commanders did.

"Chaaaaaaaaaaarge!" Yuri shouted. The first rank, greatly encouraged, surged toward their enemy. After they had gone fifty steps, the second rank began running to engage their foes, too. The third rank moved ahead as well, under the direction of Calvin, but it stopped short to await direction. Enemy commanders did finally figure out the effect of the crazy man's deed, and issued loud and urgent commands to meet their enemy, but the circumstances had changed dramatically. Now, the fine swords and shields and armor that the Shadowmen possessed were superior to the weapons possessed by their enemy. That is to say, their enemy had no swords, had no shields, and had no armor. They had various dangerous instruments, but none as efficiently lethal as those possessed by the Shadowmen. The Pledge didn't have time to reflect on that, because Yuri's wrath was quickly upon them.

Shortly after the first rank had begun thundering forward, and before the second rank had begun making its move, Fides had shouted to Jonathan and King, "First to Fermion!" The two sides had crashed into each other causing them to lose sight of where Fermion lay. Horses from the second rank were now in the full thick of battle. If Fermion was not pummeled to death by Pledge soldiers who came to him first, there was a chance he could be trampled to death by their own forces. The three of them tried to get into the area, but simply could not.

Even though the advantage had significantly changed, the Pledge remained a violent threat. The Shadowmen brought five thousand people crashing against three thousand, but the Pledge was effectively and efficiently getting their men across. In no time at all, they had four thousand, then five, and then six. Fides was now finding enemy in his area, though he was still mainly hemmed in by his own allies.

"Come on!" thundered a voice near him. The extremely large man that Fides had seen in Henryetta's contingent had dismounted from his horse and taken the bridle of Fides' ride. If Fides had thought the man to be large before, he now could be seen as positively gigantic. He was up to Fides' shoulder, and Fides was on a horse. "Let's go get your man!" the man growled.

"Getouttatheway!" the man was barking as he plowed his way through both friend and foe. They still hadn't arrived on Fermion's position, but they had definitely arrived in an area where the fight was especially intense. Fides and Jonathan were on the ground almost immediately, fighting. Fides' sword flashed in the early morning light, and Jonathan stayed near, purposely keeping an eye on his charge. King had become separated, but they could see his staff occasionally arc through the sky not too far away.

"Ee's ere some'er," the giant said to Fides, clearing a path again.

"We're with you, too, Gol!" a young man exclaimed from nearby. Two other young men, dressed in identical clothing and bearing similar appearances also informed Gol of their close proximity.

Gol was picking up men and hurling them back towards the bridge. These screamed on the journey and Fides could hear the crunch and cries of those impacted as the bodies landed. Fides found himself in a life and death battle with two strong enemies. He managed to run one of them through, but the sword was stuck in the man's body. The man fell to the ground, and Fides was left to struggle with the other one with his bare hands. Jonathan was nearby, but could not come to Fides' aid.

Fides was a man on fire, however. He was bound and determined to find and rescue Fermion, or at the very least, recover his body for an honorable burial. Fides stepped inside his opponent's overhead strike of a club and put the man in a headlock. The two fell to the ground, but Fides didn't let go. He heard the man's neck snap as they hit the ground. The man's head lolled loosely and unnaturally as Fides pushed the body away from him. It was a very disconcerting moment, but Fides didn't have time to reflect on it.

Gol was suddenly howling in pain. Several Pledge soldiers had driven daggers into Gol's legs, and others were clubbing away at his mid-section. Fides worked his sword free from the body of his dead assailant and caught the men by surprise. Jonathan had worked himself free, too, and between the two of them freed Gol from the threat. Gol was in great pain, however, as he pulled the daggers out of his thighs. He was deadly even as he limped, still sending foes flying when he could lay his big hands on them. In the midst of this, he grunted and pointed in a direction which Fides interpreted as where the giant thought Fermion lie.

Right then, Dor and Thamson had arrived on their horses. They were each slashing with their blades. "He's over here," Thamson shouted. Gol had pointed them in the basic direction, but was off by twenty feet. Twenty feet in a swirl of ten thousand men can make all the difference in the world if you're looking for something within it. It was becoming apparent that Fides was not the only one with designs to take hold of Fermion. Whether each had taken the idea in their own heads independently or perhaps because they interpreted Fides' command to Jonathan and King as commands to them as well, you could not know. The upshot, though, was the same- Dor and Thamson were right with them as they made their way towards Fermion. Fides now saw that Nagro was in the area with his men and Peder with his. He could hear Yuri shouting, but did not see him.

Loud yells from very close by alerted Fides to Fermion's precise location. There was a bloody heap of men in a rough circle around the body of Fermion. Many of these men were fallen Pledge soldiers, but many were Shadowmen, as well. However, the soldiers currently holding the perimeter around Fermion's body were citizens of Cairo. One might suppose that the men of Cairo, being the least armed, had the most to gain by Fermion's valiant and mysterious deed. When Fides got to the ring, a gap opened up so that he could get through. He and Jonathan rushed to Fermion's side. Fermion was lying there very still.

"I don't know if he is alive or dead!" Fides shouted out.

"Let's get him out of here and see about it somewhere else," Jonathan argued. The two of them scooped Fermion up and onto Fides' shoulders, but Gol had arrived.

"Lemme take'm," Gol ordered. Gol took Fermion from Fides and put Fermion on his shoulders as one might put a scarf around one's neck. Then, it was time to battle their way out. Dor, Thamson, and the first men who had called out to Gol in the first place went ahead of them, clearing out room for them to make their retreat. Fides and Jonathan were each on one side of the giant, fending off the enemy, but not exactly sticking around to deal with any particular threat. Behind them was Peder and his men, and King joined them with two halves of his staff. Fides couldn't help but laugh.

"Broke another one, did you son?" Fides called out.

King gave a toothy grin in reply, "You can't believe how hard some of these people's heads are!"

They could see the third rank ahead of them, now. Horses were brought to them and Gol laid Fermion's body over one of them.

"Here is his sword," a man said. It was one of the grateful citizens of Cairo.

Yuri had found his way back to his reserve lines and ordered Fides to take Fermion back to Cairo for care, and not to return to the battle. No sooner did he issue the command did he turn his attention back to the battle at hand. Both armies were now in full force. Sporadic rifle fire could be heard from behind them as they began making for the road.

"Take good care of'em," Gol growled at Fides.

"Tally ho!" Dor shouted out, following Gol back into the fray. As they returned to Cairo they passed dozens and dozens of wounded men, and occasionally wounded women, too. Some were on stretchers, but many were being carried, or even dragged, by their comrades. Fides and Jonathan kept the horse carrying the limp body of Fermion between them while King walked slightly ahead of them, helping to clear a path. At last they reached the hospital clearing. Men and women were working quickly but calmly to address the wounded that were laid at their feet.

Initially, they laid Fermion down there but quickly realized he didn't have any normal wounds. They grew uncomfortable just sitting there. Several attendants didn't even give them a second look so they decided to scoop him up again and head back to the inn, hoping Fermion would come to with some rest. They laid him on the floor in the main lobby, and then Jonathan and King went to the roof to see how the battle was going. After a time, they came down to report that the battle was still raging fiercely on the plain. Naturally, they couldn't see much of it from where they were, but they could get a general sense at any rate.

It was about then that Fermion whispered. They didn't recognize it as a whisper at first. They thought it was merely a deeper breath, or maybe a sigh. Then he did it again, and there were clearly two syllables to it. "He's talking!" Jonathan had declared. Fides put his ear right up close to Fermion's mouth.

"Taaaaa- sha..." Fermion whispered, ever so faintly.

"He's trying to talk to Tasha," King said.

"Tasha isn't here, Fermion," Jonathan told him, kneeling next to him.

Fermion's eyes had been closed throughout this, but with Jonathan's words, Fermion's grey eyes flashed open. He reached up and grabbed Fides by his cloak, and with apparently every ounce of energy he had left, quite audibly said, "Get Tasha!" And then he collapsed, and was very still.

"King, quickly! Go get her!" Fides commanded. King was out the door before Fides had even finished the command, his long brown hair flapping behind him in the wind.

King returned very quickly. Far more quickly than Jonathan and Fides would have expected, in fact. The door opened, and Fides turned his head to speak to King and Tasha, but it was not either of these. In the door way was a short, fat, ugly looking man. His eyes squinted as he peered into the room. He had a blade out, pointed at King's belly. King was retreating before the man.

"What is your business?" demanded Fides.

"This is one of the Pledge slaves," Jonathan blurted out, pulling his sword. The dumpy man flashed an evil smile, but didn't move. He looked familiar to Fides. Fides was pretty sure he'd seen someone looking very similar to this one in one of the crowds of people he traveled with, at least briefly, a long time ago. Fermion's body trembled. Fides thought to himself that the trembling was probably what he'd expect a death rattle to be like.

"Get out of here!" came a woman's voice from somewhere behind the man. The brute frowned, but only for an instant, because suddenly he couldn't be seen. It was as if an invisible force had picked the man up and tossed him aside from the door. In his place was Tasha, filling up the entrance, and clutching both sides of the door frame. She called out, "King! Jonathan! Be sure he keeps running!" Then she stepped through the door. Jonathan and King ran past her to drive the dumpy man off.

Fermion's eyes fluttered and his face turned pink, and his limbs began to move, and by the time Tasha had finally laid a hand on him, he was sitting up straight and looking at her.

"That was a close one, my friend," Fermion said to her.

"I do hope you had a good reason for what you did," she rebuked him. "I thought you were gone. I thought you had to be gone based on what I felt."

"Almost, my dear. Almost," Fermion said, looking much better. In fact, he seemed to be back to full vigor. King barged through the door before they could say anything else, though.

"The tide of the battle has changed! The Pledge is in the city!" King shouted. They could hear loud shouting through the open door. This also was the first that they realized that Tom, his men, and the vehicles were gone. They had been gone the whole time, even.

"We need to get out of here!" Fides exclaimed.

"I think you're right," Fermion admitted. "I feel much better, but I still lack the strength. If it seems as though we can have no more good effect here, I confess we ought to get you and that key out of the grasps of the Pledge. If the Shadowmen have collapsed, we five will not be able to resist them." Tasha helped Fermion to his feet. "We need to head north, immediately," he continued. "We shall hope that the tide changes here, but anticipate that it won't."

They quickly gathered their things, such that they were. Fermion seemed to be suddenly struck with a thought just as they were getting ready to leave. He hesitated, "There is one more thing," he said.

"What's that?" Tasha said, stopping short at the door.

"It is time for Fides and I to say goodbye to our swords," he explained, slowly.

"Are you mad?" Fides exclaimed.

"No, we must. Here. Put your sword behind the front desk next to mine," he urged Fides.

"We are going to flee a battle in progress without swords?" Fides demanded incredulously.

"Fides, you have to believe me. You must have faith in me. After what you have seen, do you still doubt me?" Fermion argued firmly, yet tenderly at the same time.

"But this makes absolutely no sense, at all!" Fides retorted. He knew that this was the moment that Fermion had alluded to some months back, but that sword had become part of his self-identity. He groped for a reason to justify saying no.

"I cannot make you. I only know that something terrible will happen if we do not leave our weapons, and something good will happen if we do," Fermion patiently pleaded with him.

"I'll leave mine," Jonathan offered.

"No, it wouldn't help. It must be these swords," Fermion replied.

"I'm not leaving behind my sword. It's all well enough for you, Fermion. You have magical powers. Or something. I'd be left with my fists, or a stick." That was the last word, because Fides had decidedly expressed his final position, demonstrating as much by striding out of the inn and walking down the road to the north. Fermion sighed: a sad sigh, not one of condemnation. The rest were confused, not knowing what to think. But not Tasha. Tasha shook her head wearily, and followed Fides out the door. They were all following the road to the north, now. Behind them was the sound of battle in the city. They joined a small but steady stream of refugees making their way out of the path of war.

That night, they set up camp about five miles away. Fides was sullen, and the atmosphere was tense. Nothing came of the tension, however. It just served as a heavy blanket over their fellowship. Nonetheless, it should be said that while trying to gather firewood, Fides had climbed out on a thick, dead branch that hung over a small river that was winding through the woods there. He had meant to try to hack off some of the smaller, yet still substantial limbs, trusting that they would be better firewood because they were dry, but the limb he was on broke and he plunged into the river below. He was absolutely fine, but angered out of his mind when he realized he had thrown his sword away from him as he fell. That part of the river was deep, and no matter how many times he dived into the icy water, he could not re-claim his weapon.

So, Fides' sword did not end up being a further use for him or anyone else for that matter.

== Chapter 10 ==

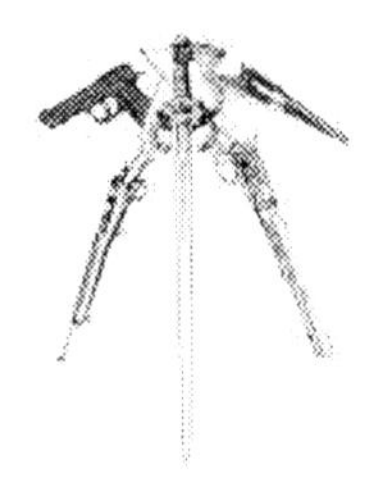

Early the next morning, the five of them were sitting around the campfire. There was just a little walking on egg shells in regards to the sword incident, but Fermion appeared to be completely over it. Only Fides' hesitancy remained, but it grew slighter each moment as it appeared to be an issue relegated to the past. They were several miles north of Cairo and off the road a little ways. They could hear refugees moving along the road. The weather had grown warmer over the last week, and Fides could not be more thankful. Upon reflection, he realized that had his journey taken place during the summer, the long passage from New Mexico to his current location would have taken place under an unbearable sun. Further, instead of arriving into the northern regions of the country while it was warming as he was now, he would have arrived right about when it would be getting frigid. It was good timing, all around.

Shortly after breakfast, they packed up their belongings and made for the road. There was a long journey still ahead of them and there was no reason to delay it. Also, they desired news about what had finally happened in Cairo and they knew there would be refugees with such information on the road. They found it and turned north. There were not many people traversing on their own particular part of the road, but they could see both ahead and behind them that there were other groups of travelers. Everyone was going in the same direction: north.

Around lunch time they stopped to have a rest and a snack. One of the benefits from their time in Cairo was that they had had time to restock their stores. Not only that, but the stores they gathered were of good quality. They had salted meats and tasty loaves of thick bread. They were able to clean out their canteens properly, too. While they were resting, they heard the familiar sound of horses trotting on pavement. Looking to the south, they saw that it was the Rangers coming in their direction.

"I don't think they have two hundred and fifty men, anymore," Jonathan said while they were still out of earshot.

"It's safe to say they've had better days," Tasha remarked. She would know, too, since she tended to many of their wounded.

The Rangers, having caught sight of them, rode over to them and dismounted. Emory and Perry approached them wearily and clearly burdened with sadness.

"Greetings," Emory called out.

"Emory. Perry. It is good to see you," Fermion replied. There were handshakes exchanged. Other Rangers whom they had become familiar with also gathered around while pleasantries were exchanged. Finally, Fermion gently asked, "What news do you have?"

"Well," Perry began, "I guess you could call it a victory. Cairo has not fallen."

"It seemed as though it had before we left," Fides exclaimed in pleased surprise.

"Well, it wasn't Cairo that they really wanted," Perry replied.

"Oh?" Fermion intoned.

"Yes, we are certain that they only wanted passage to the north. No doubt, actually taking Cairo and holding it would have been critical for them, but if they could have gotten by us altogether, I shouldn't think they wouldn't have tried," Emory explained.

"What is it to the north that they want?" Fermion wondered.

"Don't you know?" Emory threw a piercing gaze at Fermion.

"I do not understand," Fermion returned, confused.

"When we first encountered you and the Shadowmen you will remember that we had a message for the Shadowmen. After we delivered that message we learned that you had developed quite the reputation in their eyes. They instantly wanted your counsel. Clearly, they didn't have an opportunity to get it, which is one reason why I am going to share it with you now. It also seems that they think it might be relevant to you. They have instructed me to share the message with you. Here it is: We learned some time back that the Pledge had recently changed its mind about its goals and the speed in which they wanted to achieve them. That is because they learned of something in Illinois that they thought could help them achieve their final goal- world conquest, really- with more ease," Emory explained.

"So, they were actually on their way to obtain this thing, and not simply to gain a strategic hold, is that right?" King asked.

"That's right. We knew that the Shadowmen were moving to stop the Pledge, but we feared that they would go about things in the wrong way if they misunderstood the Pledge's intentions. I suppose we are lucky, all in all, with how things turned out," Emory continued.

"But what is it they want?" Jonathan pressed them.

"Come on, man. Fermion knows!" Perry blurted out.

"I only have a dim awareness of what you mean, I confess," Fermion said. "I know my own mission, and I know how important it is, but I cannot imagine how what I am sworn to protect would specifically help the Pledge."

"Alright, I'll come right to it," Emory decided. "The Pledge believes that the Ark of the Covenant is buried somewhere in the north."

"The Ark of the Covenant!" exclaimed Fermion.

"The Ark of the Covenant?" asked Fides.

"Ok, I'm going to harass you every night from here on to read some of Corrie's Bible, Fides. Believe none of it if you will, but at least you'll be informed," Fermion growled at him.

"The Ark of the Covenant was a chest carried by the ancient Israelites thousands of years ago," Emory patiently explained. "It was specially blessed by God, and God's presence went with it. Wherever the Ark was, there was success. The Pledge calculates that with the Ark, they have a win-win situation. If it is not a magical mechanism to gain success, they will be able to exploit the superstition of the masses, at least. It would be a propaganda field day for them. They could show, too, that they were not opposed to religious expression. If it does have magic then all the better."

"That is amazing," Fermion said, still dumbfounded. "How did they come to this information?"

"That, I cannot say. I do not know," Emory replied. "Is it true? Is it true that the Ark of the Covenant is in North America of all places?"

"About one hundred years ago it was claimed that the Ark had been discovered. Of course, it had been missing for thousands of years, smuggled off and protected when it became evident that the nation of Israel was going to be defeated. There was all sorts of publicity. I would not be surprised if it was really the real Ark. However, after a year it disappeared again. It was stolen from a museum in Jerusalem, and no one ever learned how or why. In fact, they were still in the process of deciding if it was the real thing or not when it was taken." Fermion paused. He thought for a moment, and then continued. "However, I know much of what is to the north, and as far as I know, it is not the Ark of the Covenant. I did not see it, or hear of it, and I think I would have. I could be wrong, but I do not believe the Ark of the Covenant is there. But I would not want the Pledge to lay hands on what is there, either."

"What is there?" Perry asked.

"I am not permitted to tell you that," Fermion reluctantly admitted.

"This is all very interesting," King interrupted them. "I still would like to know how the battle fared!"

Then Emory told the story. He told it slowly and methodically, with Perry throwing in excited interjections as he was known to do. The battle had not actually ever turned bad for them. What had happened, though, was that since the Pledge really only had wanted to get past the Shadowmen army, they had collected their wits and focused on taking the bridge that the Copperheads had escaped over, and which the Rangers had used to enter Cairo. By sheer numerical superiority, the Pledge managed to erect a wall of soldiers to serve as a barrier. Behind the barrier, the majority of the Pledge found their way to the bridge across to Kentucky. Attempts to head them off failed, even though thanks to the Ranger's message they knew the attempt was possible and even likely. In the course of this escape, the Pledge mounted a surprise attack on the opposite flank. The Pledge soldiers, along with their strange, stunted slaves, forced their way into the city, as though looking for something. Emory paused in his story.

"Slippery folks. We didn't understand what was going on. We lost some good men, there," Emory said softly. "But afterwards we learned that there was a key to whatever was protecting the Ark, and that key was with you, Fermion. Maybe they do not know about the key, but after the display you put on, my friend, it's possible they simply wanted to take hold of you. At any rate, we think they were looking for you. We chased them from house to house, but in the end, the sneaky fellahs were able to escape and get back to their own lines and then across the bridge to Kentucky."

Emory told them that the Pledge Army was now in Kentucky, though they left a thousand or more dead on the flood plains south of Cairo. The Shadowmen had lost men, too, so the break from fighting was a welcome break. Some of the neighborhood blocks in Cairo had been torched, unfortunately, so the city itself had taken a wound. Emory explained that, as far as they knew, there was no good way to get across to Illinois from Kentucky anywhere close by, but there was a lock and dam to their north-east that with some ingenuity might be re-formed well enough for the Pledge to get their army across.

With a better grasp of the full situation, the Shadowmen Army was at that very moment making plans to pursue the Pledge. However, the Shadowmen had decided that the 'key' needed more protection, and for that reason they dispatched the Rangers, who readily obeyed, to escort Fermion and his friends northward.

"So, tell us about this key you have, Fermion," Perry jumped in.

"I'm not the key. He's the key," Fermion replied, nodding toward Fides. Fides pulled the awkward necklace from out beneath his shirt. "That cannot come off of his neck without the right code being entered. Any attempt to take it off without that code will kill him and destroy the key. Any attempt to open up the structure that key was designed for, without the key, will result in that structure being destroyed."

"So, we actually need to keep Fides away from the structure?" Emory inquired.

"No. Actually, as I said, opening the structure without the key will cause the structure to explode, destroying its contents. I have no doubt that the Pledge would make the attempt. This cannot be allowed to happen," Fermion explained.

"It is your mission. Our's is to accompany you for as long as it is necessary, and regardless of our own preferences. The Rangers are at your disposal, Fermion," Perry stated.

"I take your services gladly, and consider you as free men whom I would never dispose of. Serve me while seeking to serve also the men who follow you," Fermion corrected him.

"It is well said," Perry rejoined.

"How many men do you still have?" Fermion asked.

"We only have one hundred and fifty Rangers. We count the women accompanying us in that number," Emory replied. "Only one is a Ranger. The others are friends who have come with us a long way, and wish to continue with us, but can leave whenever they please."

"I am sorry for your losses," Tasha offered gently.

"That is much appreciated," Emory returned.

"The map, Emory," Perry reminded him.

"Oh, yes. Here," Emory said, producing a map of the region. He spread it out between them and pointed at it. "As you can see, that lock and dam I mentioned is not really that far from here, and in some ways, as much on the way to Bloomington as our own way. We risk being cut off if we don't hustle. We should use our time advantage as much as possible to get past this point-" he was jabbing his finger at lock and dam number 53 "-and head for Bloomington with as much space between them and us as possible."

"The Shadowmen are going to try to stop or delay them. It is agreed that we must keep them from obtaining the Ark of the Covenant, but even more so it is our goal to put down the Pledge army altogether. So, we don't want to let them get away," Perry interjected again.

"Very well," Fermion said. "Let's finish our meals and then be on our way again. What are the chances that you have horses for us?"

"Very good!" Emory laughed. They all rose to go and get the horses that had been set aside for them. Perry led the way to the horses, but Emory turned aside to give out orders to the Ranger remnant. They found the horses lashed to three other horses, which were guided by three women.

"This is Misaluva. This is Charis. And this is Melody," Perry said, introducing them. Fides was startled momentarily. His wife's name was also Melody. He felt a pang of anguished loneliness as he thought of his wife again, and then a pang of guilt as he noticed to his dismay that all three of the women were very attractive ladies. He turned his eyes away from them and toward the horses that would be theirs. First, there were introductions all around, however, and Fides had to stew in his warring emotions for a moment longer than he really wanted to. Finally, he was released from the awkward moment- though it was only awkward for him- and they claimed the horses.

They all climbed onto their horses and situated themselves on them. Misaluva was commenting on Fermion's strange display of power, but Fermion wasn't biting. Clearly she hoped for an explanation from the wrong man!

"It is a pleasure to meet you," Charis initiated with Fides. She rode high on the horse, with pride.

"Delighted. Are you the one that Perry said was a Ranger, or one of the companions?" Fides replied respectfully.

"I am one of the companions. It is Misaluva that is the Ranger. She used to look so much more vibrant, too. I can hardly explain how much. It has been a hard time for everyone," Charis said. Fides glanced at Misaluva (not too long!) and thought that Misaluva seemed quite 'vibrant' as it was. Any more vibrant, he thought, and you'd have to number her with the Shadowmen. Charis chatted on. "We've really been running from place to place, trying to stay out of trouble. It has been very exciting. It has been much more dangerous, of course, but at least we are with others."

Fides couldn't help but think that Charis was just a bit too bubbly for his liking. He had only just thought it when Charis said, "Oh, I know I talk so much!" She said this on her own, as Fides hadn't made any changes of expression to indicate he was annoyed in anyway. "If you think I talk too much, wait until Melody gets going!"

Indeed, Melody was in a very enthusiastic conversation with King and Jonathan. Fides didn't know what they were talking about, but he couldn't help smirking as he observed the eyes of his friends glazing over. Misaluva was still plying Fermion with questions, too. Fides felt a little bad for delighting in the fact that even Fermion seemed to have been overwhelmed with the stream of sound coming from the lovely face. Tasha interrupted it all briefly to say, "I'm going to go see how soon it is before we ride!" Fides could hear her chuckling as she walked back up to the front where Emory was. Perry was laughing, too, and followed Tasha.

All that day they kept the horses on a fast walk, eager to get past the point where they were afraid the Pledge might be able to get ahead of them or even intercept them. All that day, the three women peppered Fermion, Fides, Jonathan, and King with a string of questions and comments and observations about the world. It did get better, because after all, when asked a question one is permitted a time of silence to answer. So, each of them were able to tell the ladies bits and pieces of their stories. One such exchange between Fides and Charis went like this.

"So, we are going to Bloomington?" Charis had inquired of Fides.

"Yes. You've probably heard that there is an effort there being made to re-unite families?" Fides replied.

"I had heard something. I'm really originally from the east. I don't have any family in this area. Who are you looking for?" she asked him.

"I have been away from my wife and children for six or seven years, now. It was right about just as the Disease was sweeping across the country," Fides explained grimly.

Charis' face darkened slightly. "I am very familiar with the Disease, I'm afraid."

"Oh?" Fides replied.

"Yes. I lived in Pennsylvania for a bit, but then I was living in Ohio for awhile with a job as a doctor," she explained. Fides couldn't hide his surprise at this revelation. His initial assessment of her wouldn't have allowed for such a possibility. "Well, in the old days- and I mean the real old days- I'd only know as much as a nurse's assistant, actually. Medical schools haven't been very good for a long time. Still, the training that I received allowed me to be called a doctor. Crazy, huh?"

"Wow, so you had to deal with the Disease first hand. You practically had your hands buried in it," Fides said with awe and a new respect.

Charis glowed slightly, "Well, it was a terrible thing. It was especially terrible because there was no cure, and in our area, it was one hundred percent fatal. Every person I helped, died. I expected to catch it myself, sometime, but I never did." She shuddered. "It was terrible."

"I had the Disease," Fides reported to her, almost with pride.

"Well, not *the* Disease, of course," she laughed, "because you're still here!"

"No, really. I had it. Fermion put me into the hands of some people that saved my life, and tended to me until I was well," Fides said. He could see she still didn't believe him. "Seriously. Go and ask Fermion!"

"I will!" she practically giggled, and she did. She rode up to Fermion and then rode back to Fides. This time she was the one in awe and possessing a new respect.

"It was nothing!" Fides said, brushing off her compliments. "It's not like I did anything to heal myself."

"That is wisely put. How things are healed is a great mystery. We don't understand it. We only know that it happens, and we can help it happen. Basically, our job is just to make things as best we can and then get out of the way," she said in a somewhat more serious tone he found as surprising as the fact that she was a trained doctor. Within that same serious tone, she offered her next gentle inquiry, "You must really miss your wife…"

"I do. I really do," he replied softly. That ended the conversation for awhile. Fides drifted off into thought, and Charis, as exuberant as she was, was also perceptive enough to allow the man the distance he needed.

After awhile, they began talking again, but of course, not just with each other, but with others in their group. Fides acquainted himself further with more of the Rangers, and Fermion found himself in deep conversation with Perry and Emory. Jonathan and King never quite freed themselves from Melody, but nor did they know if they wanted to be freed from her. Tasha also enjoyed the traveling conversation. All in all, it was a pleasant day for everyone. You could hardly have guessed that the day before they had all been in a great battle, and that many good people whom they called friends had been killed or injured, and were left behind. That evening, they made camp on the shores of the Cache River. They reasoned that they were probably ahead of any forward Pledge elements. It wasn't while they were on the old interstate that they were worried, anyway. Rather, they were concerned about where the interstate intersected the road that came up from the vicinity of the lock and dam. This is where they expected to have trouble, if they had trouble at all.

That night was spent in very good conversation. A dozen or more campfires were made, and everyone roamed from fire to fire, socializing. It wasn't much later than 10 p.m., that they all drifted off to their beds. By midnight, all were asleep, except for Fermion, who had agreed to take the first watch.

The next morning, the crisp and cool air filled up their senses and shook them gently into awareness. Because they wanted to be sure they were ahead of the Pledge army just in case it had managed to get across the Ohio River, they didn't bother with a full breakfast. Instead, they quietly and quickly packed up their belongings and started to the north at a steady pace. Whether it was because of the heavy, chilled air of late winter, or the apprehension about what may lay immediately ahead of them, they rode the first hours of the morning in subdued silence.

When something close to three hours had passed, they saw a rest area on one side of the road and Emory directed them all to take a break there. They were only ten or fifteen miles from the road that led up from the lock and dam, so Emory decided to send some Rangers up ahead to serve as an advance team. King and Perry joined this group, and went north at a quicker pace than they had been traveling up to this point. After about twenty minutes, Emory gave the command, and they again began moving north. The lovely forest, which ought to have made for a pleasant view, made them nervous. It could easily conceal an army.

It was well into the afternoon when they saw the signs alerting them to the coming merge of Interstate 24 with Interstate 57, which they had been following. Everyone checked their weapons one more time. Fides had been given a short knife to use as his weapon. Disappointed by this meager tool when compared to his previous implement, he satisfied himself the night before by using the knife to create a very short spear with as sharp a point as he could manage. It could serve as a club and would definitely hurt someone if they were on the receiving end of a thrust. Still, it was nothing like the premier weapon he had had in his possession for many months.

When at last they saw I-24 melting into their own road, Perry was riding back to them. Fides was too far back to hear the conversation, but he gathered that all must be well. The group continued north. As they finally passed the point they were most concerned about, Fides turned around to see King and some other Rangers coming towards them from scouting I-24. It was clear by the nonchalance of their approach that everything was alright. The conversation turned cordial.

"That's a bit of a relief, right Fides!" Charis giggled at him. "I know it would have been ok, but a little break from battle is just what I think we needed."

"I can't say that I welcomed a battle with this as my weapon," Fides said, nodding pessimistically towards his pointed stick.

"Better than nothing!" Charis replied, sprinting forward to converse with the other women with them. Fides was left alone for a short time, but not very long. King had caught up to them.

"We went south a little bit while we were waiting for you guys to catch up. We didn't see anything. I think we're safe," King reported. He didn't stay long, of course, because this was important news to report to the chain of command. The assembly began to slowly come alive in conversation as it became clear that they were not in any immediate danger.

By pushing the horses just a little bit more than perhaps they ought to be pushed, they managed to get near the little town of Marion. Perry had decided that he felt more comfortable with more of a cushion between them and their 'point of danger.' It was a hard day's ride when it was all said and done and they were very glad to be finished. The horses were treated to special treatment for their hard labor before any person served themselves. At last, though, campfires were made and late dinners were had.

Despite the fact that they knew they'd have to get up early in the morning, once again people stayed up late into the night talking. Fides found himself greatly enjoying the present company. Perry and Emory were great conversation. Emory would tell stories in his straightforward way and Perry would interject with more colorful commentary as the tale would go on. It was their way, but without the imminent threat of battle surrounding them they both gave into it whole heartedly.

In the course of the conversation, they learned that the Rangers had formed spontaneously in the hills of Kentucky after local residents grasped that there were other forces- especially the Pledge- that had designs for the country in its weakened state. These proud men and some women were not willing to standby and let that happen. Decades earlier, it had been impossible to disarm Kentucky. The citizens there had plenty of hunting rifles and knew where to hide them better than any foreign army.

Besides the Pledge, there were other forces, too, like the Copperheads, but these were much less likely to generate wide spread support. That is not to say that the Copperheads did not try. So, as the Rangers went from place to place meeting this challenge or that, others had joined them. They initially grew to have almost five hundred men, but in the course of some minor skirmishes some of their number had decided it just wasn't worth it.

Somewhere in this history Charis and Melody had joined the Rangers. That part remained unclear to Fides. The two would surprise him by contrasting what seemed like superficial chatter with some sudden extraordinary indication that they were in fact deep people. Misaluva seemed to have always been part of the Rangers, but her part didn't seem clear. What was clear was that Jonathan was falling for her. The darkness of the night concealed his constant glances in her direction.

As the night went on, residents from Marion came to visit them. The tone of the evening changed. It became apparent that some of the residents of Marion were supportive of the goals of the Pledge, even if they didn't have the nerve as yet to join them. There were some bitter words shared when it was revealed that the Rangers stood opposed to the Pledge and any group that wanted to set up anything less than a democracy on American soil. Not all of the residents felt that way, of course. In fact, when some heard about the battle and the Ranger's role in it, they slapped them on the back and offered to get for them whatever they could from their own stores.

Soon, nearly the whole town of Marion was talking with and arguing with or applauding the Rangers. The same sort of conversations that Fermion had had in Oklahoma City now took place with the residents here. This time, though, Fermion just observed.

Many of the folks the Rangers argued with felt as though democracy had only allowed rich, wealthy, and powerful people to take advantage of everyone else. People were not educated enough to express themselves democratically. When they suggested to the Rangers that it was better to have some people decide for them all and deal justly many of the Rangers became outraged.

There were plenty of murmurs supporting the Ranger position from other citizens of Marion. The internal debate of the city of Marion spilled out in the Ranger camp. By the end of a couple of hours of debate, it was clear that many were not persuaded by the Rangers, many were still neutral, but some more had decided to join the Rangers outright. These were welcomed with good cheer.

It was beginning to get late by anyone's standards. By the threes and fours they started turning in. Within thirty minutes of the first to give in to exhaustion, all but a few lookouts were asleep. For the first time in a long time, Fides took a look at his Bible before turning in. "Yea, though I walk through the valley of the shadow of death..." he read. He finished the passage, and went to sleep.

In his dreams Fides saw his wife and his children walking on the driveway coming towards him. He was walking towards them. They just kept walking. They didn't get closer or further no matter how long they walked. In his dream, Fides became uncomfortable. The joyful anticipation in the beginning of the dream turned from sweet cream to soured milk. Something was not right. His wife seemed to be warning him. But of what? His eyes flashed open just as a hard hand clapped over his mouth. He felt the point of a blade at his neck. His muffled shout got nowhere and as the tip of the knife dug into his neck he decided he had no choice at the moment but to sit still. His eyes tried to adjust so that he could see his attacker in the dark. At first, he could only see a black shape cut out of the fabric of the starlight night.

"Jack's back," he heard a voice snarl. There was a wicked snicker from the direction where Fermion had laid down. "Franklin's got himself a Fermion. What fun!" Fides could hear the sounds of shuffling but then a whisper shout by Franklin convinced Fermion to hold still, too.

"You guys killed my brother and my uncle," Jack growled. "I can't believe you guys lived this long! There is a God. He saved you for me!" Fides racked his brain for some way out of the dire predicament. Jack had obviously let his pride get the best of him. He could have killed them while they slept, but he wanted them to know. Fides knew that he had to turn this into a mistake by Jack, and quick. As he grew more aware of his situation he realized that

Jack had him straddled with his knees pinning his arms down. He didn't have many options. He only had the opportunity while Jack wasted time gloating over him.

As is so often the case in such situations, everything happened very quickly but it felt like a long time had passed. The moment was pregnant. The sound of his own breathing deafened him. Before he himself could do anything, Fides heard a shout of exclamation a few feet away from him. He heard, rather than saw, Jack jerk his head to see who had shouted. Fides used the moment to roll away from the knife, and he had a sense that Fermion had used the opportunity in the same way. There was the sound of wrestling in the dark. A number of bodies had joined the fray. The camp was coming alive, and soon someone had produced some light. The first thing Fides could make out was the forms of Jonathan and Jack in some sort of lethal embrace. But there were other forms, as well. To his surprise, there were some twenty people engaged in mortal combat all around him. Apparently Jack and Franklin had brought some friends.

However many friends they had brought, they were certainly out-numbered by the Rangers. The Rangers brought both more light to see and more men to fight. Soon Jack's gang was fighting against four men for every one of their own. Jonathan had Jack by the throat, but Jack was hacking at his arm with his knife. Every fourth blow managed to cut him but still he did not let go. Tasha had been sleeping nearby when everything started. She and Misaluva were also in the tussle. Fides shook out the remaining cobwebs and dove into the melee. It was good that they had spent some time that day getting to know some of the other Rangers or otherwise none of them would have been able to tell friend from foe.

In no time (though it felt like eternity) there were a number of men were lying on the ground. Whether they were dead or not, they were at the very least still. Fides saw Fermion pick up Franklin at the shoulder and sling him over his head. "Nice shot," Fides marveled. Fides, though, was on his way to help Jonathan. He threaded his way through the mosh pit and grabbed Jack's knife arm as he tried to bring down another swipe on Jonathan's arm. Jonathan's hands began squeezing Jack's neck with more determination. They all fell backwards. When they hit the ground Jonathan lost his grip but Fides had the knife. Jack had pulled out another from somewhere on his body but did not have a chance to use it because Fides had already plunged the knife in his hands into Jack's chest. There was a wheezing gasp, and then Jack was dead.

By this time, Perry and Emory had arranged for some of their guns. At first, it was not safe to shoot for fear of hitting their own. Jack's gang, or whatever was left of it, figured out too late that the odds had changed. Everyone else busied themselves with disentangling themselves from the fight to give their allies clear shots. Single shots rang out. Ranger snipers picked off Jack's gang at close quarters as the shots became available. Defying logic and reasoning and engulfed in a mad rage, the last three men, rather than surrendering, tried to rush the rifles. Cool to the end, the snipers waited for the clean shot and dropped each one of them in turn. For a moment there was calm, but then came a burst of orders.

"Clear up!" Emory ordered.

"Check those men!" Perry demanded.

"Sentries, check in!" Emory snapped angrily. There would be hell to pay for the sentries for letting their camp get infiltrated.

"Seal the perimeter!" Perry shouted.

Fides pulled himself over to Jonathan, who was holding his bad arm with his good one. "Many thanks," Fides said, exhausted. Jonathan didn't say anything, so Fides got close to him so he could see him in the dark. Jonathan seemed a bit pale, even in the light of the stars. Fides saw this and shouted, "Hey, Tasha! Someone help Jonathan!" Tasha came along side Jonathan as he started slipping into unconsciousness. Charis had arrived, too. Even she began barking orders.

"Put pressure on that wound there, and there. Hold the arm up. Quick, put pressure there," Charis was saying. Tasha, who needed no such instruction, took it completely in stride and did as she was told.

Jonathan looked up at Charis and saw Melody standing near, as well, a long knife in hand. "You two helped fight them, too!" Melody raised her eyebrows at him but said nothing. Charis smiled.

"Just because we are women does not mean we won't fight for our friends," Charis told him. "Or even die for them," she added.

"I'm impressed," Jonathan mumbled, and then slipped into unconsciousness. Fides was impressed too, but remained silent on the matter. After stabilizing Jonathan, Charis moved on to check other people.

Several of the Rangers had been painfully hurt, but not seriously so. Jack's gang numbered twelve. Ten were dead, but there were two left that were largely unhurt. There was some brief talk about dispatching them more permanently but Fermion argued on their behalf that without Jack to foment things, these two would find better things to do. The two nodded their heads vigorously.

"Still, we can't have them wandering around as spies," Emory said.

"I think the Marion Men might have a place to keep them locked up," Perry suggested. The Marion Men were those of Marion who had decided to join the Rangers. They would later be called "The Mighty Marion Men," but that was later, and was too long to say in normal conversation, anyway.

"Alright, send someone into town and find someone who can deal with these two," Emory agreed. Emory then gave a thorough tongue lashing to the look-outs who had allowed the gang to infiltrate the camp. After this, he turned to Fermion, "Who's Jack?"

Fermion explained the story of their encounter with Jack and his men back in Albuquerque. He omitted nothing. He explained how the last they'd seen anything to do with Jack and his men was before Oklahoma City. He concluded, "He must have known where we were going and decided it was easiest just to head us off."

"Well," Fides said, "we'd forgotten all about them, hadn't we?"

"We sure did," Fermion concurred. "But we'll be able to definitely forget about them from now on," he added.

Fides and Fermion went to Jonathan's side. Tasha and Charis were working together to stitch the many wounds in Jonathan's left arm. Jonathan was still out cold. This was good, as he very likely would not have enjoyed being awake at that moment. After he was completely sown up, he still did not wake. There were still hours left of the night, so everyone turned in to get some more sleep before the sun would rise to drive them onward. Jonathan was one of the first to wake up.

"Oooooow!" he muttered loudly. Jonathan proceeded to use language that his mother certainly would not have allowed him to use in describing his wounds, his pain, and his overall circumstances. Whatever effect Jonathan expected, what he received was a round of laughter and applause.

"Give'm hell, Jon!" Perry egged him on, scratching his big black beard in amusement.

Tasha changed the dressings on Jonathan's arm. There were some significant wounds there. He would not be able to use that arm for weeks, even months. Tasha informed him of this: he would not be able to ride a horse, either.

"There is no way you guys are leaving me behind!" Jonathan exclaimed. "Fermion, you find a way to bring me. That's the end of the discussion."

"But you are released from your vow," Fides said. "You have saved my life. You've earned the right to move along as you see fit." Jonathan considered that for a moment.

"Ok, I am free. I accept that," Jonathan replied. "And the way I see fit to proceed is to remain with my friends. I would rather go forward and face death yet again as though still bound by my oath than be a completely free man and abandon my friends to face death alone, without me," he argued.

"But you can't ride..." Fides tried to reason with him.

"You guys can find a way," Jonathan said decisively. There was nothing else they could say to him, so Fides and Fermion went to talk it over with Perry and Emory. They were in council already to consult their map and chart out the day's goals. Misaluva was there listening quietly. King was there too, ready to once again perform the scouting duties that he had happily fulfilled for the Rangers the day before. Some of the new Marion Men that Fides had not yet learned names for were there to discuss arrangements for the tattered remnants of Jack's gang. Fides and Fermion shared the situation with them.

The Mighty Marion Men thought that they could arrange for a wagon. Misaluva volunteered to hook her horse to that wagon. It was not exactly riding in comfort, but it was reasoned that if Jonathan insisted on coming with, he'd have to be prepared for the best they could arrange and the discomfort likely to be associated with it. It was quickly arranged and quickly performed. Jonathan was informed and he didn't make any kind of protest.

With their numbers increased by some thirty men from Marion, they set out north again. King and a few others laid back to form a rear guard. Perry went ahead as an advance guard. The main body escorted the key: Fides. Fides could only think about his dreams the night before. He was getting closer to his home, his wife, and his family. But was he? Was he really?

The troop continued north on the ragged remains of Interstate 57. As they passed through the demoralized Illinois towns along it, they picked up a few more people here and there who thought the Rangers were the people to be with. In fact, by the time they had reached the intersection of I-57 and I-64, they had accumulated another one hundred men. This success was due in large part to the influence of the Mighty Men of Marion. Taking into account relations and friends, the Mighty Men were familiar with a large part of the population in the region, and the Mighty Men did most of the evangelizing as they passed through various towns.

As encouraging as it was to see their numbers swelling again, it did not relieve the grief that the Rangers had for losing so many fine friends only a little over a week earlier. Even worse, as they went through each town it was clear that many residents had already left to join another army: the Pledge. On occasion, they'd pass travelers heading the other direction who looked at them suspiciously and remained quiet and unfriendly with the Rangers.

It was a little over a week after the great battle at Cairo and the troop saw the signs announcing the miles to the city of Salem document smaller and smaller numbers yet to be crossed. It had been several days after Jack's gang had been finally dispatched, and the conversation had once again become cordial. The Rangers were all eager to hear more about Fermion and the Nephilim. The spectacle that Fermion had provided could not be forgotten, and Fermion didn't even try to make people forget.

"Alright, Fermion," Perry had prodded Fermion once again. It was the tenth time Perry had tried to pry an explanation out of Fermion. "Now, this seems a good time to tell us about the Nephilim."

Fides smiled, but Emory joshed: "Yes, you've been delaying it for several days now. Perry is going easy on you letting it go that long."

Fermion could not help grinning in return. Perry hadn't exactly been going easy. "I'll make you a deal," Fermion replied.

"What are your terms?" Perry returned.

"If you can get Misaluva to sing us a song, I'll give you a hint of an explanation," Fermion replied with a straight face. Some of the others listening in laughed and some playfully taunted Fermion for delaying the inevitable. Perry turned to Misaluva with a questioning look.

"Sure. Here is my song," she smiled, clearing her throat, and tipping her head back slightly.

"Myth and matter merge
Spirit o'er the water's surge
Lords of melody and song
Lords of Blue, burning bright
will right the ancient wrong,
No Val' Is saying,
Our Life is no dream,
but it should and will perhaps become one.
I rise up from slumber to meet the light
I awake to be as I'd always seemed
and partake in the ancient victory won."

Misaluva's voice was as clear as a mountain brook. Her song could be heard by the entire company, but it did not seem like she was singing loudly. Even when she ended on a soft and tender note, it could be heard clearly by everyone. Fermion was contemplative.

"That is a lovely song," Fermion said. "May I ask where you learned it?"

"You could ask," she replied, making it clear that she would not answer directly. "Whenever I see a blue flower, though, I think of it."

"Well, at any rate, I thank you sincerely. We shall have to be on the look out for a blue flower to signify our hope in the righting of the most ancient wrong," Fermion said airily, as though trying not to call attention to Misaluva's reticence. "Well, you've kept your side of the bargain. I shall tell you more. It may even be more than my dear friends Fides, King, and Jonathan know."

"Alright then, get on with it!" Perry cried out.

"You may have guessed that I do not belong to this world, even if you were prepared to dismiss that as nonsense. But when I say 'world,' I do not merely mean that I come from some other planet in your universe. The distance between my home and this place cannot be measured; it is only declared," Fermion ignored the confused looks and went on. "Have you ever heard the argument put forward by theologians that as awful as things sometimes are, the existence of at least the possibility of awful events is what makes certain virtues possible? For example, it is difficult to consider courage a virtue if there is not the possibility of failure. And the amount of courage that might be possible is proportional to the potential depth of the failure?"

Fermion gave them a moment to respond, but those who had managed to follow along this far decided they'd be better off leaving the question as rhetorical. Fermion continued, "Well, the theologians are right about that. Courage is about overcoming fear, and unless that fear is a real thing, 'courage' is not real, either. But have the theologians considered that some of their conceptions of the afterlife in heaven with God would rob heaven of its virtues? A heaven without the possibility of fear is a heaven without courage. But we all know that courage and bravery are great and noble values. How odd to suggest that they could not extend into the next Life. But there are some differences that we need not go over now. Suffice it to say in the next Life your passions are all completely robust and capable and sustained in such a way as to deal with obstacles that would destroy you in your current state."

"Well, an adventure is a fine way for courage to be exercised. Beyond the veil, one type of adventure you may embark on is to become a Nephilim. The Nephilim consist of those who are entranced by Creation. All Creations. Every aspect of them. They are permitted to study aspects of this or that Creation, and in some cases, enter into them. I have been studying your creation from the beginning of it. As I studied it from without, I was not bound by your temporal or spatial limitations. How long I have studied it, I do not know or care. It is many times longer than your creation has even existed, though.

The Nephilim are like bookends: they come at the beginning to try to provide guidance to the budding creation- to prevent a fall, or war against the effects of a fall, so that all who will be saved, *will* be saved. Then they come near the end, to provide every last opportunity for conditions to exist so that every ounce of being that can be redeemed is redeemed. I am of the Nephilim- and I am one who comes near the end. Your time is almost up, but it is not for me to say how much longer is ahead of you. The end has been hidden from me, and it is not my business to know."

Most of those in the range of Fermion's hearing were astonished at these words. There were shouts of disbelief and even anger. They wanted the honest answer, not a fairytale. That's what they said, at least. Fermion's face got a little red with anger, "You do not believe me? Even after seeing what you have seen? Such it is with your generation. But that was the price Someone was willing to pay to accomplish what he wanted accomplished. I have seen the Joy that awaits the final redemption, or else you'd see more indignation out of me now!"

"So, what about the crazy demonstration?" Emory thoughtfully asked.

"You have to understand that there is more to your world than even you are aware of. I, however, while completely within your world am not shut off from those parts that you cannot see. Furthermore, I do not give up who I am and what I am merely by entering into your creation. I have sometimes been at war while you have been at peace and at peace while you have been at war. I am able to stand in all levels of your reality. As such, the weapons for use in some of those levels still have effect in other levels. To use them, however, requires allowing power to go out from me. In some cases that power is replenished as the normal course of things, like a person can be healed over time with good treatment and food."

"So, you can still die?" Perry wondered.

"Again? Why not?" Fermion asked him.

"Again?" Fides repeated, perplexed.

"Surely you understand that despite the fact that we are of different worlds, we are nonetheless of the same kind? In order to be resurrected, you must die. The seed that is planted dies and gives birth not merely to another seed, but to a whole plant. This is not to say that resurrection is the normal state of affairs. Life is the normal state of affairs, and death a terrible and repulsive interloper. Resurrection sets right a disgusting situation, and in that regards is mercy, but so much better it would be if there were no need for any kind of resurrection at all! However, I confess that my world never suffered a fall, so death has not made itself at home there. Most of what I know about death, sadly, comes from my observations of your world."

"If there was no 'fall,' as you say, how did you come to die and rise?" Emory pressed him.

"I fell off a horse and broke my neck in a wild charge against the Tentacles of Cthulhu-"

"Bless you!" Tasha said.

"Thank you," Fermion said, and then continued, "Yes, that was a bit of an ignominious end, but it did give me the opportunity to become a Nephilim. Since my world was unfallen, I decided to volunteer for duty on a fallen world. But every Nephilim has his- or her- own story, including individual duties, tasks, and assignments." Seeing Melody about to inquire about what those might be for Fermion, Fermion rushed to add, "Most of the time, it is for the Nephilim and the Nephilim alone to know."

"Ok, so when we die, it's not over, but you've already died, so what happens if you die?" Jonathan inquired.

"I do not know. But the one who knows me knows, and that is enough for me," Fermion replied.

"Do you know the future?" Perry wondered.

"That depends on what you mean. The word doesn't mean all that much to me. However, I know what you are getting at. Let me say that I really don't, but I do know quite a bit about the past," Fermion said, clearly coming to the end of whatever he was willing to share.

Fides prompted him to answer one last question, "So, when Corrie said to watch out because the Nephilim were on the earth, she was saying that time was short, right?" Fermion nodded.

"Now, wait a minute," Jonathan interjected. "Ok, this 'explains' you- but what are the Shadowmen?"

"I honestly don't know," Fermion said.

"How can you not know?" King pressed him.

"I am mystified about their identity and their purpose. They are not Nephilim. Indeed, I do not believe they have any existence at all- at this time, anyway- apart from this world. Perhaps it is because this is my first assignment, but I really don't know," Fermion stated. He then indicated that he was taking no more questions. That was alright, because many of the Rangers had lost interest, thinking that it was all one great big yarn. Those who believed Fermion had grown quiet, considering the implications.

Throughout the rest of the journey, few asked Fermion anything more about the Nephilim. The only exception was some of the

Mighty Men, who heard the talk but who obviously had not been in Cairo to see the event. They came and made Fermion repeat some of the account again. This had the same effect: some believed, most didn't. This did not keep anyone from having fine conversation as the trip progressed, however. Some of them especially got on well together. They became more familiar with members of the Rangers that were beyond the leadership core became well known to them, too. For example, the de facto leader of the Marion Men, Aiken Trott, fit right in with them, fast becoming King's friend.

Their travels were without further incident until they drew closer to Effingham. They had begun discussing whether or not they ought to proceed to Bloomington where the family contact center was or if maybe Fides should go home first to see if his family was there. This led to contemplating whether everyone should go on to Terre Haute if Fides went, or if it might be better to divide the party with some escorting Fides and the rest going to Bloomington. The ultimate destination was Peoria. It was in Peoria that Fides would be able to rid himself of the treacherous key around his neck, and even then he still did not have the code to open it.

However, the closer they came to Effingham, the more anxious that Fides was to go home, first. They were relatively much closer to Terre Haute than they were to Bloomington, and Fides could not help but think any trip to Bloomington without finding out what could be found out at home would only make for a longer trip later. After all, if there was no sign of his family in Bloomington, he'd have to go all the way back to Terre Haute, anyway. The counter argument was that in such a case, Fides could go on to Peoria first from Bloomington and rid himself of the key and finally be unburdened from the tie to that city. Fides was definitely leaning towards a trip to Indiana first. The matter was left unsettled until Effingham itself.

King and Aiken had taken to being in charge of the advance guard. Tasha tended to remain back with the group, and rather than being put off by King having someone else to spend time with, she seemed to be relieved. King and Aiken would begin their trip in the morning about thirty minutes before anyone else. They'd be about a mile ahead of the rest of the group before it set off. Another advanced guard would take their place around lunch time, and then King and Aiken would replace those people in the middle of the afternoon. Emory wisely kept people coming and going between them and the advance guard to make sure all was well. Additionally, Emory made sure that they maintained a rear guard as well.

Effingham was only a few miles away and it was getting dark. Emory decided that they would start camp a little earlier than normal so that they could pass through the city in the full light of the day. They had just completed throwing up their rudimentary canvas shelters after starting some fires when the group became aware of activity. One of the relay messengers between King and

Aiken had come rushing back to bring Emory a message. Emory was not happy with whatever the news was, but it appeared to be tentative, as he gave no commands except to send the relay back out along with a few more companions on some of the freshest horses. Despite the casualness in which this was done, some of the more experienced Rangers checked their weapons.

After about an hour, King and Aiken returned. They were deeply troubled and immediately sought out the fire where Emory and the rest of them had set up shop.

"What's going on?" Fides asked them. Emory had not said anything about the earlier conversation. King did not respond to Fides, but directed his comments to Emory.

"There is another Pledge army!" King exclaimed.

"You're sure of it?" Emory inquired.

"Yes, absolutely. We were right when we spotted those riders in thinking that they too were an advance guard for another party. We sent the relay back with our hunch to make sure that you did not come too close and then sought cover to watch. After about twenty minutes we saw what I hope was the full body. There were at least a thousand men," King explained.

"Why do you hope it was the full body?" Jonathan asked.

"I shouldn't like to think there were even more than what we observed," Aiken answered for King.

"We think it was the full body, though, because we didn't see any others and we watched the full force pass us heading north," King said.

"But that's not all," Aiken reminded him.

"No, there's more. Even though I think we saw the full force, I think there really must be many more. Tens of thousands more, *somewhere*," King shuddered.

Perry's face went pale. Emory spoke, "What makes you say that?"

Perry screwed up his eyes trying to make sense of the message, "How can you think there must be many more while insisting you saw the full body?"

"Well, after the advanced guard went past I thought I spied another vantage point to check things out from. So, I crept to it, and hid. Soon, the main group arrived. Well, I'm pretty lucky. I didn't expect so many people. There were so many that they walked right over my position. I heard some of them talking. Most of it was just conversation. They clearly think that they are on their way north to meet a much larger body, though," King said.

"Perhaps they are expecting the force that we defeated at Cairo?" Fermion suggested.

"That's what I thought, too, but they seemed to know about the defeat in Cairo and they included them in their estimated strength. I couldn't make out everything, of course. However, I definitely gathered that they thought that they had at least a force of some twenty to thirty thousand, not including the Cairo force."

"You're sure about that?" Emory pushed him.

"Definitely. They passed right over me. They were talking about divisions and regiments and squads and a southern force and an eastern force and a western force. I didn't look to see at the time, but Aiken told me later that he thought that their leadership went past near where he saw me hide. I am confident of this information," King added emphatically.

"This is a ruffle in our plans," Perry thought out loud.

"It sounds like they are on their way to take Peoria right now," Tasha suggested.

"It doesn't add up very well, though," Emory said. "We have been south, and I think we have a pretty good idea what is there. Though we heard of various smaller sized units of the Pledge, the groups we heard of were more often than not just like some of the roving bands of renegade Indians or Copperheads. We know of no group the size of the force at Cairo. And a western force? To the west is St. Louis and the Mississippi River. St. Louis is supposed to have been annihilated and should not have any population. I confess I know nothing about what is to the east."

"I'd stake my life on this information," King declared.

"I don't doubt you," Emory rushed to say. "In fact, I very much believe you and think you've got the right view of things. What it means, though, is that we are operating on some very bad assumptions. It would seem, for example, that we are walking headlong into an army that is overwhelmingly large. Just the unit you saw is bigger than we are."

"Time to go off-road?" Perry suggested.

"No doubt," Emory agreed. "Our rear-guards haven't been reporting anything behind us, but with I-70 passing so close we can't be sure. Let's make that our first step. Let's re-encamp just north of this little town on my map," he said, pointing to a dot called 'Watson.' "Let's break camp right now and set up camp over there and re-consider the matter," he ordered.

The orders were immediately delivered. The Rangers had complete trust in their leaders so there wasn't even any grumbling. The fires were put out and the ashes hid as best as could be done and the horses were re-packed. King and Aiken went off to the east into the fields and woods to find a suitable place that was within a reasonable distance. They didn't have to go far to find a good sized hill that could conceal their position from passerby on I-57. Camp was reset, and more armed scouts than normal were posted in a perimeter around their new position.

"Ok, what to do?" Emory opened the conversation among the leadership after the camp was settled.

Fides had been considering the issue during the whole transition to the new camp. He told them that he thought that given this new information, he really thought it was not only good on his emotions to go first to Terre Haute, but good sense. A force the size as what King's information suggested existed was far too large to try to try to navigate the key through. Yet, the very thing they needed in order to have success in Peoria, ultimately, was the key. There were comments of agreement on the point, but reluctance to totally abandon Bloomington or Peoria to the Pledge. At least, not without a fight. This seemed to be Perry's view.

As the conversation progressed, the plan firmed up. Fides, Charis, Melody, Misaluva, Jonathan, and perhaps a half dozen Rangers would go on to Terre Haute, and then seek to rejoin them either in Bloomington proper or Peoria. Tasha, King, Fermion, and the remaining Rangers under Perry and Emory would press on to Peoria. Fermion had to continue north, because except for Fides, no one else had a clue how to get to the bunker that was hidden in Peoria. Fides and Emory were the main decision makers, as everyone else was willing to abide by their judgment. In the course of the deliberations, King had grown subdued. At last, he felt he had to speak.

"I've been thinking," King began explaining some thoughts he'd developed. "That southern force we defeated in Cairo will soon be at our backs. The Shadowmen are likely to be behind them, but as it was, the Pledge force to the south is a good match in size and capabilities to the Shadowmen. What lies ahead is a force that is two or three times bigger even than the Shadowmen. Even if we had everyone available, we would not be able to successfully resist."

"My boy," Perry said somewhat ruefully, "we do not retreat."

"No, no, no," King corrected him. "I'm not calling for a retreat. I'm saying that we need more men. More armed men, preferably."

Perry didn't quite see the point, so he scoffed, "Well sure, but where are we going to get more armed men?"

"Actually, I can think of a place," King said hesitantly. There was a lingering pause.

When the pause became uncomfortably long, Perry blurted, "Well, ok, you can tell us where we can find them now!"

During this pause, though, there was a silent conversation between Fermion, Fides, Tasha, Jonathan, and King. No words were exchanged. Instead, one set of eyes met another set of eyes, as each one in turn saw the solution but also immediately the problem that it posed. Emory had noticed this, and respectfully waited for them to sort it out between them, but Perry wasn't good at seeing such nuances until they were pointed out to him.

Fermion gave the explanation: "We had an opportunity to meet with some Indians back in Oklahoma who were heavily armed and extremely disgusted with the Pledge. I do not know how many their total number would be, but they would be extremely well armed. I'm not talking about hunting rifles, here. I'm talking about military hardware."

That got Perry's attention, "Oklahoma? That seems far."

"Yes, it could take some time, and someone will have to make the trip," King pointed out.

"It could take months!" Perry objected. But the decision had already been made with silent looks.

"It very well could take months. You will have to try to postpone a confrontation if you can," King said.

"Ok, but who will go?" Emory brought the matter to the point.

"I will go," King asserted.

"You are only a boy!" Perry objected again.

King winced, and snarled back, "I am man enough for this!"
Aiken interrupted them. Though it was true that King was a young man, not yet twenty, and Aiken was in his forties, the two had become good friends in the short time they had known each other. He addressed King, "I do not doubt your capabilities. I do hope it is no slight if I say that you would want a fellow warrior at your side. I will be that warrior, if you would permit it."
"That would be fine!" King agreed.
Emory had poked Perry in the ribs to keep him from putting his foot in it anymore. He encouraged King, "I cannot keep you, of course. It is a noble effort besides. As for trying to postpone a confrontation, that may not end up being within my power. I support you in your quest."
"Tasha, will you come with me?" King turned his attention to the woman that had been his guide for as long as he could remember.
"We have come far together, King. You no longer need me. I know you aren't asking out of necessity; you certainly are man enough for this task. Still, I feel that I will be needed to the north. At the very least, to tend to the wounded: and I think there will be many. I hope you will forgive me," Tasha spoke with some apprehension, not knowing how King would respond. King was surprised- the two had been together for years. However, he did not seem especially hurt.
"It is settled, then," King said. "We'll leave first thing in the morning."
"We'll need some new people to serve as our advance guards," Emory said.
So it was finally decided that King and Aiken would leave them and try to get help from the Indians. It went without saying that they would try to enlist Chummy and his vehicles, too. Perry and Emory with their Rangers would continue north with Fermion and Tasha to find what there was to find. Charis, Misaluva, Melody, Jonathan, and Fides would go to Terre Haute to see about Fides' family.
The next morning saw bittersweet partings.

== Chapter 11 ==

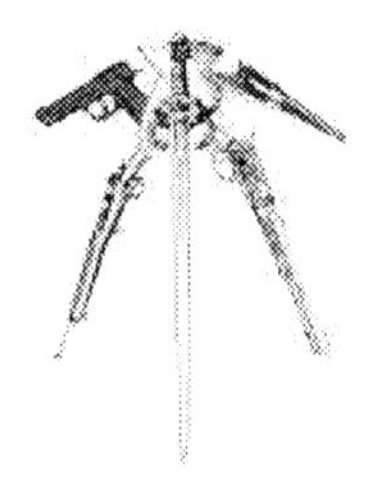

The three parties divided early on a fine spring morning. King and Aiken went west, towards St. Louis. The Rangers went north. Charis, Misaluva, Melody, Jonathan, and Fides were on their way to Terre Haute. There had been a brief argument with King about his choice of direction. St. Louis was supposed to be a nuclear wasteland. It was also the most direct route to Oklahoma. King argued that if people were coming from that direction, they had to come from somewhere. It was King's quest, after all, so he was free to do as he saw fit.

It had also been decided that no other Ranger other than Misaluva would travel with Fides (Charis and Melody did not consider themselves Rangers). Every spare man would head north. It was also reasoned that a group of five would stand a better chance evading a threat than ten or twenty would. Also, both Fides and King refused arms, arguing that they could more easily talk their way out of a situation if they seemed to only be locals. There were tears, but no weeping as the three groups parted.

After allowing Fermion to take the lead for so much of his journey, Fides felt awkward in having his small group look to him for decision making. Fides would have even let Misaluva take charge since she was clearly a warrior, but she would have none of it. Fortunately, Jonathan had been able to ride a horse on his own for the last couple of days or this trip would have been a bit slower than they would have liked. Jonathan greatly preferred being able to ride by Misaluva's side than be pulled behind her in a cart. It was strange and almost eerie to hear only five horses instead of two or three hundred horses. At first there wasn't much conversation as they absorbed the relative silence, but after a couple of hours they began again to engage each other.

They rode about fifteen miles that day, and fifteen miles the next. On the third day they were only about thirty miles from Terre Haute and Fides found himself babbling on about life in the area. He was, after all, very near home. He could point on occasion to construction projects that he had had a part in and he would chat about various events he'd experienced even decades earlier. The lurking question was left unasked and in fact Fides himself refused to ask it. He could not control whatever it was that was waiting for him in Terre Haute, so he forced himself not to think of it too much.

On the third day, there wasn't any immediate familiar place to talk about so the conversation turned to Fermion's self-revelations about the Nephilim. They were perplexed about how a person could die and then die again. It sounded like reincarnation, but Misaluva pointed out that the Nephilim didn't seem to be absorbed into the universe in one new form or another but retained their specific personality and individuality where ever they went. Jonathan carried the conversation for a time pondering whether or not the same things that were open to members of other creations would also be open to them as well.

Misaluva wisely pointed out that Fermion was only giving his own story and not their story. Fermion's own story and the story of the creation he was from was really none of their own business. Melody added that if Fermion had told the truth, only a handful of generations were even aware of any details about any other people from other creations at all. As Fermion had said, the Nephilim were only bookends, coming to help guide things in the beginning and in the end. This reminded Fides of Corrie's Bible.

The next time they took a break to rest the horses, Fides discreetly pulled it out and thumbed through it again. The old pages had a musty smell that he found enchanting. He had always thought so, but he had also always been intimidated by the book, too. He was nervous about reading it. Corrie's numerous notes dotted the collection of smaller books that collectively were known as 'the Bible.'

His eyes fell onto a passage in a book called Jeremiah: "For I know the plans I have for you,' declares the Lord, 'plans to prosper you and not to harm you, plans to give you hope and a future.'" Corrie had written the word "Context!" in the margin and underlined it several times. Reading the passage gave him a sudden comfort. Did God know the plans for him? Were those plans to prosper him? Fides felt a growing assurance that he would find his wife and family well and healthy. He had fallen into such deep thought that he didn't notice that the others had returned from watering the horses at a nearby stream.

When Charis saw the book, she was immediately taken by it and even insisted that they stay for a few minutes longer to look at it. Fides pointed out to her the passage in Genesis that spoke about the Nephilim, and then with some embarrassment admitted that he had not made it a habit to read much of what else was in it. He didn't add that he had been frequently rebuked for not reading it, or that Corrie had rebuked him for not even taking the time to read some of the other books that she had kept at her small home. Charis read a few pages of the worn book and asked Fides if she could hold onto it to read more of it later. His initial feeling was that it was a gift to him, but something inside him told him that the gift was meant to be used, and if he wasn't using it, he may as well lend it out to someone who would. With his new assurance in hand, he didn't need the book anymore, anyway.

After they returned to the road from their brief stop, the conversation turned to how there were now so few Bibles in the country in the first place. None of them seemed to possess the whole account. The events had all occurred prior to their own times, though some of the later ones occurred while they were coming of age.

The United States had given up some of its rights to govern itself in the name of world peace. Naturally, it had started innocently enough. The nation's capital had been destroyed in an act of nuclear terrorism. The United Nations had graciously offered to take over some of the functions of the government while the United States got back on its feet. Those given that authority seized even more. It was not too long before the United Nations and its International Force had decided that the problems of the world could be solved by clamping down on religion and weapons proliferation.

Experts, mainly biologists from England, argued persuasively that religion was the source of most of the problems in the world, and the use of weapons the logical manifestation in the minds of those delusional individuals. The experts at the United Nations accepted this view, and attempted to solve it. The average citizens of the United States did not abide this very well. Despite resistance, the International Force easily dispatched the unorganized armed forces of the United States in their area of control.

A coordinated invasion in the south by the Chinese and Mexicans surprised the organized armed forces of the United States, defeating them. This defeat allowed the United Nations to carry out its book burning and weapons confiscation programs throughout the country. Bibles were not the only books burned, by any means. Korans and other religious documents were also collected and burned. Ensuing riots were dealt with mercilessly. The United Nations had learned its own lessons from the past. Once the thousands of small, rebel militias had been trounced, the United Nations graciously allowed a semblance of the United States of America to continue to exist. The southern invaders withdrew.

Then, the United Nations surprised their own membership by proceeding to stamp out religious fervor throughout the world, disarming or defeating numerous countries that tried to resist. After all, the experts at the United Nations argued, religion was the cause of all the worst ills in all human history, not just American history. The consequences of this attitude would have been predictable to some, but not the experts at the United Nations.

That was the history as best as the five could piece together, and that was why Bibles were exceedingly rare and why Charis had never seen one before.

They shared various stories about how their parents or grand parents endured the various aspects of these turmoils. How it all crumbled was part of their own story, however. The Disease had loosened the United Nation's grip on the United States, and perhaps the whole world, and the nuclear attacks had destroyed centers of control, besides. In this limbo, average Americans had discovered that they had the opportunity to once again rebuild their nation.

It gave them a sense of awe as they realized that they were in a position to help affect the path of history in a meaningful way.

There were some who wanted to have a monarchy (so they had heard). Some wanted anarchy. Some wanted communism. Some wanted an Arian nation. Some wanted an Indian nation. Still others wanted a return to democracy and the Republic. Who knows what other views were out there? There was also a sense of concern that lurked in the background, too. Even the Indians, communists, anarchists, and Arians did not want the United Nations to come back. All the groups were unified in the view that they needed to get the country on its feet before an external force managed to get back on its feet and come knocking on their door once again. The quest for many of the groups was to unify the country under its own banner before the external threat made itself known.

Speaking about such matters helped keep the conversation off of Terre Haute for most of the day. However, late in the afternoon they met a farmer on the side of the road and had a brief conversation with him. For the first time, they learned that Indianapolis had been one of the cities destroyed in the wave of nuclear attacks. They thanked the man for that information and gloomily moved forward. Fides could not think about anything else, now. His wife and children not only would have had to endure the spread of the Disease, but also the problems associated with a nuclear detonation not too far away. In fact, there was the possibility that his family had been in Indianapolis. Fides fought against the despair growing in his heart. He remembered the passage: The Lord had a plan to prosper him. Doubt and faith clashed inside his soul in the shadow of his deep longing to be reunited with his family.

That night, they camped about ten miles away from his home. Fides had trouble sleeping. His dreams were filled with stories that felt familiar but ended without comfortable resolutions. He woke up once and strolled around the forest just to shake off some nervous energy. The clouds parted here and there so that dark patches punctuated with star light could be seen. After a time, he returned to his blankets and fell into a much deeper sleep. When the morning came, he had a sense of being reconciled to his fate. There was nothing to be done but to find out. Sympathetic looks from his friends greeted him as he resolutely climbed onto his horse and they began making their way towards Fides' home.

Shortly before they came to the Illinois-Indiana border, Fides guided them off of Interstate 70 and onto Highway 40. It was shortly after a brief lunch that the party threaded their way through some side streets that Fides called shortcuts and re-emerged again on Highway 40 for the homestretch. It was only a couple of miles, now. The party slowed slightly, as Fides became hesitant to go on. On they went, however. They came to Fides' driveway, and they turned left to follow it through a bit of trees. The view opened up and they could see his house tucked off into some more trees ahead and to the right.

Stillness.

Fides brought them to a small shed that they could tie the horses to and then led them to the house. The doors were locked and the windows were shut. The bars he had installed were unmolested. It did not seem as though anyone had been in or out of the house for years.
"Should we knock?" Jonathan inquired.
"I suppose maybe I should," Fides agreed, but could not bring himself to do it. Charis knocked on his behalf. There was still no noise coming from the old farm house or anything else to indicate it was at all inhabited or had been for a long time. Fides walked around to the back. As they were going, Charis suggested that they pry their way into the house, but Fides chuckled and informed them that it would take far more extreme measures than that to get in. Before they had a chance to press him for an explanation, they arrived at the back door. Instead of going to the door, though, Fides went to the rock garden and kicked at the rocks.
"A hidden key?" Melody asked.
"Nope," Fides replied. "A combination." Fides was stooping here and there to move the stones around into new positions. After a little deliberation he managed to remember what needed to be remembered. There were some faint clicking sounds. Satisfied, he went at last to the door, but instead of trying the handle he pulled down on a lever which clanked loudly. The door, instead of swinging open, slid up into the house like an overhead door.
"Not bad," Jonathan goggled. The interior of the farm house had been completely re-done. The windows had been barred, but that was not all that was barred. Though it was decoratively done, you could see that there were in fact bars all the way around the exterior walls of the house.
"Those are fire resistant," Fides said, pointing to the various support beams that reinforced the bars. "Can't tell you all the tricks, though." They lingered in the living room uncomfortably as Fides explored the house. The kitchen adjoined the living room, so they could see that it had been left as it was many years back. It wasn't as though anyone had left suddenly- it was more like someone went to do some errand or chore and left the kitchen cleaning to be done later. Some place settings were left on the table. Everything was caked in dust. They didn't need Fides to come back downstairs to understand what could be understood from the scene.
"Well, what do you want to do?" Misaluva gently wondered. Fides didn't know. Where was his family? There was no note. There was no hint of explanation. He had looked in the bedrooms. Fides felt so sure that he would find them safe and sound. He had looked in the bathrooms. There was a familiar pit forming in his stomach, but he decided to refrain from morbid thoughts until he actually knew something. He had even looked in the closets. It required every ounce of self-control he had not to give into his fears.
"Well, if you don't mind, can you help me clean up? I guess if we stay a day or two before heading to Bloomington to see if we can learn anything else it won't hurt anything," Fides replied. This

suggestion was received as a command and the five of them set about cleaning up the place. The kitchen was cleaned; the dust was swept away. The windows were thrown open so that the crisp spring air could flush out the place. About the middle of the evening they decided they ought to eat something. Fides led them to a discreet stairway that went down into the basement. It was a fortified cellar. They were able to find some of the provisions that had been left from before. Things like wheat, flour, and dried corn were sealed up in air tight containers and were still good after all this time. Everything was a little stale, mind you, but it was edible. While they ate, Fides regaled them with stories about his wife, Melody, and his children. He pointed out pictures of them from happier times.

For the first time in a long time for all of them, they slept inside a building for the night. Fides stoked up a fire that sent a plume of smoke out of the chimney for the first time in many years. His friends retired to the various bedrooms of his children. Fides reclined in his own bed. How long had it been? It was sad that he was in it by himself, but he was in it, and that was a good start! Despite his apprehensions about the future, he slept well, a voice in his head saying, "...plans to prosper you..." But maybe that was his own voice he heard.

In the morning the smells of pancakes greeted his nostrils. He quickly distinguished the smell of coffee, too. He didn't even have half a thought that his wife and children were home: he knew he had the ladies to thank. He rolled out of bed and helped himself to some fresh clothing- again, the first for quite a long time. Downstairs Jonathan was flirting with Misaluva and Charis and Melody were chattering while they cooked and cleaned. Everyone gave him a hearty hello and good morning, and Fides sat down to eat, too. Finally, all five of them were seated around the table. Fides teared up briefly as he considered the ever increasing likelihood that this was the most people to sit around this table in five or more years. However, it was too pleasant to ruin it all with such emotions, so he made up his mind to enjoy the fellowship of the moment and the first good, hot meal in a very long time.

They relaxed for about an hour after the meal but then fetched the horses, which had also had a comfortable night. They trotted into the environs of Terre Haute to see what could be seen. People who saw them didn't recognize Fides and since the city saw a lot of travelers anyway, they didn't draw much attention. After poking around the city for awhile, Fides began dropping in on neighbors and businesses looking for familiar people. The population was pretty sparse. He decided to return home for the day and tomorrow go deeper into the city to check around a little more. Turning the horses around, they returned to the Ranthem homestead.

Waiting for them was Ed.

"Ed!" Fides shouted, embracing the man. Ed warmly shook his hand.

"Fides, you're looking old!" Ed flattered him.

"Not as old as I would be had I been stuck with you these years," Fides jazzed him in return. "Come on in, let's put on some coffee!" Ed gave a sideways look at Fides companions, noting especially, but as discreetly as possible, the three ladies. Fides introduced them to Ed as they came into the kitchen.

"Ed was the foreman of the work crew that I was a part of on the Peoria project. He's a real good friend," Fides explained to his friends. Melody fired up a pot of coffee and Jonathan fetched another bag of dried corn for Misaluva to magically turn into something tasty to eat. "How did you know I was back?" Fides prodded.

"Well, I've been watching for you..." Ed trailed off.

"Well, Ed, you won't believe the story of my last few years. Let's hear yours!" Fides exclaimed, exuberantly.

Ed didn't meet Fides' eyes, "Well, to tell you the truth we thought you were dead. The plane didn't come back as had been promised, which made me a bit angry. We debated about leaving the project, but they convinced us to finish it up. A couple of days later we heard about the nuclear explosions. Well, we heard that Chicago was gone. We didn't learn about Indy until we got home, ourselves. We agonized over whether to leave immediately after hearing about Chicago, and I suppose had we known about Indy we would have left for sure. We figured at that point that if we worked double time, we could finish in a week to ten days and be off for home almost a month early. That didn't turn out to be realistic, but we were done in twenty days. We came home to find a stream of refugees coming from Indy..." Ed grew thoughtful. "They didn't look so good. We ended up burying quite a few of them. And well..."

"Go on, Ed," Fides encouraged him, now fearing news- not so pleasant news- about his family.

"Well, not too long after that most of the crew came down with the Disease. They're all dead, Fides. All of them," Ed painfully informed him. That was like a punch in the gut to Fides, who gulped hard. Still, this was better than what he had been expecting. "We got all the stuff we earned, but none of it was enjoyed. I've got your share and everyone else's stored in a couple of the guy's barns." Jonathan and the three ladies watched the scene uncomfortably. "That's not all, Fides," Ed said softly.

"Oh?" Fides replied, knowing what was coming, but disbelieving. Fides whispered to himself, "...plans to prosper..." Ed gave a nod towards the door, and got up and walked out of the kitchen and out of the house. Fides caught the signal and followed him. The rest of them looked at each other and wondered if the nod was an invitation to them, as well. They followed as far as the front window, which they looked out of to see Ed walking and talking with Fides as they walked in the prairie grass. They saw Ed stop and put his hands on Fides' shoulder. For the first time, they noticed out in the field four small, slightly raised hills. As though shot, Fides fell backwards in startled realization. He fell to the ground and laid still. Ed stood still, unsure what to do.

Jonathan had been the first to realize what was going on and was three steps out the door before Misaluva, Charis, and Melody had moved an inch. The four of them rushed towards Fides, but pulled up short. Ed was still talking to Fides. Fides was now sitting with his head in his hands. Fides responded, but the words were swept away in the wind. They couldn't hear what was said. Ed answered, and the answer too was unheard. Both were still for a time. Ed turned slowly away from Fides, gave a sorrowful nod of recognition to Jonathan and the three ladies, and left. After a time, they came around him and enveloped him wordlessly, but with the thick meaning that can never be relayed in words, anyway.

A day went by, than another. Fides sulked about the house, giving his friends little opportunity to console him. After awhile, he became anxious to leave. Two nights after hearing about the death of his family, he informed his friends of his decision that it was time at last to move on. The next morning, he arose before anyone else did with a distinct thought in mind. Actually, it was something even more robust than a thought. It was a decision, an urge, a resolve, a passion. It led him into the woods. There was someone he wanted to give a piece of his mind to.

He picked his way through the low branches, knocking them away from his face, beating them back. Finally, he stepped into a familiar clearing. Familiar, but one he had not been in for decades. The clearing seemed smaller than he remembered, but it was still a decent size. The shed was still there, but was lying in a pile of rotten pieces. He walked around the edge of the clearing for a few minutes. Finally, he sat down in the center of the clearing, facing the shed. The sun had been inching up steadily throughout his trip. The crisp, wintry air was not cold enough to freeze water, so the grass was still wet from the morning dew where he sat down. Settled for the moment, he listened to the wind.

"Where the hell were you?" he snapped into the air. He listened for a response. He watched the empty air around him for some tell-tale shimmering. "No where!" he answered for the Emptiness. "Not here!" he shouted again. His mind fell blank, as though his self was sitting on the edge of a dark abyss which was his soul. There weren't thoughts. There barely were feelings. His feet dangled over the motionless, black pit. His eyes were unfocused; he allowed them to drift on a blade of grass that was nearby, but he did not become aware of the blade even though his eyes were upon it. The autumn wind continued to yield up no presence.

Fides felt beaten. No, it was something else. He felt like he had been set up for the beating, and that was adding insult to injury. His life had been saved all those years back for what? Why ensure his safety, and his mother's, only to abandon the rest of his family decades later? It made no sense. It was infuriating, embarrassing, devastating, perplexing, and maddening, all at the same time. He gave into it all: he kicked and screamed and wept and moaned and groaned and cursed right there in the grass. He cried himself into dehydration. Finally, he'd exerted as much energy as he was in the mood to exert. He was spent. Only one thing was left, and it was a cold determination to never be made a fool of again.

"'Plans to prosper,' my ass," he muttered in conclusion. He sat quietly for so long that he lost track of time.

"Fides?" came Melody's voice, hovering on the wind like a hummingbird hangs in the air.

"Fides!" Misaluva called for him.

"Fides..." Charis yelled across the clearing.

Fides heard them. Hesitantly, he answered, "Here..." It wasn't loud enough, he thought, to attract their attention, but it did. A moment later and they were in the clearing. Melody walked towards him gingerly, not wanting to upset him. He could now hear Jonathan shouting for him, too. Charis called out to Jonathan that Fides was found, and before another moment had passed, all four were sitting on the grass near him. No one said anything, leaving it to Fides to initiate the conversation.

"She didn't answer," Fides said. His head was down. He did not want to look anyone in the eyes.

"I'm sorry," Charis said, thinking Fides meant his wife.

"She wasn't here for them," Fides complained. Confused looks were exchanged. It dawned on Fides that they wouldn't know what he was talking about. He looked at them, "Let's go to Bloomington." Without saying anything else or looking at them again, he abandoned the clearing.

"Well, let's go," Jonathan nodded to the three women. They nodded in agreement. Jonathan and Misaluva followed closely behind Fides, but Melody and Charis paused before stepping into the woods and looked back into the clearing. A gentle breeze wound its way through the branches, past Fides, into the clearing, past the two, and back into the woods. Fides turned and saw them lingering, but they didn't linger long. Soon, all of his friends were behind him. He made his way back to his house.

Fides grabbed his sack that had held his belongings the last few months and began filling it again. They retrieved 'fresh' supplies from the house, and Fides re-secured the building. In the meantime, the horses were prepared. Shortly before they were set to leave, Ed came by and bid farewell to Fides and assured him that he'd make sure that the property was looked after until Fides returned home once again.

Fides pointed them north: he reasoned that the way they had come was likely to bring them into contact with units of the Pledge rallying against Bloomington. The plan was to take route 63 north to Danville, and hopefully come around from on top of Bloomington. Route 63 roughly followed the Wabash River, and provided some scenic relief to compensate for the somber reverie that Fides had fallen into. For himself, Fides endured warring emotions. He couldn't have put anything into words if he had tried. He had been struck simply speechless. His being was thrown around by pure, unadulterated emotions. He had full throated feelings of guilt followed by unmitigated self-pity followed by helplessness followed by bitter pangs recalling that it had been his strenuous choice to leave his family.

There was also a lurking quiet rage against God. Though he very much doubted such a being existed, he decided that the beautiful woman without mercy, in the final analysis, answered to God. He need not blame her for leading him into a sense of hope, only to dash it later. Perhaps in some measure he could not bring himself to hate the lady of the wood whom he saw with his own eyes when it was much easier to hurl invective against an unseen entity. Surely, the woman of the wood would have come to his family's aid if only she had been ordered to do so. Clearly, it was God who did not issue the order.

After wallowing in such thoughts, Fides would find himself enduring embarrassment. He felt like he had allowed himself to get 'taken in,' by a book that he had once been told was nothing more than superstition. He was tempted to fetch the Bible from Charis and burn it. He scornfully decided that he now understood why copies had been rounded up and destroyed. A lingering thought reminded him that it had been his willful choice to cling to those words from some dude named Jeremiah. No sooner did he remember that, he recalled again that it had also been his choice to leave his wife and family.

What kind of man leaves his wife and family at the hour of their most critical need? He failed them, but perhaps the failure began years before when he abandoned his own mother to save his own skin. Was he perhaps still that small boy, wrapped now in a man's body? Round and around it went like a vicious circle until late in the afternoon he was just exhausted by the effort of maintaining the raw cycle. Round and round and round he went... he could perpetuate it, but it was just taking too much energy.

"Ed tells me that they died somewhere out towards Indianapolis," Fides said, breaking the day long silence. "They were at a market or something, and the bomb made the roof collapse. Melody had been out there with Ed's wife doing some shopping. Apparently, they had taken my car. Ed's wife saw the place collapse. People immediately tried to rescue the people inside the building, but most of them were dead. Ed's wife, Marcia, retrieved my family's bodies, and came home and buried them. Marcia later died from radiation poison, but not before Ed came home. He says that's all she told him."

They couldn't tell if Fides was finished, so no one said anything yet. Another floodgate burst open, though, and Fides slid off the horse, weeping. He sat down with his head between his knees and let the sorrow overwhelm him. The others dismounted and sat down near him, but again remained silent. Fides could not see their compassionate looks. Between sobs, he shared with them the bitterest news out of all of it: Marcia had not been able to find the small body of Keane, his youngest son. She had been forced to give up the search and returned to Terre Haute without him. "I wasn't able to say goodbye to him," he moaned.

Another wave of sorrow dovetailing into self-pity enveloped him. His sorrow was replaced with what could only be described as a bitter and burning anger. Life was not right, or fair, and Fides made up his mind again to make sure that it was no longer he that was on the receiving end of injustice. At least, that's what he told himself as he finally mounted his horse again. How long that emotion would sustain him God only knew, but it allowed him to be functional for the moment.

That night they pitched camp and Fides was conversant again. No one was fooled. However, they respected the man's grieving process and returned to small talk and occasional discussions about future circumstances. They had about another two days worth of riding ahead of them. It was good that it wasn't going to be all in complete silence. On the end of the third day, Danville was only a few miles away. They passed a few smaller roads that looked like they'd have been good shortcuts but one could not be sure that they were safe. Instead, the group pushed their way on to Interstate 74, which they presumed would have more travelers and perhaps even some settlements where they could get some news and fresh supplies. As soon as they got to I-74, though, they realized that things were not as they expected.

There were quite a few people in the area, but they appeared to be spectators as much as anything else. Some women were carrying French parasols. Men were carrying lawn chairs. It was quite a scene.

"Where are you going?" Jonathan called out to a man they were just passing.

"There's some fighting down in Danville. We're going to watch!" the man replied.

"Aren't you afraid of getting hurt?" Jonathan called back to him.

"Nah, the army on this side said they are support the fair and equal treatment of people! They promised we wouldn't get hurt!" the man shouted, and then was too far away to talk with.

"I'd say that the army on this side is the Pledge," Fides remarked cynically. They became more certain of this as they approached the scene of the battle, because there were many spectators coming back with juicy accounts. While they were confident of the name of the army closest to them, who it was on the other side was unclear. It could not be the Rangers, because they were not large enough to qualify as a 'mighty army,' and the spectators were unanimous that it was a large force.

They picked their way through the stream of travelers on their way to the front. It was about midday when they finally saw the Pledge encampment. Because of the great amount of spectators in the area, they were able to move without hindrance. The battle seemed to be where I-74 went over a river. When the country was at peace it forgot how important certain geographic features of the landscape around them could be during war. Innocence like that was no longer possible: the logistical nightmares involved in moving large numbers of people around and what can happen when such groups must transit narrow passes made sure of that.

The sounds of rifle fire could be heard. The Pledge was held up at the bridge over the river, and could not get over. The main body of their army was gathered around the on and off ramps of the

Interstate. They sized up the army to number in the six to eight thousand men range. After getting about as close as they felt comfortable doing, they stopped to consider their next move. Clearly, trying to cross the bridge wasn't really a good idea. It was being fired upon by the army across the way as the Pledge was trying to cross it.

They struck up a conversation with some of the other spectators. They learned that this Pledge army was composed of all sorts of men from the eastern states. There were former members of the International Force, some Europeans, but mainly just average Americans who accepted the Pledge's vision for the future of the country. They were saddened to see that the spectators were fairly indifferent, but they were not in the mood to argue with anyone.

As the evening came, they saw that a large detachment of the Pledge was coming their way. Sure enough, the men seemed to be average Americans. These seemed much less rough around the edges compared to the Pledge soldiers they saw in Cairo. Fides saw some of them consulting a map before they veered off to the north. The entire unit was on horseback, and many of them had rifles.

"I can only imagine that there are other ways across this river," Fides said.

"I wish I knew who was holding them up," Jonathan added.

"I should think that if they are friends of ours, they would like to know that they are about to be flanked," Fides said.

"I think our friends would be the sort to be prepared for such things," Melody chimed in.

"If it's the Rangers, they may not have enough men to cover their flank, even if they know about the flanking maneuver," Misaluva pointed out.

Charis had a bold suggestion, "Why don't we just go and see who is on the other side? If it's the Rangers, than we ought to try to find a way across and warn them. If it's not the Rangers, and maybe just some bandits like the Copperheads, we can just let them fight it out."

"How do you suppose we get to the river without being shot from the Pledge or from those on the other side?" Jonathan pressed her.

"We ladies have our ways," Charis winked back.

"Well, that's fine for you, but we aren't ladies," Jonathan shot back with a smile.

"It's getting dark. I suppose we'll have to wait until morning, now," Fides suggested.

"No, no," Melody objected. "The Pledge is probably not going to wait. I think we need to find out now, and then try to get across ourselves still tonight."

"This is sounding very undoable," Fides frowned.

"Hush," Charis giggled. "Come along boys. Just stay out of the way of the ladies. Girls?"

"Ride on!" Misaluva laughed. Jonathan and Fides exchanged concerned and wary looks, but the three women were already trotting out towards the bridge. Jonathan and Fides stayed close to the three so that it would be clear that they belonged with them, but could hardly stand it. The three women chattered on and giggled and twittered and laughed and otherwise presented themselves as shallow, jabbering war-gawkers. They were only challenged once, and the three ladies gave no quarter, returning the challenge with a stream of obscenities such that Fides and Jonathan joined the sentries in blushing.

"Wow," was all Fides could say. Jonathan's mouth flapped open but no words could come out. The sentries let them pass and the three ladies went back to being bubbly and obnoxious. To their great surprise, the three ladies were able to lead them right to the river bank not more than fifty yards from the bridge. Some Pledge snipers that were in the bushes in the area made it clear that they thought they were just plain crazy, but the ladies kept gossiping loudly. In the meantime Fides and Jonathan were trying to make out what was on the other side of the river. It was now dusk, so the light wasn't very good. There was sporadic rifle fire coming from the opposite shore, so Fides was quite certain that the Pledge snipers were right in classifying them as crazy: they, being on horseback, were the biggest targets.

Jonathan let out a low whistle and pointed to a large, hulking shape that suddenly stood up from behind a rocky outcropping on the other side of the river. It was clearly a huge man- the escaping light and moderate distance could not conceal that. Fides recognized the man immediately. It was the giant, Gol. Gol had been the one that scooped Fermion out of the fray in Cairo and carried him to safety. Charis gasped in recognition but Misaluva hushed her.

"I think we've seen all there is to see here," Melody said coyly.

"You call this a war?" Misaluva chided the men crouched in the underbrush. They turned their horses away from the shore and trotted back the way they came. As they were about to discuss their next move, they were confronted with a large contingent of the Pledge army marching towards them.

"This doesn't look good," Jonathan muttered. It wasn't good. Some of the men in the first rank grabbed them and took them into custody. Their horses were led away and the five of them were brought to an officer who looked them over and decided that they were not a threat. When Fides asked why then they were being held, the officer said that after the attack they were about to unleash, they could go. Fides pressed him about their horses, but the officer said he couldn't make any promises. The officer sent them to a makeshift tent where three puny looking guards kept their eye on them. That would not normally have been enough to restrain them but each had handguns that looked old, but functional.

The three guards were playing poker but eyed them warily. "Come'on Zach, bet!" one snapped at another, "Josh. Chill," sniped the third. "Junior, why do you have to be that way?" the last scowled. Fides couldn't help but laugh at their banter.

"Well, this is a pickle," Fides summarized their situation.

"Think it's worth trying to bust out of here?" Jonathan whispered.

"Honestly, I don't think so. They don't think we're a threat," Fides nodded towards the guards. Besides," he smiled, "I kind of like them.

Melody added, "Let's remember that we don't even have our horses now."

"I think I know where they are, though," Misaluva informed them. "When we were coming in I saw some makeshift stables not too far from here and I think that's a likely place to check."

"Shouldn't we try to warn our friends about the enemy trying to encircle them?" Charis wondered.

Misaluva shook her head, "Honestly, if it were the Rangers I would say yes. But it's the Shadowmen, and they've got plenty of men. I wouldn't be surprised if they've got all the bases covered."

"That's a good point," Fides concurred. "I hate to say it, but let's just wait out the night and see what the morning brings."

With that settled, the five of them tried to make the best meal that they could and then laid down to sleep. The sounds of yelling and hollering in the distance caught their attention. They strained their eyes in the dark to see the battle but couldn't see anything. Realizing that they really couldn't do anything and noticing the two guards with their pistols at the ready, they each closed their eyes, and in time, fell back to sleep. The rising of the sun revealed that the battle was still raging, but the Pledge had had some success.

The three guards proved Fides' estimate of them by agreeing to arrange to have the horses returned to them. Fides thanked them and made up his mind to not assume that every Pledge soldier was a rotten man. Fides realized that this sentiment could come back to haunt him, though, because he would not always have time to measure the character of a person before he must act.

Wishing to see what the situation was, and now released by the guards, they made their way to the river once again. A thousand Pledge soldiers were now on the opposite shore, but wave after wave of arrows were hurtling down on them. More soldiers were wading or swimming across the river, and the bridge appeared to be in Pledge hands but treacherous, anyway. Another thousand soldiers were still on their side of the bank, and they had noticed that the camp still had plenty of soldiers in it. That struck them as odd. Why weren't they attacking, too?

Some semblance of an answer to that question came when another large group of soldiers in the camp formed up and began marching north. Apparently, the Pledge had reason to think that the passage to the north held promise. This left them in a bit of a predicament. Their friends were on the other side of the river, and were apparently losing. It was a reasonable conjecture that the battle to the north was also not going well. How might they join their friends? Fides had been fairly ornery since Terre Haute, and it was this that probably prompted a brazen suggestion: a charge.

"A charge?" Melody asked incredulously.

"Yea. Just take our horses across the bridge at a sprint and either join the battle or tell Yuri about the northern flank and then join the battle, or whatever," Fides said.

"We have no weapons to speak of!" Charis protested.

"What about Jonathan's arm?" Misaluva begged him.

"Jonathan, it's your arm, what do you think?" Fides asked.

"I don't fight with that arm, anyway," Jonathan joked.

"It's a good day to die," Fides tersely offered. Welling up inside him was some of the grief and self-pity that he had been beating back. Battle was just the thing to take his mind off of such things, and possibly even end such thoughts forever. If he died and he was wrong and there was a God, he had some things that he wanted to say to him. But the ladies were not to be persuaded so easily.

"Jonathan has a knife, and we've got some heavy sticks, but you've got nothing," Misaluva protested. She put her foot down, "We're not doing any such thing unless we have better weapons." She misjudged her man. That or she judged him exactly right. Fides' anger burned inside him.

"Jonathan, give me your knife. Everyone, follow me," Fides commanded. Jonathan handed the knife over. Fides started his horse off at a jog towards the bridge. The others followed close behind. You'd think that they would have attracted attention, but the Pledge soldiers had grown used to their presence and figured there must be some right reason for them being there. Fermion spotted a handful of men off by themselves, clearly getting ready for a foray across the bridge. They had machetes. This was what he was looking for. The men were walking towards the bridge with their backs to them and didn't see Fides bearing down on them, with four other horsemen close behind him. Fides allowed his horse to slam between the men like a bowling ball crashing through pins at a bowling alley. He had been moving too fast to turn around to help claim the dropped machetes, but his companions were right on the spot. Misaluva and Charis jumped down and scooped them up and handed one each to Jonathan and Melody, and keeping one each for themselves. Fides, his eyes ablaze, was already turned back towards the bridge and whipping the horse into full speed.

"I don't think Fides is feeling well," Jonathan growled.

"Or maybe he's feeling just right for a moment like this one," Misaluva calmly replied.

The four of them set their horses racing towards the bridge after Fides, who was already fifty yards ahead of them. Fides had blown by numerous soldiers who were too stunned to do anything except gawk. They were still staring off at them when they perceived the sounds of hoof beats behind them again, only to now have four other rough riders thunder by them. There were some shouts, but there was no action.

Fides had made it to the bridge. He hadn't slowed down a bit. There were victims of Shadowmen arrows strewn throughout the length of the bridge, and living Pledge soldiers hunkered down here and there firing off into the trees on the opposite side of the river. There was a significant stream of soldiers merely trying to get across the bridge, and Fides confounded them all by suddenly racing by them, madness in his veins. No sooner did he get by them, Jonathan and the ladies were upon them as well. Some of the riflemen had turned their guns on them after they had gotten by, but the shots were badly off target, perhaps because the Pledge snipers were concerned about shooting some of their own in the melee. It seemed like eternity, but at last all of them were across. Fides kept his horse charging down the road, and didn't look back until the sounds of battle had grown softer. When he finally gave his steed a rest, he noticed his friends catching up to him.

"Looks like we didn't need these blades, after all," Misaluva smiled.

"I wouldn't speak so soon," a voice called out at them from the woods to their right. It was Redemptus. Carefully ensuring that his face was carefully concealed in his cloak, he beckoned for them to come in his direction. Their horses were glad for the break. They hadn't been in that kind of a sprint for quite awhile. They turned their steeds off the road and led them to where Redemptus was standing on a narrow trail. Redemptus' hood fell off his face, leaving the five of them in the uncomfortable situation of trying to be friendly while not staring. Redemptus surely was used to this and noticed.

"It's my face, isn't it?" Redemptus accused.

Melody was gifted in tact. "Our apologies, sir. Perhaps it would not strike us as odd except for the fact that your fellows are exceedingly beautiful. No doubt, we look the same as you look. If you were with us, I suspect we would not think any differently about your appearance. But in relief against your comrades, we are surprised," she said. Though not completely true, it wasn't completely false, either. The man would still have been ugly even set against the rest of humanity, but in stark contrast to the people Redemptus was traveling with, that reality was completely laid bare. Redemptus appreciated the attempt, however.

"They are beautiful because they are much loved. I am not as loved, but I am as real as they, and hope to one day be as real as you are," Redemptus intoned mysteriously. "May I yet be as loved as they." Redemptus had been leading them along the path during the conversation. A very small clearing appeared before them and their friends, Nagro and Henryetta, were there. There were other Shadowmen going to and fro, as well. Redemptus led them to Nagro.

"Hail, friends!" Nagro called out upon seeing them. They all shook hands with Nagro but Henryetta embraced them.

"Gol told us that he saw you across the river," Henryetta said. "He hoped that you'd notice him and try to join us!"

"That is indeed what happened," Fides explained.

"In that spirit, we have some news," Misaluva inserted. "I think with your army here you are already able to deal with this threat, but last night and today we saw Pledge men marching to the north.

We think there must be another bridge and that they have found it and are going to try to flank you."

"That is fine intelligence, and much needed," Nagro replied. His face darkened as he explained, "We do not have the whole army here, I'm afraid. We arrived near Decatur not too long ago and heard tidings about the extent of the predicament we were in. We learned about various Pledge elements converging on Peoria. Our army is mobile, but it cannot all move at the speeds we needed. Also, many of the men of Cairo remained in Cairo and did not follow us."

"Ingrates," growled Gol, who had just arrived.

"That is not ours to judge, my friend," Nagro chided him. Gol appeared in the clearing and greeted them all warmly, and then Nagro continued with the update. "So, we are only a small element. There are not more than two hundred of us. Our purpose and goal was to try to delay at least one army. We have no men defending our northern flank. I fear that we are in immediate danger of being encircled."

"This is not good," Jonathan sighed.

"No, not at all. It is good information you have brought us, though. We will have to retreat and hope that the rest of the Shadowmen army has been able to make it to Bloomington or Champaign," Nagro explained. Nagro issued orders to Gol and Redemptus who quickly left to order the retreat. As leaving their positions could mean that the Pledge would immediately launch a full scale attack, and they were in danger of being cut off from an attack from the north, they prepared to move just as soon as the rest of the group arrived.

Beautiful people started to filter through the woods. They had been ordered to try to retreat discretely, leaving the impression that they were still in their positions, so they had stayed clear of the road which would have revealed their movements, and snuck off through the trees. It wasn't too long before most of them were now in the woods around them.

The last to arrive were those that Fides and friends recognized as Peder, one of the inner council they had spoken with a long while back while Fermion still traveled with them. Peder was in company with some others that Fides recognized. There were two young men he had thought seemed as though they were princes. He knew the name of one of them was Hector, but he did not know the name of the other. Then there were two darling women. He recalled the name of one was Susanna, but did not know the name of the other. Curiously, one would think them to perhaps be husbands and wives, but in fact their fellowship appeared to be more like kin. They were ornery with each other just as brothers and sisters sometimes are and were heckling each other until Peder ordered them to be silent. Nagro allowed himself to smile faintly at the sight, but did not take too long to dwell on it. The full withdrawal was ordered.

They quickly fell back to the west where they found yet another clearing where a large number of horses were grazing. Upon seeing Nagro, the Shadowmen who had been left to keep eye on their horses began leading horses over to their riders. In about five minutes, everyone was on their horse, except Gol. Gol was too large to ride a horse, so he had two horses hitched to an old horse trailer he had turned into a chariot.

He appeared to be quite proud of his contraption, but Peder smiled and whispered to Fides, "Nagro isn't nearly as pleased with the chariot. On two occasions the chariot had been a hindrance to our journey. Apparently a 'chariot' does not work very well going through woods or crossing creeks!" Peder chuckled as he explained that each time there was an obstacle, Gol had been forced to carry the horses and the chariot for a little ways, and then he would regal them all with muttered regrets for ever creating the contraption. From Gol's pleased look right then, those moments appeared to be forgotten. He was proudly showing off to Fides and his friends. This was only possible because now that they were out of sight from the Pledge army, they were taking the road and making good time.

They didn't have time for conversation after that, however. About five miles down the road, they looked back and saw an old truck following them. It was a Pledge scouting vehicle sent out to make contact with their foes and report back. The cat was out of the bag: the true strength of the Shadowmen was revealed as well as their retreat. Nagro brought them to a stop by a small stream so that the horses could slake their thirsts and the riders could move about a little bit. Nagro spread the word that they were going to have a hard ride ahead of them. Fides learned that the rest of the Shadowmen army had been moving to old Champaign, Illinois, in hopes of battling the Pledge armies as far away from Peoria as possible. Nagro wanted to get to Champaign still that night in order to warn his fellows as well as the residents about the oncoming danger. It was doubtful that they could really make it there that soon on horses. They were about forty miles away.

Though Fides had said nothing about what he had found in Terre Haute, it appeared that the word had gotten out. Fides didn't notice the tender looks and comments directed towards him. For himself, Fides felt very much alone though he was surrounded by these great and noble friends. Whenever he had a moment that was not occupied by the thought of battle, or conversation, or some other diversion, his thoughts turned to his inward rage. He was angry at God, at circumstance, and himself. When he had charged across the bridge earlier that day he had hoped that someone would have cut him down. It was better in his mind to die at the hands of his external enemies and end the battle in his mind and heart, than to remain alive yet tormented by his internal foes.

His friends noticed the steely gloss that would cover his eyes as he fought against the various passions warring inside him. Those who tried to converse with him would have to wait for him to 'wake up' before he could attend to them.

After their short break, Nagro urged them all back onto the road. Taking the lead, Nagro led them all at an unendurable pace. They rode on the shoulders of the road so as to put less strain on the horse's hooves, but Gol was unable to extend this gesture to his own horses because his chariot did not ride well on the softer earth. They rode hard throughout the day. There was no conversation while riding because of the speedy gait. They had short breaks but nothing long enough to allow for recovery. As the afternoon wore on, Nagro's counselors began to beg him to relent. They were still ten miles from Champaign, but their horses could not possibly carry them that far at their current speed after sustaining that speed for so long already. At last, Nagro reluctantly agreed. That night, the signs for St. Joseph were in view of their camp.

== Chapter 12 ==

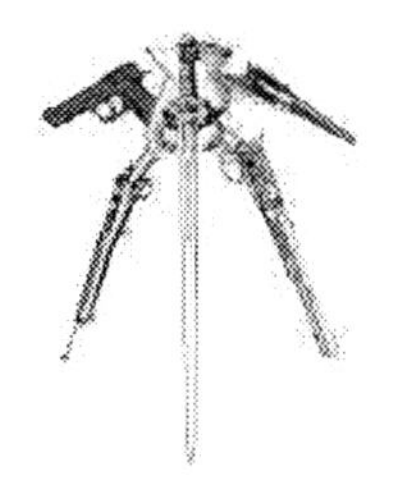

The sounds of clanking armor and horses woke them up from their deep and needed sleep. Nagro was up with sword in hand before the second cacophonous syllable was heard. The voice of one of Nagro's fellows, the night watch, called out to him and set him at ease. Allies had arrived. Soon, the entire campsite was awake to welcome their friends. It was only a small unit sent out to keep an eye on the flank of the main army. It was only a brief meeting. The main army, it turned out, was actually due south of them, just to the west of a little town called Sidney.

They learned, too, that the Pledge had been forming up to the east of Sidney, between the cities of Homer and Fairmount. This appeared to be the pre-arranged rallying point for the many Pledge units that had formed in the last few years. To some degree, everyone was a little surprised to hear that the Pledge's appeal had been so broad. Fides knew that Fermion would not have been surprised.

Upon hearing this news, Nagro ordered his men to break camp immediately. The main Shadowmen army was about five miles down the road and he wanted to pass along to Yuri whatever information he had that would be helpful. Certainly, Yuri should learn that the eastern army that they had been expecting would be on its way. Once again, not content to amble along, Nagro ordered a fast pace for the horses. In just under two hours they saw the main army sprawled out in front of them. They were quickly greeted and tended to. Nagro hastened to the council tents to give his news.

Fides and his friends were left to wander around a bit aimlessly. They were surprised to see that the main army was not merely composed of the Shadowmen. As in Cairo, area residents had joined together with the Shadowmen to defend themselves against the Pledge onslaught. Many of these folks opposed the ideology of the Pledge, but most simply refused to allow another foreign invader to come in and tell them how to live. By 'foreign' they meant even those Americans from other states. Fortunately, news and rumors about the Shadowmen had spread faster than the Shadowmen themselves. It was well known that the Shadowmen had no such designs. Nobody could quite make out what designs they did have, though.

As they explored the encampment they figured there were probably some twenty thousand men there. There were quite a few women, as well. They struck up conversations with many of them and learned that they came from as far away as Wisconsin to stand up against the Pledge. As Bloomington had become an important destination for travelers seeking news about their loved ones, the city was much larger and more populated than many American cities at the time. They learned that besides the fifteen thousand or so average American citizens fighting with the Shadowmen here, there were another ten thousand men and women back in Bloomington fortifying the city.

"So long as the Pledge does not have heavy weapons, there is a good chance that it is going to meet its match on the south-eastern plains of Champaign, Illinois," Jonathan remarked.

"I wouldn't count on that," Fides replied. Part of Jonathan's optimism was fueled by the sight of a number of their men in possession of firearms. It was only one out of every sixth man, but that still made for some reasonable firepower. They were all encouraged and impressed to learn that the people of Bloomington had re-learned blacksmithing: there were a fair number of rudimentary, but no doubt effective, swords and spears on display in the camp. Still, there was nothing here that could compete against heavy machine guns.

"Let's look for the council tents," Charis offered. This was agreed to. The camp was so large that it was in the early afternoon before they stumbled upon the council tents that Nagro had been led off to. Here they found some of their friends standing about, while others were going from place to place organizing for battle. Peder was there, standing with his apparent 'kin.' He greeted them.

"This is my beloved friend, Sapian," Peder said in introduction. "This is my sister Susanna. I don't know where my brother and other sister are," Peder said. There were warm handshakes around. There was cordial conversation between them. When they left, Charis discretely admitted that though the Shadowmen were still all lovely to look at, they also looked more like normal people than when they had first laid eyes on them. They appeared to be worn out, tired and weary. It was as though a sheen had worn off of them, or perhaps a reality had worn in. At any rate, they still had enough glow about them to reveal their strange 'otherness' to those who encountered them.

Jonathan was hungry. Misaluva spotted a mess tent and the five of them helped themselves to a reasonably fine meal. While they were eating, Fermion and Tasha came into the tent. The two had been looking for them ever since they'd heard from Nagro that they had joined them. Fermion and Tasha sat down to a warm greeting. It had been more than a few days since they'd been together.

"Nagro tells me that you've acquired a death wish," Fermion said to Fides. Fermion was never one to beat around any bush. Fides looked away.

"We missed you," Tasha said to them all.

"So what happened? Where are the Rangers?" Melody asked.

"They stayed in Bloomington to help fortify the city. The further north we got, the more we learned how dire the situation is," Tasha explained.

"What's the situation?" Melody prompted.
"The Pledge is much shrewder than anyone expected," Fermion told them. "The Shadowmen had meant to follow the leftover Pledge army from the battle at Cairo, but that army managed to slip by them. They didn't know how or in what direction and then they learned about the existence of other armies. Well, the target seemed to be the same, so the Shadowmen made right for Bloomington. It turns out that they had actually been moving parallel to us during our trip north into Illinois."
Tasha interjected, "We are aware of Pledge armies from the west, east, and south. Plus, there have been smaller units coming in, too. It's really quite amazing that none of us have officially met, yet."
"So how many are we talking about, here?" Fides inquired.
Fermion made a clicking sound with his tongue. He was either stalling or making fast calculations. Finally he answered, "My estimate is in the forty to fifty thousand range. Yuri thinks it's closer to thirty thousand. More accurately, he *hopes* it is closer to thirty thousand. What we *know* is thirty. What I'm concerned about is what we don't know."
"And any word of King?" Fides asked.
Tasha had a stern look, "No, none."
Jonathan had been eating the whole time and now felt satisfied. He cracked his knuckles and got a steely look in his eye. "Ok, enough of the preliminaries. When is the battle?"
"Tomorrow. Day after tomorrow more likely. Perhaps the day after that. I'm sure they'll want to get that eastern army into the area and that may take a little time," Fermion explained.
"We can use the time, though. We are getting the lay of the land and besides that still equipping some of the men," Tasha said.
"Not that we're fighting, though," Fermion fished. "We're going with you guys to Peoria." A pause.
"I'm not going to Peoria," Fides muttered. His friends sat back in shock. Only Tasha and Fermion were not surprised.
"But Fides," Charis argued, "you've got to go to Peoria to get that thing from around your neck and use the key for what is made for."
"No, I don't," Fides returned. "No doubt Fermion and Tasha here have already learned about the fate of my wife and children. I intend to fight in the coming battle, and I intend to die in the coming battle. I've had enough of this world." His mind completed the sentence, "I hope there is a God so I can give him a piece of my mind."
"Wounds acquired in this world are trophy scars in the next," Fermion gently said. "It is alright to be fed up with this world. We don't belong to it, anyway. But there are things that transcend it that still matter: loyalty, honor, bravery, and duty."
"Ha!" Fides exclaimed, standing up abruptly. "Duty? I did not ask to be involved in any of this. No one asked me to be involved in any of this. If I had any duty at all, it was to my wife and family.

Now, they are gone on account of my disloyalty." He said 'disloyalty' in a sneering way. "I do not deserve to live, but perhaps in fighting a noble cause I can at least have a meritorious death."

"My friend," Fermion soothed, "there was only one meritorious death. None here deserve to live. The life we live is by grace. For you, for me, for our friends, and for our enemies. But not every noble cause is accomplished by bloody warfare. Some noble causes are fought for and won inside a single human heart. Others are fought for using words of persuasion. Others are fought using kindness, or gentleness. What you need to do in Peoria is in fact a noble cause, and it is no less noble simply because it can be achieved just by showing up!"

"I betrayed my family."

"You betrayed no one. You did what you thought was right at the time," Fermion said firmly.

"It was the wrong choice."

"You could only say such a thing if you had known the future. You didn't," Fermion countered.

"I have made up my mind." With that, Fides stood up and stalked out of the tent. He wandered the camp for a long time. He really wanted to be alone, but that didn't seem to be plausible with all these people around. Though he told himself he wanted to be alone, he found himself wandering back to the mess tent more than once to see if his friends were still there. He wanted to know if they were still agonizing over his decision. For some reason, knowing that he had perhaps caused them consternation gave him some sort of satisfaction. He knew it was sick, but he couldn't help it either. Or, perhaps he could help it, but didn't want to. At any rate, word must have spread pretty quickly about his decision, as insignificant as he thought it was, because he suddenly found himself face to face with a short, stocky man. He had big feet.

Fides was sauntering along the outskirts of the camp when the man stopped him, "Fides!"

Fides thought he had seen him before, but couldn't remember where. "Yes?"

"Fides, my friend, I am very sorry to hear of your losses. Truly, I am," the stout man said compassionately. Now Fides remembered: it was at the battle of Cairo. He was one of the Shadowmen, but like so many of the others, his 'glow' had nearly worn off.

"You know my name. May I have yours?" Fides asked, refusing to be comforted.

"My name is Dor. I have come to look for you because I heard about your decision," Dor explained. Fides now recalled him with clarity.

"You don't approve, either?" Fides snarled.

"My friend, please. Don't hate me until I give you reason to hate me!" Dor pleaded. Fides couldn't help but be won over by the man's earnestness. His tone softened.

"My apologies. You must have sought me out for a reason," Fides said.

"Please, let's sit over here," Dor said, pointing towards some barrels that would allow for comfortable conversation. Situated,

Dor continued. "I don't know if you remember me from the battle at Cairo. I lost a very dear friend there. His name was- is- Lobi. It took us a little time to figure out that our armor did not have the capabilities we thought it would. Lobi was among those who made it real to us. He was dear to me- to us- and it was sad to lose him. We thought we were on this grand adventure at the time. It didn't seem right that any of us might actually die on it. It was a grim moment for us."

"I am sorry for your friend," Fides said, and he truly meant it.

"Thank you. He is not why I sought you out, though. I understand what it is like to lose loved ones, that is true. But I also know what it's like to fight a battle raging inside rather than outside. I know what it is like for others to gain obvious glory in valiant thundering warfare while for my own part, my task was simple. I had only to get from point A to point B. Don't get me wrong, it was a dangerous journey, but it was dangerous in different ways. The fate of many depended on my steadfastness. I confess I nearly failed." Dor stopped for a moment, drifting into a thoughtful contemplation. "You might say I did fail, actually. In all honesty, I can't say I was faithful to the end. I suppose that is for the better, though. It was never me, anyway, and had I remained completely steadfast throughout perhaps I would have lost sight of that fact. My dregs were enough, though. There is a power that is made perfect in weakness. There is a power that can only exist with full surrender."

"My friend, I must confess that I do not know what you are talking about," Fides said.

Dor jumped up and slapped him in the arm. "That is because you do not read!" Dor chuckled, and returned to his barrel.

"Is that about that book? That one that Corrie gave me? How would you know about that?" Fides demanded.

"Never mind, that. Why do you think this is about you?" Dor asked, but then did not give him a chance to respond. "There is an author who sustains everything by his word, and by everything, I mean everything. Within that story, there is no unimportant battle. No unimportant wound. No unimportant duty. This is true no matter how far removed you are from that author."

Fides grumbled. "It's like talking to Fermion," he said under his breath.

"I've already told you more than I ought to have. We aren't supposed to talk about these things with anyone outside our community," Dor confided.

"So, you think I should go to Peoria," Fides concluded.

"Without a question. This battle is not your battle. Your battle is not my battle. I had my turn fighting the internal battle, now I get a turn at the sword. Each has its own dangers. Today, it is your duty to do the right thing in the small way. Tomorrow you might get a turn at the sword. You must understand, we may come out of this battle victorious, but I fear that if we win, but you fail to make it to Peoria, it will be for nothing. It is all around your neck, if I might put it that way," Dor urged him.

Fides reached up instinctively to his burdensome necklace. He fingered it carefully. His brain went through a checklist of excuses: "I can't make it to Peoria, anyway. I don't even know the combination. I don't know the way, anyway." Against them all was a quiet, still voice that said, "Do good as you have opportunity: do this good, as I have given you, and only you, the opportunity to do it..." Dor put his arm on Fides' shoulder.

"I wish I could join you on your quest. I am on my own, now, though, and must see it to the end. I hope you understand," Dor said.

"I do understand. I will think about what you have said. No promises, though," Fides said, regaining some of his earlier determination.

"I leave you to fight your battle," Dor replied. After that, they shook hands and Dor disappeared into the mass of soldiery that was constantly churning around them. Fides sat for a little while, thinking. Words can not describe the terrible battle that was raging inside of him. In one moment, it was a series of unrighteous arguments railing against perceived unrighteous demands on him. In the next, he had righteous rebuttals to the righteous duty laid upon him. In the next, he knew it was all tomfoolery and he really ought to just be getting on his way to Peoria. This was happening on the inside, but on the outside he just looked like a man at rest. It became difficult to sustain this internal running argument, though.

He got up and began to look for his friends, his mind still not made up. The sun was starting its descent when at last he found them. As he expected, but not exactly as he wished, they all received him warmly even after he told them that his mind was still made up. They brushed that aside but at the same time heaped a little more weight on his shoulders by easily promising to follow him wherever he goes, whether it be into battle or to Peoria. This was too much loyalty for Fides to handle. Plus, he was uncomfortable with Fermion deferring things to Fides at all, now. Fides much preferred it when Fermion was calling the shots and making the decisions.

There was casual conversation as the night finally came upon them. There was even laughter. A large party of Shadowmen came by to revel in the fellowship. They were a delightful bunch, and Fides could not help having his heart lifted. These appeared to belong to Henryetta, whom Fides and the rest had met in council just west of Cairo some weeks ago. There were two twins who got on marvelously telling jokes and doing pranks. One was named Frederich and the other Gregory, but you couldn't tell them apart. A somewhat slower member of their number, named Newt, was their constant victim. Dolam came by a little later, accompanied by Falda. They were still smoking their pipes and furtively trying to make smoke rings with them. A very pleasant looking lady, whose name they learned was Sharon, seemed to flirt with Fides. That could not be, one of the twins informed him, for she was already committed to another.

The merrymaking had to end eventually, and Henryetta and her friends left. It was quite dark, and the fire had gone down quite a ways, too. Fides curled up in his blanket, shut his eyes, and was fast asleep. When he awoke, there was a moment when his mind was clear and his heart was new but with a brute declaration by the will, his heart was hardened and his mind entrenched once again. He would not be going to Peoria on his own power. It just wasn't going to happen. He thought it wise not to share this information with his friends who he did not doubt hoped that the new morning would change Fide's views. When he rolled out of his blanket, though, Fermion was sitting up already (still?) looking at him.

"So?" Fermion asked him.

"I stay," Fides muttered. Fermion sighed. A sour look washed over his face but was gone in the next, replaced by Fermion's own sort of positive attitude.

"Can't worry about the things you can't control," he said, whistling to himself.

Soon the whole camp was awake. Horses were tended to, breakfast for thousands was made, armor was polished, counted, or distributed, and a myriad of other chores were completed, as well. Around lunch time, the chores were done. It seemed as though their army was as ready as it was going to get. A sense best described as boredom overtook the camp. Even Yuri and Nagro were seen socializing. There simply wasn't anything to do. The only real exception was the man they recalled was named Calvin. Calvin was still busy organizing and planning, but mainly it was perceived as just senseless reminding.

"Come on, Calvin," a scrawny, yet sturdy young man said to him. "Give people a rest."

"Chuck, the rest comes after the six days of work, not before," Calvin rejoined. Chuck left him and stood by a pretty girl that Fides remembered seeing working on the hospital field in Cairo.

Only two things worthy of mention occurred that day. First, the Pledge army had finally begun assembling for battle within their sight. Most of the Shadowmen army was encamped to the west of the small town of Sidney. On the east side, there were wide open plains that had formerly been used for farming. It was flat, without any unique geographic features. It was ideal for cavalry. To the north, running roughly east and west was a small river that wound its way towards Danville. It formed a natural wall to contain the coming battle. It looked as though Sidney would become a fulcrum in the battle. Already, the Shadowmen (presumably under instigation of Calvin) and allies who had guns had taken up position in the town. It was one of the few areas of cover and a strategic asset for that reason.

The other thing worthy of mention is the visit by Perry and Emory. They had each acquired an old motorcycle and could not contain desire to ride them. They left Bloomington to find out what could be found out, but Yuri chastised them. Emory received his rebuke a little sheepishly, but Perry brushed it off. Misaluva was very enthused to see her old friends again. Perry and Emory were sad to learn about Fides' wife and family, but glad that Fides and friends had been able to rejoin them. Charis asked Fides if he'd be willing to go to Peoria on a motorbike, which prompted an uncomfortable discussion about Fides' decision. Emory frowned at Fides but Perry looked him in the eye and said he liked what he saw in there, even if it was obstinate. Or, especially because it was obstinate.

"Fides without a certain obstinacy is no Fides at all, that's my view," Perry told him. This encouraged Fides some, but he knew in his own heart that if there was a good sort of obstinacy, this current expression of obstinacy wasn't it.

Yuri came by to see if Perry and Emory had left yet. Seeing that they weren't started on their way back to Bloomington, he unleashed a tirade upon them that would have made a certain general of a past European war blush. The defense of Bloomington was in the hands of the Rangers. It wouldn't be good for its two leaders to be caught in the battle at Champaign. So, reluctantly, Perry and Emory left and all their friends reluctantly let them go.

The Pledge army continued to assemble off in the distance. Calvin's spyglass seemed to suggest that they had at least another day before the full force was there. Yuri readied two thousand men after lunch to serve as a safe-guard against a surprise attack. These men, along with the snipers Calvin had posted en masse in Sidney, would give the rest of the army time to react if anything sneaky happened. But nothing sneaky did happen. The night came without any further incident.

That night the camp went to bed without any joy or frolicking or laughter. There was a good chance that the next day would bring battle. Battle might bring death. It might be one's own death. Weapons and armor double-checked, the horses inspected once more, and then fitful rest for all. Just as the army was drifting into uneasy sleep, one voice sang out,

One breath is all it takes
One mighty breath to come
And makes the stone arms move
And gives the Shadow form
It lives, it lives, and it lives, because he lives.

Both camps were up and awake before the rising of the sun to prepare for battle. Horses were fitted. Armor was put on. Weapons were quadruple-checked. How the men were to be situated had been decided and communicated days earlier. Nagro's delaying tactic in Danville had won valuable time. Calvin rode up and down the front line communicating final instructions.

Men of Champaign, Bloomington, Danville, Kankakee, Peoria, Decatur, and cities and towns in between stood alongside soldiers of the Shadowmen. Facing them were men of the Pledge. No doubt, its army drew men from the same region, but for the most part it appeared that they had assembled in the states to the east, to the south, and mysteriously, to the west. The Pledge now intended to gather up for itself the crossroads of America. That, at least, was the more immediate strategic objective that the average person could discern. There were some in both armies that knew that this strategic objective was second in importance to another objective to be had in Peoria.

Until the last waking moment the night before, Fides had insisted that he would be fighting the next day. In the morning, there was slim hope that he would relent and do his part by going to Peoria ahead of the rest while the Pledge was still blocked from influencing the journey. If Fermion had hoped to keep the Key out of the hands of the Pledge by positioning the Shadowmen army between it and the Key, the hope failed by the Key's decision to march into the Pledge lines with sword swinging.

Upon hearing of Fides' decision, Yuri insisted that Fides come to his section of the line. Yuri and Nagro were disappointed along with the rest of the Shadowmen that knew of the situation about Fides' decision, but they respected and honored the courage of it. Fides' friends were also asked to join their section. Yuri solemnly charged them with protecting Fides to the best of their ability. Each of them pledged to do just that.

The Shadowmen army moved their lines towards the Pledge lines until the small town of Sidney, which they held, was only about two hundred yards ahead and to the left of them. The riflemen in Sidney were to hold their northern flank. From this new position, and because the sun had risen high enough, they were able to see the full scope of the Pledge lines. An exact analysis was impossible, but it was apparent that the Pledge outnumbered them by at least a three to one ratio. There was still wet dew on the old overgrown farmland when the Pledge line sent out a party with a white flag to the center of the field of combat.

Yuri sent Nagro out to negotiate with the Pledge delegation, so there was time for conversation. The negotiation dragged on for a half an hour with both armies lined up against each other, separated by no more than about a thousand yards. There was anxious banter by some, but steely silence by others, during this delay. Fides' friends used the opportunity to try to persuade him to the last.

"It is not too late," Charis told Fides. "We still have time to go to Peoria. We- or I know I, at least- will go with you." The others nodded, indicating their own willingness.

"I deserve to die on this field. I hope I die. When I am dead you can lop my head off and take the key from around my neck that way. Or, if it is easier for everyone, you can do that now," Fides returned curtly.

Charis was visibly hurt by this remark, but she was quick to reply. "The only one condemning you at this point is you. You must forgive yourself before you can forgive anyone else. No one else is condemning you, and no one else is passing sentence on you. Be merciful to yourself: if you are, I believe we shall all share in the overflow of that mercy."

But Fides did not answer her. Instead, he turned to Fermion, and said, "Look at this fine blade I have now, Fermion." He pointed to the machete that he had picked up in Danville. "Why I am reduced to *this* after having such a fine blade before, I don't know."

Fermion glanced at him, "We are already prepared to endure imminent suffering and death to abide with the consequences of your decision, must we also abide you being an ass as well?"

Fides' face flushed with anger but then he regained his composure and apologized, "I am sorry. That was stupid of me to say. Charis, I apologize to you, as well." Charis's beautiful, long brown hair had been brushed into her eyes to conceal the single tear that had emerged there.

She gave a muffled, "It's alright," but said nothing more.

There was a long an uncomfortable pause. "I truly am sorry," Fides said again.

"If you are sorry, my friend, then shouldn't we even now be turning towards Peoria?" Jonathan asked him.

"We are all prepared to die along side you today, Fides. If you live, and we die, will you be able to console yourself with the consequences of that decision? You left your wife and family using your best judgment," Misaluva joined in, "and you condemn yourself viciously for that. Here your self-condemnation itself has clouded your judgment. If you cannot forgive yourself for your decision in regards to your family which you made in good faith, will you be able to forgive yourself for your decision today that was not made in good faith?"

This appeared to sting Fides, but he did not make any indication that he had changed his mind.

"Today is a good day to die," Melody said, shrugging her shoulders.

Fides turned his thoughts back to his old sword which Fermion had asked him to leave back in Cairo. In a moment of clarity, he realized that it was not Fermion's fault that he did not still have that sword, even though Fermion had implored him to leave it behind. Fides had chosen at that time to take the sword with him, with no visible consequence, and lost it, anyway. He had no grounds for condemning Fermion for no longer having it in his possession. In the end, the effect to him turned out to be the same. Didn't it?

This line of thought led him to another line of thought, though. He recalled that the sword had seemed to impart a sense of strength to him, merely by having it in his hands. The few times he had held a gun, something like that emboldening had entered into him, but it wasn't the same. Of all the people who might have thoughts on such an issue, Fermion jumped out as an obvious one. With a little bit of humility in his voice…

"Fermion. Tell me, why is it that a blade in my hands gives me more of a sense of worth than nothing at all or even a gun?" Fides asked him.

Fermion thought for a moment. His hesitancy could not be because he did not know, but only because he didn't know the best way to explain it. Finally, with others nearby interested and listening in, too, Fermion spoke. "This is a profound question you ask, actually. What you have here are three, general positions. Two are at the extreme, while one occupies the center ground. A weapon is an extension of a man's will, just as an army is the extension of a commander's will. Obviously, the extent of the capabilities is different, but it is the same sort of thing.

"A man who must fight without the use of weapons, relying only on his own limbs, is in a desperate position. To have your hands around a man's neck is to have direct sensation- and control- of life coming and going. To will yourself at that point to bring about the man's death is to cross a threshold in your own mind. Woe to us all when anyone crosses that threshold and enjoys it. It is a grotesquely intimate moment. On the other hand, a man who shoots another with a firearm, and in some measure, even with a bow and arrow, delivers death by messenger. There is no physical sensation involved for the messenger in the moment where life and death meet. This diminishes a person's sense that the person whom they have just wounded, perhaps mortally, is in fact another person. Woe to us all when a person loses sight of the personhood of the one he fights with. A person as an abstraction is easily dismissed. A person who throttles another has himself to credit- his brute strength, his physical prowess, whatever. A person who shoots another does not require any special exertion either physically or mentally. The weakest person can pull a trigger. The most indecisive can yet decide to pull a trigger," Fermion explained.

"But with a sword... with a sword you have an extension of your will that allows for both distance and physical sensation. You cannot forget it is another man you are contesting. You can feel the weight of him even if you can't feel him. And unlike pulling a trigger, to bring your sword up for a stroke enjoins your entire being. A man might be physically weak, but he is able to train himself to compensate for such weakness. A man might be physically weak, but impressively brave. Bare hands and guns equally bring a person in contact with brutality. So, even though war is a terrible thing, and it can make a man terrible, the weapons they use can have other consequences, too. A sword makes it easier to keep a man from becoming a monster or making his enemy into one, either," Fermion concluded. "That is not to say it is not possible for either to happen," he added.

"Am I nothing without a sword?" Fides persisted.

"You are everything without it," Fermion replied. "Woe to the man who measures his worth, his value, and his being, by the inanimate objects he uses to exert his will. Better, much better, is the man who is master over himself, who understands that he is not the things around him, and that his very body is nothing more than God's gift of dignity to man- for without anything at all to manifest the consequences of a decision of the will, it is impossible to distinguish a free will from an enslaved one. Without a body to reflect your decisions, your choices are meaningless, as you have no means to carry them out. You- each of us- are entrenched inside our bodies, but you cannot actually add to it, neither with a sword or a stick. You are no more or less a man because of the weapons you hold. That measure is always taken by looking at the choices you make, even though the weapons we use can help facilitate certain choices, or give us a sense of our own potency that we'd otherwise not suspect we had."

Nagro was returning to the lines, now. Some of the eavesdroppers had drawn closer during the conversation. Dor had come closer, too. He heard Fides ask about having a sword and formed the wrong conclusion that Fides had no weapon at all.

"Where is your fine blade we heard so much about, Fides?" Dor asked him.

"I lost it in a river near Cairo," Fides explained. "It's a bit of a story, because Fermion had told me to leave it at an inn in Cairo itself, but I refused. Then in the end, I lost it anyway." Fermion was watching both Fides and Dor closely. Dor's face turned sour.

"Leave it at an inn...?" Dor stammered.

Fides wasn't looking at Dor, so he didn't know that Dor's countenance had changed. Fides didn't feel like elaborating on this embarrassing story, though, so he merely replied, "Yea. Odd, I know. Just leave it in an inn? I thought it was crazy, too."

"Something terrible happened there," Dor reluctantly told Fides. Now Fides looked at him. "Simus..." Dor hesitated.

"Simus? Perry and Emory's friend. Yes, where has he been?" Fides wondered, aware with a start that Simus had been absent and unmentioned for many weeks.

"I don't think it is my place to say..." Dor stated, his eyes shifting towards the earth. Fides had the sudden realization that his failure to leave the sword was somehow connected to whatever terrible thing had fallen upon Simus. Fides looked to Fermion, but Fermion was wearing a stony expression.

"Why didn't you just tell me that I would be helping to save a life?" Fides rounded on Fermion, angry beyond words.

"I didn't know," Fermion replied dispassionately. "I only knew that obedience was called for. It was not for me, or you, to know why."

"Obedience to who?" Fides shouted. "You? God? Perhaps I would have more willingly 'obeyed' if I had been given a compelling reason!"

"A 'compelling reason,' as you call it," Fermion said coolly, "would have robbed your obedience- if you had obeyed- of its virtue."

"Of its virtue?" Fides exclaimed bitterly.

"You deny that it speaks well of your son if he obeys you, even if he doesn't understand the command?" Fermion challenged him.

"My sons are dead," Fides snarled. Fermion was unfazed.

"Answer the question," Fermion insisted. For a time, nobody said anything. All of Fides' friends and many of the Shadowmen were captivated by the exchange. Dor was looking around uncomfortably.

"I don't understand," Fides said at last.

Fermion still maintained his stony expression, but his eyes softened. "That is because understanding is like a destination. Your journey to that destination cannot be completed all in a step. Also, if you do not obey the signs as you are going, not only should you not expect to arrive at the destination, you can expect whatever consequences that follow from leaving the road."

Fides was not satisfied, "What I don't understand is why the safety of one man was made to depend on my obedience, and why the so-called 'virtue' of my obedience was more important than the life of a man. The price of this virtue is too high, I say!" Fides was shouting, now. "How little God must care for life- what a tyrant, he much prefers blind obedience!"

At this, Fermion looked positively angry. Fermion had seemed annoyed and angry on occasion, but for the most part he didn't let the words and actions of other people dictate how he was going to feel and respond at a given moment. But as Fides glared at Fermion, he saw that Fermion was truly enraged. Fides was glad.

"The only reason why I don't..." Fermion began.

"Is because my history has been robbed of me, blah blah blah," Fides sarcastically replied. Fermion now looked as though he was making every effort to retain self-control. When he finally spoke, though, it was with a visible tremble.

"The price is too high, you say? What makes you think you are the one paying it?" Fermion demanded. "You only have some abstract notion that your own action, or inaction, led to the hurt of another. You feel guilty, but wish to justify yourself. Is your guilt the price to be paid for this virtue? The arrogance. The insolence..." Fides thought he saw a shimmer of light rippling just outside the contours of Fermion's body. Fermion continued, "The price you are paying is nothing compared to the price he has paid, and is paying, even to this very moment. Look around, Fides. There are currently thousands of people gathered on a plain to fight and kill each other. Do you weep for them? Billions of people have lived and died, many of them in various forms of agony. What price are you paying for them? All this because of a series of acts of disobedience by your race, narrowing down through time and history to the first act of disobedience."

Fides did not wish to give in so easily, "But why? What is so valuable that such pain and suffering is allowed to persist?"

"Is it not obvious?" Fermion put back to him. "It is not blind obedience that he wants, but noble sons and daughters, free people, free men, free woman. Lords and Ladies. Kings and Queens. Is the price too high? It is not for you to decide! He has made many pilgrims princes, though they were beggars born. If he is willing to endure their beggarly behavior in the meantime, what is that to you? But do not think that merely because you do not think the heartache worth it, he must share the same view!"

Fides had never considered the possibility that God wanted him to be a king. While considering the ramifications of that sentiment, he asked Fermion, "If what you are saying is true, than even the smallest deed can have great impact. I don't know if I can wrap my mind around all the things I am responsible for."

"You are so tiny, you can't detect the ripple effect of your actions beyond one or two concentric circles around you. Beyond your inability to detect them, those you detect you do not understand," Fermion was softening. "But God detects them out to where the wave circles are no more, and he understands where they stop, and why. Not just for you, but for every man, every incident, every event in the universe. It is not your job to understand all this. Your job is simply to accept the gift, fall on grace, and obey. Certainly, some understanding will follow. That, however, is incidental. On the other hand, apart from that obedience, there cannot be understanding."

There were sounds of movement around them. The battle was poised to begin. Throughout the conversation, it had slowly dawned on Fides that he had been wallowing in self-pity.

"But you don't understand," Fides moaned. He was considering how such a small thing like leaving behind or not leaving behind a sword could have such tremendous consequences, but he was also reflecting on the ripple effect of his actions had impacted his wife and children. If even the smallest and most innocent of decisions can have far-reaching consequences, who would dare lifting even their finger? There were more noises signaling that the battle was nearly at hand.

"I think I do," Fermion said to Fides tenderly. "Realize that there are both good and bad consequences to nearly every human action in this broken place. It is too much for any one of you to comprehend, at least not now, in your current state. That is why you are not expected to understand all these things. Small requests that require your obedience is a mercy. Yet, if you make a habit of obeying in the small things, perhaps you will be trusted with a great matter. Your duty is the same in either case."

"What will happen if I do not go to Peoria?" Fides asked Fermion.

"Some good prepared for will not happen. Some evil will happen that would not have happened otherwise. But if you do not do this small thing, another good will be worked out of your disobedience. It will not be the same good as the one if you had obeyed," Fermion explained. Now there were shouts up and down the line. The command to charge was now nearly upon them. Dor brought his horse close to Fides.

"Please, my lord, take my sword," Dor begged him. He held the sword out to Fides with the handle facing out. Fides instinctively took hold of it, but protested.

"Lord? How can anyone call me a lord? I'm a buffoon, as everyone around me can clearly see!" Fides argued. "I am not worthy of another man's weapon!"

Yuri was heard nearby shouting for a signal to be given. Melody called out that the Pledge was moving, now. Dor and Fides were still in argument.

"I insist! You have the Key, and deserve the best protection. I admit my sword is not the likes of Nagro's or the one you used to have. But it has served me well. Its name is Glints, and it will serve you well, on my honor!" Fides opened his mouth to object, but then Dor said, "For Lobi, then. Take it for Lobi." Fides could not say no to that. Finally, the command was given to the army and it now surged around and behind them, pushing them towards the Pledge.

Fides had, in fact, changed his mind. He realized in a single flash of perception that he had hoped to redeem himself in his own mind by demonstrating that he was still a Man, but in fact he had only been showing himself to be an enslaved Man. To be a Free Man, he'd have set his mind on the duty he knew ought to be done and kept the duty itself distinct from his own identity. Doing the thing, rather than the thing itself, was the actual measure of his Manhood. This all came in a flash, but it was not possible to leave now.

He and his friend's horses were being driven now towards battle. The sound of rifle cracks from Sidney came into his left ear. His eyes beheld that the Pledge was likewise rushing towards them. Most were on foot, some were on horseback, and there were some vehicles, too. Fides was not in the very first rank, but he was in the third. Fifty ranks or more were behind him. Just ahead of him was Gol in his chariot forming the equivalent of the first and second ranks. Fides heard Gol let out a shout as the two armies collided in the middle. Gol brought his weapon, a club, thundering down on the first rank of the charging Pledge.

Fides quickly felt himself pulled off the horse and to the ground. Before he could be dispatched, though, Jonathan and Melody were off their horses and at his side. The three men that had dismounted Fides were themselves laid low in seconds. Fermion and Misaluva were now nearby, as well, but they were still on horseback. Fides' friends tried to form a protective ring around him, but it could not be maintained. One or another of them would often lose sight of their charge for a few minutes before finally finding him again. Dor and his fellows, Blessed, Greene, and Thamson had taken it upon themselves to also protect Fides. It was not easy to protect the one man while also fulfilling obligations to further the objectives of their portion of the line.

After his initial fall, Fides arose armed with Glints. The two fought marvelously together. Many Pledge soldiers died because of their partnership. The Pledge soldiers in their area were discovering that the silvery armor of the Shadowmen in their section was effectively deflecting cuts of their blades. Some had had success with clubs: Jonathan stepped over Sapian who had been clumped on the head and now lay still.

Gol had taken his chariot deep into the Pledge line with much success, but now that his momentum was stopped, he found himself in need of abandoning his chariot altogether. Thanks to his armor, slashes and jabs of the enemy were not having any effect. Thanks to his great size and bulk, clubs were barely bruising him. Still, he found himself alone around a surging mass of soldiers trying to take him down at his knees or pulling his arms down. He could be seen by his fellows on horseback, towering above his enemies in plain sight of them, but inaccessible. There were shouts among Gol's friends to do something about it, but Fides did not see how the thing turned out.

Peder and Hector passed within their sight and wept when they found Sapian on the ground. Men of Champaign passed them on their way to push deeper into the Pledge lines, but Peder and Hector scooped up their brother and tried to make it back to the hospital area. Tasha was no doubt their ultimate goal. She had won a reputation for her skillful medical skills at the battle of Cairo.

Charis would have helped some of the wounded around her as well if it were not for her pledge to help protect Fides. She was not by any means as strong or as skillful as the men fighting around her, or even Misaluva or Melody for that matter, but she was as loyal as them. She was willing to die for Fides, if it came to that. She had come up a little after the others because of the way the armies had moved. She also dismounted and stood with Dor and his brethren and Jonathan and Melody in battling with and for Fides. She was injured, however, when a Pledge soldier jabbed her with a pitchfork. One of the prongs got her in the arm and another in her side. She gasped out loud in shock and pain. Melody was quickly at her side: Fermion dealt with the man wielding the pitchfork.

The surge had now diminished and it became possible for them to withdraw if they wanted to. Fides realized this, and having a moment to assess the situation, he called out to his fellow warriors that he had in fact changed his mind and was ready to head to Peoria. He had already said as much as they were being pushed toward the coming line, but he repeated it now. Fermion brought his horse over to Fides.

"We'll try to get you out of here, but it will be at some risk. We'll need to tell Nagro or Calvin that this section will need reinforcement!" Fermion called out over the din.

Fides nodded in acknowledgement, but he was stunned to observe something strange happening to his sword. After he had shouted out his decision to move on to Peoria, there had been a convergence on his position by some within the Pledge. In particular, some of the strange, dumpy looking Pledge 'slaves' had filled in some of the spaces in the area and were pushing their way towards Fides. Fides didn't notice that, and even if he had, he probably wouldn't have made the connection with what he saw with his sword. It appeared to have a faint glow about it at that point in time.

"It's not supposed to do that, here!" Dor said, from nearby.

"No kidding!" Fides returned, staring at it in awe.

Thamson hastened over to Fides, "No, it's not supposed to work. Not here."

This made no sense at all to Fides who found himself staring dumbly at it. Thamson and Dor were now frantically scanning the soldiers around them. They saw nothing out of the ordinary, but they were able to see that there were more enemy soldiers collapsing onto their position. Fermion, who had at first tried to relay to Calvin or Nagro the turn of events, had caught pieces of the exchange between Fides and Dor, turned back in time to respond to the developing threat. He gave a shout and Jonathan and Misaluva were quickly at Fides' side. Sensing the increase in enemy strength in that area, more allies entered the section, too. This was just in time, because everyone who had sworn to protect Fides now found themselves in frantic and mortal combat for their own lives. Fides had become separated from them, and potentially exposed, but men from Champaign and Bloomington caught up to him and passed him in beating back the enemy surge.

In fact, these men so successfully pushed the enemy back that Fides was left sitting on the ground in exhaustion and practically alone. He was in a very nice sized pocket where there was no battling at all. His friends clawed into the pocket in short order and rallied around Fides, but then the pocket began to collapse. Fermion's arm was bleeding profusely, but he used his other one to pull Fides up to standing. Fermion's horse was nowhere to be seen.

"Where is Jonathan?" Fides shouted frantically.

"He was over that way," Misaluva shouted back. Fides staggered in the direction that Misaluva pointed. Thamson and Blessed were near the spot and were hacking and slashing madly. Other men were around, wrestling to the death with their bare hands, having been disarmed. Fides found the spot where Jonathan lay. A sharpened rod jutted out of his chest. His decapitated attacker was nearby.

"Thamson got him," Jonathan gurgled faintly. Fides got on his knees by him and wept bitterly.

"I am so sorry I made you do this," Fides cried out. In the back of his mind, he knew that this was the sort of result that Fermion meant about an evil happening if he did not do the small good before him.

Jonathan pulled Fides' head down so that he could speak into his ear, as it was becoming difficult for him to talk. "It was my choice, I made it of my own free will," Jonathan stuttered. "You are not responsible for my choice," he finished. Fides tried to pull the rod out of Jonathan's body, but it was lodged. Fermion had arrived now, and the two of them tried to sit Jonathan up to try to take him back to the hospital tents, but the rod had gone clean through his body and stuck in the dirt. Jonathan gave a great gasp of pain, but then closed his eyes, and stopped breathing.

Fides stood up, shouting. He shook his fist at the sky and cursed it. Then he cursed himself. Then he plunged Glints into the belly of a Pledge slave. Then he kicked another in the knees. Then he cursed the ground. Then, in a rage, he waded into the area he thought he saw the enemy at its thickest. Fermion and Misaluva tried desperately to try to join him but Fides was not stopping to do battle with any single soldier. He was instead stomping further up and further in, slashing and jabbing, and shouting, and cursing, and weeping. Pledge soldiers turned their heads as Fides went by, because in some cases Fides just walked right by them without taking any notice of them at all, which confused them.

Fides soon stumbled onto Gol's toppled chariot, though Gol himself was nowhere to be seen. There were many battling around him, but many of the men around him were Pledge soldiers pushing up and pushing back into the Shadowmen army. Fides sat down on one of the wheels of the chariot and waited for some Pledge soldier to come by and run him through. For whatever reason, none did. Perhaps it was because he couldn't easily be distinguished from the rest of the Pledge soldiers, or perhaps because he sat so still on the wheel, hunched over, that they thought he was already dead. At any rate, Fides sat motionless on that wheel for more than a few minutes before Misaluva found him.

"Fides," she said to him curtly. "You need to get a grip. Unless you want Jonathan to have died in vain, it's time you and I left this field and did what you still have time to do. Get a hold of yourself."

"He's dead because of me!" Fides exclaimed.

Misaluva would have none of it. She lifted Fides head, and before he had a chance to do anything, she brought her fist around in a round house and punched him as clean hard as she could. Fides found himself tumbling off the wheel and face down into the dirt, where soil stuck to the blood now running from his mouth.

"Get a grip. Be a man!" Misaluva shouted at him. Her golden hair flashed in the light of the sun, but not nearly as brilliantly as her eyes flashed in anger. "Stand UP!" she shouted again, catching him by his armpit and hoisting him up in a single motion. "Here. Is. Your. Sword." She punched the words out, handing Glints back to Fides. Fides appeared to be coming to his senses, but not quite as fast as Misaluva would have wanted.

"If I had not..." Fides began.

"If you complete that sentence, I may kill you myself," Misaluva muttered.

"But..." Fides tried again. Misaluva turned around on him again, but this time instead of using a fist, smacked him across the face just as hard with the back of her hand. Fides' face snapped around. Something like cobwebs began to fall out of his thinking. He sort of staggered forward again as he caught his breath.

"Fides, you're getting your butt kicked by a woman. Let's go already. Step up and do the right thing," she snapped at him. She grabbed his arm and pulled him back towards where they were not so out-numbered. Some of the Pledge soldiers that Fides had passed earlier and left in confusion were confused again to see Fides, this time with a beautiful woman, being pulled back the other way.

Some lingering obstinacy remained in Fides, though. As they reached the area where Fides was much safer, he managed to say to her, "I deserved to have his fate." Misaluva whipped her head around and gave him the world's iciest stare, ever. There was a moment as she sized him up, as though trying to consider how best to end his life while maximizing his pain, and then at last reached out and grabbed his bloody shirt with both hands and pulled his face into her face. Her lips met his lips with such force that he was knocked backwards and the two fell to the ground with Misaluva on top, straddling him, and still kissing him. At first, Fides struggled. It was not much of a struggle. In fact, it was really quite feeble. She kissed him- or they kissed- for a full minute before finally she broke the connection.

She let her lips hover over his just about an inch or so. Fides could feel her warm breath on his cheeks. Her eyes glittered with mirth.

"Do you feel like a man, now, Fides?" she murmured. Stunned into silence, and with a slightly embarrassed smile, he could only nod. "Good! Now get up, shut up, and let's get out of here!" she ordered him. She yanked him to his feet, and as though speaking into the heavens muttered something like, "No, the daughters of God will not be marrying the sons of men!" but Fides really couldn't be sure that's what she said, because it made no sense at all to him.

Fermion had re-appeared, now. Peder and Hector were with him. "That was an interesting tact," Fermion whistled at Misaluva.

"To each their own," she replied coyly.

"I let Nagro know that we were going to try to get out of here," Fermion said, ignoring her remark.

"I've been stupid," Fides said, giving his clearest assessment of things in days.

"Yes, we know. But hopefully you've had your fill for the time being," Fermion answered him.

As they talked, though, the battle intensified around them again, and they found that conversation with each other had to wait again. There were now many hurt and wounded people from both sides lying around them, moaning. Many more were lying, dead. A general exhaustion began to consume the fighters on both sides. However, to their astonishment, there was the sound of several prolonged trumpet calls in the direction of the Pledge.

Fermion glanced over at Peder, who was nearby. "I think we are about to see what difference being out-numbered five to one makes," Fermion said. Indeed, by straining to look over the heads of the people fighting around them, they could see another wave of Pledge soldiers running at a sprint to join in the battle.

"This is not good," Hector remarked. Peder flashed his noble sword into the sky as if to egg the next wave on.

"I do not know if we have any reinforcements to expect at all," Fermion said ruefully.

"We've got to get him out of here," Hector replied, nodding towards Fides. They continued to battle their way back in retreat, but in only a few minutes they found themselves swamped like the rest of the Shadowmen army by the fresh Pledge soldiers entering the battle. These new entrants seemed to have driven almost completely through the line, but Calvin had a few ranks of archers held back that dropped the ones that did get through. The hole was sealed up somehow, and the battle again turned into a massive, swirling pit of combatants. After some time, the tide changed again in favor of the Shadowmen and Men of Champaign, but Fides was nonetheless trapped within the battle. Now that he was willing to go to Peoria, he was unable.

The battle had been raging for several hours and the sun was beginning to reach its place directly above their heads. The Pledge's next wave was well met but Yuri and Nagro received reports that more waves could be seen in the distance assembling into lines. The riflemen in Sydney were the ones mainly responsible for allowing them to endure the additional influx of Pledge soldiers. Within the small town, some of the riflemen had re-deployed so as to pick the enemy off even while they were in the midst of their allies. There were no reports of wounds from friendly fire, but even if there had been it would not have been held against the riflemen. Still, it was becoming evident that they were not going to be able to hold their ground against the Pledge.

Yuri and Nagro now made the difficult decision to order a retreat. One of the questions that had pervaded the pre-war considerations was the matter of how many firearms the Pledge had. It was known that they had at least some from the delaying action in Danville where they saw some Pledge riflemen. Oddly, the only rifles firing in this battle were their own. Where were the Pledge's guns? How many did they have? It was a mystery that they were not being used against them, especially since their own riflemen had been having a great impact. Yuri and Nagro thought it likely that the rifles were being held back even though they couldn't fathom why. The bigger guns that were seen in Cairo crossed their mind, too. What if some guns like these were out there somewhere? None of their scouting had revealed any such weapons, but that didn't mean they weren't out there.

Shortly after the decision for retreat was made and signals were being sent, the Pledge did unveil one surprise. Fides and his friends had finally managed to claw their way out of the main battle and were in sight of the hospital tents when they heard the sounds of pounding hooves and shouting to their left, from the south. Someone gave a shout and those in the vicinity turned their heads to look. Bearing down on the camp were about two hundred Pledge soldiers on horseback. They had apparently flanked wide around. Within two minutes they were in the perimeter and charging into the hospital areas. The two that tried to enter Tasha's tent, however, met Tasha and rode no more.

Upon seeing the coming threat, Fermion and Fides sprinted the remaining distance back to the camp's tents to try to meet the enemy. Hector, Peder, and Misaluva were not far behind. There were plenty of other soldiers in the camp, so it wasn't completely defenseless. Some of Calvin's archers and some other horsemen were dispatched by Yuri when he finally saw the danger, so there were men to meet the riders. The riders, however, did not seem to be looking to engage the defenders. They seemed to be looking for something, or someone.

Fides remembered that Charis had been wounded and made his way quickly first to one hospital tent, and then, finding that she was not there, to another. The second tent contained a wrathful Tasha, but Charis was not there. Hector and Peder had Sapian in mind and were close behind Fides with the same sentiment. The third tent revealed a startling scene. Charis and Sapian were in fact there, along with quite a few other wounded people, but some of the Pledge riders were charging up and down the rows of cots shouting and heckling the wounded. The nurses laid their bodies over their charges and shouted for the burly men to leave them alone. An extremely powerful looking man was looming over Charis' cot, his sword hovering a few feet from her chest. She was holding her own sword weakly above her, but it was all for show. At any rate, as they came on the scene the man didn't seem to be concerned with actually killing her, but was talking to her. They couldn't hear the words, but they caught the threatening and even deriding tone well enough.

"You there!" Fides shouted at him. The man's head whipped over to see who was challenging him. Some of the other riders also noticed the newcomers for the first time, now. As these were well armed, as opposed to the frightened nurses, the riders peeled out of the tent. The burly man did nothing, however. Instead, he glared at the newcomers, sizing them up. Fides thought that there had once been a gleam of something noble in him at one time, but it now seemed dead.

Misaluva apparently recognized the man. "Mirbor," she growled.

An apparent sense of recognition came across the man's face as he looked at them all. He shouted, "Here is the one!" and kicked his horse to charge them. Charis shouted after him but in less than a few seconds the horse was upon them all. Fides was in a state of disbelief, unwilling to believe the man would charge the five of them by himself. The horse's chest hit him in the shoulder and he found himself spun around. The sounds of yelling were around him, but as he shook off the cobwebs to try to assist he received another tremendous blow. Fides fell to the ground with a tremendous thud, and that was all he would remember from the battle at Champaign.

== Chapter 13 ==

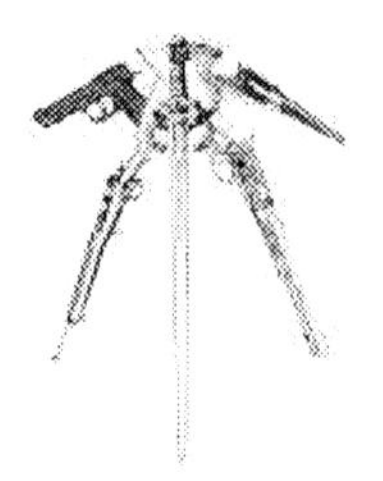

The next few days were experienced in a murky mist that Fides recalled was similar to his awakening in New Mexico. He was being transported. The jerking of the wagon occasionally jarred him into consciousness but it was never for long. In one of the instances he turned his head and saw Charis lying next to him. He couldn't see who was hauling him. He didn't know what direction he was going. Besides Charis, all he could see was a blue tarp that stood between them and the elements. Fides thought that maybe he was a captive, but he knew he didn't know really anything. In another instance his hand went up to his head and he felt a great sticky lump, the size of an orange, underneath his scalp. He could feel a gash that had been sown up, cutting across the middle of the bump. He drifted off again.

After some time had passed, he woke up and he could hear voices. He heard Fermion for sure. As he grew more alert, he developed a disquieted concern that they were all prisoners. Knowing that Fermion was there- prisoner or not- gave him peace, and he drifted into a much longer blackness than some of his earlier lapses, but it was much more restful than the earlier ones. There came a night, though, when his consciousness also brought an awareness of an extraordinarily painful ache coming from his head and his shoulder. He grimaced and made a noise. Of course, he'd been making noises all along, but he hadn't realized it.

He opened his eyes and saw that he was in a tent. He could see the light from the setting sun cast a light on the tent as though it were a lamp shade. He could hear some voices nearby. One of them was Fermion's. He thought he could also make out Nagro's. His eyes shut again as he tried to come back to his senses. He heard the tent flap move. Someone came near him and touched the bandages on his head. The tenderness of it made him sure it was probably Tasha. He left his eyes shut, though, and allowed himself to be tended to.

His confidence that it was Tasha was confirmed as he heard her leave the tent and say, "He's fine. I don't think he's coming out of it yet, though."

"Alright, then, we can still talk," Fides heard Nagro say. There seemed to be an edge to his voice. Fides' ears perked up instinctively, the way one's ears become alert when they sense hostility or a secret about to be told. With this new attentiveness he could hear the crackling of a fire.

"I understand what you are saying," Nagro continued, "But we have received words that lead us to look for and expect a king, Fermion."

"Then you misunderstand the words," Fermion countered in his characteristically matter of fact and emotionless manner.

"They don't strike us as something easily misunderstood," another voice said. After thinking hard, he thought he recognized it as Falda's.

"And yet you must have misunderstood. I am confident that another monarchy is the last thing intended for this country or the world," Fermion replied.

"We must obey the word we have received," Falda replied.

"Obviously. But tell me the word you have received. Perhaps I can help you understand where you have made your mistake," Fermion invited them.

"I fear that such advice is not the sort of advice I would have expected from you, Fermion. Do you tempt us?" another voice asked. This one was Dolam.

"Yes, that is a dangerous invitation, Fermion," Nagro added. "Why don't you tell us the word that *you* have received?"

"You know that I cannot tell you that," Fermion retorted. "I would think that I have established my repute with you all well enough. I can understand that you do not wish to tell me the word you have received. Did you receive orders not to reveal the commands given to you, though?"

Here there was a bit of silence. Apparently, no such command had ever been given. Falda at last offered, "You may have a point there. Still, I think we must wait and discuss it with the full council to see if there is wisdom in this. You have to understand that up until our conversations with you we had no reason to doubt the commands that we have received."

"I trust you to use wisdom to the best of your ability. However, I hope it has occurred to you that your prisoner has almost certainly passed your commands along to the enemy. It strikes me as an opportunity squandered to conceal it from me, your trusted ally, while the councils of the enemy already have gained knowledge of these same commands," Fermion replied with a mixture of perceived absurdity and hurt feelings.

"But we do not know that he has shared our commands with them," Nagro replied.

"You don't?" Fermion said bemusedly.

"I see your point again," Falda said to him, agreeing that this was likely.

"I would invite you to examine the commands you have received to see if perhaps the commands themselves have not merely been misunderstood, but even corrupted," Fermion said. There was an outburst of indignation at that.

"I should think that we at least got the words right!" another voice interjected, angrily. Whoever this person was, Fides had not heard the voice before, so he didn't know who the speaker was.

"You know better than me that your prisoner's heart was bent long before he left you. A little yeast works through the whole loaf! Was he not at one time a trusted advisor of the council?" Fermion pressed them.

This was again received with silence. It was true, after all. The quiet was sustained for so long that Fides began to drift off again. However, the unknown speaker spoke again, and brought him back to attention.

"I know him best," the speaker said. "As I think we all recall, it was he that pressed us to keep looking for a king from the very beginning. It was he that suggested that perhaps the king might come from among us. He never said it, I'm sure because of Yuri's presence, but even more so because of Nagro, but I fear he thought that he himself was the king to be looked for."

There was another thoughtful silence. Fides could smell pipe smoke, now. The conversation made him think of King and wonder how he was doing. Nagro broke the mood this time. "Such a thing is terrible to consider. He himself has received visions before, so he knows how they are to be treated. It would not be an accident if he has guided us into some misunderstanding. It would have been purposeful. His thoughts must have turned against us very early on. But if the words themselves have become corrupted, how are we to regain them?"

"You should assemble the full council as soon as you reach Bloomington," Tasha spoke for the first time. "Bring in even those who are your trusted servants that are out doing various tasks for you. Have everyone sit down by themselves without any discussion amongst yourselves about it to write down the message as best as all recall it. That should give you some forty to fifty different scripts. Then, compare the different accounts and see if you can sort out from the various recollections where the errors, if any, have occurred."

"That is good advice," Dolam said.

"I think it is advice we should follow," Falda added.

"Now, what shall we do about the prisoner?" Nagro asked them all. This question was met with a very long and heavy silence. By this time, the sun had fully gone down, and Fides could see the light of the fire flashing across the tent. The silence went on and on and finally Fides could not keep his attention fixed, and he fell back into unconsciousness.

When the sun came up Fides opened his eyes to greet the morning as though it had just been another long night's sleep. He could hear the sounds of the camp around him, but he was alone in the tent. His hand went up to his head where he had first felt the large lump and the stitches. He gingerly touched it. The lump had gone down quite a bit, but it still hurt to the touch. Then his fingers went to the necklace around his neck. Still there. He had a sudden desire to get up and get moving. He threw off the blanket and saw that he was already dressed. Perhaps he'd never been undressed. He got up and pulled the tent flap back so he could see out into the camp. People were bustling about tearing down the camp in preparation for leaving. Fermion spotted him peering out of the tent.

"Get out of the bed, you sluggard! Learn from the ant and be wise!" Fermion called out to him with a grin.

Nagro came over and wished him a good morning, but then hastened off to some other duty of apparent import. Tasha approached him and inquired as to his well-being. He assured her that he was feeling fine. His shoulder hurt quite a good deal and his head ached but he was ready to join the functioning world. The slumber was over. He looked around.

"Where is Charis?" Fides asked.

"She is watering some of the horses at a nearby stream," Tasha said.

"Is she ok?" Fides asked her.

"Well, we think so. She nearly had a lung punctured. Her arm hurts quite a bit, though. The prong from the pitchfork grazed a bone. Plus, we're battling infection," Tasha said. "But her spirit is fine." Tasha left to help pack up some tents.

The sudden recollection that Jonathan was dead struck him. "Jonathan!" Fides exclaimed.

"He lived and died nobly, Fides. Do not grieve as the rest of men do," Fermion comforted him. Fides nodded. He knew that he could try to make himself feel guilty for his friend's death but his friend's last words forbade him from doing such a thing. He brightened up. Melody brought him some water and a piece of bread. She seemed less and less perky since he had first met her. The realities of war, perhaps, were starting to wear in. Still, she offered the breakfast merrily enough.

"What's going on? What happened?" Fides asked as he was led to a seat by one of the campfires.

"We are just a few hours away from Bloomington," Falda said, coming to sit near Fides. As was Falda's habit, he was smoking a pipe. He was a wizened old man. The war had been relatively gentle on him as far as physical combat had gone, but he showed the signs of stress that came from constantly worrying about the doings of the enemy.

"But what about the battle?" Fides persisted.

"Well, that didn't go so well, all in all, but it could have been much worse," Falda confided to him. "Yuri signaled a retreat, and to our surprise, the Pledge armies let us go. Most of our army is behind us, about a day or two behind. We are riding ahead of the army to get you closer to Peoria and warn Bloomington of the situation."

"How bad was it? Did we lose many?" Fides asked him, a pang of sorrow shooting through his heart as he saw Jonathan die again in his mind's eye.

"We did lose many, but not as many as the Pledge. Still, like I said, it could have been worse. The Pledge could have swarmed us and ended us, I think. We don't know why they didn't press their advantage," Falda said, pausing to reflect on the conundrum yet again. "We probably lost only three hundred fine men, with another three hundred wounded. But there were some losses grievous to some of us. Peder's friend, Sapian, died in the hospital tent. Gol, Henryetta's charge, is missing. It is odd that a man of that size, even if he fell in battle, could not be found. They have hope that he is still alive since they can't find him. My dear friend Gratus has been hurt terribly, and is being tended to by Lucas, Leredo, and that healer, Tasha. Ah, but of course, you don't know most of those. Dear friends, though," Falda concluded, and sighed.

"And the prisoner?" Fides ventured, catching himself too late. Now they'd know that he overheard the night's conversation. Indeed, Falda's bushy eyebrows lifted curiously and an impish smile flashed across his face. Fides decided not to say anything else about what he heard.

"Ah, so you joined us a little sooner than we knew!" Then Falda's face turned grim. "The prisoner is being released as we speak. He is being escorted, by his own brother, back to the main body of our army and then released back to the Pledge."

"Why would the prisoner be released?" Fides wondered. Fermion and Melody were sitting with them, now, too.

Falda frowned. "It was Nagro's decision. I only have wisdom these days, not far-sightedness. Nagro thinks it's important to give him one more chance. We all spent time talking to him, pleading with him to reconsider his behavior and choices. I only just came from talking with him when I came and sat down with you. As we speak, Nagro is riding with him and his brother back a little ways towards the main body of the army. I suspect we'll be leaving shortly, ourselves, and Nagro will re-join us soon before we reach Bloomington. It was a hard decision. Whatever may come of it, I do not fault Nagro for making it the way he did."

"It is hard to accept forgiveness when one does not even acknowledge the error of one's ways," Fermion offered.

"That is the truth," Falda agreed. "In this instance, the problem is that and more, I fear. Still, perhaps there will be a sifting and something of substance may yet fall out."

At this, Charis and Misaluva joined them.

"Charis!" Fides exclaimed. He leapt up and embraced her. Fides had a growing appreciation for the loyalty and kindness and affection displayed by his friends. They truly were his friends.

"Don't hurt her, Fides!" Misaluva warned him. Fides and Charis looked at each other. They were both glad the other was alive. Both had worried about the other, though in different ways. Fides suddenly recalled Misaluva's unexpected display of affection back in Champaign, and started to turn shy but then noticed that Misaluva was no longer looking at him at all. If she had any recollection of the incident, she was not showing it. Fides relaxed.

"It's about time that you woke up," Charis chided him. Falda chuckled. She continued, "We've been on the road for four days now, and I've been up and about for two of them!"

"My deepest apologies, my lady," Fides grinned, giving a teasing bow. Then he remembered the last scene from the battle and he was going to ask her about it but he decided it wasn't the right time or place.

Tasha came over to the campfire. "Ok, we just have a few more tents to fold up. The horses have been watered and harnessed. We'll be leaving in about twenty minutes."

"I will help with the tents," Fermion said.

"And I will speak with the horses," Falda added. The two stood up and went to help with the packing. There were a handful of Shadowmen that Fides had not seen before- or at least he hadn't noticed them- with them, helping them pack. Dolam took Falda's spot, but only nodded a greeting and didn't say anything. It was soon time to leave. The fire was put out and Fides and Charis were helped into the wagon. Fermion took the reins of the horses with Tasha sitting next to him. They were off.

After several hours, they saw the buildings of Bloomington in the distance. Ranger scouts intercepted them while they were still a ways off, checked their identities, and allowed them to pass. As they drew closer, they could see that Bloomington had been fortified in much the same way as Oklahoma City had been fortified. It was ringed with old tractor trailers. Nearly all of the trailers were on their side. Guard posts were erected on some of them, and all of them were manned. When they drew nearer, they were met by a messenger and led off the interstate to the north. After a time, they saw a large military encampment spread out before them occupying an old airport. The camp had many more tents than the Champaign force had, but there were not as many people around to fill them. As they drew closer, a Ranger came out and greeted them, and brought them the rest of the way in. Perry and Emory's meeting tent was before them.

"I hope this isn't all that's left of the army!" Perry exclaimed with a smile but a trace of concern. Fides felt a deep pang of guilt at the sight of Perry, recalling that it was his friend that was affected by Fides' disobedience not too long ago. Perry did not seem to have any knowledge of the matter, and Fides decided it was better left that way. At least for now.

"No, Perry. The rest of the army is following about a day behind us," Nagro replied.

"Victorious?" Emory asked.

"I'm afraid not," Falda said, getting down from his horse.

"Yuri and I ordered a retreat when we saw that the enemy had as many men in reserve to commit to the battle as we had in total, and our total was already engaged with its equal," Nagro explained.

"Misaluva! The Woman Ranger returns!" Perry rejoiced. The two embraced. The group began to divide according to the various tasks that they had to do. Some of the escorts took the horses off to be fed and watered. Tasha led Charis away to have her wounds tended but told Fides that his turn would come soon and not to stray. Melody went with them. The rest were standing outside the meeting tent, talking.

"Is Bloomington ready?" Nagro asked Emory.

"As well as we can be at this time," Emory returned. "We sent Rangers out to all the small towns as far out around as Peoria. Many of the men who would stand by our side had already joined us and fought with you in Champaign. Still, we were able to get maybe three or four thousand more. Bloomington itself has a large population because of the nature of the place. A large portion of noble travelers that delayed here fought with you in Champaign, but the natives were just as noble, and they have allowed us to take charge of the city defenses. They have been very helpful, but the city has had a few years of peace, and I don't know if I'd say that they are battle ready. They had once started a wall, but when we got here it was only partially completed. Let me tell you, it is a chore moving these trailers around and knocking them over."

"What is your total, then?" Nagro wondered.

"All told, perhaps twelve thousand fighting men. Some of them are younger men. Their mothers couldn't constrain them. The city has a population of some twenty thousand if we include the women and children. Even if all of them had a weapon, we cannot completely defend every part of the surrounding wall. What strength is left of the Champaign army?" Emory asked Nagro.

"It is not nearly as bad as that," Nagro said. "I am unsure about the totals, but killed was only about five hundred and wounded about the same. Of our total, we probably have nineteen thousand still, eighteen thousand of which has a weapon, either a sword or rifle."

"That will help!" Perry clapped his hands.

"The Pledge lost at least twice as many as we did, but they had more than twice as many as we had, too. We still may not have enough even with our numbers combined," Nagro sighed.

Emory looked at Nagro thoughtfully. "If we have maybe fifteen thousand defenders and combine them with your roughly twenty thousand, that puts us at close to thirty-five thousand fighters. If I understand you correctly, the Pledge army was only double the army there, which would make them out to be about forty thousand. But we have a wall. It seems an even match to me, with an advantage going our way. I sense a lingering doubt."

"They let us retreat," Nagro tried to put the doubt into words. "Something is not right. They had twice our number on the field but when we began falling back, they did nothing more than occupy the small town that was nearby. Otherwise, they watched us return to our camp. They let us pack up our things- we were able to get nearly all of it- and leave, all uncontested. We had a retreat plan in place to fight our way all the way back to Bloomington, but when we left we did not have to make use of the plan. There is something more to this story, and I am greatly concerned by it. Yuri is as well."

"How far back did you say the main army is?" Emory asked him.

"We are probably a full day ahead of them, if not two days," Nagro said.

"We have our Rangers out scouting, and they should be able to give us a report when they get close enough. But look at the sun! It is time to eat," Emory said, pointing in the direction of some campfires where food was being made. "Let's go have lunch, and then perhaps Nagro can inspect the defenses and give us instruction as he sees fit."

"That sounds good to me!" Fides said, realizing his hunger in full, now. However, Tasha had arrived with Charis and Melody.

"You'll have to wait," Tasha told Fides. "We need to look at that lump on your head and see how the bruising is doing on your shoulder." Fides grinned at the attention and allowed himself to be led away. Everyone else walked towards the mess tents. As Fides looked back, he saw Emory and Nagro talking privately with each other just behind the rest of them. Whatever else there was that Nagro was concerned about, it was evidently very serious. But Tasha took hold of him and led him to a hospital tent where she could clean his wounds. After he was washed and bandaged, the two went to lunch, where the rest of his friends had set aside the serious matters of the day for a time and were enjoying the camaraderie.

The rest of the afternoon, Charis and Fides remained inside the camp. Fermion was invited by Nagro to join him as he inspected the city defenses, and Fermion accepted that invitation. Charis and Melody spent some of their time tending to the horses, and were joined by Falda. Misaluva accompanied Perry on whatever tasks he was on for the day, but Emory was with Nagro and Fermion. For her part, Tasha was in the hospital tent talking with the nurses and preparing them and the facilities for the coming mass of wounded who were on their way from Champaign. After the horses had been tended to, Charis and Melody joined Tasha, but Tasha would not let Charis do anything. This meant that Fides was actually alone for the afternoon.

He found a tree just a little ways off and, having recovered Corrie's Bible from Charis, decided to sit down and read a little of it. He recalled Corrie's note by the Jeremiah passage that he had latched onto. The single word had been 'context.' Reading that part more closely, he realized that the passage was dealing with a specific set of circumstances. He had been foolish to so quickly apply it to himself. It occurred to him that he might have to use his brain to understand the book. Fides wondered if maybe he had expected to be suddenly filled with the 'spirit,' or whatever that meant, when he read the book. He had used his feelings at one particular moment as some sort of guide to his interpretation. Clearly, his feelings had not been a reliable guide. As he examined it more closely, he realized that 'context' would be important for understanding much more than single passages.

This was the first time since traveling alone with Fermion many months earlier that he had invested any time reading it. It had an overwhelming and intimidating size, but with 'context' in mind, he discovered that it was composed of smaller books, most of which were self-contained. They would have to be understood both on their own terms and in context with the whole. Since he had some free time, he thought he would try to get a grasp of the whole. He started in the beginning, but then he skipped ahead and read bits and pieces that he found interesting. He found himself entranced by a book called 'Judges' and read it all from beginning to end.

One thing written at the end of it caught his attention and held him riveted, recalling the conversation he had overheard the previous night. It said, "In those days Israel had no king; everyone did as he saw fit." Had America been thrown back into the same situation? Everyone was doing as they saw fit; was a king the solution? Was Fermion right to tell the Shadowmen that their command could not possibly have directed them to look for a king? He pondered these questions for a time, and then continued his random readings. Eventually, he fell asleep.

The rest of the day went by fairly lazily. The newcomers were assigned tents to be theirs for sleeping in, and in the evening Fides and the others emptied their bags out on their cots to try to clean and organize them. Fides reflected on the fact that he had at last reached the destination he had set out for many months earlier, but there was no longer any purpose to it. He had discovered the fate of his family, so Bloomington offered nothing for him. After he gave up the necklace in Peoria, he had no other goals or objectives. Where would he go after that? He let out a long sigh. Sometime later, he went to bed, forgoing the conversation that was going on around the campfires around him.

The next morning the first elements of the Champaign army could be seen. They had fallen a full two days behind, but apparently Nagro had taken a longer way into Bloomington, not knowing where the camp was. The Champaign army had been met by scouts, though, and brought in more directly. A great number of wounded were in the first elements, and they were quickly ushered into the waiting hospital tents to receive whatever care could be offered. Word had gone out the day before, so the hospital tents were well-staffed, even if not well-supplied.

Sometime in the afternoon, the command elements of the army could be seen coming their way. Horses were hauling wagons full of supplies and there were large groups of armed riders on both flanks. Yuri was in this section, along with Calvin, and the two quickly sought out Nagro and Emory. Many of the Shadowmen that Fides had come to know were in this section. Fides was sitting with Charis and Melody as they marched in.

Peder, Hector, Susanna, and a woman that Fides recognized but did not know the name to, were carrying a litter between them. There was a body laying on it, covered in a blanket. Fides knew that this was Sapian. The three of them stood up to pay respects. They remained standing as Dor and his three friends came bearing their own litter. Who was underneath that blanket was not something that Fides could guess. The litter bearers were sad as they bore their friend's bodies into the camp, but they did not seem dejected, either. Instead, they were singing a little song that Fides recalled hearing sung the night before the battle at Champaign. Fides thought he should talk to Dor sometime about whether or not he should share with Perry and Emory his role in Simus's apparent demise.

As the day was coming to an end and the sun was beginning its march into the shallows, the remaining part of the army arrived. This was a great mass of soldiers, mostly on foot. Fides recognized many of them as the riflemen that had formerly held the town of Sidney. They were grimfaced and proud: ordinary men from the area who refused to be cowed into turning over their property for 'equal distribution.' Few of these last stragglers had a chance for rest. They were quickly sent to various places along the wall, though Fides didn't learn until the following morning what hasty threat prompted this immediate deployment. Still, once the men had spread out along the wall, they were at least able to take their boots off.

The next morning, the camp that had once been barely occupied now brimmed with activity. There was a steady stream of traffic between the camp and the city, proper. Soldiers were being re-supplied, and it was clear that a siege was expected. Shortly after breakfast, Fides was summoned, along with others, to a war meeting. He tried to protest his worth, but the messenger would have none of it. When he arrived at the meeting tent, he found that an area had been cleared around it for more than fifty yards. A perimeter was set to keep unauthorized individuals from getting close and so able to hear the proceedings.

He found that his own friends had all been invited: Charis, Misaluva, Melody, Tasha, and Fermion were all seated in some of the old folding chairs that had been produced. Besides them, there were the nine members of the inner council of the Shadowmen that they had first sat with while Fermion discussed his sword and won the trust of the Shadowmen. Perry, Emory, and Misaluva, were there representing the Rangers. Then there were another thirty or forty people. Fides recognized most of them as being part of the group of Shadowmen that had met them in the center of the highway many months ago. Others he didn't recognize, though. After all had assembled, Yuri stood on a wooden box to address them all.

"Greetings, friends! It has been a long time since we have all been together like this, and even now some our friends are not here. We long for the day when the full assembly shall meet. Let us enjoy the substantial company that we have now, though, and not take it for granted. We have many things to discuss. Not all of it will concern all of you. We will give you leave when we get into those matters. We consider you all captains, fellow workers, fellow citizens. We all seek truth, and freedom. We all stand against sweetened lies that conceal oppression. We come from different places, practically different worlds, even, but we are all in this place to do good as we have opportunity," Yuri encouraged them.

"Our situation is dire. The Pledge Army is much bigger than we expected it to be. Many good men have believed their stated good intentions without thinking about the consequences of their stated beliefs. It is sad to have to fight against brothers. Nonetheless, we must. We also have reason to believe that the number of our enemies has grown, overnight, as it were. Our scouts have reported that there is yet another great army standing opposed to us. We are not certain if it stands also against the Pledge or not, but as our scouts were mercilessly attacked, it is certain that it stands against us," Yuri said to them.

"What is this new army?" called out a representative of Bloomington, standing up to pose his question, and then sitting back down.

"It would appear to be a unified army of American Indians. We are informed through other dealings that they wish to re-take the United States and drive out or subdue the rest of America's inhabitants, which they consider invaders. They have guns. Not hunting rifles, but old military style rifles. How many, we don't know. Several scouts were shot at and were lucky to get back to us to tell us anything of it," Yuri answered the man. He continued, "They were pursued by the Indians for quite a ways but a unit of Rangers heard the gunfire as the pursuit came in their direction, and the Rangers were able to respond to fire with fire. It was enough to send the Indians away and let the scouts get through."

"What strength?" Emory asked, standing up to make his question.

"Your own Rangers could not tell us, as they only saw the pursuing Indians. Our scouts inform us that they number in the thousands. How many thousands is unknown, for the scouts never saw the end of the column," Yuri said grimly.

"From what direction, then?" Emory asked, sitting down, now.

"From the west, apparently. St. Louis was supposed to be impassable according to all the lore. It was supposed to be a nuclear wasteland. Our communication lines stretch back to Cairo. No Indian army has come up that way. Some way through St. Louis or some other way across the mighty river must exist. The scouts report that they are on horseback, without a vehicle among them. This gives us an idea of how fast they can move and permits some guesses as to their ultimate origin. However..." Yuri paused. "These guesses would only be speculation. However, this next assessment is also a guess, but we think it a very likely possibility. As you all know, we met the Pledge Army in battle at Champaign and were forced off the field. The enemy allowed us to go, prompting us to wonder why. Now that we have heard about this Indian army, we think it probable that the Indians were late to a pre-arranged meeting. Why have their army picked apart piecemeal when they can wait for the heavy arms of the Indians to come and more quickly and efficiently dispatch us? That is what we think," Yuri concluded.

At this, Nagro stood up. "This means that we are truly at great peril," he continued the analysis. "They let us go, seeking only to stall us so that we might be slaughtered with less cost to themselves, later. When the Pledge Army comes next, they will not let us retreat. They will pursue us, and eliminate us." Somebody caught his attention, and he nodded to him. The young man stood up. It was Harold. Fides could see he had received a vicious cut on his forehead. It had completely healed, so Fides supposed the wound was not received in Champaign but rather in Cairo, or perhaps earlier and he simply hadn't noticed it in Cairo.

"Nagro, how do we know that the Pledge Army itself might not be able to resist these 'Indians,' as you call them? Even if they were working together, why should the Indians submit to them?" Harold inquired, and sat down.

At this, Fermion stood up, and stopped Nagro from answering. "My friends, we should not think that the Pledge does not have its own heavy arms. Nagro can testify to the fact that the Pledge Army in Danville certainly did have some weapons. They chose not to deploy those weapons in Champaign. Let us keep the two matters distinct- the Pledge certainly has weapons. The Indians may very well not be aligned with the Pledge, but we shouldn't entertain even the faintest hope that the two will battle it out amongst themselves before they dispatch us from the face of the earth."

"Hear, hear!" a short, but incredibly stocky man called out. He rose slowly, careful not to disturb his many bandages. "They may very well hate each other, but neither can risk fighting the other until we are out of the way. If either side suffered too much loss fighting us, they might then not possess the strength on their own to overthrow us. Nay, I smell treachery between them, but it won't bear fruit, yet!"

"I have to say that I agree with Gratus," a taller man sitting next to him agreed.

"Alright, that is Lucas and Gratus and Fermion's view," Yuri said. "I think I am compelled to agree as well. However, I would be pleased to hear what Falda or Dolam has to say? Or perhaps Peder or Henryetta?" All four of the ones that Yuri addressed signaled that they were in agreement with Fermion. "Calvin?"

"I think it certainly is the case, sir," Calvin reported to Yuri.

"It really is a dire predicament," Yuri sighed.

Dor stood up to speak his mind. Not quite as tall as Gratus, and not as stocky, he nonetheless seemed just as valiant. "If I may, my lord, it seems to me that there is hope in this man, Fides. Around his neck appears to be a key to something tremendous. Do we not all agree that this is really what the Pledge aims to get at this particular moment? Is that not what we learned from the Rangers not too many weeks ago that sent us hither to the north as fast as we can go? Their intelligence was correct up to the point where it predicted that the Pledge armies would amass in the north. Why shouldn't it be correct in regards to the sought for treasure in Peoria?"

"What do you propose, dear man?" Falda said, urging him to complete his thought.

Dor pondered a half a moment, and answered. "The situation seems so similar, except it's not me! It seems clear to me that Fides must get to Peoria and unlock the treasure and if it is something that can be wielded in battle, bring it to battle on our side. And if it is not the sort of thing that can be wielded in battle, but is still a thing of inestimable value, perhaps it is better for us all to die on the field of battle if it means we can prevent the enemy strength from reaching out and corrupting it."

"I know something about the treasure in Peoria," Fermion interjected. "Unless there is more to it than I know- and I don't think there is- it is the latter case and not the former. Nonetheless, I agree with Dor that Peoria is in fact the primary objective for the Pledge. There is little reason for the Pledge and the Indians to empty their lands and come north except for something they think, or hope, is in Peoria. After all, we came chasing them. They did not come chasing us, even though we managed to arrive first."

"It seems to me that it should be a matter of no controversy at all to conclude that Fides should go as soon as he is ready and able and achieve whatever it is to be achieved in Peoria. The only question is whether or not Fides will in fact, go?" Yuri said, gazing at Fides.

"I will go," Fides said, sheepishly.

"Very fine," Yuri smiled. "Assemble a party to your satisfaction and depart as soon as you wish. It is my hope that you leave sooner rather than later."

"Yes, my lord," Fides agreed.

"So what about us?" the man from Bloomington blurted out.

"Well, for one thing, sir," Nagro set his steely eyes on him, "You won't be telling a soul about Fides' departure and destination."

The man scowled, as much offended as anything. "Not at all! I don't know what you folks have been blathering on about for the last ten minutes. Ever since you stopped talking about Indians with guns I thought you stopped talking about anything important. Never mind Peoria! What about Bloomington!"

Yuri chuckled, "Alright, Bloomington."

"There is a fine chance that at least some of our enemies will be trying to go around Bloomington altogether," Calvin said. "We will need to station well-armed parties along some of the roads that go around the city. The enemy will quickly grasp that we have guessed their true intentions, so we will need to be ready to deploy some other armed units to wherever they try to go around next, for it is sure to be an attempt made with stronger forces. That said, I have been looking at the map. If the Pledge wanted to seriously get to Peoria, given its large numbers, Interstate 74 is their way to go. Holding Bloomington is a very important step in preventing the enemy from obtaining its goal."

"I didn't think there was any doubt that we were going to try to hold Bloomington," growled the representative from the city.

"My apologies, sir. That is not what I meant to communicate. My point is that Bloomington will certainly be a target for them, and it must be held," Calvin tried to explain.

"On the other hand," Nagro said, "It may very well be a bloodbath. If the Indians have military firearms, they will outmatch our own capabilities quickly. If the Pledge have significant weaponry of their own, as Fermion suggests, it might be the same situation. Can Bloomington's Wall protect us from the enemy's weapons?"

"Sandbags. We need sandbags," another representative from Bloomington said.

"Sandbags?" Nagro asked him.

"Yes, they'll help keep the bullets out. Their bullets may go right through the skins of the trailers, but if we can put in some sandbags that'll take care of that. They're men, just as we are, and they'll not be able to go through the trailers' walls. If we can be alive when they start coming around, through, and over the trailers, we have as good a chance as any," the man said.

"That sounds like the best plan, then," Yuri said. "Leave us now with your fellow representatives and begin assembly of an earthen wall to supplement your current defenses. Calvin will go and order as many men as he can find, which ought to be in the thousands, to help you and your citizens in this project."

"That sounds fine," the man said. "How much time do you think we have before our attackers come?" Nagro didn't have an answer to that. He nodded to Yuri.

"Well, if the Indians are working by themselves, they might be expected as early as tomorrow," Yuri said. "They were encountered not more than a few miles from here, to the south. However, if they are working with the Pledge, we have four or five days before we see them, I think. The two armies will have to meet and there will have to be councils, just as we are having this council. Let us count on the former and hope for the latter so that we might have time to get those sandbags filled! Calvin, begin immediately!"

"Yes sir," Calvin said, exiting the tent with a handful of men who belonged to the city. When they were gone, Yuri climbed back on top of a box and looked out at them.

"Fermion and Nagro have been carrying an argument between them for many weeks, now. Of late, Tasha had suggested a possible resolution to that argument. The argument has centered around whether or not we have understood our commands properly, or even got them right. So, at this time, we will have to ask those who are not of our number to exit at this time so we can pursue Tasha's course of action," Yuri explained to them. Before anyone could stand up to leave, Fermion stood up to address them.

"If I may, my lord," Fermion said.

"Of course," Yuri returned.

"I confess that you have all fascinated me. I am convinced that we serve the same Master, and though I have long studied this world, I have not seen the likes of you hinted at in any time or place. But you have received commands, and orders. I won't ask you to tell me what they are. I definitely hope that you will re-evaluate what you think you know about them, but you're about to get down to that in a few moments. There was a day when a word passed down from father to son was well preserved. It was the way of the world. The children were trained to receive the word, and remember it, and recall it with great accuracy. The Evil One, of course, wished to thwart that, but it was not something that could be thwarted easily. This transmission went on for hundreds of years, but the skill that made it work has been lost for hundreds of years, or more. In you, and in me, we have new words issued.

Effort and care must be taken to preserve the words. I have heard your songs! They have a beautiful glory about them. A song is a fine way to remember a word," Fermion said to them.

"Well, one of my orders was to give a word of my own when the time seemed to be right," Fermion continued. "That time seems to be now. I shall deliver it to you as a song, and I plead with you to write it down and commit it to memory: everyone in the room. Are you ready? Does someone have a pen?" A pretty woman got out a pen and a scrap of paper and indicated she was ready. Fermion began to sing…

Hope comes from the west,
Yet despair in those who have been,
No, look for love's unborn, together with them.
The sound of swords against shields!
The mighty swell, countless on the plains
Summoned to possess at last
the desire to all once proffered,
to them thwarted once but not again
Their mighty one declares:
Claim the greatest treasure ever offered!
None shall stand against them now
A noble race, they shall make
Time will end when their time ends when
Their own gift received, they forsake.

His voice was clear and beautiful. The young woman wrote as fast as she could, but was enchanted by the song and could not get it all. She asked Fermion to repeat it, which he did twice. The assembly was in awe, but Fides did not think it was merely because of the quality of the singing.

"Is this message for us?" Yuri asked Fermion incredulously.

"It is for everyone in the room, as far as I know," Fermion said, nodding in the direction of Fides and Charis.

"We will commit this to memory at once," Nagro said.

"You are right, Fermion," Falda said. "I am embarrassed, because I, of all, ought to have been more scrupulous. Hopefully we will be able to set things right."

"That is my hope as well, Falda," Fermion told him.

"Can you tell us what it means?" Yuri pressed him.

"No, I am ignorant. There are mysteries afoot. You, in fact, are mysterious to me. I have carefully memorized this and kept it close to my heart over these long years, waiting for the moment that seemed right to deliver it. I believe that moment has arrived, but it was not given to me to understand it, though I can make some guesses."

"Why don't you make some guesses, then?" Gratus asked him.

"Some people made some guesses many hundreds of years ago and they guessed wrong. When the fulfillment was upon them, they didn't recognize Him. It is wise not to make the same mistake. The meaning of the words will be known immediately to you, if you keep them pure, when the right moment has come. And perhaps parts of it will mean more to some of you and not much to others. This is not for me to judge. I have done what I was commanded to do; I have but one last command to obey," Fermion replied to Gratus, though he was speaking to them all.

"You are a wise man," Dolam told Fermion.

"Only a servant. Some day I hope we will stand together at a grand assembly. But be content, now," Fermion said. "I suppose this is where we must leave so you can complete Tasha's suggestion."

"I am sorry for that," Nagro said, sincerely embarrassed that they felt they needed to exclude Fermion and others that had become dear to them.

"I understand. Come, Fides, let us go," Fermion said to Fides. Charis got up with Melody and Tasha and followed them out of the tent. They walked a little ways until they were well out of range of hearing what was going on in the meeting tent.

"That was a very lovely song," Melody told Fermion.

"Neither the words or the tune are my invention, though I am the first to put them together, I think," Fermion smiled.

"So when shall we leave?" Charis asked Fides.

"We may as well leave right away," he replied. "How about tomorrow morning?"

"That is fine," Charis said.

"Will you all be going with me?" Fides asked them.

"Certainly I will," Charis said.

"You can count on me," Melody said in the bubbly way Fides recalled used to be her fashion.

"I will go," Tasha said, to Fides' surprise.

"Won't you be needed to tend to the wounded here?" Fides asked her.

"They have many fine men and women to do that. For the sake of King and Jonathan, I wish to see what is at the end of the matter which brought us together," she explained.

"Well, Fermion, there we go! Three fine friends to see us to the Peorian bunker!" Fides said, actually looking forward to it. But Fermion had a pained look on his face. Fides frowned, "Fermion? What's the matter? Are you not coming too?"

"I'm sorry, Fides. You know the way from here. I know now that my last task is to be completed here. It is really for your sake that I must stay. I must obey the last word given to me. You will need time. My obedience, I think, will buy it for you," Fermion shared with him solemnly.

If anyone thought about trying to persuade him otherwise, they dismissed the thought as a fruitless waste of time right from the start. Fides was crestfallen for a few minutes, but eventually regained his humor. "Very well, Fermion. I trust that you will at least see me off?"

Fermion smiled, "Absolutely. I wouldn't come this far and miss the final farewell!"

The rest of the day was spent in the camp exchanging farewells with the people that they had come to love. There was a sense amongst them all that there was a final farewell awaiting all of them. Even so, amongst the Shadowmen there was the sense of a first welcome awaiting them, too. As the day wore on, thousands of men were filling up whatever bag or container that they could with dirt or sand and stacking them up against the insides of the trailers. Fides tried to help them but Yuri rebuked him and insisted that he enjoy the fellowship while he could. Fides obeyed him. It was the first time in a long time that obeying any command had brought him pleasure.

Later in the evening Dor found Fides and offered to go on to Peoria with them. Dor's close friends were bent on going to. At first, Fides thought it would be better to journey only with the ones he'd journeyed so many days before with, but when Dor gave the signal, his friends, especially the one called Greene, peppered him with requests and pleas and beggings and insistings until at last Fides acceded to the mirthful request.

"It's one short, but perhaps we'll get a ninth yet," Dor had said, as he left to make sure Yuri approved of their deed.

== Chapter 14 ==

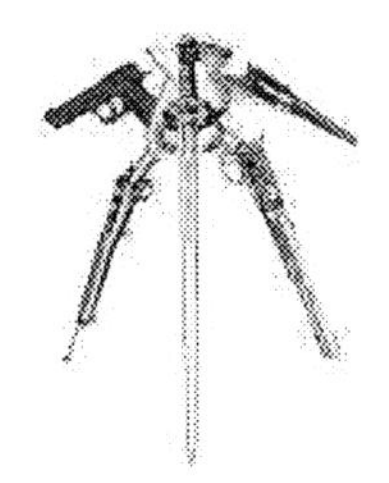

The night came too quickly. There were long and lovely conversations around the campfire and some of the ladies of the Shadowmen sang Fermion's song long into the night. The outcome of the end of the council was not made known to them, but a merry spirit seemed to permeate the entire camp, even as the end drew nigh.

The following morning, the camp came alive while it was still quite dark. Men from the city joined with the Shadowmen army to hastily fill with sand or dirt whatever would hold it. There were many shovels and wheelbarrows in sight when the sun finally gave enough light to see them. It was impossible to tell how much progress had been made during the previous day's labor, but it wasn't for Fides to know. He had his own duty to fulfill. As the smell of coffee began wafting over the mess tents, Fides was finishing his packing. When he emerged from his tent to go and eat, he found that his traveling party was already assembled. Melody and Charis were there, eating. Tasha was in line to get her own food. Dor, Greene, Blessed, and Thamson, were standing and talking with Nagro, Dolam and Falda. Fermion came along side Fides as Fides deposited his gear at a table and got in line to get some food.

"It's been a journey, my friend!" Fermion said, clapping his hand on Fides' shoulder.

"I have much to thank you for, I think. I would not be alive if it weren't for you," Fides said.

"That is true, I think, in more ways than you know," Fermion told him. "But thank me not! All I ask is that you give to others what you yourself have received."

"I will. And I'm sorry, too, for all the trouble I've been," Fides said, sloshing some eggs onto his plate.

"Don't you fret. I was ready for anything, though I confess you still found ways to surprise me. I don't think fear will be a hindrance for you any longer," Fermion said.

"You have great confidence in me. More than I have in myself, I think," Fides replied.

"I've seen many instances where you set aside fear and faced challenges with courage and honor. These were times when the challenge came upon you and you acted instinctively. It was when you had time to ponder what was coming, even when it was completely out of your control, that you struggled. That gave me hope that the deepest parts of you were centered. Now you march off to the unknown with a smile on your face! I suspect you might be a good Nephilim some day!" Fermion said.

"Will you join us for breakfast, at least?" Fides asked him.

"I will do that and go with you to the edge of Bloomington and see you off," Fermion said. That made everyone happy to hear, and not only Fides. As they ate, many people came to bid them farewell. In fact, so many people came to see them off that it took Yuri to notice and say a word so that they could get free to actually leave. Calvin had brought them their horses while they ate, so after Yuri had won them the ability to finally get away from all of the fine people wishing them goodbye, they threw their packs onto the horses, climbed up, and were off. A great multitude was behind them, waving, as they left.

"It must be because of Dor that so many have turned out to wish us well," Fides thought to himself. But it was not true. They had all come to love and respect each of them, and that included Fides. There was also a belief among them that somehow their fate was tied to whatever Fides found in Peoria, so in some of their minds Fides was like a noble knight heading off to slay a mysterious dragon that they themselves could not touch.

They entered the outskirts of the residential section of the city after only a short ride. They passed hundreds of citizens busy with wheelbarrows or shovels or both. Also, there were members of the Shadowmen that saw them and bowed their heads slightly as they passed. They began passing signs labeled 'Family Reunification Registry' shortly after getting into the actual city. Their path to the west was the same path to the Registry, so after about an hour or so they were in the downtown area of the city and in front of them was a massive sign indicating that they were right on top of the Registry. They decided to turn into it and look at it even though they had nothing to look for.

The 'Registry' was actually a series of long plywood walls that had been erected using any kind of available lumber that had been around. There were innumerable pieces of paper or photos stapled, nailed, glued, or some other way stuck onto the walls. Columns held up more sheets of plywood that shielded the various notices from the weather. It resembled a long, narrow, twisted, pavilion. The walls were only separated from each other by about eight feet. The rough ceilings were no match for the elements: many of the notices could not be read any more. People had clearly taken that into account early on, and more permanent measures had been used to secure the messages, like using clear plastic wrappers to cover them. The narrow corridor only went the width of a football field.

"Surely, this is not all it is?" Charis asked incredulously.

"No, look," Fides pointed. They had come about to the middle of the corridor, and an opening could now be seen. As they looked down it, they could see that there were rows upon rows upon rows of these narrow outdoor 'hallways.' In fact, they could not see where the last wall was from where they were standing. Large signs stuck out like tabs on the walls, labeled with the letters of the alphabet. The corridors for people with names beginning with 'A' seemed to number a half dozen. But before the letter 'A,' there was the section that they were still standing in, which was labeled "Miscellaneous," and it had a half dozen of its own rows. Every wall was covered with pictures, drawings, scribbles, names, directions, maps, and any other type of thing you might think of that might help people identify loved ones and reconnect. For example, on one wall they saw a hat nailed to it, with a description below it.

Now seeing just how vast the registry was, the members of the party split up and spread out to read some of the writings on the wall. Though none expected to learn of any family of their own from the Registry (and especially not Dor and his friends), they were enthralled by the extent of the brokenness, pain, loneliness, and suffering, that the numerous entries represented. The feeling that one was looking at tombstones of the living came over them. When Tasha called out to them that there was another section called 'Success Stories' the reaction was bitter-sweet: Here were rows upon rows of people who had managed to re-unite because of the Registry, but it was still only a small number of rows compared to the size of the Registry itself.

After about an hour of scanning the walls of the Registry, it seemed to be a mutual agreement that enough was enough and it was time to be going on. They exited the Registry maze and mounted their horses, and again made their way west. After about an hour, they found an entrance ramp for I-74. The interstate was raised at that point, so when they got up to the top finally they could see for a ways all around them. There were quite a lot of people moving in either direction up there, as well.

Little markets and shops were spread out on its length, too. It appeared that some people even lived on the interstate highway. Even though they saw quite a few people traveling, they knew that there had been a time when many more travelers had used this route. For one thing, the citizens of Bloomington had long since begun screening travelers, forcing the ones who were only passing through to go around the city altogether, and only allowing citizens or people looking specifically for the Registry to come in. It was a dangerous time.

They finally reached a place where the road veered off to the left, with signs directing travelers looking for I-55 and I-39 to head to the right. There was a make-shift sign that had been erected: "Bloomington Safe Boundary: 2 Miles." Sure enough, after about a mile, they could see where the wall of tractor-trailers completed their circle around the city. Soon, they could see troops and armed citizens busily moving dirt out to the trailer wall. As they came closer to the boundary, they saw that a gate had been constructed. Perry and Misaluva were at the gate and saw them. There were greetings exchanged, but because the party had already been so delayed, the conversation was short, even if it was affectionate. Fermion agreed to go another mile down the road with the party, but after that he could not be persuaded to go further. They dismounted in order to give a proper farewell to Fermion.

"Will we ever meet again?" Fides asked him.

"I do not know. I think it likely, but we'll have to be patient. There will be other joys while we wait for that one, though. This moment's sorrow cannot be allowed to overthrow future joys," Fermion replied.

"Can you not tell me more?" Fides pressed him.

"No. Your story and my story briefly intertwined. No one is told anything but their own story. Their own story is enough to grapple with, why divert your attention on the stories of others? Our curiosity knows no limits, but when the predicament is dire, one does not have time to explore every curiosity. Focus on the matters before you. I do not know if we will meet again, but we both shall certainly meet the one in which we have our being, and that will be more than enough to satisfy us," Fermion explained gently.

"Shadowy to the end!" Fides laughed.

"I do not think it is the end, as you should well know. But you may understand more sooner than later, and wish you'd have remained ignorant. We shall see," Fermion smiled cryptically.

"What about us?" Greene asked him.

"I still don't know who you are! Whatever story it is that you belong to I do not doubt that there is only one storyteller! Let us content ourselves with that," Fermion laughed. They were all off their horses by now. Fermion reached for something on his horse, "Now..." he said, pulling out a long, narrow bundle. "Fides, you need another sword, I think." And it was true. Fermion handed the bundle to him. Fides unwrapped it gingerly.

"My sword!" Fides exclaimed upon removing the sword from the bundle of cloth. "I didn't see you stow this!"

"Now, where did you get that?" Tasha gazed at Fermion with steely eyes.

"Maybe I just found it in the woods," Fermion winked at her.

"Clever boy," she replied coolly.

"Now, remember Fides. Always, always, remember to clean off your sword!" Fermion told him.

"I will. Do you think that I will need a sword still?" Fides wondered.

"At least once more, I think," Fermion replied.

"Very well. I shall be ready when the moment arrives," Fides said.

"I pray you will, Fides," Fermion said. "Well, I need to get back. You will be closely watched from here to Peoria, I assure you. Danger will be all around you, but so too will protection. Do not be afraid to call out in your hour of need."

With that, Fides embraced Fermion. Charis and Melody joined in the embrace, too. Thamson shook his hand, "It's been an honor, Fermion." Dor agreed and shook Fermion's hand too. Blessed and Greene also pumped Fermion's arm. Having said their farewells each returned to their horses. Fides was the only one close enough to hear a brief between Fermion and Tasha when they said their goodbyes.

"Now, my dear. Tell me, what is your real name?" Fermion asked her.

"My name here or the one written on the white stone?" she replied coyly.

"You know that the latter is not for me to know," he said to her.

"I am known here as Trina," she smiled.

"That is enough," Fermion grinned at her.

"I will see you at the great table, then?" she asked him warmly.

"Indeed. Farewell," he replied tenderly.

"Farewell," she responded in the same spirit. With that, Fermion turned and rode back in the direction of Bloomington at a fast pace. Fides, realizing that he was now the one in charge, ordered everyone forward. His sword hung at his side as in former days, and he felt that he had at last come to a point where he was worthy to wield it. It did serve as a reminder, though, of Cairo. He still thought he needed to say something to Perry and Emory about the matter, but the opportunity had not arisen. Nor had he talked to Dor about it again, though Fides perceived he might be able to do that soon.

They moved at a fast walk. Their map showed that there was a rest area not too far ahead of them and that seemed like a very good place to stop for the night. There was still enough light that if they had wanted to they could have gone another four or five miles fairly easily, but Fides didn't recall there being any decent places of shelter after the rest area until they reached Peoria itself. In fact, his recollection about the geography this far seemed to be about right. On either side of the road there was desolate farmland. On occasion they would see a farmhouse that still had life in it, and there would be signs that a crop was about to be planted on the land near it. However, these were the exceptions, and not the rule. As vulnerable as it made them feel to know that they could be seen from a great distance, they knew that the flip side was that they could see others, too. There certainly was no way that an army could be concealed where they were at present.

As the afternoon wore on, they passed what had at one time been truck weigh stations on either side of the road. One of them had been turned into a rest area for horse travelers. A small body of water was nearby. Even as they passed by they could see some travelers giving their horses drink. But this was not where Fides had in mind to stop for the night. The terrain changed a little bit as the road shifted from a north-west bent to due west. There were groves of trees within sight here and there on each side of the road. It was also clear now that early evening was on its way. Soon after rounding the bend, though, they saw the sign for the rest area. Fides decided to not use the one nearest him. It was hemmed in on all sides by ominous looking trees. He hoped that the next one would provide a better view of the surrounding area. His memory was coming back even more. It had been more than five years, but he had been this way before.

The rest area on the other side of the road could be seen in the distance on the south side. It was only a thirty minute walk for the horses. As he had hoped, it was easier to see the environs around it than from the other one. Still, there were more wooded areas within view compared to the other rest area, they just weren't right on top of the rest area itself. The other rest area, with its ominous looking trees, was not that far away, either. All in all, they were not far from the bunker that was their destination. Fides felt apprehensive, though. It had been a long time, and even though he knew that the bunker was on the other side of the river that divided Peoria, they had gotten there by twists and turns. It might take a lot of scouring of the countryside to find the right place.

They made their way to the back of the rest area where there were trees enough to conceal them if concealment became necessary. They strung up hammocks and then set about starting a fire in order to cook dinner. Greene and Blessed walked around the grounds in order to get a feel for the layout of things. There were a handful of other small campsites in the area, too. Other travelers were starting to fire up their campfires for dinner, too.

"It is a nice evening," Charis said, breathing in the cool air.

"It is hard to believe that not so far from here, two or maybe three vast armies are arranging to meet each other," Fides said.

"How long of a journey is it to get to this bunker we seek?" Melody asked Fides.

"Well, the first time I was through here I was in a vehicle. It was only a couple of hours, then. In fact, we stopped to rest and check the map back at that other rest area when we did come through. If we knew right where we were going and had no interruptions, I'd say we have only one more day's ride, maybe two. But as I don't know right where we are going, and I expect to be interrupted, I'm thinking we have three to four days ahead of us," Fides replied.

"The air smells clean here, Dor," Thamson remarked to his friend.

"It does. It is these trees, I think," Dor replied. Greene and Blessed returned from their survey.

"It seems like a pretty laid back place," Blessed informed them.

"We'll blend in here fine," Greene added. "There are quite a few parties at least our size."

"That is well," Fides said. "It appeared to be some concern that our mission might be compromised. If this mission were important enough to be kept secret, perhaps there are already spies in the land that will quickly guess the fact of our going without it necessarily being betrayed."

"That is a fair concern," Tasha said. "Have some bread."

"I think I should like to sing the song that Fermion sang for us," Charis said. The warmth of the fire and the full stomachs and the good fellowship was having its natural effect.

"I do not think that would be wise..." Melody began, but was cut off.

"A song! Why, a song is just what these times need!" exclaimed an old man who had wandered by them but stopped when he heard what Charis said. He was a big man, and adorned with many layers of clothing. The exterior layers were rags, mainly. It was clear that he had been carrying his wardrobe on his back for some time. He had a long gray beard. His hat looked like the bowl he used for cooking. More long and gray hair, in curls, flowed from out from under the hat.

"We're not very good singers," Greene said, trying to deflect the man's interest.

"We don't want to call attention to ourselves, anyway," Blessed said before realizing what he was saying.

"Blessed!" Dor exclaimed at him.

"Oh, trying to be covert, are ya?" the old man smiled knowingly at them.

"Or, perhaps we do not have enough food to serve every beggar we attract, sir," Fides offered, trying to make it sound jovial. Even while he said that, Fides knew that the man was more than he seemed. In fact, anyone observing the scene would have known that right off, and that is no compliment to Blessed's powers of perception.

"Beggar, eh?" the old man snarled. He had a smile on his face, but it was definitely a snarl that came out of his mouth. "I assure you that I am no beggar. If I am a beggar, it is only that I am the same as you, but I can tell you where the bread is."

"Come again?" Dor asked the man.

"I'm just one poor beggar leading other poor beggars to bread," the old man repeated.

"What bread?" Blessed asked.

"Living bread," the old man winked.

"Bread with yeast is alive in a sense, isn't it?" Greene wondered aloud.

"Do you still not understand?" the old man laughed.

"These riddles give you away, old man," Fides declared. "What is your business? State it so we can settle it and part company."

"Yes, that's right. Let's barter. Let's see what the 'beggar' has to offer, eh? What's he trying to get? What's his game? I can see it in your eyes. Let me go get my horse, and then I'll show you my wares and you can show me yours and then we can both be happy and call it an evening," the old man's eyes gleamed.

"Alright, but don't dawdle. We mean to have pleasant conversation tonight still," Fides bluntly told the man.

The old man muttered something, then picked his large body up off the ground where he had dropped himself, uninvited. The old man's tattered gray clothing nearly shimmered it was torn into so many pieces. However, he seemed to be wearing so much clothes one couldn't be sure that he was really in fact a large man, or just a man wearing far too much clothing.

"Well, Fides. What do we do here?" Dor asked him.

"We play the man," Fides replied.

"What do you know about him?" Melody suddenly asked him.

"His eyes say more about him than his clothes. I know it," Fides replied.

"Well, not to be contrary, my friend, but it is getting dark," Thamson said.

"Yes, it is getting dark. Still, you watch," Fides said. The man could be seen bringing his horse over to them. There were just a few shades of crimson sunlight left on the horizon. Earlier, the old man seemed to be hunched over and beaten. Fides felt this was a façade: in the evening light, silhouetted against the horizon, the man could not conceal the proud way he carried himself. At last, the old man arrived at the campfire.

The man's eyes grew big: "What? You've not laid out any of your wares!"

"Everything we have we mean to keep," Fides informed him.

"Everything?" the old man persisted.

"Everything."

The old man sat down and was quiet for a minute. Then, he jumped up and said, "Well, maybe you just need to see some of the things I have to offer!" He rummaged around his bags for awhile. Finally, in a low voice, as though showing them something that could get him in a lot of trouble, he threw a package into Charis' lap. "There ya go, little lady," he said proudly. "Tell me what you think of that? Surely you want it- what will you give for it?"

Charis removed the old rags that the object was wrapped in. "It's a book!"

"Sure, but not just any book," the old man replied.

"She can't read," Fides told the man sternly. He got up and took the book from Charis and tossed it back to the man.

"A hard bargain! A tough sell!" the old man guffawed. "I took you for the educated type. I see I was wrong. Now, what else. Well..." the old man sized the eight of them up, going over each of them with his probing eyes. "Maybe not educated, but definitely wise about the ways of the world. Don't want to attract attention, is that right?" the old man said, making clicking noises with his tongue. The group sat silently. Blessed cursed himself for his thoughtless comment.

"Don't want to attract attention... warrior types, perhaps. Soldiers, maybe? Traveling with women, though? Spies for the Pledge, possibly?" the old man hissed at them.

"You watch your mouth!" Dor snapped at him, leaning forward and reaching for the handle of his sword.

The old man whipped out a shining short dagger and held it up in Dor's direction, "Sit down, Dor," the old man hissed again. Dor was taken aback.

"How did you know my name?" Dor demanded, eyeing the blade pointed at his chest only a few feet away.

"Oh, come now. What did the other short fellow say? 'The air smells clean here, Dor,' as I recall," the old man snarled. "That's rock solid military discipline you got here," the old man heaped contempt on them.

"That is a very fine blade," Fides said, studying it carefully. It was, after all, fully extended in Dor's direction. "In fact, I think that I can say that I have only a few that are its like." Tasha also studied the blade carefully. The rest of the party had their hands on the hilt of their respective weapons, crouched, as it were, ready to spring.

The old man smiled and relaxed, turning the blade around and offering the grip for Fides to take, but Fides declined. The man shrugged and set it down in front of him.

"So, not interested in fine blades, either, then?" the old man winked.

"I wouldn't say that. Rather, we already have the arms we need," Fides informed him.

"You have a blade as fine as this one?" the old man said incredulously, throwing his bearded head back in a guffaw. "I think not."

"I think so," Fides replied coolly, pulling his own sword out, and laying it down in front of him so that the old man could see the blade flicker in the firelight.

"Well now. I stand corrected," the old man leaned back in surprise. He stammered for a minute and then got quiet. Finally, he spoke. "Well, this might very well be a first. Have I nothing to offer the weary travelers? Have I nothing to offer them that they don't already have?"

"We have been well provided for, I'm afraid," Fides said, putting his sword away.

"No, you are not afraid at all. That much is clear. Still, there must be something that you don't have. I'm sure of it, now," the old man said, staring right into Fides' stern eyes.

"I can't think of a single thing that you might have that we don't already have but that we need," Fides said, waving his hand in the air as if to dismiss the man and bring the encounter to an end.

"Oh, no. That is not true," the old man replied firmly. "I think I have at least one thing you need..."

"Speak up, old man, so that we can finish this," Fides demanded.

The old man leaned far into the firelight so that everyone could see the light shimmering on his gray head and beard and mustache. He looked right at Fides. "I have the combination to that necklace you're wearing around your neck and hiding underneath that cloak!"

The old man had his eyes locked on Fides' eyes for a long moment before the significance of the statement finally was understood by everyone in the circle. Tasha had quietly taken out her own short dagger before the rest. When Thamson figured it out, though, he leapt to his feet with sword drawn: "It's some murderous spy, I'll wager!" But the old man didn't take his eyes away from Fides' eyes. Fides returned the probing gaze, but did not reach for his weapon.

Fides spoke finally, "Greene and Blessed, I want you to take another walk. See if anyone is lurking about waiting to ambush us. Return when you can." Greene and Blessed reluctantly agreed to that, but saw the wisdom in it. Thamson was still standing over the fire with his sword out.

"So, you carry around books, have a beautifully crafted short sword, and know not only that I have a necklace around my neck, but that it requires a combination to unlock it that I do not possess. Those are a lot of interesting things to encounter in a single old beggar only a few miles from Peoria," Fides said to him.

"Yes, Fides, I know a bit about you," the old man replied.

"And you know my name as well!" Fides muttered. "What about the rest of my party? Do you know their names, too?"

"No, I don't. Well except for Dor, and now Greene and Blessed too," he winked. "But I've been waiting for you. We all have. Your situation is dire and you must overcome your doubts about me very soon or it will all be for nothing," the man asserted.

"For some reason I had thought to trust you from the beginning, but now you've only raised questions," Fides replied.

"Ah, very good. No blind Fides here! You seek a solid foundation for trust. Yes, yes. I'm asking you to have faith in me, and that means establishing a pattern of trust from what you do know to take action on what you do not know. Very wise. I am afraid that I only have two last cards to lay out, though. Well, maybe three," he laughed, "Depending on how you count them. You'll have to decide quickly."

"Lay out your cards, then," Fides invited him.

"I know that you were sick down in New Mexico. Fermion traveled from New Mexico while you were sick and met me and those I am with. That is how I know about you and your necklace. Fermion left, but we have been waiting and watching. I am among those defending the bunker you seek," the old man said, pulling back some of the layers of his clothes so that they could see underneath what seemed to be shining armor with a red cross on it.

Just then, Greene and Blessed returned. "We see nothing to fear!" they reported.

"But you do have much to fear," the old man replied. "Our mutual enemies are already in Peoria looking for the bunker which you and your fellows helped to conceal."

"Before you go on, don't you think you should give us your name?" Thamson demanded.

"John Henry Lambert, if you will," the old man replied. "Call me John, John Henry, Lambert, anything you want, but not late for dinner," he winked.

"Sit down, Thamson," Dor ordered. "Fides will decide the man's fate."

"My fate was decided long ago! But it's your fates we must concern ourselves with, now," John said to Dor.

"How is it that Peoria is already dangerous when Bloomington is where the Pledge army lies?" Fides asked John.

"The Pledge is not so stupid as to constrain itself to Bloomington. You have to understand, the Pledge consists mainly of average citizens who think that they are doing the best thing for their country. They look like any other member of the population. Pledge soldiers have been infiltrating the area with ease for many months now. You can't tell them apart, right? But we know them," John said.

"I have heard Fermion speak against the principles of the Pledge for some time," Charis interrupted, "But they seem to treat everyone fine. They do not seem wicked, or evil."

"That is the case now, my lady. But you wait! It's all honey to attract flies. The time will come when the leadership of the Pledge will run out of patience playing their game. The people who started the Pledge are mainly true believers. They think that they can steer this country and perhaps the world on a new and moral course by making sure that everyone is treated fairly and equally. Not all of the members of the Pledge have such sincere notions, but it doesn't matter if they do or not. Ultimately, all systems eventually have power gravitate inwards. Someone, some person, eventually decides what is `fair' and what is `equal.' *Someone* has to make that decision. The Pledge is right now making the same fundamental mistake of history of assuming that humans are in the main, good. They are always so surprised when a bad man suddenly is in the position of power deciding what is fair and what is equal! But then it is too late! The bad man has the power! Already, there are many bad men in the Pledge. And I am not talking about their so-called 'slaves,'" John said.

"I don't want to sound argumentative, but if what you say is true, then why do they seek the bunker and... I think I heard it called the Ark of the Covenant?" Charis pressed him. "Are they religious?"

"Only as it suits them. They think that religion is all a fraud, of course, but a necessary one. I think they are afraid that if there really is an Ark of the Covenant that might mean some of their truisms are not so true. But they will not find any such object. Right now, they have positioned themselves to appear spiritual in the eyes of men, so long as they think that the object may exist, and especially just in case they manage to get a hold of it. When they find that it is not attainable, they will set aside any pretences about spirituality and instead make their appeal to 'humanity,' which again begs the issue of who decides what constitutes 'humanity.' In either case, this time is coming. Right now, many of the Pledge soldiers have joined thinking that they are fighting for the cause of righteousness. When they learn that this cause was misguided, some will feel betrayed and try to desert, but most will be trapped. Still others will wallow in the freedom that comes from believing that they answer only to themselves. So, men will repeat the mistakes of history, thinking yet again that if they try a rotten principle out in a new way this time it will taste good for all. But let's not be too hard on them, or all of them, at any rate. They do not know much about history," John argued.

"I have some of my own reasons for resisting the Pledge," Charis explained. "I don't want you to think I'm sympathetic to them at all. I have firsthand experience with their cruelty. But you answered my real question, I think. It just seems that in general, the ideas seem good, it's only in the implementation that they are cruel- but what if wiser and more just men were doing the implementation? Your answer seems to be that even if wise and just men begin the implementation, it is inevitable that some wicked man will pick up the task and bend it towards his own purposes."

"Yes, I'd say that is about right. In a broken world, any system for governing others must be realistic about that brokenness and build that awareness right into the system. Many years ago, this country did exactly that, and then forgot the lessons of history. As a result, later generations reap the consequences of that amnesia, and much suffering is the result. Utopian idealism is more dangerous than the most cruelly stated truth. Better to cruelly state that all men are wicked, plan around that assumption, and then hope that some will rise above their wickedness than to naively state that all men are good, plan around that assumption, and then discover that in fact, all men are not good at all," John went on. "Let's keep in mind that there are threats besides the Pledge loose on the land, too!" he added.

"Well, you definitely speak as Fermion did," Fides told John. "I'm inclined to trust you, but I don't know what that means. What is it that you propose I trust you about?"

"A few things, but let's start small. You cannot continue along this road. It is being watched. And you cannot travel by day. It must be by night, and we must leave here very soon. Every moment along the main routes is a dangerous moment. I've tarried this long in conversation only to justify your trust in me. We can talk more, later, but we must move soon!" John insisted.

"You are asking much of us," Tasha said, breaking her long silence. "I will follow Fides, for that is what I am tasked to do. I have faith in him, and if he decides to take you as our guide, I will trust his judgment. However, all we know is your name and some bits and pieces of information that you could perhaps have gathered through superior intelligence gathering. Perhaps answer this question, and I will submit my judgment to Fides, and he can do as he pleases with it."

"Dear lady, truly time is getting short," John objected.

"Tasha is among those who, as you said, established herself by a long pattern of loyal behavior, and so deserves my trust. Speak hastily if you wish, or dare, but we won't go until I have heard the answer to her question," Fides firmly informed John.

"Ask your question," John relented.

"You said that the Pledge will not find any Ark of the Covenant in the bunker. You seem to know what is in fact in that bunker. I should like to know how you have come to know what is in that bunker," Tasha asked him.

"I belong to a military order which was formed a thousand years ago or more in order to protect... certain things. History, if you will. The real facts of history have always been under attack and suppressed by whatever forces were undermined by those facts," John explained. "There are things of great power in that bunker. I know that, because I helped deposit them. That is how I know what is in there. And that is why I know there is no Ark of the Covenant, too."

"This answer satisfies me. I believe that I know which military order it is that you belong to. I think scholars a few generations back will be disappointed to learn that the charge you were given to protect was not flesh and blood," Tasha said.

"Scholars? Conspiracy-mongers who believed that something was a fraud because it contained information that only the authentic would have! How then would one ever recognize an authentic thing?" John's blood began to boil. "Only the Beloved records a spear thrust! Evidence of tampering because it fits so well? Or the sort of thing that shows the Beloved was really there? The march of history has been greatly hampered by historians! History is written by the victors, they say! If true, how then can we ever know the real story, as any counter historical claim would itself be written by victors! The supposition cannot be demonstrated! Insanity! Idiocy! Lunacy!" Fides thought he saw frothing at the mouth, but it was just a trick of the mind.

Tasha laughed, "Fides, his answers satisfy me a great deal. I will gladly throw my lot in with him."

Fides laughed, too. "You seem to be a cross between our friend Fermion and our friend Perry. Very well, John. We'll go. Right now. But if every road is watched, how will we get across the river? Surely the bridges are being watched, too!"

"We've been roaming this area for more than a decade. I know it better than any. What you say is right, but it would not be wise to say anymore until we were away from here. It is good that you have sent your friends out to scout the area, and in fact I scouted it myself before approaching you. Still, we cannot be too sure. Let us put out the fire and saddle up. We have a hard journey tonight, but if we reach the end of it we can sleep well in safety during the daylight hours," John said.

John's plan was agreed to. They put out the fire and packed their gear. Blessed and Greene continued to patrol the area while they packed, just to be on the safe side. When they were ready to go, they were surprised that John led them due south through the woods instead of taking the Interstate another foot. After about an hour, they heard the rippling sounds of a small creek or river, but could not see it well. John used the river as his guide. Because of the great black night, they could move only slowly on the horses. John led them true, though.

The river turned towards the south-west, and after what had certainly been hours and hours of plodding, John brought them up onto a dark road. They followed this road for another hour, but then he veered off of it to the north. After about forty-five minutes, they figured out why. They came across some other interstate blocking their way. They had avoided the crossroads of the interstate, which was more likely to be watched then the stretches in between the crossroads, at least at night. They crossed this highway. After forty-five minutes of travel west of the interstate, John led them south again, where they picked up the road they had found earlier. After several hours on this road, they picked up a smaller road that went due north. Right about the time they found that road, the sun began making its presence known.

Everyone was exhausted, but John encouraged them and pushed them forward. Finally, they turned abruptly off the road just short of a small town that they could see coming up in front of them. John picked up a small dirt road, and led them to an abandoned farmhouse. Weary beyond words, they forced themselves to water the horses at a small pond nearby, and then they tied the horses up inside a dilapidated barn. Each fell asleep wherever they could find a place to lay down, except for John and Thamson, who kept watch.

Any refreshment that had been gained by their time in Bloomington had been wasted on twenty hours in the saddle. Others in history had had worse situations, though. John let them sleep. Even Thamson couldn't hold his head up beyond noon. They began waking up on their own late in the afternoon but John told them to get some more sleep if they could because they had another hard night ahead of them. As the afternoon dissipated none could sleep any longer. They yawned, and stretched, and snacked, and as the sun started to go down were once again sitting around a fire. John was explaining the situation.

"There are quite a few bridges across the Illinois River, and almost all of them are sure to be watched by spies. There are more than spies in the area, though. There are some pretty good sized units in the area, too. They are waiting to snag you, I think." That was directed at Fides. "That's not their only purpose, of course. Obviously, some of them are trying to find the bunker, too. They know it's around here, but they don't know where. That in itself is a victory for us, but it makes our situation somewhat more precarious, because there are lots of search parties out and it will be difficult to avoid them. That's why we are traveling by night. There are so many of them, though, that we are sure that there is a much broader strategy at work. For example, if your friends in Bloomington try to retreat to Peoria, they are sure to find that the small towns nearby are not friendly at all. In fact, beginning with the town of Morton, they are all heavily fortified with Pledge soldiers. My friends have found that it has been easier to avoid the towns altogether. We get peppered with questions if we don't, and the people asking the questions are quite menacing."

"At any rate, the bridges being watched are old automobile bridges. There is one bridge that as of two weeks ago was still not being watched. It's an old railroad bridge just south of the city. It won't be easy to get there on the horses, but there is a good chance that for that same reason we might be able to get there undetected. And once we get across, we are only one more night's ride to the bunker," John concluded, stroking his gray beard.

"How do you know that the bridge isn't being watched now?" Melody asked.

"Well, obviously I don't. But I have some friends that are watching for watchers, and watching for you for that matter. When we get there, they'll let us know if it's safe to give it a go," John replied.

"You've mentioned these friends," Tasha interjected. "Are these all from the same military order?"

"No, actually. But we all have the same goal. You could say that the bunker project was quite ecumenical," John smiled. "You'll have a chance to meet one of them when we get to the railroad bridge, if all goes well. Well, for that matter, the bunker is not unattended. You'll meet more of my friends there for sure."

The sun was starting to dip down even lower and John told everyone to start packing again. The horses were fed and watered and packed up, but John said it still wasn't dark enough to start their night's journey. For that reason, even though everyone was ready they found themselves sitting around the campfire still, chatting about various things.

The last groping rays of the sun had just disappeared when there was suddenly a shimmering and pulsing silver light that seemed to wash over them from the east. Their cloaks flapped and the horses neighed and their tin cups rattled. Their hair stood on end. A single tear gathered in one of Tasha's eyes.

"So passes Fermion, son of Marleigh," John said quietly. Each person contemplated the significance of the event and statement in silence. After a few quiet moments they gathered up their things and began their dark journey to the Illinois River.

== Chapter 15 ==

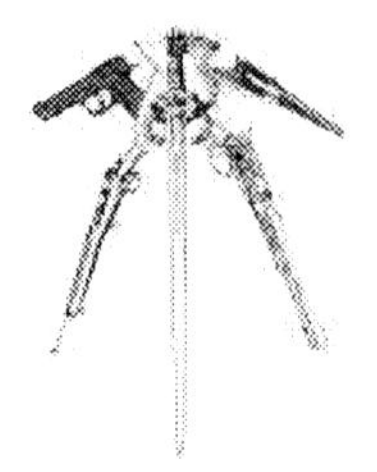

After about an hour John let them take a break. They all carried with them the thought of Fermion as they went. They each knew that the rippling wave of light that flashed over, around, and through them, was an emanation of Fermion. He had demonstrated such power once before. John's claim that this latest wave marked the end of Fermion was startling, but they knew in their hearts it was true. Fides remembered how after Fermion had exerted himself on the plain at Cairo he had been reduced to unconsciousness. They had been within one or two hundred yards of Fermion in that instance, and the wave that washed over the field then paled in comparison to the wave that overwhelmed them earlier this evening- and they were miles and miles and miles away. If the first time had drained Fermion, this one no doubt had extinguished him.

As they stood in the dark, Fides felt a number of emotions clashing within him. There was shock, despair, rage, loneliness, grief, and more. Fermion had become the most genuine friend that Fides had ever known. He was simultaneously devastated and... his other feeling congealed at last into a word ... proud. Fermion had no doubt expended himself for his sake. This raised a very troubling concern, however. What threat had arisen that required such an expending?

The group was lingering in the dark. Fermion's fate was clearly on their minds. John felt that he had to address the matter.

"Every man dies, friends, but not every man has the opportunity to die for his friends. If we must die, what a privilege to die for such a cause, and not alone and forgotten by humanity," John comforted them.

"He didn't really seem like the sort that could die," Dor confessed.

"This world is a broken place. All but one simply *had* to die. Everything will come to an end, but then all things will be made new. But what comes new will be what remains when the old is sifted away, purified. Things that you lay your hands on now, like a blind man stumbling across in a room, will be things that you can see with your eyes, then. The rot will be washed away, allowing the seed to grow into a fine plant. You have some sense of these things now, but then you will know fully, even as you are fully known," John continued. "Do not begrudge Fermion his joy. He is going further up and further in, and we will, in our own time, follow."

As strange as it may seem, these hard words brought comfort to them. There was much that some of them did not understand, but they could feel in their bones that it was right. If a skeptic had approached them at that moment to try to offer a different view, even armed with a thousand evidences, the skeptic would have had no success. It would be asking them to deny their own experiencing of reality. Indeed, the skeptic could only hope to try to offer a different explanation for that experience. But if one is asked to deny their own experience in order to accept someone else's claimed experience, what hope for knowledge remains? No, they knew that in this brittle moment, time and experience was snapped taut and they could feel the vibrations of something more robust in the world coursing through the line. They didn't need to know *what* was on the end of the line in order to know that there *was* something on the end of the line.

John allowed them a few moments of reverie but knew that there was no time to be spared. He gave out a tender, yet firm command, and the nine began their dark journey anew. In honor of their fallen friend, they found themselves singing Fermion's Song. They worked from memory to piece it together. After about another hour of traveling, they came to another interstate. Fides didn't notice a sign saying which it was. John was a little jittery as they crossed through the area on their way north, but once it was behind them he relaxed considerably. They continued on the road that they were on for a little ways longer but then John led them off the road. He said something about 'cutting the corner.' This was a very difficult part of the journey because they were winding their way along a path that they could not see at all. There was just enough starlight for each person to see the other in front of them, and so stay straight. John assured them that this was just a brief part of the trip. Brief or not, it took another hour. Suddenly, they were among houses. It was a residential section of the city of Peoria. None of the houses had lamps shining, so it was impossible to say whether the houses were empty or if instead the inhabitants were sleeping. John led them through the quiet neighborhoods with ease. He knew exactly where he was and where he was going.

Their time in this particular subdivision was short-lived, however. After just a short while they were in an old industrial complex, and somewhere in there- no one knew how- John found railroad tracks. He followed them west. A gust of wind offered them the hint of a nearby river. Then they were out of the industrial complex, still following the tracks, but now in woods again. John had slowed the pace down some, proceeding cautiously. He made them stop and rest near the edge of the woods and then went further by himself. He was gone only for a short time. He returned accompanied by another man, who was on foot.

"All is well, it appears," John informed them. "This is my co-laborer, Sal Hasan. A fine old man who has come down from the mountain to help us. He has been stationed here for a day and has seen nothing. We can proceed."

"Greetings, my friends," came a firm voice from out of the pitch dark. They could not see him at all. Nonetheless, the man literally reeked of honor, courage, and nobility. They instantly trusted him. "I must now depart my post and assemble the rest for the next task. You will make good time from here, God willing."

That was the extent of the exchange. Sal Hasan melted into the darkness and John gingerly led them to the railway bridge. There were no visible signs that they were being watched. Even if someone were watching the bridge, because of the darkness of the night they would have had to be laying right on the bridge and catch their silhouettes against the horizon. Otherwise, there was no way to detect them. They crossed the bridge and in no time found themselves once again in a residential section.

"Where is Sal going?" Fides asked John.

"He is going to go roll up the picket line, both to the north and to the south, and other parts. Everyone will be heading towards the bunker within an hour to exert all their strength to ensure your safety," John explained.

"In an hour?" Tasha inquired. "That is fast communication."

John only laughed and said, "We will have to pass over the Interstate two more times in order to arrive at our destination. The first time will be within the hour. I expect this to be a very dangerous part of our journey, for it is all within the city. Once we cross the Interstate, we will be out in the country more, and we will not travel by road any longer. So, keep your weapons ready!"

The journey had been so easy up to that point that this new warning made them feel uncomfortable. For a city allegedly swarming with enemy patrols, it seemed eerily quiet and practically abandoned. John took advantage of the reasonably decent roads that they were on to set the horses on a faster gait. Two hours later, John called out that the Interstate was before them. They had been riding for some five hours. Crossing the Interstate proved to be uneventful. John led them along the road that they were on a little ways further, but then turned them due north. They were heading due north.

They quickly came upon a series of open plains. John had them set the horses off at a gallop on these plains. There was less concern about waking up sleeping residents or sleeping patrols out on the open countryside. It was a good opportunity to make up time, but the poor horses certainly would not have agreed with the plan. They did this fast gallop followed by a fast walk cycle a fair number of times over another two hours when John suddenly pulled them off to the right. They went north-east for about fifty yards, and then John commanded them to dismount. There was a small creek or river running roughly parallel to them. They watered the horses and tried to tend to them as well as they could while they themselves stretched or fetched a small bite to eat from their sacks.

"Ok, we are not far, now," John revealed to them. "The problem is that I make it out to be three or four in the morning- closer to four, I reckon- and that means that the sun may very well come up just as we are crossing the Interstate. That is intolerable to me, but I can't see any way around it except to sleep out here somewhere during the day and make the last leg of the journey tomorrow night. If we don't arrive at the bunker tonight, my friends are sure to be concerned, though."

"How much further to the Interstate?" Dor asked John.

"One hour at a sprint. At the rate we've been going, tack on another thirty minutes. It might take two hours. Then, after we cross the Interstate its another one to two hours," John replied.

"It would be unbearable to be this close and yet have to wait another full day," Fides said.

"I wouldn't be able to sleep!" Charis exclaimed. "I'd be too excited and filled with anticipation!"

"She'd keep the rest of us up, no doubt," Melody laughed.

"Well, as I recall, this little creek we are watering the horses with runs right to the Interstate, and in fact, runs underneath the Interstate. So, we wouldn't have to actually go up and over the road. If we are very unlucky, there might be enemy camped in the area just waking up and looking to get some water themselves, but if we made haste we might be able to still just get by under the cover of darkness," John reflected.

"Then let us go!" Fides blurted out. "I am weary of this journey and should like to sleep with the bunker as a pillow for my head at least."

"Very well. But let us ride with great speed up until the last hundred yards or so, and then proceed slowly, with weapons drawn," John said. There were mutters of agreement from the rest of the party. Everyone had the same sentiment in mind: "Let's get to this lousy place already." The horses shuddered upon learning that they would be asked to carry freight a little longer. It's a good thing that they didn't have the sense to know how fast they were going to be asked to perform their next duty, because they would have refused to participate. Once everyone was back on their saddles, John led them to a small road that ran more or less parallel to the creek, and set them at a run. It wasn't so fast that it wasn't unsustainable, but it was so fast that when thirty or forty minutes had gone by and John allowed them to slow down, they had already slowed down considerably on their own.

"This is no road!" Melody exclaimed. "You've had us on the edge of a another railroad track! And for how long?" The sun was now providing the first rays of light, allowing them to each make out the railroad ties in the track. Fides had thought the road they were on was a bit softer than he expected a road to be.

John chuckled, "Now, dearie. This is no time for such discussion. We are less than two hundred yards away from where the creek goes under the Interstate. Here we turn due north and leave the railroad track completely. Let us give the horses some water one more time, and then get it over with." These orders were quickly obeyed. It had been another hard ride so everyone was eager to walk around. Greene and Blessed took the opportunity to scout out ahead a little. They returned with the news that as far as they could tell, everything seemed clear. After not more than ten minutes, they were back in the saddles and riding again. This time, they were plodding along fairly slowly to try to cut down on any noise that might alert or awake any patrols or travelers who might be in the area.

They kept close to the creek. Though it was still quite dark, there was enough light that if anyone had looked their way from the Interstate, they would have been spotted, even if it wouldn't have been easy to tell who they were. John had recalled correctly: the creek went under the Interstate. In short order, the massive concrete columns were in sight, and not very long after that they were among them. They rode in single file with hands on their weapons. Unfortunately, they ran out of dry land in one place and had to slosh along in the creek, which had widened into a small river at that point. John motioned to them to remain quiet even after they were some forty yards away from the Interstate. A quick look over their shoulders revealed why: they could still be seen from the overpass if anyone had bothered to look. But finally the waters narrowed again and the creek bent so that the overpass could no longer be seen. John told them that they were not more than one or two miles away from the bunker.

They continued to follow the creek for another hour or so. They maintained their leisurely pace, because John had only urged them ahead earlier out of fear of passing the major road in broad daylight. Now that that danger was behind them, he didn't mind allowing the horses to recover. The creek veered abruptly to the east so John kept them heading due north. The creek returned to them after a short ways, but when it did John led them across it. A large field greeted them, and on the other side of it, their creek crossed their path again. John led them across it again. A much larger field was discovered here. A little nervous about passing such an expanse without any kind of cover, John made them pick up the pace. When they reached the tree-line, John brought them to a path. John dismounted, and everyone else followed suit. They walked the horses from here.

Another twenty minutes went by, and the path opened up into yet another clearing. In this clearing, though, was yet another old homestead that had been abandoned and fallen into disrepair, but now served as a waypoint for the defenders of the bunker. A dangerous looking barn was nearby, but John assured them that it was not going to fall down around their ears. They tied up their horses. John informed them that they would travel no more that day.

"But where is the bunker?" Thamson asked him. John smiled.

"I thought you said we'd make it to the bunker by this morning," Melody persisted. John only smiled again. Naturally, they began scanning the environs for anything that might look like a bunker. Fides knew that if there was any bunker here, that house had something to do with it. He couldn't say that he recognized the landscape, though. He marched over to the farmhouse. The walls were bent in and out and were grey-colored from the passing of time without adequate care. He found the door nailed shut and the windows intact. He peered inside them. Tasha joined him, and soon the others had followed, too. The place seemed to be completely barren. From one window, you could see from one end of the house to the other.

"So, this is the bunker?" Fides said to John. "My fellows did a fine job, it seems."

"Oh, definitely. A lot of fine craftsmanship went into this structure," John explained.

"So, after we give you the key, what happens?" Fides asked him, and then suddenly realized that there was still the little matter about the combination to the key. "And how are we going to get the key off?"

"One thing at a time," John countered. "After we get the key, of course we'll make sure that it works. Most of us from a safe distance, of course," he smiled. "Then, you can see what's inside it if you like, but you must continue to guard our secrets. There will be an appropriate time for the contents to be revealed and given to their rightful owners, but that time is not immediate, I'm afraid. As for the matter of the key, and the unlocking, might I suggest that we wait until this evening, or even perhaps tomorrow morning?"

"Why?" Tasha asked him.

"Well, for one, I would like to have more of the bunker's defenders present, just to be on the safe side. For another, I think the removal of the key might be best handled when Fides and everyone else involved is well rested."

"More defenders? More than us?" Melody inquired. John smiled again.

"More than us? We are not alone. The trees are keeping a close eye on us," he said to her. "It would not be wise for them to reveal themselves too hastily, though. They will be checking to see if we were trailed, or to see if I look like I am in fact a captive, things like that. And of course many of the defenders, if not most, were scattered around the countryside looking to meet up with you. It will take some time for all of them to re-converge here. I should think by tonight nearly all of them will be here, though," he finished. Fides had been thinking this through as John explained his proposal.

"Alright, I agree," Fides said. "Let us sleep for awhile, and then deal with the important matters after we have all rested. As much as I am dying to see it all play out, and especially to see where the bunker entrance is in this large, glorious, rundown shack, and even what is in it, at the same time my eyes insist on shutting."

"Will it be safe for us to sleep, then?" Charis wondered.

"We will stay up a little while," Greene said, referring to himself and Blessed.

"That is very kind of you, but unnecessary," John answered them. "You can stay up if you like, but I assure you, we are well protected."

"Be that as it may, I appreciate having our own men about," Dor said.

"Show us the way to the sleeping quarters!" Thamson said wearily, and relieved, really, that resting had been the decision. John led them all back to the barn. Seen from the inside, it was clear that there were solid timbers supporting the walls and the ceilings. In one section there was fresh hay, which Melody and Charis led the horses too. They did not all spend that much time getting situated, though. Their bodies were tired and sore from the long rides. One by one, they found flat, dry, places to lay down. And that is what they did. They slept peacefully, even as the barn grew stuffy as the sun came out and baked it.

In the late afternoon, they started waking up again. A campfire was started, and food was cooked. They found some old stumps in the woods to use as seats. Greene and Blessed teased John about the alleged defenders in the woods, as they had been up and down through the surrounding trees gathering firewood and secretly trying to sneak up on some of the defenders and had seen no sign of any hidden warriors. John deflected their taunts with his knowing smile.

As the sun started making its descent, Sal Hasan joined them. Good conversation followed, but no other defenders of the bunkers showed their faces. The sun was hanging low in the sky, now, and Fides turned the conversation onto the subject of the necklace around his neck.

"Well, we've come to it, haven't we?" John replied.

"Yes, we really have. So, how about that combination so I can get the thing off my neck!" Fides returned.

John looked at him carefully, "Do you trust me?"

"What do you mean, 'Do you trust me?'" Fides replied. He fiddled at some of the cylinders that clearly rotated around on both sides of where the necklace joined together. The cylinders all had what looked to be computer chips on them, and numbered about twenty in total, ten on each side.

"Well, I don't know how to break this to you, exactly," John said, "But I really don't want to tell you the combination!"

"You are being very confusing!" Fides exclaimed.

John chuckled, "Yes, that's true."

"I don't understand," Fides said, clearly dazed.

"Well, it's like this," John began. "That necklace really is the only key into this bunker, and it really does contain explosive material on event of the necklace being unlocked by force or unlawful means, but the code to that key is the code for other things, too. Things you have no part in. Things that need to be protected."

"So what is it you propose?" Fides demanded to know.

"I propose that you just let me reach up there and dial the code for you," John told him.

"This all seems very strange. Just how did you get the code, anyway? Wasn't Bill Huxley the only one that had the combination?" Fides asked him, beginning to get a little angry.

"You're just going to have to trust me," John said again. "I think I've given you good grounds to trust me."

"But it's not your neck at risk!" Fides exclaimed. "If you're wrong, I'm a dead man!"

"Well, as you know, we are all dead men, so that is not much of a punch," John replied, kindly. "But what do I have to gain by lying about the matter?" John patiently inquired.

"So... you want to enter the code yourself to make sure that it remains secret, is that right?" Fides put it to him.

"Absolutely. Right now if you like. On each side of the connecting latch there are two little buttons that can be depressed. I'll just align the cylinders, depress those buttons, and it will pop apart," John explained to him.

The sun had gone down, now, making the primary light the campfire that they all sat around. Fides' friends and escorts had observed the conversation in tense fascination. There was nothing for them to say. The two men appeared to be like great giants sparring with each other. Fides looked as though he was a man face to face with his mortality. John had a steely look in his eyes, and he directed them right at Fides and never took his eyes off of him. Sal sat nearby, looking down or into the fire.

It was quiet for awhile as Fides pondered the decision before him. Lurking ominously in his brain was the thought that the whole thing was just one big set-up. John said that the old farmhouse was the bunker, but he couldn't see anything that would indicate that this was so. The landscape seemed slightly familiar, but quite a bit different, too.

What if John had brought them all to this place with the idea of ambushing them? What if he was not who he said he was? For that matter, who did he say he was? Fides didn't know! And what about the alleged defenders in the thicket? Greene and Blessed had teased John about the lack of any sign of any such defenders. What if they were just part of the story that John was weaving? What if they were actually there, hidden very well, but waiting for a sign to leap in and dispatch them and take the key for themselves?

The idea that these last two questions were at odds with each other barely crossed Fides' mind. Despite all of these questions, John had known his name, about his necklace, and about the combination. Plus, he knew Fermion. If it was a great deception, then it might mean that removing the necklace would kill him- but wouldn't it then destroy the necklace, too? In that case, what would John hope to gain? But what if John knew something about how it dispatched its wearer that Bill did not know about to pass along to Fides? Or, what if Bill had told him that, too, but he had already slipped into unconsciousness?

John broke the silence, "Unless I free you, you cannot be free."

"I have no choice but to believe you," Fides acceded. "However, to tell you the truth, if my judgment is in error, I'd rather die in the light, and I would want everyone to see how it happened. That sounds negative. I do trust, you. I want to assure you of that. I just would feel more comfortable waiting for the morning."

"That is perfectly fine with me," John replied. "There is no rush. At least, not yet."

With that settled, the tension dissipated and the good conversation started up again. Sal spoke rarely, but when he did it was always insightful. John laughed often and boisterously. Blessed and Greene would join in the laughter in the same manner, but would occasionally turn serious and make another patrol. As the fire started to go down, despite the fact that they had slept most of the day, they began to get tired.

Charis was the first to excuse herself, and Fides watched her go. A strange and sudden sensation struck him as he realized again, for the first time in a long time, that she was quite beautiful. Confronting imminent death had apparently awakened some desire to live, and some of the pleasures of life appeared to awaken in him at the same time. But she went to bed and the conversation moved along, and Fides forgot about the moment. Soon, everyone was crawling off to bed. Fides and Dor were the last ones.

Dor looked at Fides and said, "Well, in the morrow your quest will be over and your burden will be lifted. I'm proud of you for doing this seemingly small yet undoubtedly important duty."

Fides smiled at him, "I appreciate that." Fides couldn't help but remember a previous seemingly small duty he had failed to do. He had been meaning to ask Dor more about what he knew about Simus and Cairo. This was as good a time as any. "Dor, can you tell me more about what happened to Simus?"

Dor became glum, "I'm sorry, but it is not my place to tell you more. It is Perry and Emory, or perhaps some others of the Rangers, who deserve to have that conversation."

"Do you think I should bring it up? Is it worth damaging my friendship with them?" Fides asked him.

"I do not think it is my place to tell you that, either. They will find out someday, though. Whatever hurt they have when they learn the details of the matter, it will be even worse if they hear it from someone other than you. I think that's all I can say," Dor advised him.

"One more duty," Fides muttered to himself.

"You must not beat yourself up, Fides," Dor argued. "The past is the past. This present moment is the only moment you can act in. It is one thing to allow the past to inform this present moment, it is another to let the past dominate every present moment that follows. Do not became the slave of the past. Learn from it, and so make it your servant."

"Those are wise words," Fides agreed. "But easier said than done."

"I realize that," Dor affirmed.

Fides looked at Dor and became aware of the deep affection and loyalty that the man had demonstrated towards him. "I've welcomed your companionship on this journey. Tomorrow I hope I do not disappoint," Fides said to him.

"It will be a simple matter, will it not?" Dor replied. "Nothing more than John reaching up and unlocking the necklace, and then its over."

"Yes, but somehow I fear that there is more to it. In the morning we find out," Fides said.

"Indeed," Dor replied, excusing himself for bed. Fides was left alone by the embers, but did not remain long. His exhaustion overcame his doubts and his concerns; he, too, went to bed.

With all of the time available to catch up on their rest, everyone was awake and active as soon as the sun popped its head over the horizon. Their four noble escorts from the Shadowmen immediately launched themselves on a patrol. Naturally, when they returned they reported that they couldn't see any of John's alleged defenders. They all only laughed about that, because everyone pretty well accepted that John was telling the truth about them. Tasha cooked breakfast for everyone over the fire that Sal kindled for her. The moment was rapidly approaching. Fides simultaneously felt apprehensive and carefree about the matter. He felt attached to the bunker and even perhaps its contents because he had held the key to it for so long, yet in fact he had no right to the contents of the bunker, and no real obligation to it. In a sense, he was a mere courier. It was a strange cocktail of emotions.

"Well. The sun's up," John told him. "Are you ready?" Everyone was sitting around the fire, now.

"Yes, I suppose I am," Fides replied, feeling the necklace latches under his fingers.

"Yep, that's right. Lift up your head a little," John said, taking the necklace in hand. John dialed in the code. "Ah, yes. Here we go. Ok, well, here goes!" John exclaimed. There was a definitive clicking sound and then the necklace became unlatched. Everyone looked at each other, waiting for Fides to blow up or perhaps sprout flowers from his ears. Anything would have better met their expectations after this long journey. When nothing happened everyone laughed.

"Now it's time for the next important test. We've got to try it in the bunker," John informed them. "But you know, your duty and obligation is done now. All of you. You are free to go, if you like. On the off chance that the self-destruct mechanism doesn't work properly, you might want to be a long way from here. What're your thoughts?"

"I've got nothing to return to, myself. Let's just do it," Fides said. The others agreed. They followed John over to the decrepit house, where he unlocked the front door, and led them all inside. The thick dust on the ground fluttered into a cloud as they walked across the floor. John led them to a hallway that was on the main level. From outside one of the windows, Fides had noticed the hallway but had not been able to see down it. Now in the hallway itself, they could see that there was a closet door. It, too, was locked. Like the front door, this one did not require Fides' necklace. The closet was empty and dark.

John took the necklace from Fides, who was standing crowded with the others in the hallway. John fumbled in the dark, out of sight, and they heard a loud snapping noise, and then the whir of wheels, and other mechanical sounds. There was a second snap, and another whir of wheels. A gust of wind came past them, rushing into the closet. Then, a breeze seemed to blow back into the hallway. It carried some familiar scent that Fides couldn't put his finger on…

He didn't have long to think about it because there was suddenly a shout from outside. It was Sal. Then there was the sound of horses galloping. Everyone ran outside, although John seemed to take a moment longer. He was probably locking the door again. When they emerged from the building there were about fifteen riders bearing down on them. Some had clubs, a few had swords, but others had crossbows. Arrows whizzed past them, lodging themselves into the walls around them. Most of them had left their own weapons in the barn!

The nine of them scattered. Only Tasha, Melody, and John had something to fight with. It was only their daggers, though, and it wasn't quite enough. Sal, on the other hand, already had a sword in hand and was rushing to meet the attackers. Those armed with daggers rushed to help him, while the others quickly tried to get to their weapons. The horsemen were among them, trying to strike them.

"Where are your defenders?" Fides shouted at John. John was no less surprised, and it showed on his face.

The attacking horsemen quickly divided into groups. Some dealt with Sal and those who had joined him but other riders pursued the rest towards the barn. Fortunately, the barn was not too far away, and those that could make it found protection while they re-claimed their weapons. Greene, however, did not make it. He was clubbed in the head and fell to the ground, and was still. It did not take long for Fides and the rest to sortie out of the barn, though. The flash of their weapons quickly greeted the assailants.

Dor, Thamson, and Blessed, were on their horses, and came out the back side of the barn in fury. They were all out-numbered, but they were not out-matched. While those armed only with daggers had found themselves unable to be more than be a nuisance, with the rush of their friends they too were able to lay hold of their own more formidable weapons. A crossbow bolt did catch Thamson in the gut and dismounted him, but apparently it had not penetrated into him, because he was on the ground howling in pain but not stuck with an arrow.

If the fury of Dor and his comrades had caught their assailants by surprise, enraged at the fall of his friend, the fury of John could not be opposed. Pride seemed to drive him on: they were supposed to be safe. It was inexplicable, and the anger which he unleashed on the men he could reach was unassailable. When it was all over, John stood, soaked in blood, in the midst of a pile of three dead horses and three dead men. Fides was the one who dispatched the last of them, ramming his sword into the man's chest after Tasha had knocked him off his beast.

"What of the defenders!" Fides demanded of John again, angrily.

But John and Sal were far angrier than Fides was and exchanged words with each other as though Fides had not just said anything. Dor and Blessed tended to their fallen friends, with the assistance of Tasha and Charis. John and Sal were still arguing with each other bitterly when they heard the sounds of gunshots in the distance. The assembly grew quiet, listening.

"Those are military arms," John said.

"And not just ours," Sal said.

"This is not good," John concluded.

"Not at all," Sal agreed.

"What now?" Fides demanded impatiently, laying his sword against one of the pillars supporting the porch. Thamson and Greene were being laid down on the other side of the porch. Thamson was still obviously in pain, but Greene was motionless.

"We need more information," John told him. "But I think one of our questions has been answered, even though it raises others. The defenders were not lax. The defenders had become aware of some other threat and had rushed to meet them."

"Without telling us, though! Isn't that odd?" Sal said to John.

"Maybe they didn't have time," John said, shrugging his shoulders as though to say that he didn't really know the answer.

Of course, this was not an answer to Fides' question. "Ok, but what are we going to do?"

John ignored Fides, but asked Sal, "Do you make these out to be Pledge?"

"They had crossbows. It would be my guess that they are," Sal replied. "As to the weapons we hear in the distance, they sound like they could belong either to the rebel Indian tribes who we know have weapons or to the Pledge, whom we are sure had some. These are not Indians," he concluded, pointing at the dead horsemen that had charged them.

"We must remember our primary obligation, here," John said sternly.

"Indeed," Sal returned. Fides looked at them both in exasperation. However, before Fides could say anything else, there was the sound of gunfire much closer to them. It was just inside the woods of the clearing. The gunfire received an answer from other guns, and there was the sound of people crashing through the woods around them! They could faintly see human forms in there. John leapt up.

"Take the wounded to the barn and secure it the way you know how!" John ordered Sal. "Fides, you are going to learn how to fire a better gun than you've ever laid eyes on before!" he said to Fides. Sal was helping Dor and Tasha and the rest carry Thamson and Greene to the barn, but John grabbed Fides by the arm and pulled him into the house. Fides had just managed to grab his sword, but John stopped him in the hallway. "You can't take that down into the bunker like that!" He yelled (not in anger, but merely in urgency) at Fides. Fides looked at his sword. It still had the blood of men on it. Fermion's last words came to him suddenly:

"Always, always, remember to clean off your sword!" Fides wanted to argue with John about it but John pushed him back towards the door, "Hurry up and clean it!" he commanded him.

Fides ran through what was probably the living room and out the front door to find some grass to wipe off the blade with. As he burst out of the door, he suddenly found himself face to face with a troop of men, most of which appeared to be well-armed with military style weapons. A man stepped from among them that Fides recognized. It was the man who had clobbered him over the head in Champaign and had been captured, and released. Fides let the sword hang at his side with the tip of the sword pointed to the ground, signaling surrender. He had to: except for the guns pointed at the barn, the rest were all aimed at him. But he did not drop it.

"The necklace, if you please," the man commanded him, motioning for Fides to turn it over.

John answered from behind him, though, "As you can see, he no longer has it. Why don't you let him go?" Fides turned and saw that John was now armed with his own high powered weapon, but this was of course temporary, for as he saw the threat he lowered his weapon carefully to the ground and put his hands out so that they could all see he was unarmed.

"Where is the necklace, then?" the man replied.

"Mirbor!" a woman's voice yelled from the barn. It was Charis. Mirbor's head whipped around to see where the voice was coming from. They could see Charis leaning out a window. "Do the right thing!" she yelled over at them. Mirbor was not fazed.

"Bring them here," Mirbor commanded his men. He turned again to John, "The necklace, please," Mirbor demanded.

"You know that I would sooner die than tell you where it is," John replied, stubbornly

"It will give me no pleasure to torture it out of you, but it may give pleasure to some of my companions here. If it comes to that, we certainly will do it," Mirbor told him. He was a proud looking man, with shoulder-length hair. His chin jutted out when he talked, but his eyes appeared hollow.

"You are one of the Shadowmen, are you not?" John put to Mirbor.

Mirbor laughed. "Of their sort, perhaps, but more realistic, I think."

"More realistic but I wonder if they are not more real," John retorted.

"We shall see how well such arguments fly after… after the Pledge commands this world," Mirbor told him.

"After the Pledge, you say? You mean after you command the world," John snarled at Mirbor.

"Naturally, every organization needs a leader. The buck has to stop someplace. Someone has to be in a position to make the hard decision for the benefit of everyone," Mirbor replied cunningly. But John waved him off.

"Enough of that jazz. Let's cut to it," John snapped.

Mirbor appeared to be perfectly happy to cut to the heart of things. "Of course. We'll take you all into custody and bring you back with us. You will all be educated in the values of communal democratic thinking. But first we will take possession of this house, which as I have guessed actually conceals something quite different and very likely of great value. And you will give us the key, or else you will lose your friends one after one until only you are left, and you will suffer terribly, and we will still get what we want. It is up to you, I suppose, whether or not we get what we want after much pain and sorrow or without it. We will get what we want in either case," Mirbor grinned at him. The occupants of the barn had now been brought nearer. Mirbor's men had their guns aimed at them.

The sounds of gunfire in the distance had persisted throughout this conversation, but they all realized that it had begun to draw closer and closer. Mirbor glared at John impatiently as he realized that perhaps they didn't have as much time to work with as he had initially thought. Then, as suddenly as the gunfire had first started up, it stopped.

"I wonder who won," John muttered at Mirbor.

"If you had won, you wouldn't be in this situation now," Mirbor retorted. "But enough of all this! It's time. Where is the key?"

"I won't tell," John said.

"Mirbor, do the right thing," Charis again pleaded with him.

Fides looked at Charis. "You know this man?" he asked her.

Mirbor sneered. "Know her? Why, Charis is my lover. Didn't she tell you?" he laughed.

"Lover?" Charis snapped. "No honorable man would consider that love."

"Well, I enjoyed myself, at any rate," Mirbor snarled again.

Charis appeared to be engaged in an internal struggle. She spoke, "I forgive you, Mirbor." Mirbor looked at her, unsure what to make of this turn of events. She continued, "I release you from my hate." Mirbor looked as though he were going to murder them all. He pulled his gun up but before he could pull the trigger (if he was going to pull the trigger) one of his men grabbed his arm and hissed something into his ear. Mirbor yanked his arm away and growled at Fides and John.

"I'm going to just start killing people," Mirbor snapped at them.

"Isn't it the breath you seek?" Melody prodded Mirbor. "Why settle for mere power?"

"What do you know of it?" Mirbor sniped back. But right then, Mirbor noticed Fides' sword. "That sword... that sword looks familiar." Mirbor seemed to be dazed again. He jutted out his chin, "Throw that ahead of you!"

Fides could not do anything but comply. He tossed the sword a few feet ahead of him, into the dirt. Mirbor nodded towards one of his men, who went forward and brought it back to him. There were close to forty gunmen keeping Fides and his friends subdued. Mirbor examined the sword carefully. A sudden look of recognition came over his face. "Is it?" Mirbor cried out, his eyes going wide. He fell onto his knees with the sword laying on his palms. "Narsalion, aner andane," he whispered.

"Arise and repent, Mirbor!" John declared. "Don't you know that in this place the darkness is on the inside of a man and not on the outside? When it is plain as day on the outside it is easy enough to stand against it. But when it is hidden inside someone's heart, it is a much different matter. It is easy to slay what are obviously monsters. It is a different story to recognize that just because you don't see a monster in a mirror, it does not mean you are not looking at one. Look inside! See it! Arise and repent, and slay the troll you have become!" John again proclaimed.

"What do you know, old man?" Mirbor glared at John, trembling under the weight of what he had in his hands.

Charis answered for John, "He knows that it is not too late. You can turn back, even now!"

But Mirbor did not seem to want to hear any of it. A vile look came into his eyes. He stood up suddenly, with the sword stretched up into the sky. He shouted, "My time has come!"

John dove for his gun. Fides leapt at Mirbor. This was obviously foolish, but Fides was not thinking clearly, even if perhaps he was acting on a noble principle. John was an old man, but he hit the ground rolling so that he came up with his gun and hunkered in firing position. Rounds from the men started embedding themselves in the walls around him so he didn't bother trying to fire, though. Instead John shot his way through one of the windows and dived through it. He popped back up and fired into the enemy. The enemy, however, had scattered and sought cover. At the very least, they laid down on the ground. The prisoners were stuck out in the open, though. Mirbor managed to throw Fides back onto the porch, where Fides quickly rolled inside the house.

Mirbor shouted: "Stop firing, old man, or we'll kill them all!"

John stopped firing, and hunkered down underneath the window. Fides had a bruised eye and a bloody lip, but he was more or less alright. He sat with his back up against the wall. John was hunkered beneath the window. He looked at Fides. "Don't worry, the walls are bullet proof."

Fides laughed. "Why not the windows?"

"That sort of thing would be too conspicuous, don't you think? Stranger comes by and throws a rock at the window but the window don't break? They might not get in, but they'll take note." John smiled, catching his breath.

"Can't say I understand," Fides said.

John just shook his head, "It's real simple. We've changed a lot of windows. Strangers come by, sneak in, poke around, don't see anything of value, and leave. They never mention it to anyone because it's not worth mentioning."

Fides shook his head in amusement. The bullet-resistant properties of the walls couldn't occupy them indefinitely. He quickly realized how absurd it was to be having the conversation at all. Fides peeked around the corner of the doorway. Most of Mirbor's men had their weapons trained on Charis and the rest of the prisoners. Some of them had their weapons facing the house.

Some were on the ground, dead from John's bullets. Mirbor was running his hand along the blade of the sword.

"What do you know about Mirbor and that sword?" Fides asked.

"I only know that Mirbor is from among the Shadowmen and that that blade is one of theirs," John replied.

"Surrender!" Mirbor shouted at John and Fides. Suddenly, though, Mirbor was distracted. He addressed himself to some new entrants on the scene. "Stand back or we'll kill them all!" he shouted in a new direction.

Fides and John both stole a glance at the scene. "Looks like the rest of your lot has arrived," Fides said. Men on foot and on horses had crashed out of the woods far off on the other side of the clearing.

"This is a pretty predicament," John frowned.

Mirbor addressed Fides and John again. "I want that key, you understand? How can you deny that fate is establishing me?" he shouted.

"Do you know what he is talking about?" Fides asked John.

"No, I told you just about all I know," John replied.

"Come out, or we'll kill them!" Mirbor repeated his threat. He also turned again to John's fellows, "I said stay back!" Fides stole a glance and saw that Mirbor and his men were now well outnumbered. His men were looking around, nervously.

"We can't let them have the bunker," John said to Fides.

"We can't let them kill our friends, either!" Fides replied, firmly.

"If we can get them to the barn, they'd be safe there," John informed him.

"I'd like to hear how you plan to pull that off," Fides shook his head, doubtful.

But John was already on his feet. The military rifle was on the ground, and in its place was a handgun. He produced the key, which he re-locked. Then he put the gun to his head, and stepped out into the opening. "I'm the only one with the combination!" John shouted at Mirbor. "I'll blow my head off and you'll lose the combination forever, and consequently, access to the bunker."

"Maybe I can live with that," Mirbor laughed. Mirbor did care, though.

John continued, "Let the prisoners go. Send them to the barn. Let Fides go, too. You can keep me. You and I can enter the bunker together, and you can see that there is nothing here for you. I will be your bargaining chip and you and your men will be our bargaining chip. As you can see, you are completely surrounded."

"I don't think so, friend," Mirbor snarled. "It is only a matter of time until the rest of my forces arrive. "If you are in fact the only one with the combination, I'll be sure that if we die in the battle that comes when they arrive, you will die, too. The contents of the bunker will be lost to everyone. I am content with that. You?" Mirbor growled at him.

At that moment, the men that Mirbor had mentioned began emerging from the forest opposite from John's soldiers. Before long, there were hundreds and hundreds and hundreds of armed men lined up with guns aimed at each other. It was an impasse.

John realized that his gambit was failing. He returned back to the cover underneath the window of the house. They could hear Mirbor laughing.

"This is a pretty pickle, Fides," John said.

"Ideas?" Fides asked him.

"Only one. It's risky. My men withdraw. Your friends become prisoners. We dive for the bunker. Then, we hope that they don't shoot your friends and Sal. Mirbor is unstable. He might kill them, he might not. But they'll be cut down for sure in the crossfire of the two groups," John explained.

"Uh, what do we gain by diving into the bunker other than securing it?" Fides asked him.

"Don't worry. We can live a long time down there," John answered him.

"That leaves only one question. How do you plan on telling your men to withdraw?" Fides pressed him.

John winked. He produced a small object from his cloak that looked like a radio. Fides looked at it, curiously. John pressed a button and whispered into it. There was a whispered reply. A brief conversation ensued like that. Finally, John shouted out to Mirbor, "Ok, look, my soldiers are going to leave, now. Ok?"

"I'll believe that when I see it!" Mirbor laughed in response. But one of his men blurted out to him that John's men were in fact withdrawing. "What is the meaning of this?" Mirbor shouted at John after all of John's soldiers had disappeared into the woods.

"Now, Fides!" John shouted. John jumped up and threw a knife at Mirbor. Fides did not see where John got the knife, but he did hear the exclamation of pain. Mirbor had been struck. Still, Fides hadn't moved. John shouted at him again, "Move, Fides!" John was now rushing towards the hallway where the entrance of the bunker was. Fides was now right behind him. Bullets whizzed by them both. Fides turned to look back.

It was all in an instant: He could hear the screams of a woman. Charis? He felt John's arm pulling him forward. But then... an uncomfortable pinch in his leg... and in his shoulder... and another in his shoulder. John was lurching now, trying to push Fides with one arm while aiming his gun back in the other direction. They collapsed into the closet. The key was above John's head, both ends situated into two innocuous looking grooves. He felt light headed. John was standing above him, now. John grabbed the key and the wall of the closet turned into a black chasm. One of his last conscious experiences was of suddenly finding himself tumbling down and down and down into a black pit. One of the other last experiences was the thud as first he landed on a level section and then John fell onto him and went limp.

He smelled that familiar smell again. As fog rolled into his thoughts he tried to figure out what it smelled like. Like Corrie's house maybe... Yes... something from that old house down in New Mexico. Something old and musty... but here was the stench of it. Was he unconscious? Is that why it was black? Or was it black because it was black? I think therefore I am, he told himself, but then… there weren't many thoughts. There was the muffled sound of wheels whirring and spinning and clanging above him.

He could hear Mirbor cursing above him, outside the bunker door, "I've got them all now, you hear? They are all going to pay! The woman-" But it was muffled, and Fides was drifting off, so he didn't hear the rest. He knew he had been shot. He could see… John… John, looking at him over a fire in the night… and saying… (or was it Fermion?) … saying "So passes Fides, son of Christopher Ranthem…" But Fides knew that was a lie. That wasn't Fermion. That wasn't John. That wasn't his own voice. Who was that liar? Fides fought back. Maybe Mirbor's voice had been a lie, too. Maybe his friends weren't prisoners, either. Fides continued to fight. The phrase, "Plans to prosper..." came into his mind. He stifled them, and replaced them with other words, "Yea, though I walk through the valley of the shadow of death..." Fides mustered his will, and repeated it over and over again.

He could hear John working near him, now. "I'm coming, Fides," he was saying. Fides laughed silently as he realized how many times he had faced that creeping darkness already. And came out of it, he told himself. He started to feel pain, now. In the midst of a swelling agony he suddenly heard Fermion's prophetic song in his ears:

Hope comes from the west,
Yet despair in those who have been,
No, look for love's unborn, together with them.
The sound of swords against shields!
The mighty swell, countless on the plains
Summoned to possess at last
the desire to all once proffered,
to them thwarted once but not again
Their mighty one declares:
Claim the greatest treasure ever offered!
None shall stand against them now
A noble race, they shall make
Time will end when their time ends when
Their own gift received, they forsake.

Fides was proud of himself for remembering it all. The song brought peace within the pain, but then a thick, heavy, black curtain fell across Fides. In due course, he would either find out what Fermion was talking about from the other side of the veil (if there was another side) or he would wake up, repaired by the diligent hands of John Henry Lambert.

+ + + + +

Charis threw her body between Fides and Mirbor. Mirbor was furious. He hit her in the face with a closed hand and she crumpled to the ground. Mirbor fired into the bunker but he was firing aimlessly because he had lost sight of the old man and the one called Fides. He ran up the steps to the porch and into the house, looking this way and that for where the two went. They weren't in the kitchen. He raced through a hallway and then stopped. There was a closet in the hallway. He ran back to it, opened it, and stared at the back of it. The back of the wall was moving. It slammed against the interior walls with a clank and Mirbor threw himself against it. It did not move. He threw himself against it over and over again. Angry beyond words, he began firing at the wall, but to no effect.

Furious, he finally gave up. "I've got them all now, you hear?" he shouted at the wall. "They are all going to pay! The woman will be the first! I swear it!" Maddened, Mirbor left the closet and traced his way back out of the house. His men were still out there with their guns aimed at a small group of prisoners huddled not too far from the house. Charis was still lying in a heap. One of the women was tending to her. Mirbor strode over and picked up the sword which had fallen to the ground.

"Narsalion," he smiled, examining it carefully.

"That's not yours!" Dor shouted at him.

"It's not yours either!" Mirbor replied, laughing.

"What are we going to do with these?" one of Mirbor's men asked him, pointing at their captives. Mirbor's men appeared to be quite nervous.

Another one added, "Our enemy out-numbers us. If they return, we will not be able to defeat them."

"Cowards," Mirbor snarled. He looked around. His eyes settled on the barn, "Go check out that barn. Let's see if we can lock them in there." Several of Mirbor's men made for the barn. The rest of his men watched the woods carefully, certain that they themselves were being watched. The men returned.

"Some hay. Otherwise, it's empty. Easy to bar the door, too," one of them told Mirbor.

"Lock them in there," Mirbor instructed them.

Charis had regained consciousness. "Mirbor, what hate has so filled your heart? Why do you behave like this?"

"I am only reclaiming what was taken from me, my dear," he replied darkly. "See this sword? This should have been mine. At least, that which it represents should have been mine. The fact that it now is in my hands is proof that I am fated to rule. You cannot stand against me." Mirbor's men were now pushing the prisoners towards the barn. The prisoners were pulling some of their wounded. Mirbor followed them to the barn.

"Even now it is not too late," Charis pleaded with him. She was kneeling inside the entrance to the barn, her arms around his legs.

"I agree, completely!" Mirbor shouted triumphantly. He used his foot to shove her backwards. "Close the door! Lock it!" he told his men. Charis locked eyes with him just before the door shut. Mirbor turned away from the barn, "Now burn it." There were shouts of horror from inside the barn, but Mirbor merely laughed.

Suddenly, the woods exploded into gunfire. Some of Mirbor's men were killed immediately. The rest rushed towards the outside of the barn walls for cover. Mirbor shook his hand at the woods and yelled, "We'll kill them!" Of course, he had made it plain he was going to kill them anyway, so this was little incentive to stop.

"The barn door won't open!" one of Mirbor's men shouted at him in fear.

"There goes our leverage," Mirbor muttered. "Come on! Let's get out of here!" Mirbor led his men into the woods away from John and Sal's friends. Several fell before getting into the cover of the trees, but most of them managed to make it. They didn't stop to return fire. Mirbor led them away.

John and Sal's men entered the clearing. Clothed in camouflage with dark red insignias, they rushed to secure the buildings. There were orders shouted out. Some of the men rushed into the woods in pursuit of Mirbor and his men. Finally, one of the soldiers knocked on the door of the barn, his assault rifle slung over his shoulder.

"It's safe, Sal!" the soldier shouted. After a moment, the door slid open. Sal was beaming.

"I knew this barn would come in handy," Sal chuckled.

"We've got to get some medical treatment here," Charis reminded them.

"Of course," Sal said, issuing the command. Some of the other soldiers rushed inside the barn to provide first aid.

"What about Fides and John?" the soldier asked them.

"The bunker," Sal answered.

"I think Fides is dead," Charis exclaimed sorrowfully. "I saw him get shot at least once before Mirbor clobbered me."

"If any man can help him, it's John," Sal comforted her.

"Can't we get into the bunker?" Dor asked them.

"No, I'm afraid not. John took the key with him into the bunker. Our radios do not work through the concrete. There is a way to send out transmissions, but it requires power. We didn't have a chance to power up the bunker before all the shooting began," Sal explained, worried.

The soldier gasped, "It's got to be pitch black!" Sal nodded.

"So, now what?" Charis asked them.

"We must go!" the soldier answered. "We must go to Bloomington to warn them about what is coming."

"What is coming?" Sal asked. Then, Sal remembered that his men had allowed the enemy to attack them. "Where were you?" he inquired, angrily.

"Too much to explain!" the soldier replied. "We'll have to explain on the way." The soldier was already moving around, encouraging the freed prisoners to stand up and get ready to walk. Some litters were produced to put the wounded on.

"What about Fides and John?" Charis persisted. "Shouldn't we leave some people behind for when they come out?"

"What about the bunker?" Sal challenged him.

"Every man is needed! Please!" the soldier replied earnestly. Though Sal was confused by the urgency of his friends, he assured Charis that if they did get out they would be able to talk to them on the radios. The soldiers were already moving with urgent haste towards the road, so even Sal had to relent from his questioning. Dor and Melody helped Charis walk, for she was a little wobbly. Tasha was tending to Thamson and Greene as they were being carried by the soldiers.

They were nearly out of sight of the house and barn. Charis looked back over her shoulder. Dor comforted her, "Try not to worry, Charis. We don't know that Fides is dead. Have hope." Hearing this, Charis steadied her heart. She turned her attention to the road and the urgent march back to Bloomington, but couldn't help glancing one last time behind her, trying to glimpse the house through the trees. It could not be seen anymore, though.

The barn and the house, with the bunker hidden beneath it, were alone. The spring air meandered through the branches of the trees. The scents of newly born flowers went unappreciated since there was now no one left to enjoy them. Or so it seemed.

The light around the house seemed to shimmer and shake, appearing very much like what you would see if you were watching heat rise off of a hot road. The house itself seemed to tremble, and then suddenly twelve fearsome figures materialized outside the perimeter of it. Some of them were men and others were women. Their swords were out and at the ready. Their countenances were as kings and queens. Light passed through them like light passing through a prism, casting vibrant colors in a dance on the ground around them. Their glistening appearances suggested that maybe they were not clothed at all, but rather naked. Naked or not, dignity radiated from out of them. Draped over their shoulders were purple garments with gold threads that dripped with silvery strands of faith, hope, love, strength, courage, justice, substance, truth, and victory.

Their stern eyes looked left and right, scrutinizing the surrounding wood vigilantly. Then, there was a sudden gust of the wind, and their appearances faded like sand being blown away. They appeared only for a moment, and then they dissipated from view, leaving no trace of the warriors behind. A breeze whisked through the trees and around the house, carrying a whispered message, "Praestet fides supplementum sensuum defectui..."

TO BE CONTINUED IN ANOTHER BOOK

About the Author:

A.R. Horvath is married and the father of four children. He is a graduate from Concordia University Wisconsin with a pastoral ministry degree. Having nearly abandoned Christianity in college, he credits C.S. Lewis and J.R.R. Tolkien as baptizing his intellect and his imagination. Anthony has been active on the Internet as an apologist and evangelist for more than a decade.

You can contact the author at www.birthpangs.com.

Concise Index of Names

Bill Huxley - the man who hired Fides' crew to build the bunker in Peoria.

Calvin- the Shadowman responsible for tactical affairs, a member of the Shadowmen council.

Charis- A fellow travelers with the Rangers, and an eventual companion to Fides.

Chummy- owner and operator of a ferry service out of Tulsa, Oklahoma.

the **Copperheads-** a group evidently bent on creating a racially pure country.

Corric- Las Cruces resident that helped nurse Fides back to health after he became stricken with the Disease.

Dietrich- Las Cruces resident that helped nurse Fides back to health after he became stricken with the Disease.

Dolam- a member of the Shadowmen council.

Dor- a trusted warrior among the Shadowmen and eventual companion of Fides and his company.

Ed- Fides' long time friend from Terre Haute and in charge of their 'crew.'

Emory- one of the leaders of the Rangers.

Falda- a member of the Shadowmen council.

Father Frederich- the name that Fermion went by while impersonating a Catholic priest.

Fermion- One of the 'nephilim,' whatever they are.

Fides- the man burdened by the key to a mysterious bunker.

Franklin- one of Jack's cohorts and antagonist to Fermion and Fides.

Gol- a giant among the Shadowmen who rescued Fermion from the plains of Cairo.

Gongral- she is a member of the Shadowmen council.

Jack- a scoundrel, really. Someone who enjoys reveling in the anarchy of the times.

John Henry Lambert- a later companion of Fides as he journeys to the bunker.

Jonathan- a traveling companion who Fides rescued on the journey to Bloomington.

Henryetta- she is a member of the Shadowmen council.

King- a traveling companion of Tasha's, and later of Fides and Fermion.

Leredo- a member of the Shadowmen council.

Melody- Fides' wife.

Melody- a companion of Charis and the Rangers, and later part of Fides' company.

Mirbor- a bent man whom the Shadowmen and Charis appears to know about.

Misaluva- a member of the Rangers who eventually becomes close friends with Charis and Melody, and eventually forms part of Fides' company.

Nagro- a member of the Shadowmen council, and apparently the second in command.

Peder- a member of the Shadowmen council.

Perry- one of the leaders of the Rangers.

the **Pledge-** an organization that has formed an army to install its own ideas about government on the country.

Redemptus- an apparent exception to the rule that the Shadowmen are a wonderful sight to behold.

the **Rangers-** a group of men and some women who rallied together informally to resist various groups angling for control of the country.

the **Shadowmen-** a mysterious group that also appears to have a beautiful radiance about them, at least initially.

Simus- the Ranger's acting general, though he defers to Perry and Emory.

Tasha- King's traveling companion, and later Fides and Fermion's companion, too. She rescued King while he was quite young.

Thamson- a Shadowmen that is a close companion to Dor.

Tom- Chummy's appointed man to escort Fides and his company to Bloomington.

Yuri Ryson- the apparent leader of the Shadowmen.

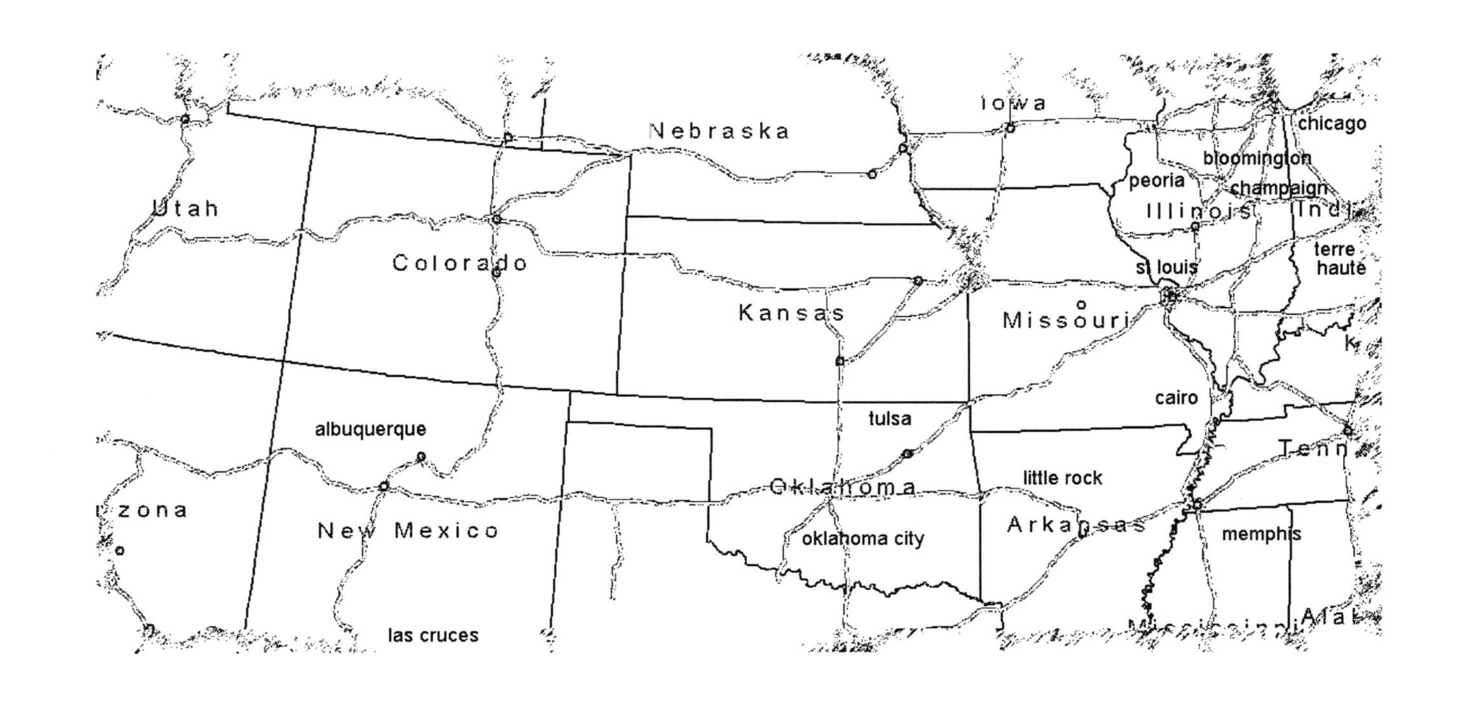

Utah
Nebraska
Iowa
chicago
bloomington
peoria
champaign
Illinois
Colorado
terre haute
st louis
Kansas
Missouri
cairo
tulsa
albuquerque
Tenn
little rock
Oklahoma
zona
New Mexico
Arkansas
oklahoma city
memphis
las cruces

Printed in the United States
68947LVS00004B/64-75

9 780979 127618